LETTERS FROM LYDIA

LETTERS FROM LYDIA

KENT KAMRON

FIVE STAR

An imprint of Thomson Gale, a part of The Thomson Corporation

THOMSON

GALE

Detroit • New York • San Francisco • New Haven, Conn. • Waterville, Maine • London

LIBRARY OF CONGRESS CATALOGING-IN-PUBLICATION DATA

Kamron, Kent.
    Letters from Lydia / Kent Kamron. — 1st ed.
      p. cm.
    ISBN 1-59414-528-8 (alk. paper)
    1. Western stories. 2. Saint Louis (Mo.)—History—Fiction. I. Title.
PS3561.A445L48 2006
813'.6—dc22   2006021450

U.S. Hardcover:
ISBN 13: 978-1-59414-528-5
ISBN 10: 1-59414-528-8

First Edition. First Printing: December 2006.

Published in 2006 in conjunction with Tekno Books.

Printed in the United States of America on permanent paper
10 9 8 7 6 5 4 3 2 1

To my dear wife Verlene and our two sons Kamron and Kent. And a special thanks to my great-great-grandmother Katerina, whom I never knew. She *lived* the times I love to write about.

ACKNOWLEDGMENTS

My special thanks go out to John Helfers of Tekno Books who believed in my work. And to Alice Duncan, my editor, I offer a hearty handshake. You have a wonderful knack for putting the right words in the right places.

ONE

Seven years had passed since the fighting. The two generals had signed the peace at Appomattox, and the war was over for most, but not for William Pearlman. Those who knew him said he never was the same. This small mining community of Grundy, located in the extreme westerly corner of Virginia, had been his lifeline ever since he immigrated to America. He worked in the mines before the war, and afterward he returned to them, but this deep hole in the side of the mountain was not near as deep as the hole in his soul.

Some said it was the confining tunnels that did him in, so claustrophobic, reminders of the confined space at Andersonville, which had been his misery for the last thirteen months of the war. The fifteen-foot barricade around the perimeter of the prison camp packed thousands of northern prisoners inside a hellhole of filth, where the only air one could breathe was filled with the constant smell of death. Every morning began with comrades collecting the dead—those ravaged in the night by the cold or dysentery. Some died from lack of food, others were beaten to death by fellow prisoners, and many simply chose to cross the killing line, an unmarked but acknowledged boundary twenty feet from the inside walls of the camp. Anyone who stepped over it was immediately shot dead.

Somehow William Pearlman survived those several months and returned home to the same dingy, dilapidated shack on the Louisa River Fork. To his dismay, his wife had died from a putrid fever seven weeks earlier, and any sanity left in him slowly eroded away.

Every day before he headed for the mines, he would visit her grave and offer a quick prayer. At the end of the day when he returned home, he would sit on the ground next to her plat for hours at a time, his legs folded underneath him, his head dipped into his hands.

"Oh, Lord," he would ask. "Why have you taken her from me?" With red and swollen eyes, his mind would delve into the past, trying to relive the precious times they had spent with each other.

It was the memories of her lovely face that had kept him alive in the camp, the one thread that seemed to hold his life in balance. William Pearlman and his wife were blessed with only one child, Lydia, but the lament over his wife's death was so strong, it was as if Lydia didn't even exist.

Actually, it was during his prison stay when the memory of having a daughter slowly began to disappear from his mind. "Who is this?" he would ask his fellow prisoners as he studied a picture from his wallet.

Those who lived in the depths of despair alongside him kept reminding him, "It's your daughter, William. It's Lydia, remember?" Over and over they would remind him, even though they never knew the girl. "She's nine years old now, remember?"

But he couldn't remember. It was as if bits and pieces of his memory had been blotted out, and when the peace came, it was his comrades who made sure he was placed on a train and headed in the right direction. They had even written notes and stuffed them in his pockets so that along the way, if he became more bewildered than he already was, someone might find the notes and help him reach Buchanan County, Virginia. His friends believed that when he reached home, his life, as he once knew it, would return to him full force.

But nothing was ever normal for him again. Lydia, who by now had reached the age of sixteen, was in the woods when she heard the gunshot. She ran up from the river and came upon her father slumped over her mother's grave.

"Papa!" she screamed as she rushed to his side. Blood from his temple was already oozing into the dirt, and as she lifted his head, more blood spilled onto the front of her dress.

Outside that lonely house deep in the woods, she screamed and screamed, but no one was near enough to hear her cries.

Those in Grundy who knew the Pearlman family were amazed that Lydia shed so few tears at the funeral—all except Eugenia Calhoun, who, over the years, saw the gradual change in Lydia after her father returned from the war. For Lydia, visits to Mrs. Calhoun in Grundy seemed to be the only respite from the loneliness and monotony of living on the small acreage along the river. Until the age of fourteen, and dressed in what most considered nothing but rags, Lydia's life revolved around this one-room shack in the woods outside of the small mining town. To escape the boredom of a lifeless existence and a father who didn't even know her, she would often retreat to the river where she sometimes fished. Mostly, she simply sat on the bank and watched the fast-flowing water slip by, and she would daydream, fantasizing about building a raft and sailing downriver. "I wonder where this river goes?" she often asked herself.

For her short lifetime, this little spot on the earth was all she knew. Her schooling was mediocre at best, taught during the war years by her mother, who was terribly unaware of the world surrounding her. What little Lydia learned about life surfaced within the last few years because of the many long visits she spent with Eugenia Calhoun, a widow of fifteen years, herself childless. Eugenia possessed an innate kindness that recognized the deprivation Lydia was going through, and she simply took it upon herself to make a lady out of this young miss.

"It's important that you learn to read and write," she emphasized. "You need to learn about the history of this country in which you live."

Eugenia procured geography books, maps and simple stories from school readers. Lydia's father didn't seem to care that Lydia spent so much time in town, and she loved the attention, which she never received at home. Though Mrs. Calhoun had not been schooled, she was a very literate person, and if nothing else, she impressed upon Lydia that an education was as important as life itself.

On one of those days when Lydia came to visit, Mrs. Calhoun had a dress laid out on a bed for her. It was the first that possessed any modicum of style, compared to the near rags she normally wore.

"Grandmama!" she exclaimed, as she would call Mrs. Calhoun. "What a beautiful dress! Thank you! Thank you! I love you for it!"

It was not at all an elegant dress, nor was it made of quality material, but it was for her. It was a gift beyond expectation. Her earlier life had been nothing but abject poverty, living with a mother who worried every day of the war that her husband would never return—a woman who was so dependent upon a man to make her decisions that she could hardly fend for herself. At home, Lydia had become the introverted young lady that most folks knew, but on those days when she visited Mrs. Calhoun, she exhibited some shining moments.

Lydia whirled around and studied herself in a mirror. "It's wonderful, Mrs. Calhoun. Do you think I look pretty in it?"

"You do, darlin'," came the response, but Lydia was not a beauty in any sense of the word, and in fact, some went so far as to say she was homely. She was dark-haired with dark brown eyes on a round face, but she rarely smiled. It was this glum face with a turned down mouth that was Lydia's demise. However, inside this young lady, Mrs. Calhoun envisioned a young heart that was ever thankful for any kindness or the smallest of gifts.

No, she wasn't a beauty on the outside, and during her short time on earth, she led an unhappy life. Who could be otherwise with a mother who worried from morning to night, who bickered and complained daily and found little good to say about anything?

Many wondered how William could even love such a person, but he did. There were periods of time when life was at least bearable for the Pearlman family, but that was before William went off to war.

During the first few years when her father was a soldier, Lydia, as young as she was, easily recognized her mother's shortcomings, and though she tried to help hold the household together, every day became an ever growing challenge because of her mother's incessant worrying and crying and lamenting.

The only reprieve Lydia received from this daily drudgery was to spend as many hours as she dared with Mrs. Calhoun, who provided the motherly care that the young girl needed.

On William's funeral day, there were those who quietly questioned William's death.

"Why did he do it?" one whispered.

"He was lonesome for his wife."

"But she died seven years ago!"

"It was the mines," said another.

"It was the war," said still another.

"Yes," someone agreed. "He never was right since the war."

After William was laid to rest next to his wife, Mrs. Calhoun turned to Lydia. "Get whatever you need from the house, darlin'. You're coming home with me."

Lydia's face blossomed with a wide smile, something those

present at the funeral had rarely glimpsed before, and while she was gathering up some of her personal belongings, Reverend Stilter hugged Mrs. Calhoun warmly. "This is wonderful what you're doing for Lydia."

It was not at all a surprise that Mrs. Calhoun took Lydia in, since everyone expected she would. One afternoon, within a few weeks of the funeral, Mrs. Calhoun summoned Reverend Stilter to pay her a visit, arranged at a time when Lydia was conveniently away.

The reverend entered her home, which was small and simply furnished. He was aware that the two upper bedrooms were rented out to lodgers. What little compensation she received from them was barely adequate to sustain her daily essentials, but she was a frugal lady, and her needs were few.

"A spot of brandy in your tea, perhaps, Reverend?" she inquired.

Reverend Stilter, a small, robust man, smiled underneath his bushy lip when he heard the offer. "Mrs. Calhoun, you are after my soul."

She had a twinkle in her eye when she tipped the carafe and quipped, "If God doesn't get it first." After a glance at his receptive smile, she tipped a bit more brandy into the cup and then eased her plump body into a soft chair.

"Very good," he said as he savored the tea and looked about. "How is Lydia getting along?"

"As well as can be expected."

"Well, she's a bright girl," the reverend commented.

"Not yet," Mrs. Calhoun countered. Reverend Stilter's eyes widened as he grunted out a sound of indignation. "She has the potential," Mrs. Calhoun clarified, "but not if she remains in this godforsaken community. There's nothing here for her but memories of her dead parents and a life of despair."

The reverend could hardly believe his ears. As the pastor of the Baptist Church circuit for many years, he had an attentive flock of parishioners by serving three different churches in Buchanan County. A delightful wife and five children rounded out his pleasant place in society.

"A life of despair?" he questioned.

"Reverend," she politely answered, "this girl needs an education in a community where she can blossom and grow."

"I thought you loved this young lady?" he charged.

"I do," she responded. "I love her like my own daughter, and that's why she needs to leave this den of drunken miners."

The reverend set his cup down, his jaw hanging.

She went on, "There's no school, there's not a man around who doesn't drink away his paycheck week after week, no culture of any sort, and nothing to look forward to but a life of bleakness and boredom. She has no friends, and there isn't a boy in town who has remotely paid attention to her."

"Mrs. Calhoun, how on earth can you utter such words?"

"Very easily, because I've wasted my life in Buchanan County, and I'm damned ashamed I didn't leave after Harold died, and I still might. In the name of God, let's give this girl a chance for a life that isn't laden with poverty and sin."

She sat on the edge of her chair and waved a finger at him. "Reverend Stilter, the sun doesn't rise and set on Grundy. In fact, it never rises and sets down in this valley."

"Eugenia!" he said, completely taken aback with her comments.

"Well, have you ever seen a sunrise or a sunset in Grundy?" she pressed.

The reverend was at a loss for words, since she was right. The sun came up late and set early in Grundy, but this was his community, his charge for the ministry. His job was to make saints out of sinners, and this town lent itself handily to that challenge.

He thought a moment, realizing that he had in large part just agreed with her. He slowly nodded, now thinking about his own family. Three of his children were girls, and what she was saying made good sense. He had already given some thought to their education and where he might send them when they were of age.

"I don't quite understand why you asked me here today," he finally said.

She smiled, poured some more tea, and when she held up the carafe of brandy, she eyed him and smiled again when the receptive nod came. "William Pearlman has a sister in the West," she went on. "I sent her a letter the day after the funeral and informed her that Lydia needs a place to live now that her parents are dead."

"And you think William's sister will respond favorably?"

"I think so."

"How can you be so sure?"

"Because I told her Lydia will have enough money to sustain herself for the first few months, which includes a train ticket to St. Louis."

"St. Louis?"

"Yes. I should think St. Louis has a great deal more educational opportunity than Grundy."

The reverend's eyes slowly looked downward. There was no mistaking that. "How much money would she require?"

"Two hundred dollars would be sufficient."

"Does Lydia have two hundred dollars?"

"No, and neither do I."

"Then where do you expect to get the . . ." He stopped in mid-sentence. "Eugenia, I certainly do not have the money to afford such a journey, and even if I did, I'm certain my wife would question such a donation. I'm afraid I cannot provide you this service."

"Perhaps not, but your church parishioners certainly could."

His mouth dropped again.

"She has no parents and no future. Surely your flock of churchgoers would find it in their hearts to donate this paltry sum, which will be this girl's salvation."

He eyed her suspiciously.

"Especially if the suggestion comes from one so highly respected in the community."

His eyes remained fixed on her as if he had just received a blow on the back of his head. "This . . . will require a bit more study," he mused.

Eugenia Calhoun smiled and poured some more tea, and without asking this time, she slipped in some more brandy.

Almost three weeks to the day later, a letter came back from St. Louis, from Almetta Boggs, William Pearlman's sister. Eugenia Calhoun read over the response, and when Lydia returned later in the day, Mrs. Calhoun sat her down and placed the letter in front of her.

Lydia could read some, and as she picked her way through each sentence, her eyes slowly saddened. When she finished, her mouth was quivering. The pitiful look on her face was almost too much for Mrs. Calhoun.

"You don't want me to live with you anymore?" she asked. The tears came, though she tried to hold them back.

Eugenia slipped an arm around her and hugged her ever so tightly. "Darlin', it's for your own good."

In between the tears, Lydia blurted out, "But I love it here. I want to stay with you forever." She was sobbing now.

The charge in Eugenia's heart was fierce as she forced herself to restrain her own tears. Lydia was, for all practical purposes, as close to her as a daughter could be, and though she hated to give her up, it was without a doubt the best for her.

"I don't even know where St. Louis is," Lydia said. She could not understand why she had to leave. It was as if this grand old lady, who could well have been her grandmother, had stuck a dagger in her heart. For the last few years, Mrs. Calhoun and her home had provided the only semblance of normality in her life, and now Lydia realized that was coming to an end.

During the following week, Lydia's moods wavered up and down, but she slowly resolved herself to the fact that she would be headed for a faraway place to live with someone she never knew. "Look at it as an adventure," Mrs. Calhoun told her, but Lydia wasn't sure she was ready for this sort of adventure.

"I ain't never been farther than Card," Lydia responded. The little town of Card was eight miles away, a trip she had made with her father in a wagon, but that was before the war when she was no more than five years old. What lay beyond the mountains was a mystery to her, and if anything, her curiosity did get the better of her. She likened the journey to the flowing river—wondering where it would lead.

As a result, she spent a few hours daily reading what information she could find on this strange, new city called St. Louis. She discovered it lay on the Mississippi, a river she remembered reading about some time ago. It seemed so far, halfway across the continent, and she had heard stories about wild Indians that scalped people for no reason at all. *Savages* was a word that seemed to linger in her mind, a term she thought she once heard in church.

Packing for the journey was the easiest task before her, since Mrs. Calhoun told her she could only take what she could carry. That reduced her clothing to one extra dress, an extra set of underclothes, some personal hygiene items and a photo of her mother and father taken sometime before the war. But as the day neared when she was to leave, apprehensions and fears set in uncontrollably, unrelenting to the point that she had a difficult time sleeping at night.

On the day she was to depart, the sun had risen over the eastern hills with a grand brilliance. It was June eleventh, a date she knew she would never forget. Mrs. Calhoun walked Lydia into the heart of the small town of Grundy to the livery where arrangements were made for Jonathan Girt to drive her to Glade Spring. That was some forty miles away to the south, the closest point from where she could depart on a train.

She was dressed in a long beige skirt with a gray vest jacket. A wide-brimmed straw hat with a red band and a few feathers sticking out of it adorned her head. She kept some food, some personal items and nearly two hundred dollars in cash in a large purse with straps that ran up over her shoulder. She had never possessed so much money and really had no idea what this amount could purchase.

"You're very special," Mrs. Calhoun told Lydia. "The church parishioners took it in their hearts to raise this money for you." What Lydia did not know is that Mrs. Calhoun had contributed thirty of her own dollars, and at the last moment, Reverend Stilter added forty of his own personal money, since the donations from the parishioners had come up short.

"Don't you pay any more than thirty cents for a meal," Mrs. Calhoun advised Lydia as they stood next to Jonathan's dray. "Don't ever let your purse out of sight, bathe as often as you can and don't talk to any strangers."

Lydia found the advice somewhat confusing. Between Grundy and St. Louis, she was sure she would not meet anyone she knew, so it appeared she would be making a trip without talking to anyone.

"Grandmama," she said as the tears once again came involuntarily, "I'll miss you so very much."

"I'll miss you, too, darlin'," she said. "You write as soon as you arrive."

"I will, Grandmama."

Jonathan gave her a helping hand up into the dray, and when he clucked his teeth, the matched pair of draft horses marched off at a steady trot. Mrs. Calhoun stood for the longest time watching the wagon, and when it disappeared over the hill, it was then she broke down and cried. No one had ever called her grandmama before, and she doubted anyone ever would again.

Two

Jonathan Girt was one of the few in Grundy who didn't work in the mines. His father ran the livery, and like his father, Jonathan was carrying on the tradition. He was about her age, Lydia judged, and she knew who he was, but she had never spoken to him before. His coat and pants were dark colored, but his shirt was white and appeared clean. A floppy hat with a short brim shaded his eyes, and the knee-high boots that he wore were splattered with manure, probably from cleaning the livery stalls, she guessed.

He was nice enough and quiet enough, since for the first six or seven miles, he said hardly a word. As the dray lumbered over another hill, he finally spoke a full sentence.

"I was sorry to hear about you losing your pa."

"Thank you," she responded. She had been teary for the first few miles, but the tears had left her now. "It's no never mind. Momma never was right in the head, and daddy wasn't much better." She quickly changed the subject. "Have you ever been to Glade Spring before?"

"A couple times with my pa."

"Is it a big town?"

Jonathan smiled. "No. A bit bigger than Grundy, but only because it's on the railroad line."

"Have you ever taken a train trip?"

"No."

"Me neither."

The set of dirt tracks that they followed meandered its way over the hills and through a countryside of thick trees and wildflowers. When they passed the cutoff to the little town of Card, she realized that everything she would see from now on would be new and fresh. How strange, she thought, to be sixteen years old and never having been more than eight miles away from where she was born. She wondered if the entire country was this hilly, and whether these kinds of wildflowers were so prevalent everywhere.

She looked at Jonathan and made a face. "How far have you ever been from home?"

"Glade Spring's it."

Lydia let the answer digest. Jonathan hadn't been much farther away from home than she, but within a few days' time, she would be halfway across the continent. She wondered if Jonathan would ever make a trip that far during his lifetime.

Later in the day, and after they had stopped for a quick lunch she had packed, she excused herself and disappeared into the woods to relieve herself. Once back in the wagon, they drove on, the sounds of birds and a gentle wind the only sense of movement about them.

Just short of Saltville, they began to meet a few wagons and an occasional rider on horseback, each person giving a nod and a greeting.

Saltville was a few streets long and lined with more buildings than Grundy, and it was flatter. From here, Lydia was sure, one could easily view the sunrise and sunset much earlier than in Grundy.

When Jonathan stopped to water his horses, Lydia splashed some of the cold water into her face. "Now, ain't that refreshing," she said. As she dabbed her face dry with a handkerchief, she realized that she had been sitting next to Jonathan for several hours. She had never been that close to a boy before, at least for that length of time, and now as she smiled at him, he was smiling back.

Five miles later, the small depot of Glade Spring appeared ahead, its dark siding blending in with the dusky color of the day.

Jonathan helped her down from the dray and handed over her bag. "I wish you a nice trip," he said as he tipped his hat. He crawled back in the wagon and turned the wagon for town. She looked after him for the longest time, her face taking on a sorrowful look. He had touched her hand when he helped her down from the wagon. No boy had ever touched her before.

Inside the station, a few people sat on benches waiting for the train. She set her bag down at a counter where she was to purchase a ticket.

"St. Louis, please," she said to the man. He narrowed his eyes underneath a green visor. "The Tennessee and Georgia don't go to St. Louis."

She was stunned, and the fright in her eyes caught the agent's immediate attention.

"Miss," he said, "I can get you to Chattanooga, where you'll have to change to the Memphis and Charleston." He ran his finger on a wall map. "At Corinth, you'll change again. The Mobile and Ohio will get you to Cairo, and from Cairo—well, ain't no easy route from there to St. Louis."

She couldn't remember everything he said. "How much is a ticket to Chattanooga?"

"Eighteen dollars and fifty cents."

She handed over the money while he was writing out the ticket.

"When does the train leave?" she inquired.

He glanced at the clock on the wall. "Was supposed to leave an hour ago, but you're in luck. Track separated about four miles up. Some boys are working on it now. Soon's it's repaired, we'll sort of be back on schedule, like as we ain't never been off schedule b'fore." He handed her the ticket. "You watch out for those Yankees when you get to St. Louis. They ain't to be trusted."

As she seated herself next to the others waiting for the train, she mulled over what the man behind the counter had said. He evidently favored the South, but her father had fought for the North. What a difference forty miles made, she was thinking.

Three hours later, the train arrived with a thunderous roar and several long blasts from its whistle. She had never heard such a noise, and in fact, she had never seen a train before, other than in a picture book. No trains came through Grundy, not with the Cumberland Mountain Range so nearby.

With smoke bellowing out of the stack and steam shooting out from the sides of the wheels, she was sure the engine had caught fire and feared she would have to wait for a new engine. The other half dozen passengers, who were waiting for the train, rose to their feet and headed for the outside platform. She fell in line, and like the rest of them, she eventually climbed the few metal steps to the passenger car.

When she entered, she gasped in astonishment. The interior was decorated in red and green colors, and oil lamps, every so many feet on each side, dimly lit up the inside. She had sat on wooden benches in a church before, but these seats were all adorned with green velvet-like material, and so comfortable when she seated herself. She bounced a few times, hardly able to believe that any seat could be so soft and inviting.

A sense of euphoria ran through her as she stashed her bag beneath her and removed her hat. She primped her hair and sat back, and when she looked up, she gasped again. "My God!" Swirling flower designs painted in green, yellow and gold adorned the ceiling. The dazzling effect left her mesmerized. Her eyes traced every line, and it wasn't until she felt the train lurch beneath her, that she cast her gaze outside. The dark of the night had taken over, and as the train slowly pulled away from the depot, she strained to watch the passing landscape. Her heart skipped a beat when she realized that all night long, she would not be able to see a thing. She could only think about how much of this vast continent she would miss seeing by morning.

Simply riding on a train kept her in a state of nervous excitement, and unable to sleep because of it, she turned her attention to the other passengers. She counted them, twenty-three in all. Most were men, some dressed quite stately, others in work clothes. Four were black men, all dressed in shabby attire, not at all unlike what she usually wore before she met Mrs. Calhoun. Two young ladies, perhaps in their twenties, she guessed, were dressed in bright clothing, their faces covered with rouge, their lips painted. Two younger men were engaged in conversation with them, and Lydia could only guess by their laughing and giggling that some sort of interesting conversation must be taking place. In the far corner, and bent over examining some paperwork, sat the conductor, an older man with a full gray beard and dressed in a dark blue uniform.

Even though the iron wheels beneath her gave off a rhythmic clank, the sound still offered some solitude, and every now and then the wheels would hit an uneven rail, and when they did, everyone inside swayed from left to right. The acrid smell of smoke from the engine was now sifting its way into the car, but wasn't so unpleasant as to bother her.

No one was sitting directly across from her, but she didn't mind. The phrase that Grandmama Calhoun told her, "Don't talk to strangers," kept reverberating through her mind, but monotony soon set in and sleep eventually overtook her.

In a short time, she woke when she felt the momentum of the train suddenly slow. She peered out and saw the sign of the station stop flit by, but she was unable to read what was written. She soon discovered that every twenty miles or so, the train stopped to take on water for its boilers. On some occasions, a lone water tower was the only structure along the track, and after enough water was jerked, the train moved on. She soon became accustomed to the frequent stops, and after a few more, she began sleeping through them like most everybody else on board.

It was early morning when the wheels below emitted a hollow sound and woke her. The train was crossing a trestle over a wide river. She didn't know the name of the river, but she guessed it was at least five or six times wider than the Louisa Fork back home. Once on the far side of the trestle, she marveled at the patchwork of forests that ranged across the rolling hills. She was amazed at how far she could see. Never had she glimpsed so much blue sky at one time.

"Knoxville next stop. You have thirty minutes," the conductor hollered out as he came down the aisle. "Knoxville next stop, thirty minutes."

As he passed her by, she stopped him. "Sir, can one purchase a breakfast meal here?"

"Certainly can, Miss. You have thirty minutes." He started to move on.

"Sir, can one purchase a meal for less than thirty cents?"

He smiled and adjusted his glasses. "You certainly can."

When the train came to a halt, she filed out with the rest of the passengers, taking her bag with her. Once outside in the open, she could not take in enough of the sprawling city beyond. Here and there some buildings were reduced to rubble. All that remained intact were their brick chimneys towering upward like huge tree stumps. It seemed that everywhere in the city, men were building or rebuilding structures. Supply wagons moved up and down the street, and many of the people that she saw walking on the boardwalks were black.

"Good Lord," she whispered. This was the first devastation she had seen—remnants from the ravages of the war. She wondered how many other communities had suffered like this one, and for a moment, she reflected on her father, who had more than likely been involved in this kind of destruction. She could not help but wonder what sort of insanity must have filled his mind, or anybody's mind, for that matter, who had been a soldier.

She stared across a field to where she saw several wooden boards poking out of the ground. The conductor from the train came up behind her and noticed her fascination with the strange set of markers.

"Eight hundred and twenty-three soldiers are buried there," he said as he focused on the graveyard. "December, eight years ago. One of them is my boy, and he wasn't much older than you."

He seemed in a trance for several seconds.

"I'm terribly sorry to hear that," she said. "My papa . . ." She hesitated. "My papa was killed in the war, too."

He offered a warm smile. "Come along. I'll show you where you can freshen up, and then we'll get you a good breakfast."

She ate, paid twenty-five cents, used the utilities and was back at her seat before the half hour was up. Occupying the seat across from her was a young man with his arm in a sling. She looked about for other free seats, but she had started her journey in this seat and decided she would continue from here, so she excused herself as she squeezed by.

As much as she wanted to keep looking out the window, she was drawn back to the young man, and after two or three glances when their eyes met, they both involuntarily smiled, but she said nothing.

When the train pulled out, she retrieved a book from her purse and opened it. It was far too difficult for her to comprehend, so she pretended to be reading. Her view was slightly raised, focused on the sling that supported the man's arm. His pants were woolen gray, and his shoes were brogans, army issue, she was sure. He wore a black, wide-brimmed hat and had a short, black coat, one arm inside the sleeve, the other sleeve dangling loosely.

His entire arm was wrapped in a bandage, and as unobtrusively as possible, she searched for blood spatters on the cloth, but she could not see any.

She put away the book and when she glanced up, their eyes met once again, and again they both smiled.

"You should smile all the time," the man said. "It becomes you." He removed his hat and placed it on the seat.

She looked down, embarrassed by the remark. Nobody had ever said anything like that to her before. She mustered up some courage. "You're a soldier?"

"Was," he answered. He saw her eyes focus on his bandaged hand and gave a broad smile. "It isn't as bad as it looks."

"My father was a soldier in the war," she said.

"I hope he survived it."

"He didn't," she answered.

"Killed in battle?"

The war indirectly did kill him, but she was ashamed to tell him how he died. "Yes," she finally said.

They both became silent, and now she noticed that the young man was looking out the window. He couldn't be much more than twenty-five or so, she guessed. Underneath his thick, straight, dark hair, his ears poked out. His face was long with a pointed chin, and his dipped eyebrows now offered some mystery about him, which she couldn't understand. As he looked out the window, he bit his lip occasionally, and if Lydia was any judge of body language, he seemed somewhat nervous.

He pulled a watch from his pocket, looked at it, then glanced outside again. She looked outside, too, and in the distance, coming from a copse of trees, four men on horseback were riding hard toward the train, each trailing an additional saddle horse.

When the young man glanced at Lydia, she saw the fear in his eyes. At that moment, a man sitting further down in the coach yanked a chord that ran the length of the car. Almost immediately, the train shuddered to a stop.

Those facing forward slumped across their seats, and with the sudden halt Lydia flopped across into the arms of the young man.

He was suddenly on his feet, and with a twist of the sling over his shoulder, the white wrap dropped to the floor, exposing a pistol.

He suddenly shouted out, "Everybody stay where you are!" Three men, who had been riding in the car, were on their feet with pistols drawn.

"Nobody move and nobody gets hurt," the young fellow shouted again. Everyone froze in place, and then, for at least a minute, the four men remained rigid, holding their pistols firm, and nobody inside the car dared move. Lydia thought for sure they intended to rob the passengers and was dumbfounded why the four men did not act.

Suddenly, from a forward door, two more men entered with pistols drawn.

"Ain't no payroll!" one of them shouted.

"What?" the young man near Lydia asked.

"Ain't no payroll, nothing!" the same man hollered.

The young man's face went blank, and then suddenly he waved his pistol and shouted at the passengers, "Your wallets and your jewelry! And be quick!"

As if the robbers had done this many times before, they moved methodically throughout the car, tossing aside any weapons they found on the passengers and collecting what loot they could find.

Lydia froze, her hand pressed against her chest. The young man near her saw the fear in her face. "Don't worry," he said. "We won't bother you."

When one of the robbers approached Lydia, the young man commanded in a soft voice, "No, not her." The one intent on robbing her didn't even question the command and moved on. Hardly another minute passed and they finished their job.

"Everybody stay inside!" the young man shouted. "First man that pokes his head out gets it blown off."

The robbers scrambled out of the train, taking their treasures with them, and seconds later, all were mounted and riding off.

Pandemonium broke out at once inside the passenger car. Ladies screamed, men scrambled for their weapons, but long before any of the men could get themselves assembled, the riders were well on their way and had disappeared into a thicket of trees.

Lydia sat, her hand still pressed against her breast, stunned from the occurrence. The riders had come from a copse of trees on the north side of the tracks and disappeared into the trees to the south. She drew in a deep breath, happy nobody was hurt and relieved that she still had her money.

The next major stop was Loudon, where a telegraph operator sent out an alert about the robbery. Inside the depot, Lydia remained with a crowd of other passengers until a sheriff and a deputy arrived.

One by one, the passengers were ushered into a smaller room and asked for descriptions of the men and their horses, and the general direction they were headed.

In time, the deputy summoned Lydia into the small room. He was carrying a shotgun, but the sheriff, who sat across from her, didn't have a weapon on him, at least not one that she could see.

The sheriff eyed her suspiciously. "Some folks said the robbers did not take anything from you personally, Miss, ah . . ."

"Lydia Pearlman," she answered in a nervous voice. If he hadn't been wearing a badge on his coat, she could easily have mistaken him for someone off the street. Her idea of a sheriff was not a man who was short and pudgy with patched pants and a smear of tobacco stain on his mustache and beard.

"You sat across from one of the robbers, I understand."

"Yes."

"Did you by any chance hear a name mentioned?"

"No."

He squinted at her. "You rode nearly twenty miles with this individual. Did you have any conversation with him?"

"We talked about the war."

"But he never mentioned his name?"

"No."

"You didn't introduce yourselves?"

"No."

"Hmm. Strange. You sit across from him for twenty miles, engage in conversation, yet, you don't get his name?"

"I'm sitting across from you and I don't know your name," she answered. The sheriff sat stiffly, insulted by the retort. She went on, "Besides, if I was going to rob a train, I wouldn't give out my name. Would you?"

The sheriff eyed his deputy and rolled his eyes. "Interesting that you're the only person on the train they didn't rob. Do you have an explanation for that?"

"They didn't rob the black people, either."

"Blacks don't got nothin' to rob," he countered.

"Do you think I had something to do with the robbery?" she dared to inquire.

The conductor, who had been standing nearby stepped into the conversation. "Elmer, this lady got on at Glade Spring. She ain't no part of this."

The sheriff nodded. "Could you describe this fellow who sat across from you?"

She smiled. "He was good-looking."

The sheriff looked up with a blank face. He already had fair descriptions of the robbers. "You're free to go."

A half hour later, most had boarded the train, a few remained behind. When she entered the car and passed by the conductor, she thanked him for his support.

The robbery was the topic of discussion all the way to Chattanooga, and now and then when Lydia looked up, several of the passengers gave her a wary look. They were suspicious, and rightly so, she thought, knowing that she was the only person who had escaped losing some money or jewelry—besides the blacks. She didn't possess any jewelry, but none of the passengers knew that, yet, she, too, wondered why the robbers never searched her purse.

At the Chattanooga depot, she purchased another ticket for the second leg of her journey to Corinth, Mississippi, not having the faintest idea that the line traversed the entire northern edge of the state of Alabama. For all she knew, as she looked out the window, she was still viewing Tennessee. Very few of the same passengers were in the car with her, which offered her a continued journey fairly free from glares or gossip.

Lydia began keeping track of the distance she had traveled and realized that when she reached Corinth, she would have traveled nearly five hundred miles.

It was evening when the train arrived in the city, a good-sized railroad hub, and it was the first night she spent in a hotel. It was also the first time in nearly three days that she was able to give herself a decent sponge bath. Refreshed but tired, she slept soundly.

She had accustomed herself to rail travel, and the stops and holdovers were becoming commonplace, with very little worry on her part that she would miss a departure. Even if she did, she'd figured out the system and felt relatively safe and secure on her journey.

In the early morning after a simple breakfast, she boarded once again, and a few hours later as the train passed through Jackson heading north to Cairo, lumber mills began showing up along the way. The rolling hills teemed with oak and maple and occasional stands of pine. The lumber mills were a familiar sight, since Grundy had a sawmill of its own. On this leg heading north toward the Mississippi, she saw very little destruction from the war, although she overheard someone mention that a fierce battle had cost the lives of many soldiers at a place called Shiloh. She surmised that the battlefield was considerable distance from the railroad, since it could not be seen.

Every glance outside provided a new experience. She wished she could remember everything she was viewing and be able to picture it later on, but the passing glimpses were too fast and furious. Since she doubted she would ever pass this way again, she regretted that she was unable to spend any reasonable amount of time in the many towns she had passed through.

The novelty of the trip made her forget about home for hours at a time. As shameful as it seemed, she even let the thought of her dead parents slip away for almost as long. To a certain degree, she felt as though this trip had come about by a kind of divine intervention, as if some sort of compensation was being doled out to her for the loss of her parents.

That was nonsense, of course, yet she could not shake the feeling.

Hour upon hour passed as she stared out to open meadows, to the hills beyond filled with endless trees. "Jonathan," she mused, "you don't know what you're missing."

She reflected once again on the robbery and wondered whether the young soldier who'd sat across from her, had gotten away. Certainly, the sheriff from Loudon must have assembled a posse and gone after the thieves. Earlier, a passenger on board had remarked that the robbers would never be caught, since they were headed toward the Smoky Mountains, an entanglement of forest and hills that could hide a person for years. She had never heard of the mountains, but however high they were, she imagined they might be similar to the mountains near her home in Grundy.

As the train pulled into the railroad station at Cairo, she could easily see the river shoreline laden with steamships and their towering decks, two and three stories high. She had never seen a riverboat longer than fifteen feet, nor did she ever think that she would witness something like these monsters that appeared to be nothing more than floating hotels.

Her energy level was as high as the decks of the steamers, and inside the railroad station, she inquired about the best passage to St. Louis.

"You can continue on by rail on the Illinois Central," the agent informed her, "but you'll have to change at a crossroad and catch the Ohio-Mississippi."

She remembered that the man in Glade Spring stated there was no easy route north from Cairo. "Is there an alternative?" she inquired.

"Stage," he said, "but that don't go but once a week." He waited, expecting her to purchase a ticket.

St. Louis was on the Mississippi, and even now she could hear the mournful sound of a steamship horn. "What about a steamship?"

"Yes, ma'am, that's a possibility."

She discounted the stage. Either of the other two options would allow her to reach St. Louis in about two days, but the steamship was three dollars cheaper than the train. Besides, a steamer left about every three hours, whereas the train didn't depart until the next morning.

"Can a person get a meal on the steamer for less than thirty cents?" she asked.

"Basic meals come with the fare. If'n you're picky, you can order extra," the clerk answered. She thanked him, grabbed her bag and started walking toward the pier.

Several hours of daylight still remained when she boarded. She found her quarters, left her bag after freshening up and made her way to the top deck where she had a grand view of the countryside. Traveling on the river was smooth, and only a few hours out of port while rounding a steep bend, she heard someone remark that on this particular curve, more than a hundred steamboats had been sunk or lost in the channel.

When she inquired about the facts, a steward told her, "Miss, you're on the safest steamer that ever traveled the Mississippi." However, she had reason to believe that the man probably delivered the same sort of assurance to every passenger on board.

That evening, she enjoyed a meal of bread, meat and cheese and apple cider. Although her fare included spending two nights sleeping in a small but comfortable cabin, the constant growl of the exhaust and paddle wheel kept her from falling asleep immediately. But to her delight, the daylight hours were warm and filled with sunshine, so she spent every moment on the upper deck.

As the ferry pushed along, she kept her eyes glued to the landscape, fearing that if she ever shut them for even a moment, she might miss something.

THREE

Mid-afternoon on the third day, the steamer approached the levee of St. Louis. A few miles earlier, from the upper deck, Lydia had been admiring the outline of the tall buildings from this sprawling city. In her wildest imagination, she'd never conceived that the city of St. Louis could be so large. Along the levee, hundreds of workers were busy constructing limestone pylons, the foundations for the Eads Bridge, she had learned. The bridge would eventually provide service for the railroad as well as wagon and pedestrian traffic.

As the steamer passed by, she heard another passenger remark that the massive bridge was to be built out of steel girders, and that upon completion, it would be the longest span across a river in America. The bridges she had crossed so far since she left Virginia were trestles made of logs. She could not help but marvel at the size of this project, nor could she fathom in the least where the steel girders for this bridge came from or how they were manufactured.

As soon as the river wheeler docked, Lydia walked down the gangplank, her heart beating with excitement every foot of the way.

Once on the levee, the multitude of travelers in front of her slowly dwindled. A number of carriages were on hand to pick up friends or relatives. Some passengers just walked off, and others simply put down their bags and waited as if they would be picked up shortly.

She searched in her handbag for the address of Almetta Boggs, but had no idea where Market Street was located. As she looked about, a frightening spell swept over her. Cobblestone streets lined the levee front, with huge four- and five-story warehouses in an unending row as far as she could see. In front of these massive buildings, bales of cotton and animal hides by the hundreds lay in stacks. Some distance away, she spotted a train at rest, and from the sidecars, men were wheeling goods off into more warehouses. Everywhere, it seemed, wagons were hauling goods—lumber, barrels of wine or liquor, wooden cases and boxes, and several wagons moved along with goods stashed under canvas covers. She had never seen so many carriages, buggies and wagons at one time.

The noise from the wharf crowded her from all directions—men shouting, horses clipping along the cobblestones with iron shoes on their feet. Steamboats whistled, and their churning paddlewheels gave off the rushing sound of a continuous waterfall. In the air, she could smell a strange combination of burnt wood mixed with a somewhat familiar odor like wet grass or dead fish, and everywhere she looked, squawking seagulls floated aimlessly on a slight breeze searching for morsels of food.

Even with all this activity around her, she suddenly felt alone, and as she again reviewed the piece of paper with the address on it, she mumbled, "Grandmama Calhoun, what do I do now?"

Across from her, a sign above the door of a small station house read *Colson Steamboat Line—tickets*. She headed for it, and once inside she showed the address to the man behind the counter. He was an older man with round, wire glasses and thick, gray muttonchops.

"Almetta Boggs?" he inquired. "How do you know Almetta?"

"She's my aunt," Lydia answered. "Can you tell me how to get to her home?"

He looked up from the piece of paper, rolled his eyes and pointed away from the wharf where a set of iron tracks were imbedded in the cobblestone. "See that set of tracks over there? You wait there. When Curly arrives with his streetcar, you tell him you want to go to Almetta's."

Her curiosity was growing as she headed for the intersection. It seemed a strange coincidence that the man in the station house knew her aunt Almetta, and, according to him, so did the man driving the streetcar.

When she reached the intersection, she drew in a breath of relief. The two signs labeled the crossing as Broadway and Market, and Market was the street on which her aunt lived.

From up the street several blocks away, she saw the horse-drawn streetcar coming, a novelty in itself. Grundy was far too small to even consider a streetcar. She wondered if it would ever grow to a size that demanded a streetcar.

The driver eventually stopped his streetcar directly in front of her over a set of rails that broke apart. He got out, and as he pulled his horse around by the bridle, the streetcar rotated fully and was facing the reverse direction. He locked the rails in place and greeted her. "A fine day to you, mum." She knew an Irish accent when she heard one.

"Almetta Boggs," she said as she plunked herself onto a bench seat.

He gave her a curious look. "Yer a wantin' to go to Almetta's, are ya?"

"Yes. I was told you could get me there."

"Aye, but it'll cost you a thin dime, it will." She stared at him, not understanding. "The fare's a dime to ride the streetcar, mum," he clarified.

She had not even thought about that. She paid him and sat back down, and as the car moved along the street, she became fascinated with the tall, multistoried buildings. She had never seen such huge hotels. One block held more shops and stores than the total number of buildings in Grundy. Carriages and buggies of every kind moved effortlessly along, hundreds of people were on the boardwalks, and now she was curious to know how big this city was. To her surprise, she saw very few black people, but after some thought, she did recall that this was Union country.

After a twenty-minute ride spent taking on and dropping off passengers, the streetcar angled across a main thoroughfare labeled as Jefferson and continued on. After another five minutes or so, the driver stopped just short of a cemetery and pointed to a huge, two-story colonial home.

"Here it is, mum," the man said.

A giant pillar rose majestically upward on each side of the steps. She had seen pictures like this structure before. If she had been in a country setting, she would have considered this huge dwelling to be a plantation home, and for all she knew, it probably was at one time. By the scarcity of homes surrounding her, this area seemed like the edge of the city.

She stood before the massive home for some time before she mustered up enough courage to approach the door. This was, after all, her father's sister, so why shouldn't she be well received?

At the door, she set down her bag and took in a deep breath. She twisted a door ringer, which emitted a growling noise, and after waiting what she guessed to be a half minute, she tried the ringer again, expecting that a maid might well answer the door.

The door suddenly swung open and startled her. An older lady with a heavily wrinkled face and tangled hair loosely tied up in a bun cast her a suspicious glance. One of her eyes was squinted nearly shut. Lydia wasn't sure it was anchored in that position because of some affliction or that she forced it shut. But it gave her an evil look that caused Lydia to shudder.

The old woman wore a puffy, black dress, and the only bit of color on her came from a dull, jade-colored necklace. What intrigued Lydia most about the lady was the long slender cigar that hung on her lip. The woman removed it and snarled, "What is it?"

Lydia was practically speechless. "Does Almetta Boggs reside here?"

Her lip curled up, and in a gravelly voice, she snapped, "You affiliated with that bunch of hyenas downtown on the water-front?"

Lydia had no idea what the question meant. "No, I'm her niece, Lydia, from Virginia."

One of the old woman's eyes widened, while the other remained almost shut. "Well, damned if you don't resemble William," she said with a hint of a smile. " 'Course, I ain't seen him in over twenty years." She opened the door wider. "Come on in, child."

Lydia stepped into the interior. Directly ahead, a flowing staircase swept up and around to the second floor. To her left was a huge, spacious receiving room with several gigantic windows, but most were draped with a material that kept the interior dark and dingy. To her right, a double set of doors led to a room of some sort.

"I was about to have some tea," Almetta said. "Drop your bag and come on." Without waiting, Almetta turned and headed down a corridor. Lydia quit gawking, dropped her bag, caught up with her and entered a long, narrow kitchen. Almetta set a cup next to hers on a table and poured in hot tea from a silver server, then flopped on a chair. She produced a small bottle from her pocket, uncorked it and poured a milky liquid of some sort into her cup. After a puff of blue smoke from her cigar, she snuffed it out in an ashtray, and slurped her tea.

"How'd William die?" she asked.

The question surprised Lydia. "He shot himself."

"And your ma?"

"She died from a fever shortly before pa came home from the war."

"God works in mysterious ways," she said. " 'Course, your pa never was right in the head." Lydia remembered using the exact phrase. Then, in lengthy detail, Almetta spilled out how in England, when she and William were growing up, he fell off a wagon and struck his head.

"He smacked it good," she said. "Didn't seem nothing was wrong but a bad bump, then later in the day he just plain fell down and went into a coma. A few days later he came out of it, but he never was the same." She sipped at her tea. "He was only seven. Surprised he lived this long."

"Did you know my mama?"

"Nope. Letter said you had enough money to stay for two months."

The statement shook Lydia. She was not sure what her aunt meant, but she had visions of having to find new lodging when the two months was up.

Lydia was about to respond when Almetta interrupted. "How old are you, young lady?"

"Sixteen."

"Hmmm." She abruptly got up and headed back to the front door. "Well, let's get you settled in." Lydia quickly trailed behind, having had no time to finish her tea.

"Can you cook?" Almetta asked as she started up the staircase.

"Some," said Lydia.

"Can you clean?"

"I reckon."

"Well, then," Almetta said, as she reached the head of the staircase and opened a door to a bedroom, "we might get along after all. Cass Brohm brings ice three times a week. On Wednesday's he brings groceries. On Fridays, he brings milk. I don't garden no more, so I buy vegetables whenever I can. Got some canned meat in the cellar, but most of it ain't good. Be sure to check the pickles before you eat 'em. Applesauce should be okay, and your own pee and excrement's your responsibility."

The last sentence took Lydia by surprise, but then Almetta opened a commode door and pointed to a chamber pot. "Everybody in this household is responsible for their own pee and excrement. Outhouse is out back." She slammed the commode door shut. "House rule."

Since she and her aunt were the only two living in the home, Lydia found the house rule rather comical, but she kept a straight face.

"You'll be expected to pay for your keep," Almetta said as she left the room. When she was gone, Lydia looked around, overwhelmed. Her aunt had expounded on a great deal, but all Lydia seemed to recollect was pee and excrement.

A week slipped by so quickly, Lydia could hardly believe it. She had her own room now, with a large bed of her very own. The room contained a dresser and wardrobe, but of course, she had nothing to put in either, except her extra dress and underclothes. She placed the framed picture of her mother and father on top of a chest and emptied her personal belongings into one drawer.

Lydia didn't have a nightgown, so Almetta supplied her with one. Even though it was several sizes too big, Lydia didn't care. No one was going to see her in bed, anyway.

The dwelling was indeed a former plantation home. Of the five bedrooms that occupied the second floor, only her bedroom and Almetta's were fully furnished. The other three each possessed a bed and very little additional furniture.

The downstairs consisted of three good-sized rooms besides the grand room and the kitchen—a den, a dining room and a music room. Most space in the music room was taken up by a gigantic, black grand piano. A small washroom off the kitchen contained nothing more than a bathtub and basin, but it was convenient, since the pump for water was in the kitchen.

She soon discovered that every square foot of the house was covered with grime and dirt. Lydia's two-room home back in Grundy was nothing in space compared to this mansion, with hardly any amenities or furniture, but at least it was clean. What furniture the home possessed seemed in good shape, and it was colorful. Lydia could not help but feel that once she had scoured and cleaned everything, life here could be quite comfortable.

She fell into a daily routine. Almetta had set aside cleaning utensils, mainly a bucket and soap and rags, and since these items were in a closet off the kitchen, that's where Lydia began.

Cleaning soon became the easiest of her duties; deciding what to throw out was more critical. Every time Lydia opened a chest or cupboard, a peculiar odor would waft out at her, and a quick search would usually produce the foul item. The icebox shelves held sausage, cold meats and cheeses and some vegetables, but some of the food smelled stale. At the end of the first day, and while Lydia was still in the process of cleaning the kitchen, Almetta came home with two fresh loaves of bread, plunked them on the table and eyed the heap of collectibles piled in a corner.

"What the hell's all that?" she snapped.

Lydia was careful with her answer. "It's stuff I would like you to go through, to see if you want to keep it."

"I don't do cleaning," Almetta said. "If it needs to be throwed out, throw it." With that, she lit up a cigar and went upstairs.

That made things easier for Lydia. During the next few days, she piled up anything and everything that was old, grimy and unusable, and if she wasn't sure what an item was used for, she simply threw it out.

Over the week, as Lydia moved from room to room, the pile of junk outside was growing to an unsightly height. She heaped on chairs without legs, old dress material, shirts, pants and worn out shoes, canvas, piles of newspapers and catalogues, moldy side covers of leather, which she supposed came from a buggy of some sort. She discovered pots and pans with no handles, broken dishes, window frames with glass panes missing, rugs that resembled rags. The list of items went on and on, and finally, the pile outside had become so high and ugly that she needed to get rid of it.

She had seen a black man driving a wagon along the street periodically, and judging by the items he hauled, she assumed he was a junk man. She stopped him one day as he came down the street.

"Sir," she said to him. "May I have a word with you?"

The man, dressed in work clothes, of which nothing matched, stopped, startled by her call.

"Yes, ma'am?" he said as he took off his hat and gave a slight bow. He was bald on top with slightly grayed hair over his temples, and he possessed the largest brown eyes Lydia had ever seen. He was a bit portly, and his nose was flat, as if somebody had pounded it with a rubber mallet, but he had a kind face and a warm smile.

"I could use some help if you're willing."

The man looked around suspiciously, not sure he should be talking to this young white woman, even though he knew she was Almetta's niece.

She could see that he was apprehensive. "I'm throwing some things out and I need someone to remove them. Is that in your line of work?"

His face softened a bit. "Yes, ma'am, that's what I do best."

"Come," she said. "And bring your wagon."

She led him to the backyard to the rising mountain of junk. If his eyes were big before, they became bigger when he took in the huge pile. He gave a wide smile, showing a large set of white teeth.

"I want all of it hauled out of here. Can you do that?"

"Yes, ma'am, I can."

"How much would you charge me?"

"For what?" he inquired.

"To haul it away."

He hadn't anticipated receiving any money for this, since there were a number of items he could use or repair or even sell.

His long silence made Lydia think he was contemplating a price, and when the man slowly shook his head, still deciding on an answer, she said, "Would fifty cents be an adequate amount?"

"Oh, yes, ma'am, that would be very fair."

"Good," she said. "I'll get the money for you."

"Ma'am," he said, "I got two or three good loads here, and you doesn't got to pay me till I'm finished."

"All right," she agreed. "What's your name?"

He removed his hat again and crunched it in his hands. "Amos Jefferson. Most folks around here know me." He offered the statement as if it might lend some credibility.

"Amos, I'm Lydia Pearlman."

"Miss Lydia, I'm glad to meet you." He hesitated, and then, "Ma'am, I don't mean no disrespect, but does Missus Almetta know you's throwing all this out?"

"She sure does, and there's more coming. Mr. Jefferson, I think I can keep you busy for a week."

He flashed his white teeth again, and as she headed for the

door, he started loading his cart.

A week was barely adequate. After cleaning the home from stem to stern, she decided to examine the cellar. With a kerosene lamp in hand, she retreated to the cellar doors at the back of the house. A steep set of steps led her into a dark and dank atmosphere, and the deeper she went, the heavier the smell of wet, damp dirt and spoiled food became.

She counted sixteen steps to the bottom, and once there, she let her eyes accustom themselves to the dark. She turned slightly, and a lump ripped into her throat as she stared into the glaring eyes of a lizard on a shelf. In seconds, it retreated out of sight.

A few shelves were lined with sealed jars of pickles. Some looked green and fresh, and others without a doubt had lost their seal and color. She discovered jars of applesauce and pears and peaches, which all looked good for the most part, but she knew from experience back home that it was best to taste a small piece before engaging a mouthful. Other jars contained what appeared to be pickled beef or pig hocks. She wasn't sure.

At the far end of the cellar, several bottles of red wine filled a rack. She guessed these were home brew, not at all unlike what she remembered her father making.

Other than being musty and chilly and with a smell of stale vegetables, the cellar seemed solid. The walls were smeared with a sort of cement finish, and the ceiling was braced with heavy beams. She guessed the cellar had been here ever since the home was built.

She retraced her footsteps back up the stairs with a few jars of fruit in her hands. She left them on the veranda and retreated to the carriage house at the back of the yard. A row of trees around the premise marked the size of the lot. Huge oak trees here and there provided constant shade over the entire yard throughout the day.

Inside the carriage house, she discovered an elaborate buggy that appeared to be in good running order. An inside wall held an assortment of harnesses, which she presumed belonged to the buggy. Numerous cans and containers in various sizes and boxes filled with odds and ends lined some shelves. Along the side walls, pieces of flat metal, wire springs and an assortment of tools were strung out in haphazard fashion.

She entered a small partitioned-off room, which housed a tool shop and workbench. Two dusty saddles hung on wooden posts, and above them reins, bits and bridles hung on wooden pegs.

She came back into the livery. The floor area, which could easily accommodate two more buggies or wagons, was packed dirt. Harnesses, leather straps and iron rings were pounded into it and had been run over so many times that they'd become a part of the floor.

"Good Lord," she mumbled to herself. It would easily require another week just to set the carriage house in order.

When Amos returned, he and Lydia began sorting through the junk. She charged Amos with singling out what he thought was in good working order and should be kept, and what should be thrown away.

"I'll be happy to sort it," he told her, "but you make the final decision what gets throwed."

In his judgment, the saddles could be reconditioned, but the only good harness set was that on the wall, which he said could be softened for use with a little oil, and he could repair the leather reins.

He looked the buggy over with a critical eye and ran a hand along the leather seat. "Yes'm, Miss Lydia. Mistah and Missus

Boggs rode in this buggy many a time. In them days, they had a big, black Tennessee walker. Oh, he was a beauty!"

"What happened to the horse?" Lydia inquired.

"Mistah Boggs, he one day up and sold him. Such a shame. Oh, yes, he was a beauty."

"Why'd he sell him?" she inquired.

Amos made a face. "Miss Lydia, I don't think it's my place to discuss what Mistah and Missus Boggs done and why they done it."

"Then you knew my uncle?"

"Yes'm."

"Is he still alive?"

Again Amos shrugged. "Miss Lydia, I don't mean no disrespect, but it ain't my place to talk about that."

The defiant look on his face told her he wasn't about to go on, and although she let the subject drop, it didn't diminish her curiosity any. Once again, she turned her attention to the interior of the livery. A thick crust of age-old horse droppings caked the stalls, and beyond them, several bins were stocked with hay.

"What are we going to do with that hay?" she asked Amos.

"It's old and moldy, Miss Lydia. Best burn it."

"Then burn it. And you keep track of your time. I don't expect you to do all this work for nothing."

"Yes'm."

"And when you find time, Amos, that outhouse has to be moved. Dig a new hole and cover up the old one. Can you do that?"

"Yes'm, be happy to."

Lydia smiled to herself, wondering how anyone could be happy digging a new shit hole. The old one was full, and although Lydia had doused it with lye, it was long overdue for a new location.

★ ★ ★ ★ ★

July 8 1872

Dear grandmamma Ugena,

I am in St. Louis and ok. It is very big over 250,000 peapl. Most of my day is bizy clening. Aunt Almetta smoks seegars so the er stinks. I rod a streetcar puled by a hors. It is on traks. The trantripp was long but I saw a lot. Ther was a robery. Aunt Almetta is strang but kind. She is gone everday somwar I dont no war. She has a bathtub I never saw won befor hav you? I met a nis blak man Amos. We saw a paraid on July 4. Lots of horses and I saw a fir ingin and som generals. Everday they bild the bridg. I am fin.

Lov Lydia

Almetta was not at all surprised to see Amos haul the junk away. She had hired Amos on numerous occasions in former years, but she was not happy that Lydia paid him fifty cents to do it.

"He would have done it for nothing," she scolded. "You threw away fifty cents, child. No sense in wasting money when we haven't got much."

Lydia wondered what she meant by that, since it appeared she had money. She owned this plantation home, she didn't work, and every day she was off somewhere, and she usually returned by streetcar, which cost a dime.

"Why you spending your own money on this old place?" Almetta asked her.

That was a good question, and Lydia was surprised she hadn't asked earlier. "Aunt Almetta, I ain't never had things so nice. I just want to keep this home nice and clean. Is that so bad?"

The question seemed to slip right past Almetta. "What's Amos doing in the carriage house?" she demanded.

"We're cleaning it and throwing stuff out."

"It's full of horse shit," Almetta said. "I ain't paying nobody to haul away horse shit."

"I'll be responsible for that."

Almetta fixed her eyes on Lydia. Her bad eye was twitching heavily, and then in a much softer voice and as if in a dream world, she said, "Big Mike could really pull that buggy. He was fast, too. Should have never sold him." Her mind had wandered, and a few seconds later, she abruptly returned to the house. At the veranda, she wheeled around and hollered at Lydia, "I ain't paying to haul no horse shit away!"

The total money Lydia paid Amos was only a few dollars, and it certainly wasn't wasted. Amos realized that Lydia had an interest in reading, so whenever he acquired any sort of reading material or books while scrounging, he dropped them off for Lydia, and if nobody was home, he left them on the veranda, where Almetta and Lydia sometimes sat in the afternoon enjoying the warm sun.

By now Lydia had gathered up quite a few books, and they were filling a shelf in the grand room, where she often read in the evening.

A month had passed since Lydia's arrival, and one afternoon Almetta confronted her as the two sat in the grand room, sipping tea. Almetta was eyeing the collection of books Amos had brought. "What the hell's this obsession with reading?" she demanded.

"Grandmama Calhoun used to help me with reading and writing back home." Lydia waited some time for a response.

"Learn anything?"

"I try reading these books, but they're too difficult. I need some simpler books and I need to learn writing. And I don't have any maps."

Her aunt's eye was twitching again. "You ain't got no grand-mama."

"She's as close to a grandmama as I have," Lydia answered.

Almetta gave a cold stare, as if the answer annoyed her. Then, almost scolding and with the demeanor of a charging bull, she said, "I ain't no teacher. You want books and maps, go see Bertha Ginghold at the library. Tell her I sent you."

Lydia was slowly becoming accustomed to the sometimes brash and abrupt speech that Almetta blurted out. She appeared to be thinking one thing and then answered with something else. It was as if her mind lingered a sentence or two behind what was being discussed.

"I don't know where the library is," Lydia confessed.

"Curly does." She poured herself some more tea, removed the bottle she kept in her pocket and added some of the milky-looking substance. She practically drank the tea down in one gulp, then got up and went to the window. "Somebody move that outhouse?" she asked.

"Yes," said Lydia. "I had Amos dig a new hole."

"Thought so." She looked around. "Sure is bright in here," she remarked as she climbed the staircase to her bedroom.

Lydia couldn't help but laugh a little. She had opened the drapes wide and washed the sheer curtains during her first week at the home. Every day since, the grand room had been so much brighter. Equally funny was the fact that her aunt had been using the outhouse for almost a month at its new location, yet it was only now that she realized it had been moved.

The suggestion to visit the library was something Lydia couldn't refuse. The next day, Amos arrived to do some yard work, so Lydia stayed around to give him instructions. Mid-morning on the day after, she was on the street waiting for Curly to come along. Although this was the first trip she was making into town on her own since she arrived, it was her third time riding in the streetcar, and Curly, the jovial driver, remembered her.

"Mornin', Miss Lydia," he greeted as she paid her fare.

"Aunt Almetta said you would take me to the library."

He laughed as he snapped the reins on his horse. "Aye, mum, I certainly can. If that's what yer aunt Almetta wants, that's what yer aunt Almetta gets."

She was curious. "How did you know my name was Lydia?"

He laughed again, his thick mustache bouncing. "On me route, I know just about everybody. Aye, that I do, mum."

Lydia got off on Fifth Street with directions to walk four blocks to Locust, where the Mercantile Library was located. Along the way, she passed the Everett House, not realizing it was one of the major hotels in the city. Her walk was invigorating, the morning filled with an air of excitement and sunshine, and she enjoyed every step along the way.

The Mercantile was a large, two-story corner building. Underneath sweeping arcades, a sheltered walkway ran the entire length along both sides of it.

She entered into a large room that seemed to stretch forever. She never dreamed that she would find so many books in one place. The lady behind a desk had her face buried in a book when Lydia approached. She was older, like her aunt, with dark hair tied in a bun. Pearl buttons ran up the front of her blouse all the way to her neck, which, to Lydia, appeared most uncomfortable.

"Can I help you?" she asked when she looked up.

"Are you Bertha Ginghold?"

She scrutinized Lydia for a moment. "You must be Lydia."

"Yes," answered Lydia, amused that she knew who she was. "How did you know?"

"You fit Almetta's description. I understand you would like

some special reading material?"

Fit her description? thought Lydia. Her aunt had described her to this lady, Bertha? She came back to the initial question. "I would like books and maps and anything else that could help me with reading and writing."

"Follow me," she said. Surprisingly, Bertha very quickly gathered up books with maps and some workbooks that were school readers, not unlike the readers Mrs. Calhoun had supplied for her. As Lydia trailed Bertha around the various stacks, she eyed the few individuals who were seated at tables. Some were reading books, others were engrossed in newspapers, and still others were apparently just lounging.

Back at the counter, Bertha checked out the material. "Tell Almetta the temperance meeting has been changed to Saturday night."

"Temperance?" repeated Lydia. She did not know what the word meant.

"Yes." Bertha, hinting at a smile through her thin lips, handed over the reading material. "I hope these are what you are seeking. And read a newspaper once in a while," she suggested.

Lydia did not catch the streetcar immediately; rather, she walked to Fourth Street where she discovered several small shops, among them Scruggs, an appliance and clothing store, and the Barr Drygoods Company. She mostly window-shopped and stopped in front of one store where a few colorful dresses were displayed in the window. What she was now wearing was very plain compared to those on display. She wondered how much one of those dresses might cost, and as she stared in the window, she noticed her reflection in the glass. She twisted and turned slightly, watching her dress swirl, and then she stood perfectly still examining her silhouette. At that moment, two young ladies passed her by, chatting as they went, both dressed in very fashionable clothes, and both with pretty faces, or so she thought. Once again, she studied her reflection in the window. "I wonder if I'm pretty," she said in a low voice.

For most of the day, she wandered the streets. On Washington, she came upon the Lindell Hotel, and out of curiosity she entered long enough to glance at the elaborate and huge lobby, then returned to the street. Farther up she sat on a bench in front of the university, where she spent some time simply observing those who passed by. She was enthralled with the size of the city and the heavy traffic. Grundy would never grow to this size, she was sure. In a valley with steep hills surrounding it, it had nowhere to expand.

Rather than take the streetcar home, she walked the entire distance and arrived late in the afternoon and very hungry. She could smell something good cooking, and when she reached the kitchen, Almetta had the table set.

She spoke brusquely, "Where you been all day?"

Lydia usually prepared the meals, so she thought she was in for a scolding.

"I went to the library."

Almetta eyed the books. "I can see that."

"I met Bertha."

"Figured so." While Lydia washed up, Almetta dished up two bowls of soup and set a plate of sliced bread alongside with a jar of jelly.

Lydia savored the soup. It contained onions, potatoes, some green tips which she couldn't identify, and bacon bits or ham. "This is delicious."

"Used to have it on hand when Elmore came home."

"Who's Elmore?"

"My no-good, drunken husband."

Lydia looked up.

"Good, huh?" Almetta asked.

"What?" inquired Lydia.

"The soup."

Lydia smiled. "How did Bertha know I was coming today?"

Almetta spooned in a mouthful of soup and tore off a piece of bread, and as she chewed it, she looked across at Lydia. "He fell down the steps once too often."

Lydia realized this was another one of those moments when her aunt was a few sentences behind with her response. "Bertha told me to tell you the temperance meeting has been moved to Saturday night."

Almetta held her spoon steady, letting the information sink in. "Good."

"Aunt Almetta," Lydia inquired. "What does temperance mean?"

"Moderation!" she blurted out. "Especially with drinking!"

The sudden outburst startled Lydia. Almetta went on eating, but under her breath Lydia was sure she heard her say, *the son of a bitch.* She guessed she was talking about her husband, and if she was, Lydia now had a fair idea of what temperance meant.

Almetta finished her soup, and after she lit up a cigar, she left the room. Lydia heard her footsteps as she ascended the staircase.

Lydia finished eating, and while she was gathering up the dishes to wash them, she discovered her aunt's teacup was still half full. Knowing that her aunt habitually would add some ingredient from a bottle she kept in her pocket, Lydia's curiosity was at a pique. She first smelled the tea, and then drank the remainder. It had a tea flavor, but there was a definite bitter aftertaste. Lydia guessed her aunt was spiking her tea with some kind of liquor. Yet, if it was liquor, how could her aunt justify being a member of a temperance group, which was against drinking?

The thought remained with her for a while, and after she put away the dishes and cleaned the kitchen, she retired to the grand room where she lit a pair of oil lamps. She had perused the library material while she was sitting on the bench in front of the university, but now she could study it in depth.

She read through one of the school readers, and when she practiced writing, she concentrated specifically on her spelling. She became so engrossed in her study that three hours had passed before she realized it.

With tiredness working its way into her system she put out one lamp, and with the other, retired to her bedroom. She thought about taking a warm bath, but she would have to pump enough water, and then heat it. If she had wanted a bath, she should have been heating water while she was reading.

It was an especially warm night, even clammy, and when she opened a window, a fresh breeze swept through and cooled her. She removed her dress and underclothes, and with room temperature water in a basin, she sponged off her body.

Next to her wardrobe was a full-length mirror, where she stood completely nude. She observed her reflection for some time, wondering if she would remain this thin forever. Her breasts were beyond budding, but far from full. She grasped each and squeezed them, staring at the small, brown nipples, wondering whether her breasts would grow faster if she massaged them.

The hair around her pubic area was but a tiny wisp, hardly covering anything at all. She dropped her hands to her sides and twisted her body to produce a profile. She turned the other way and raised a hand behind her head to strike a pose, and she smiled.

When she reflected on the two young ladies she had seen on the street earlier in the day, her smile slowly faded. "I wonder if I'm pretty," she said. After she crawled into her nightgown, she picked up the picture of her mother and father from the night-stand and studied it. "Momma, you were so beautiful." She glanced at herself in the mirror again. Her facial features definitely resembled those of her father. She put out the lamp and lay on the bed, staring at the strong ray of moonlight coming through the window. Crickets were chirping now, something she had never noticed before, and then she heard an owl call out. Grundy had owls, too. And crickets.

The next afternoon, a letter arrived from Grundy, Virginia. Hardly able to contain her excitement, she ripped the envelope open and read the contents.

August 1, 1872

Dearest Lydia,

I am relieved to learn that you reached St. Louis safely. Praise the Lord! I did not realize St. Louis was so large. I am sure Mrs. Boggs will treat you like a daughter, as I am aware that she never had any children.

You mentioned a robbery. I hope it did not involve you and that your money is still in safekeeping. I'm sure if anything was stolen, you would have told me.

You are fortunate to have parades in St. Louis. For our 4th of July celebration, the Grundy band played at Spicer's Bar. Those who attended brought food to share. Afterward on the way home, Reverend Stilter fell and broke his leg. Mrs. Stilter said it was slippery after a mild rain, but many said he left Spicer's bar a bit tipsy. I don't know which is true. I'm sure the Lord knows.

I miss you very much, but am happy you have found a new home. Write soon.

Your loving Grandmama Eugenia

Lydia placed the letter back in the envelope and looked up, her eyes tearing. "I miss you, too, Grandmama."

FOUR

The temperance meeting came and went, and so did three more, a week apart. This group of ladies, who seemed to meet on a fairly regular basis, were all members of the Women's Temperance League. The group usually met at one of the members' houses, and tonight, a hot and humid August evening, the meeting was held at Almetta's home.

The front street and backyard were filled with buggies, surreys, flatbed wagons and even a few saddle horses on which women arrived. The official count was thirty-two women, and although Lydia helped serve cake and tea along with Almetta, she chose to remain in the kitchen most of the evening, but she kept her ears cocked, catching whatever she could glean about the strange conversation going on.

Although the doors and windows were wide open to let some air circulate, the ladies were constantly fanning themselves. Those who didn't bring fans had handkerchiefs out. With all the fans and handkerchiefs waving back and forth, the grand room seemed in constant motion.

"We need more members," someone suggested.

"One for every household," another added.

"What about another march?"

"That's a good idea," came a response. "When's the next holiday?"

"Columbus Day," someone answered.

"Too far away," another commented. "How about something sooner?"

One older lady complained that they should have marched on Independence Day, but that was already long gone.

"Bessie Allen," someone said. "Your husband's the circuit judge. He wouldn't object to us setting our own march, would he?"

Bessie practically choked. "Not if he's drunk when I ask him."

Hearty laughter followed, and on and on the discussion went, and when it appeared that all were settled on a Tuesday, two weeks away, Almetta called for more iced tea. After all the ladies were served up, Lydia retired to the veranda outside.

The air was fresh, and in spite of the humidity, a slight breeze out of the south was gently flowing over the yard. Across the way among the many wagons and carriages, where a lantern burned, Amos Jefferson and his son were sitting on a few stumps. Both had been hired to watch the horses during the meeting. Just to be friendly, and mostly because she was bored with the temperance meeting, she wandered over to them, enjoying the breeze of the night.

"Evenin', Miss Lydia," Amos greeted as he stood up and removed his hat.

"Hi, Amos," she greeted back. She had not met his son. As she moved into the light of the lantern, she could see that he was a good-looking man with a smiling face just like Amos' and muscular like Amos. When he stood and removed his hat in respect, she had an even better look at his face. He might have been twenty, she judged, but a black face for her was hard to judge.

"This is my boy, Calvin," Amos explained.

"Good evening, Calvin," she said. "It was nice that you and your father were able to help us out on such short notice."

"Yes, ma'am," he said with a nod. "We were happy to. My

daddy speaks highly of you and Missus Almetta."

She addressed Amos again, "Had I known earlier the meeting was to be held here, I'd have notified you sooner."

"That's no trouble, Miss Lydia."

"Do you mind if I sit for a few minutes?" she asked.

The lantern light caught Amos' bulging eyes as he looked at his son, his hands still twisting his hat. "Oh, I don't know as that's a wise thing, Miss Lydia," he answered. "I don't mean no disrespect, but sitting here with two, ah . . ."

"Colored men?" she finished. "In the dark, we all kind of look the same, don't we?" She smiled as she sat on a stump.

The men eyed each other, and feeling more comfortable, they chuckled as they sat.

"Amos," she said. "I have a question for you."

"Yes'm."

"Is laudanum a liquor?"

Amos' eyes flashed in the dim light. "Laud'num?"

"My aunt Almetta puts laudanum in her tea. I discovered a bottle with that word written on it. Is that a brandy or whiskey?"

"No, ma'am, that's a medicine. Your auntie is takin' a medicine. It's for a sickness."

That seemed to solve the problem for Lydia, but she wondered what sort of sickness her aunt had. "She uses it in her tea all the time."

"All the time?" Amos asked.

"All the time," she answered. Amos was shaking his head, but she didn't know why.

"Lydia!" she heard Almetta shout from the veranda. She excused herself from Amos and his son and ran back to the house.

When she was gone, young Calvin looked at his father. "What's the difference between liquor and laud'num, Daddy?"

"Well, son," Amos said, offering his best explanation. "Too

much liquor makes you temp'rarely funny. Too much laud'num makes you perm'nently funny."

Two weeks later, on Tuesday, the Women's Temperance League convened on the street along the waterfront. At least seventy-five women of all ages were in attendance. On a wooden crate, which had been hustled into position, several ladies in turn delivered their lectures on the evils of drinking. After practically every sentence, the listeners in the group cheered and waved their makeshift signs that labeled various slogans against drinking.

Lydia was not a member of the league, but Almetta suggested it would be good for her to attend the rally, and that it would be a good education for her. She did not feel she could decline, so she accepted, but she stood off to the side far enough away from the throng of leaguers so as not to be associated with them.

The last to speak, and not too surprisingly, was Almetta Boggs. Halfway through her lecture, a man near Lydia grunted and remarked, "Jesus Christ, she's at it again. Somebody ought to stuff a rag down her throat."

The man next to him hollered out, "Almetta! Whyn't you get on your broom and fly out of here?"

She heard the comment from the heckler. "Jack Sutter, you drunken sinner," she shot back at him with a pointed finger. "What are you going to tell your wife when you go home drunk tonight? That you been fornicating with that whore at Darby's?"

The crowd of women turned and jeered at him, some of them bold enough to take his name in vain.

"Good God!" the man named Sutter said to his friend. "How the hell'd she know about that?"

A few other men not too far away were laughing at the comment, but Lydia was embarrassed for both her aunt and the young man next to her. She reasoned that Darby's must be a saloon or a house of ill repute or both, and when she looked down the wharf, she spotted the saloon.

Almetta delivered a few more scathing remarks at the man known as Jack Sutter, her wicked tongue driving him into a shell of silence, and then she was back at the crowd, lecturing again about the evils of drinking.

Jack Sutter turned to Lydia, his face flushed. "Are you with this group of women?" he asked.

"No, I'm not."

"Well, I'm glad to see at least one woman here has not lost her senses."

She appreciated the fact that he addressed her as a woman, but she did not agree with his assessment. "Sir," she said to him. "I do not believe these ladies are against men who drink in moderation."

"Oh?" he said. "Than what are they against?"

"They're against married drunks who fornicate with whores. That's the message I got."

The man grunted. "Be a good idea if you joined this bunch of jackals." He nudged his friend, and the two walked off.

When he was gone, Lydia surmised that if these ladies were the jackals, then he must have been one of the hyenas her aunt had alluded to some time ago.

When Lydia turned her attention back to the meeting, one of the steamships anchored at the levee blasted a horn as the ship backed away from shore, drowning out Almetta's speech. She held up long enough until the horn abated, but when she began anew, once more the horn sounded, its deafening roar making it impossible for anybody to hear anything. She again stopped and stared at the steamer with eyes that would kill an attacking bear, and as if her glare had got through, the deep horn blast finally abated.

As soon as she finished her speech, the ladies cheered and waved their signs. Then, like a flock of sheep, they all turned and marched to the street running beside the levee and proceeded to parade along the fronts of all the saloons and whorehouses. Lydia trudged behind, giving herself plenty of space so as not to be identified with them.

Down the street the ladies marched, chanting phrases in unison, occasionally stopping in front of a saloon, drilling their message home.

Lydia was so intrigued with the rally that she really hadn't been paying attention to the weather. When a few drops of water fell, she thought nothing of it, but like a wave of running animals, a wind swept in over the Mississippi, and she saw the wall of rain coming.

Most of the ladies were in the middle of the street, and the stacks of bales and goods toward the levee side prevented them from seeing the rapidly approaching onslaught. When the rain struck, it struck with a devastating fervor. Women yelled and screamed as they scrambled for shelter. A few had umbrellas, but as soon as they extended them, the heavy wind whipped them away. Like a herd of stampeding cattle, the ladies scrambled en masse for the sides of the streets. For twenty minutes straight, the drenching rain pelted every square inch of open space.

Ironically, the only escape from the storm was along the saloon fronts under the overhangs. It was a most comical sight for Lydia to see some of the ladies secure their safety at the very doors they had formerly been protesting. Even those under the overhangs did not escape the rain entirely. The wind was so fierce that dresses flew, bonnets tore from heads, and every placard and sign was whipped from their hands.

At the end of the first wave of rain, several of the saloon doors opened, and out came some of the marching ladies, the few who had escaped the rain entirely. And right behind them were the saloonkeepers and drinking patrons.

"Come back any time ladies," someone shouted.

"Next time, the drinks are on us," shouted another.

It was a sad state of affairs for the marching temperance ladies. The march, as seriously as it started out and as comically as it ended, was sure to make the headlines in the newspaper the next day.

Almetta and Lydia were a couple of miserable wet hens when they finally returned home. Curly, the streetcar driver, usually was quite talkative, but he said nothing during the entire trip that day.

The two took hot baths that evening before they settled in for the night. In the morning, Lydia was up bright and early, but when she checked on Almetta, she was still in bed.

"You've got a fever, I think," Lydia said as she felt her aunt's forehead.

Scraggly hair hung down over Almetta's face, like it usually did. "Get my medicine," she said as she motioned to a drawer. She drank a swig straight from the bottle, corked it and placed it under her pillow.

"Are you going to be all right?" Lydia asked.

"Where are my cigars?"

Three days later, Almetta was up and around again.

October 2, 1872

Dear Grandmama Ugenia,

Thank you for yor letter and forgiv me for not riting sooner. I was sorry to hear Revernd Stilter brok his leg. Tell him so. I atended my first temprans march with Aunt Almetta last August. It went well as cud be expected altho it rained. Almetta took il but Laudanum duz wonders for her. It is good medicine. I am studying riting and reading almost every day and I atend the library offen. I wons talked to a young man ther but I have not seen him latly. I eat well and have ganed a few pounds. But I am not fat so dont worry.

I have some money left but it soon will be gone. I dont think Almetta rememberd I was to pay for to months. She forgot. She forgets a lot. I think Elmore was her husband. Last week Almetta sold the piano. I got work as a waitres at the train stashun, and I get a tip sometims and won free meal each day. I like it.

Almetta has anothr march on Columbus Day so I hop it dozent rain. I hop you are well.

Love, Lydia

FIVE

When the cold weather set in, they shut off the upstairs and kept the kitchen and den doors closed downstairs. Almetta took over the den as her bedroom and Lydia utilized the music room as her place to sleep. Without the piano, the room now offered a lot of space, and a couch became her bed. It was simply too much trouble keeping up fires in the three fireplaces to heat the entire home, and this was the arrangement Almetta had made over the past several years.

November was exceptionally chilly, and keeping up with the one fireplace was becoming a chore. On a cold, Saturday morning, Lydia watched out the window, waiting for Amos to drive up in his wagon. When he arrived, she greeted him at the back door and ushered him into the kitchen where she had hot coffee brewing.

"S'good to see you, Miss Lydia. I's wondering how you's getting along this winter."

"That's why I asked you over, Amos. We've closed most of the house down, but we can't keep up with one fireplace. In the morning, I can stoke the fireplace and the kitchen stove, but I'm working now, and during the day Aunt Almetta needs help."

He nodded. "I know'd you got a job at the railroad place, and I'd like to help, but I's got permanent work now for the winter, Miss Lydia, a good job working the stables at the Wilkinsons'. And they's three miles from here." He saw the sorrow crawl over her face.

"But, if you gots no objection, I think Calvin would attend the fire for you. He ain't got no work now, and he wouldn't charge much. Jes' his keep would be good enough."

Her face brightened. "Amos, that would be wonderful, but I'll pay him, and he can stay in the carriage house. The upstairs quarters has a stove, and he can eat with us here."

"Miss Lydia, that would be a fine arrangement."

The next day, Calvin brought over his personal things, and inside of a few hours, he had a fire going in the carriage quarters and was settled in.

"Not much to do but haul wood and keep the fire going," Lydia instructed him. "Aunt Almetta pretty much takes care of herself, but she needs watching occasionally."

Calvin nodded, his whole being as attentive as could be. "Yes'm, I can handle that."

"And if Aunt Almetta asks you to run errands for her, I hope you will accommodate her."

"Yes'm."

Over the next week, Calvin faithfully kept the fires going in the fireplace and the kitchen stove, and he watched over Almetta like a hawk. She loved being pampered, and as a result she began to spend many hours of her day in bed.

"Calvin," she would holler. "Bring me a cigar." And Calvin would bring her a cigar.

"Calvin! Tea!" And he would bring her a cup of tea.

"My medicine," she would say, and he would fetch her bottle, and though he offered to pour it in, she took that small chore upon herself.

One late evening, hardly a week after Calvin started work, Lydia arrived home to find him in the kitchen with an apron draped around him. Usually by this time, he had retired to his room in the carriage house.

"Evenin', Miss Lydia," he greeted. He was stirring a soup

kettle with a wooden spoon.

She easily recognized the aroma from it. "Calvin," she chuckled. "What on earth are you doing over the cookstove?"

He hunched his shoulders. "Miss Lydia, I ain't so sure myself. This morning your Auntie sort of gave me instructions how to prepare this soup for her. It took me some time to find all the fixin's and I'm doing the best I can."

"I believe it's a special soup she used to make," Lydia commented.

"Yes'm," Calvin responded. "She says she has to have it for Elmen or Elmer or somebody when he comes home. I don't know what she means."

Lydia knew. "Has she been asking for her medicine today?"

" 'Bout every hour with her tea. Miss Lydia, I don't think she should take that medicine. It does funny things to her head."

When Lydia walked into the den, Almetta was sprawled out on her cot. Her eyes were shut, but she must have heard Lydia's footsteps.

"Is that you, Elmore?" she asked.

Lydia sat next to her. "Aunt Almetta, it's me, Lydia."

She opened her eyes, and then, for the longest time, she held a blank stare on her face as if she were trying hard to concentrate on where she was or who Lydia was. "Well, I know that!" she finally said, and then she slumped back against per pillow, sound asleep.

It was definitely the laudanum. Lydia knew Doctor Regenfeld, who lived a half dozen streets away, so she sent Calvin to summon him. Inside of an hour, she heard a horse and buggy drive up, and Calvin ushered the doctor in. He was a big man, heavyset, with a nicely trimmed mustache and goatee. After he removed his coat and hat, he sat by Almetta and lifted an eyelid with his thumb. He felt her arms, examined her palms, then pulled a stethoscope from his bag and listened to her heart for a few moments.

He dropped the stethoscope down. "Are you Lydia?" he asked.

"Yes."

"She's lost a lot of weight. Has she been eating regularly?" Lydia realized now that she hadn't. "No."

He nodded. "Calvin says she's been hallucinating."

"I believe she has," Lydia responded.

"She's been taking laudanum again, I'm guessing," he said.

"Yes."

He shook his head. "She took up with it after Elmore left." He lifted her hand to find a pulse again and sat for several seconds counting the beats. "Where's her bottle of laudanum?"

Calvin produced it for him.

"Empty the contents, then pour in a mixture of water and milk to give it a translucent color. Add a tinge of vinegar and a spoonful of this." He produced a small bottle of castor oil from his valise. Every time she asks for her medicine, give it to her in coffee or tea, but not straight. Understand?"

"Yes, sir," Calvin answered, although Lydia thought the doctor was talking to her.

"In two or three days, she's going to figure it out and get cranky. You call on me when she does and I'll bring over something to calm her down. It's going to take some time to straighten her out."

"And then?" Lydia asked.

"One way or the other we've got to wean her from it or it'll kill her. She's halfway there already." He stood up and put his coat and hat back on.

"What do I owe you?" she asked.

"There's no fee, Lydia. There was a time when Almetta did a lot for this town, but she never did receive her proper accolades.

Send Calvin when you need me."

He was gone just as quickly as he had arrived.

"What's an accolade?" Calvin asked Lydia.

"I don't know," she answered. "I was just going to ask you the same thing. How about some of that soup?" she suggested as they returned to the kitchen.

"Yes'm, I think it's ready. I sure hope it's good."

After they ate, they talked for some time, and to Lydia's amazement, she discovered that Calvin could read, and that he had already read several of the books that his father had sent over.

She felt jealous to a certain degree, to learn that a colored man could read better than she, but she said nothing. "There's a lot more books in the other room," she said.

"Yes'm, I've seen them."

"You feel free to read any of them you wish, Calvin."

"Yes'm, thank you."

She liked his charm, and he was always so polite like his father. "You can call me Lydia, if you wish, Calvin."

"Yes'm," he said. And then he smiled. "Yes, Lydia."

Almetta turned downright mean after a few days, and she might have been even meaner if she wasn't so weak. Doctor Regenfeld prescribed morphine in very slight doses, which Calvin began administering according to his instructions. Almetta remained confined to bed, where, over the next few weeks, she mostly slept. She did, however, eventually regain some appetite, and when she felt the urge to eat, she took mostly soup and bread.

"And don't forget my tea," she would add.

Calvin made sure that Almetta had meals on time, no matter how meager they were, and on his own accord, he had supper meals prepared for Lydia when she arrived home. She'd had no idea he was such a good cook. He could whip up dough for bread, make cookies and rolls and grits and fried chicken, and he had his own special recipe for beans and mushrooms in some kind of sauce that he concocted.

"Momma had lots of good recipes," Calvin said. "Momma done fed us good!"

November 20, 1872
Dearest Lydia,

I received your letter some time back, but time passes so quickly. It makes me feel good to learn your Aunt Almetta is a member of the temperance league. Her involvement shows she cares about this terrible vice, and as a member, it may fare well for you, too.

You said Elmore was her husband. Are they not living together? Did he die? If your aunt is taking laudanum, she must have an ailment of some sort. I hope it is temporary at best.

You are working at a train station restaurant! Good for you!

Reverend Stilter is back on both feet now, but he has a slight limp. I'm sure the Lord will provide. Jonathan Girt got kicked in the head by a horse at the livery. They took him to Glade Spring to a doctor and he is back now. He seems all right. Our prayers were answered.

If the city officials decide to build a schoolhouse, I will remain in Grundy as the schoolteacher. If not, I may be moving to Philadelphia to stay with my sister, but you can still send your letters here. Reverend Stilter will forward them if I make the journey. Your writing is very good. I am very proud of you. Always study and bathe often.

Your loving Grandmama Eugenia

Every week, Amos brought a wagonload of wood, and Lydia

could not have been more pleased how Calvin took to his responsibilities. If something required fixing, he made the repairs without question, and he could even sew buttons on a coat.

She was glad to have acquired work at the railroad restaurant, but what money she earned each month was completely used up, spread among the cost of wood, groceries and a few dollars for Calvin. She lamented over the fact that her earnings were spent simply trying to stay even. She left early on the streetcar every morning and came home late the same way, and each day cost her twenty cents in fare. In summer she figured she could maybe walk to and from work, but it was two miles and too cold during the winter months. The temperature usually rose to the forties during the day, but in the evening, the temperature would often drop to below freezing. The secret to making it through a cold day was to dress warmly.

On one cold evening, she and Calvin had just finished a meal of beef, potatoes and gravy, and afterward, she spent some time with a pencil and paper making some calculations. She looked up at Calvin. "Do you realize it costs me over five dollars a month for transportation to and from work? That's sixty dollars a year."

"That's a lot of money," he agreed. "If you had a horse for that buggy out there, I could drive you to work and pick you up every day." He gave a wide grin, exposing his shiny white teeth.

She had no idea what a horse would cost, but that thought had crossed her mind. "Are you happy working here?" she asked, even though she knew what his answer would be.

"Yes'm, I'm very happy. It's a fine job."

He was good for Almetta, and for her, too. She gazed at him for the longest time, and when she realized she was staring, she felt awkward.

"What is it?" he asked.

She felt a certain attraction to him, but to cover her thoughts, she said, "I just wish I could pay you more."

Christmas came on quickly and passed by just as fast. She had Calvin procure a tree, but Almetta had no decorations, so Lydia strung popcorn on a string and cut some figures out of colored paper.

Almetta hadn't celebrated one Christmas since her husband, Elmore, left. Lydia made inquiry from some friends if they knew why he had left, but she received no response. When she asked Calvin, it was obvious he knew something, but he was as mum as his father.

Almetta was still weak, and although she was off the laudanum, her mind still wasn't functioning very clearly. For Christmas, Lydia gave her a purple shawl and a red-colored necklace, two items, which she thought would brighten up the drab, black dress that she wore every day. She wore both gifts daily through New Year's Day, and after that, Lydia never saw her wear either again.

Lydia had fallen into a routine at the depot restaurant. Luckily, Mr. Devon, the restaurant manager, supplied all his waitresses with uniforms—black dresses, white aprons and a simple white hat. In the morning, he carried out a ritual. He would line up the girls and inspect them for clean hands and fingernails.

He was coming down the line now, inspecting them, he himself dressed in black pants and vest and a white shirt and bowtie. He was overly skinny and wore round spectacles, which no one believed did him much good, since he would have to bend way over to examine their fingernails. For being in his early thirties, he had already lost a lot of hair.

"Colleen," he blurted out as he slapped her hand and pointed to the washroom. Little Colleen, about the same age as Lydia, tore off to wash her hands once again. By the time he finished inspecting the rest of the girls, Colleen had returned. Mr. Devon examined her hands and scowled, "One more time, young lady, and you're out."

It was impossible for Lydia not to overhear the comment, and when Mr. Devon left the room, she threw an arm around Colleen. "Don't let the bully bother you," she consoled her.

Colleen was almost in tears. "My hands were clean, and he knew it, and I need this job!"

"I don't understand," Lydia said.

"He hasn't got around to you, yet," she said. "When he does, you'll understand."

Almost all of the girls who worked as waitresses were twenty years or less in age, and most were very attractive, Lydia realized. Colleen, so petite, with coal black hair and a figure that was stunning even underneath the bulky uniform, was definitely a beauty in Lydia's estimation.

That evening, Lydia was asked to stay on later to help clean up, and while she was mopping the floor around the tables, she happened to see Mr. Devon leave the station. As he passed under a lamp pole only a block away, he was joined by one of the other waitresses who worked in the restaurant.

What Colleen had alluded to earlier became clear. Lydia couldn't believe that she hadn't earlier recognized the pressure that Devon placed upon the girls.

The next day, all the girls lined up again, and Mr. Devon made his morning inspection. He examined Colleen's hands for a few more seconds than normal, and then moved on to the next girl.

"Well, I made it for another day," Colleen said to Lydia.

"Did I see Margaret join Devon last night?"

"Yes," said Colleen. "And you can imagine what for. Oh, God, I need this job so badly but . . ."

"But what?" Lydia asked.

"What do you think?" she answered.

Mr. Devon suddenly appeared. "You girls get on the floor!" he scolded. "The seven-ten is early."

When a train arrived, the passengers who were traveling through had less than a half hour to consume their meals before the train moved on. Usually three different offerings were on the menu for quick service, so it was imperative that all girls were on the floor taking orders.

Lydia liked her work, though it was a far cry from a good-paying job, and although she had never really had a run-in with Mr. Devon, she did not like him. Most of the girls didn't. He was picky and curt with his orders, and if one of the girls dropped a tray or spilled a drink, she would privately receive a reprimand before the day was over. Even though the door was shut in his office, one could hear his caustic comments when he berated someone.

And usually, whoever Devon berated was gone within a week, which didn't seem to bother him, since he had a steady line of young girls applying for the vacated position.

The following Sunday, Lydia had a day off, and on Monday morning when she arrived at work, Colleen was gone.

"He let her go," said Selma, one of the girls.

"Why? Because her fingernails were dirty?"

"No," Selma said as she wiped her hands in her apron. "Because she wouldn't let him screw her."

Lydia's mouth hung open. "He's never approached me."

"Me neither, and we've both been here a couple months."

"Why do you suppose that is?" Lydia questioned.

Selma grunted. "Lydia, neither one of us is much of a beauty, and he needs some good regular workers. That's what we are—good and regular." She gave a contemptuous laugh again. "Look, honey, we ain't his screwing type. The reason we're keeping our jobs is because rouge and face powder wouldn't do us much good."

When Selma walked away, Lydia felt almost limp. During her nearly seventeen years, no man had ever entered her life, and now Selma, having no idea how much the comment had hurt her, made it quite clear why.

That night on the way home in the streetcar, she sat far enough away from Curly so he would not hear her cry.

Within a week, Colleen suddenly showed up for work again. Her arrival stirred a few comments among the girls, and when Mr. Devon made his habitual morning inspection, he had a smile on his face when he passed Colleen.

Later in the day during a break, Lydia took Colleen aside. "I can't believe you came back to this position."

"I need the money," she said. "Daddy's got pleurisy. He's been out of work for months. I've got momma and four little brothers and sisters. We need the money."

Over the next few days, Devon had put the pressure on her. Colleen was a changed girl, her face molded into an expression of permanent sadness, and even when Lydia approached her, she was reluctant to speak.

"Please," she said. "It's difficult enough living with myself. I can't talk about it."

Lydia felt so sorry and even grieved for Colleen. At first she could not believe that a person with such high morals could be pushed into such a corner. But Colleen was desperate, and desperation forced people to do desperate things. Lydia decided she could not chide her for making such a decision, yet she herself often wondered what it would be like to sleep with a man.

Over the next month, Colleen came to work like everyone else, but there were occasions when Lydia knew that she had spent a night with Devon. On the following morning, the guilt was written all over her face.

Lydia no longer attempted to console her. For both of them, their lives had fallen into a daily routine that depended on survival more than anything else. The only fun either had was during the breaks with the other girls, where they could laugh and joke, and where their conversations were usually restricted to family.

The days had become too routine for Lydia. At home, one day in her life was not much different from the day before. Almetta was no longer dependent upon laudanum, but her personality had not changed much. Doctor Regenfeld said that she had been on the drug too long, and that her ability to come back to a normal life was unlikely. Thank God for Calvin. He carried on his duties like the tactful and responsible person he was.

The entire month of March was colder than normal; however, most of the snow flurries, which earlier marked the tail end of the winter, had disappeared. On this, the last day of the month, a cold wind whipped over the Mississippi levee, even colder than on the preceding several days. At the station restaurant, it did not at all go unnoticed that Mr. Devon failed to show up for work, nor did he appear the morning after.

Mr. Longhorn, a short fellow with a pointed handlebar mustache and a pointed beard on his chin, was summoned to take over Devon's duties. His was a welcome change from the former management style. Longhorn was purely business and commented on how well the girls handled the customers. Nobody could remember receiving a compliment from Mr. Devon.

Everyone surmised that Devon was ill, something Mr. Longhorn did not confirm or deny. In fact, gossip spread that the little, wiry manager had been relieved of his duties, which, if true, was welcome for everyone.

Though Colleen had been to work every day, Lydia noted that she seemed nervous. If someone dropped a glass, she jumped. If a door slammed, she whirled around to see who had entered.

"What is it, Colleen?" Lydia pressed her.

"Nothing," she answered. "It's just that . . . my family, you know. They . . ." She stopped mid-sentence when she saw two police officers enter the restaurant. They immediately sought out Mr. Longhorn, and after a short conversation, they disappeared into his office. For the longest time, the three remained inside, and when they finally emerged, Mr. Longhorn summoned the girls. "I've just learned that Mr. Devon was found dead this morning."

The girls could hardly believe what they heard, and when they started talking among themselves, Lydia saw the fright on Colleen's face.

"These two officers would like to ask you ladies a few questions," Mr. Longhorn went on. "They'll be interviewing you during the afternoon one at a time, so go about your work, and please come when you are summoned. They tell me this is purely routine, so nobody should be alarmed."

Mr. Longhorn singled out Selma. "Selma, we'll begin with you, if you will, please," he asked.

"Somebody shoot the son of a bitch?" she inquired as one of the policemen escorted her into the office.

"As a matter of fact, someone did," the policeman answered. "How did you know?"

"Just a good guess."

When the door shut, Lydia grabbed Colleen by the arm and ushered her off to the washroom. Inside, Colleen's face was as white as a sheet of paper.

"You did it, didn't you, Colleen?"

She nodded, her face unchanged. "And I'm not sorry. I couldn't stand his filthy hands all over me. My God, I can't believe I slept with him."

Lydia held her by the shoulders. "That was two nights ago. Did anybody see you leave with him?"

"No. I met him a few blocks away on the levee. I waited until nobody was around, and when a steamer blew a whistle, I took a derringer from my purse and shot him twice. I don't know how I had the strength, but I dragged his body in between some bales out of sight and then I went home."

"Good," Lydia said. "No matter what the policemen ask you, you and I both left together after work that night. We walked to where I catch the streetcar and talked with each other until the car arrived. That would have been about nine. When I got on, you walked home. Is that clear?"

A slight smile appeared on Colleen's face. "Lydia, why are you doing this for me?"

"You heard Selma. He was a son of a bitch. Nobody around here is going to miss him."

When the two girls walked out of the washroom, Mr. Longhorn summoned Lydia, and when she sat down in the office across from the two officers, they introduced themselves and were most polite.

The police chief's name was O'Fallon, who asked all the questions. "Miss Pearlman," he addressed her. "We should like to inquire about your whereabouts two nights ago, after you left the restaurant."

Lydia was as calm as could be. "Let's see, that was Wednesday, was it not?"

"Yes," he answered.

She hesitated long enough to indicate she was thinking about that particular night. "That was the night Colleen and I left together."

"And Colleen is . . . ?"

"One of the girls who works here."

"I see," he said as he jotted something down on a piece of paper. "She could substantiate that?"

"I'm certain she will," Lydia answered.

"Very good. Tell me, did you have any sort of relationship with Mr. Devon?"

"I worked for him. We all did."

"Of course," he said. "But other than that? Perhaps you met privately with him on occasion?"

"For what purpose?"

Chief O'Fallon shrugged. "That's what we should like to find out."

She dipped her eyebrows. "No. I never had any occasion to meet with him privately, nor did I have any desire to."

"I see." He asked a few more simple questions, and then dismissed her.

By the end of the day, all the girls had been interviewed, including Colleen, and when she came out of the office, Lydia was happy to see that she had maintained her composure. What conclusion the two police officers drew was announced in the newspaper the next day.

During a break, Lydia, Colleen and a few other girls listened while Selma read the article. " '. . . that the murder was probably committed last Wednesday evening,' " she read. " 'Although numerous individuals have been interviewed concerning the dastardly deed, the police have no suspects. Officials believe the motive may have been robbery. Police Chief O'Fallon stated the case will remain open.' "

"Dastardly deed," said Selma, as she put the paper down. "Serves the bastard right. I'd like to give a medal to the one who killed him."

Lydia and Colleen eyed each other.

"Girls," said Mr. Longhorn as he clapped his hands. "The seven-ten's on time and the breakfast menu is ready."

A month later, Devon's murder still wasn't solved. It wasn't unusual to find a dead man along the levee; it happened often enough, and many of the perpetrators of such crimes were never brought to justice. Too many transients passed through St. Louis, making it impossible for the small police force to track down every lead. In many cases, before the police even learned about a murder, the murderer might well be long gone on his way north or south by steamboat, or by any other means. The city was simply too big, and there were too many hiding places.

August 6, 1873
Dear Grandmama Eugenia,

I reread your last letter. I hope Grundy decids to build a schoolhouse and you will be the teacher. Poor Jonathan Girt. I hop his hed improves so he can travel west like I did. My work at the depot station is going very well. Our maniger, Mr. Devon was found murderd some months ago, and his murder is stil not solved, but noone hear at the restarant misses him.

I have a good frend, Colleen, and we spend lots of time together. For my 17 birthday, she gave me a beutiful braslet, and Calvin baked a cake. Amos cam to. Aunt Almetta took ill last winter, but she is now better. She sold the piano a long time ago, and last week some men came for more furnicher. She is slowly selling everything for money. I wish I could help with more, but work dos not pay much.

I continew to study and read almost every day. I even lerned a new word, accolade. Aunt Almetta wons took in orfans, and that is a accolade. I hope you can see som improovment in my writing. Calvin has a summer job, so he dos not work with us any mor.

I miss you and will never forget you.

Love Lydia

Six

With Calvin off for the summer, the burden of taking care of Aunt Almetta increased immeasurably, but Lydia dealt with the situation as best she could over the next several weeks.

It was an early October day, and due to a break in the track over a railroad bridge south of St. Louis, the trains were off schedule. As a result, the only customers eating in the restaurant were locals, so business was not booming, as Mr. Longhorn called it. Half of the girls had been sent home and the other half were not near as busy as they might have been.

Colleen and Mable Dee were off in the kitchen somewhere, and Lydia and Selma were sitting at a table near the window.

"Ain't much in the paper," said Selma as she puffed on a cigarette. Very few of the girls smoked except for Selma, who rolled her own, and since she was such a good worker, Mr. Longhorn let her get by, especially when only a few customers were in the restaurant.

Selma suddenly looked up. "What do we have here?" Outside, two men had just ridden up on horses. Both were wearing long coats and had wide-brimmed hats pulled down snugly over their heads. It was windy, and as the two slipped from their horses, one of their coats whipped up, and Lydia glimpsed that he was wearing a pistol belt and revolver underneath. From this distance it was difficult to make out their faces, but as they neared the restaurant, she could see that both possessed heavy growths of beard.

"Cattlemen?" Selma mused.

"Either that or a couple of cowboys," said Lydia.

"If they're cattlemen, I'll take 'em," said Selma. "If they're drifters, you take 'em."

Selma was still smoking a cigarette and didn't want to waste it. "I'm guessing they're drifters, so you take 'em." Then, with a laugh, she added, "If they're big tippers, I get half."

Lydia gave the two strangers enough time to find a table before she approached them, and when she did, they were already reading the menu. "Afternoon," she said. "You boys look a little windblown."

The younger of the two removed his hat and hung it on his chair. "Yeah, I guess you could say that. What's good today?"

"Everything," she answered. "Home-fried chicken or meat-loaf. Comes with potatoes and gravy, beans and coffee and a piece of pie."

"No steak?" he asked. "We ain't had steak in two weeks." He smiled under his heavy beard. The fellow next to him was quiet and still had his hat on. The way these two were smiling, she was sure they were just a couple of fun-loving cowboys.

"I think I can rustle up a couple of steaks for you. You want them cooked or raw?"

Both laughed as she left to place their order. She came back in a minute with two cups of coffee and set them down, and as she walked away, they were still smiling.

She returned to where Selma was sitting. "Cattlemen or cowboys?" Selma asked.

"Neither one, I don't think," said Lydia. She continued to study the two men for the longest time, and ten minutes later she carried the two steaks over to them and refilled their cups with coffee.

They were hungry all right. They charged into the beef like it was their last meal, and they were gulping the coffee down at a

85

rapid pace. Halfway through their steaks, Lydia grabbed the coffeepot and returned to their table. As she gave them refills, the younger of the two looked up.

"I don't mean to be disrespectful, ma'am, but I do believe we had the pleasure of meeting somewhere before."

"We did," Lydia said with an eyebrow cocked. "You boys rob any trains lately?"

They both stiffened and dropped their forks. In unison, they looked around and unbuttoned their long coats. She had never seen two smiling faces disappear so fast.

"Don't worry," Lydia said. "I won't tell anybody. After all, you never did rob me, and I had nearly two hundred dollars on me."

The younger one softened his look. "You were the one sitting across from me, down near . . ."

"Loudon, I believe was the town," she finished.

He picked up his fork and knife, and as he cut off a piece of steak, he was still looking around as if somebody was watching.

"How come you never took my money?" she asked.

He kept chewing as he answered. "You said your daddy was killed in the war, and we weren't about to rob the daughter of a fellow Confederate soldier."

"My daddy fought for the Union side."

He stopped chewing, and with a silly grin on his face, he said, "Should'a robbed you."

The man across from him chuckled.

The younger one wiped his lips with a napkin. "But I am sorry you lost your father. I'm sincere about that."

"I believe you are. My name's Lydia Pearlman. What's yours?"

The two eyed each other but said nothing.

"Well, I can understand," she said. "If I was a train robber, I guess I wouldn't give out my name, either. That's what I told the sheriff who interviewed me."

The younger one nodded. "I'm Jesse Woodson, and this is my brother, Frank." He offered his hand, and so did his brother. Frank had a long nose and a rugged face that didn't at all resemble the baby face on the younger man, which made her believe that the two probably weren't brothers. And for sure, that wasn't their correct names, either.

"Well," she said with a smile, "if you're planning on robbing the seven-ten, it's going to be late. There's a trestle south of here that needs repair."

They both chuckled, and now the fellow whose name was supposedly Frank, spoke for the first time. "That wasn't what we had in mind. We're just sort of passing through."

"Where's the rest of your boys? Sheriff catch them?"

The one named Jesse just laughed. "No, afraid not. They've all got ranch jobs now, just like us."

"They carry big guns under their coats like you two?"

Jesse shook his head, as if he couldn't believe the conversation they were having, and then, just as it appeared he was about to respond, a policeman entered the restaurant. The two men kept their eyes on him like an eagle eyeing a rabbit from five hundred feet.

"Don't worry none about Homer," Lydia said. "He comes in regular about this time. This is his beat along the levee. He'll be back in about eleven tonight for a piece of pie and coffee. Speaking of pie, you boys got a piece coming. Hope you like pumpkin. Our cook makes the best pumpkin pie this side of the Mississippi."

They kept their eyes on Homer for a few more seconds and seemed relieved when he sat and began reading the menu.

"Pumpkin pie it is," said the man named Jesse.

She brought the pie and filled their coffee cups again, and inside of another ten minutes or so, the two called for their bill. It came to slightly under three dollars, but Jesse handed over a five-dollar bill. "The rest is for you," he said, and as they got up and put their hats on, they again eyed Homer, who was only feet away. He was sipping coffee and reading a newspaper, not giving the slightest hint that he was interested in them.

"Lydia, glad to have met you . . . again," Jesse said. His partner tipped his hat, and as they walked out of the restaurant, Lydia stared after them. They climbed on their horses, gave a wave and then rode off at an easy pace toward the center of the city.

She had just received over a two-dollar tip, the largest she had ever received since she started working here, and she was feeling good.

As she began cleaning away the dishes, she was sure that she would never see these two men again, and they needn't worry; she wasn't going to tell anybody about them. Of course, they wouldn't know that.

When she lifted the plate where Jesse had been sitting, her mouth hung wide open as she eyed a twenty-dollar gold piece lying underneath. Then, as she lifted the second plate, she gasped again. Another double eagle, so smooth and shiny, glittered back at her! She looked up through the window to spot the two riders, but they had disappeared down the levee road.

She picked up the two coins and dropped them in her apron pocket, and all the way back to the kitchen, she wore a large smile.

"What?" asked Selma when she saw the wide grin. "The boys leave you a good tip?"

"Two dollars," she said with a smile that was still stretching from ear to ear.

"Whoa," Selma retorted. "Must have been cattlemen after all."

"No," Lydia answered. "I think they make their living off the railroad."

For the next several days, Lydia checked the newspaper to see if a robbery had taken place on the railroad line in the St. Louis area, but none had occurred. It crossed her mind that perhaps the two men had decided to go straight, but then she figured not. Two cowboys wouldn't each leave a month's wages as a tip.

She had plans for the forty dollars, so that evening as she rode home on the streetcar, she passed word on to Curly that the next time he saw Calvin, he was to tell him to pay her a visit.

"I will, mum, that I will. And how's Missus Boggs getting along these days?"

"She's doing fine." It appeared to Lydia that Curly was fishing for a bit of gossip, so she slipped him a line. "She's thinking about making a trip to California next spring."

Curly's mustache bounced. "Is she now? And for what purpose might I ask?"

"I think she's going to try panning for gold."

Curly said hardly a word the rest of the way. When Lydia got off the streetcar, Curly kept his eyes on her for the longest time, and just as she reached the door, he hollered, "Hope she strikes it rich!"

On the following Sunday afternoon, Lydia had just finished washing Almetta's hair and wrapping a towel around her head when she saw Calvin pass by in his father's wagon. Almetta had just left the kitchen and was headed up the stairs when Calvin knocked on the back door.

"Come on in, Calvin," she said as she opened the door.

"Hello, Lydia." He removed his hat. "It sure is nice to see you again."

"Calvin, it's always a pleasure to have you visit. Almetta and I just had some tea. Would you like some?"

"I sure would. It's a bit chilly out today. Feels like winter is going to come on early." He removed his coat and hat and sat at the table.

"Sorry I haven't got any laudanum to put in it," she quipped, as she poured the tea.

"Lordy," said Calvin with a grin. "How is Missus Almetta these days?"

"She still isn't right in the head, but her brother—that is, my papa—never was, either. She has given up on her temperance meetings." She paused. "I'm not sure she can even remember that she belonged. She spends her days at home. Sometimes some lady friends visit, but not so often anymore."

Lydia drank a bit of her tea and started a new train of conversation. "Did you know that Almetta used to take in orphans at one time?"

"My daddy told me that. But that was when I was young. I really don't remember much about it. In them days, daddy worked for her more often, but then, he . . ."

"He what?" she asked.

Calvin twisted his head to the side. "Something happened, and Mistah Boggs one day just up 'n left."

"Why?" she asked. "Calvin, you can tell me." He dropped his head as if he was thinking about answering. Lydia placed her hand on his and squeezed it. "Calvin, we've been friends long enough to share our thoughts with each other."

"Miss Lydia," he said using formal speech. "All I know is Mistah Boggs was a drinker. I think something bad happened here, but I swear, I don't know what it was, and my daddy never talked about it. And he wouldn't be happy to know we were having this conversation."

Lydia smiled and patted his hand. "That's fair enough." She let a few seconds pass. "Do you know why I asked you over today?"

"I ain't so sure now."

"Are you finished with the cotton harvest?"

"I am. Jes'a few days ago."

"With winter coming up, we could use some help around here again—that is, if you might be looking for work."

His face lit up. "I certainly would welcome the work."

"Good," she said with a lighthearted laugh. "I have another question for you."

"Yes'm."

"If I wanted to purchase a horse to pull that buggy in the carriage house, how much would one cost?"

His eyes went wide now, and he grinned. "Miss Lydia, you really thinking of buying a horse?"

"How much?"

Calvin sat perfectly still, as if he was calculating.

"Show me your palms," she told him. When he did, she placed a twenty-dollar gold piece in each one.

"Lordy!" he said. "Been a long time since I seen a double eagle, and I don't think I ever seen two at one time!"

"Will that buy a good enough horse?"

"Oh, yes, if you ain't fussy about looks."

"Looks means nothing to me. Just make sure he's gentle. Can you find one for me?"

"I know I can."

She folded over his fingers and held both hands for the longest time. "This winter, you're going to drive me to work and back and I'm going to save five dollars a month. By spring, that horse will almost be paid for."

"Yes'm. That's a real good idea."

She was still holding on to his hands. "More tea?"

Two days later, Lydia and a few of the girls were cleaning up toward evening after a throng of customers had left, when Colleen pointed out the window. "Who do you suppose that is?"

A buggy had just pulled up along the restaurant, drawn by a huge horse under harness.

"My God!" Lydia practically screamed. "He got one! He got one!"

None of the girls had any idea what Lydia meant as she ran for her coat and tore out the door.

"Calvin!" she greeted. "You got a horse!"

"Yes'm, I sure did, and he's a good one, too."

She pranced around the animal, running her hand alongside his neck, over his muzzle.

"Name's Jake," said Calvin. "Cross between a quarter horse and a draft. That's why he's so big."

"Is he gentle?" she asked.

"I rode him bareback from the Wilkinsons' to your home. He hitched up inside the livery like he'd lived there all his life. He's smart."

"Calvin!" she said as she threw an arm around him and hugged him to death. "Be right back!"

She ran into the restaurant and headed for the changing room. As she was changing out of her uniform, Colleen came in.

"Lydia, how can you get so excited over a horse?"

"Did you ever own one?" Lydia asked.

"No."

"Well, change your clothes, and Calvin and I will give you a ride home."

Five minutes later, the two girls ran outside, and immediately she introduced Calvin to Colleen. "This is Colleen, one of my best friends. Colleen, this is Calvin, my very best friend!"

"Glad to know you, Miss Colleen," Calvin greeted. He helped the two up as the girls chatted between themselves, and when all three were settled in the front seat, Lydia was squeezed into the middle. Calvin clucked his lips, snapped the reins, and old Jake took off into a light trot.

"Where we going?" he asked.

"Utah and Lemp," Colleen said. Calvin made a face. "The old Westerman Cemetery's on Lemp," she said.

Calvin nodded. "I know it."

He headed along Broadway, and although the sun had long gone down, enough lights coming from the various saloons and bawdy houses, as well as a strong moon, helped light the way.

They could see their breath, and although a chill crept underneath their clothes, Lydia and Colleen laughed and joked along the way, as giddy as two girls could be.

Inside of ten minutes, they reached Colleen's home, a small, two-story affair, surrounded by a picket fence, both dearly in need of paint.

"Thank you," Colleen said as Calvin helped her down. She hurried up the walkway to her home and disappeared inside.

When Calvin crawled back into the seat, he was surprised that Lydia had remained in the center of the cushion. As he snapped the reins, she grabbed onto his arm. "This is wonderful, Calvin. You don't know how happy you've made me."

"You the one who come up with the money," he retorted. "I jes' got my daddy to find old Jake for you. Daddy, he knows horseflesh, and he knew the Wilkinsons was considering selling old Jake. This ol' boy's nigh on to sixteen years old, but he's got a lot of walking left in him, jes' like my daddy."

Sixteen, Lydia was thinking to herself. Jake was one year younger than she was. When they reached Jefferson Avenue, Calvin turned on to it. "Do you suppose they named this street after your daddy?" she asked.

Calvin laughed out loud. "Lord, no. I'm sure President Thomas Jefferson gets that credit."

On Market, Calvin turned left. Within a few blocks, he

overtook Curly and his streetcar, and as they went by, Lydia waved at the Irishman.

"This horse was a good investment," said Lydia. "He's not only going to save me money, but a whole lot of time, too. No more waiting for the streetcar."

"Yes'm, Lydia, but don't forget, jes' like the rest of us, this ol' boy's gotta eat."

She'd never even given that a thought.

"I already got some hay and oats for him, and you even got a few dollars left over."

Inside the livery, Calvin lit two lamps and told Lydia he would unharness old Jake and put him in his stall.

"I'll have supper ready for you when you're finished," she said.

"I already ate, Lydia. No need to fix nothing for me."

"All right," she said. "Then you unharness this old fellow and tell me what you're doing."

"Yes'm. First thing, gotta unbuckle the belly band." He loosed the strap that ran under the horse's belly. "That frees the hold-back, what keeps the britchen seat in place, then you lift the crupper, like this." He loosened the leather strap that ran under the horse's tail and proceeded to point out how the harness was attached to the long wooden shafts that came off the buggy. She heard more words like *terret* and *overcheck rein* and *breast strap*, and although she was engrossed in the process, by the time he removed the harness and hung it on the wall, she couldn't remember a thing he'd said. All the while, she marveled at how calm he was, and how precise he was with his explanation, and how he kept saying to Old Jake, "Thas a good boy, thas a good boy."

"And then you put him in a stall, give him some hay, and pat him on the neck, because he done good."

"I wonder if I'll ever be able to hitch him up."

"Oh, yes," Calvin said, his teeth flashing. "I'll be happy to teach you."

Every Saturday night, the Planters Hotel on Fourth and Walnut held a dance in their ballroom. It was just a few blocks off the levee, an easy walk from the railroad station. Lydia knew about the dance, but she had never attended, mostly because the only dancing she had ever indulged in was by herself, while humming a tune.

The last time she had heard a band play was in the Fourth of July parade, and that was months ago. On this particular Saturday, a Bohemian band was staged for an evening of fun, and several of the girls from the restaurant decided they would go after work. Lydia, Colleen, Selma and Margaret got off shortly after eight and walked the distance to the hotel. For late November, the night was rather nice. The air was brisk, even refreshing, and the absence of wind held down the wind-chill factor.

Lydia's ride home afterward was already arranged. Calvin was to pick her up at eleven o'clock. The livery behind the Planters provided ample space for buggies, which was where Lydia was to meet him.

The girls each paid a dime to get in. A dimly lit dance floor spread out before them with several couples dancing a two-step to the five-piece band—a tuba, trombone, cornet, accordion and drums. As the girls charged across the floor to find a table, the rhythmic thumping of the music grabbed their senses. A polka resounded loud and clear, and every now and then, one of the men hollered out, "Hoo, hoo, hoo, hoooo."

Chatter was coming from everywhere, and Lydia loved it.

"Good, huh?" said Selma as she garnered a table for the foursome.

The girls giggled incessantly until a waiter came around and asked for their orders.

"Sarsaparilla," said Colleen.

Lydia had no idea what a sarsaparilla was. "I'll have the same."

"Me, too," said Margaret.

"Make mine a beer," Selma said. She had barely ordered when a sporty young man in a striped jacket grabbed her by the arm and whisked her off the floor.

"That's Danny McFarland," said Margaret. "He's a dance nut, and so's Selma."

A minute later, another young man pulled Margaret off her chair, and in no time she and her partner disappeared into the crowd.

"Have you ever been here before?" Lydia asked Colleen.

"Once in a while. Not much to do on Saturday nights if you don't have a man hanging on your arm."

Lydia knew Colleen well, or at least she thought she did. Her eyes sparkled day or night, and in a crowd of women, she would easily be picked out as the charmer. In that sense, it was strange that she hadn't swept some beau off his feet already. Then again, Colleen possessed some temperament. After all, she had killed a man.

Margaret, too, had a special charm about her. Her sparkling blond hair could be spotted from a mile away. She had a turned-up nose, and the light color of her skin went well with bright, blue eyes. She was shapely, too, something Lydia had noticed long ago.

Selma was the hard one of the bunch. She was twenty-six, one of the older girls at the restaurant. She had flaming red hair and a thousand freckles on her face. Although she always seemed to wear a scowl, she was delightfully funny. Her rough language was often sarcastic, yet refreshingly comical. Her nose was long and pointed, and her eyes were sunk back, giving her high cheeks prominence. Whoever married her would be up against a very independent woman with a very independent mind.

"I don't even know how to dance," Lydia said to Colleen. She laughed. "Half of the people here don't, either. But keep your eye on Selma and Danny. Those two are like two peas in a pod when they're together."

They were good, Lydia determined after watching them. Danny whirled Selma around with such ease, his guidance appeared almost effortless, and she flowed with every movement.

For the next half hour the other three girls were up and down dancing, but Lydia sat, mostly by herself, watching the couples move their feet and trying to gain some confidence that someone would soon ask her to dance.

"May I?" came a voice from behind her. The man was short and stocky, with a bushy beard. In her estimation, she wouldn't be far off judging him to be about fifty. She got to her feet, and after the gentleman gave a bow, he eased up against her and moved off into the center of the floor.

She felt awkward at first, knowing her feet weren't matching his steps, but she persevered, and at the end of the dance, he escorted her back to her seat, gave another gracious bow, and he was gone.

The girls were back. "I see the judge picked you out of the crowd," said Selma.

"Judge?"

"He's the circuit judge. Gerard Featherstone. He's usually drunk about this time, but at the moment, he looks like he has some spunk left in him."

"I could smell liquor on his breath," Lydia said.

"You're lucky," said Selma. "Whenever I danced with him, I always smelled puke." The girls laughed so hard and so long that tears came to their eyes.

Lydia remembered the man's name. "Isn't his wife a member of the temperance league?"

"Yeah. Ain't that ironic," Selma said.

Lydia learned a considerable lot that night. Selma and Danny were great dancers, but Danny was married, and this was the only connection she had with him—on the dance floor.

Several men asked Margaret to dance, and before the night was over, she was sitting at a different table with a fellow named Charlie.

Colleen, it seemed, had a man at the table asking for a dance every number, but after a half dozen rounds she began declining when asked, and Lydia knew she did so because no one since the judge had asked her to dance.

When a waltz came up, a familiar young man came over to the table. "Go, Colleen," Lydia said. "I'm perfectly fine."

Colleen waltzed off with him. It was the third time he had asked her.

Three more numbers played, and close to eleven o'clock, Lydia put on her coat and hat. The other three were dancing, and while the Bohemian band was still blasting away, she slipped through the crowd to the back door that led to the livery.

Several lamps gave the interior a dull glow, but from a short distance she saw Calvin standing with a few other men.

"Miss Lydia," he said as he removed his hat. He helped her up into the seat of the buggy, and once he was in place, he flipped his reins. "Did you have a good time?" he asked. She dipped her head, and softly began crying. "Oh, my," Calvin said as he put an arm around her. "Oh, my."

Several more Saturdays came and went. Lydia had no intention of attending another dance, but the girls always begged her, so on another occasion she gave in. An Irish group of four men attacked their music with a variety of instruments that Lydia had never heard of. Dancing jigs of some sort seemed to be the mainstay of the night. Lydia had no idea people could look so stupid the way they jumped around, but when asked by a nice-looking fellow to dance, she entered the floor and acted just as stupid as the rest.

It was a strange night of entertainment, and before the night was over, even Selma was grumbling. "For Christ sake. I've seen chickens with their heads chopped off dance around better than this crowd." The girls could hardly contain their laughter.

The beat of the Irish music was not the easiest to dance to, and when the dancers on the floor became sparse, a few young men slowly inched their way up to the girls' table. One of them was a good-looking fellow who had asked Lydia to dance earlier. His name was Matthew McGrath, but before the evening was over everyone was calling him Matty. Lydia judged him to be about thirty. He was well dressed, had long, curly hair and was so quiet that one had to prod him with a question to get him to speak.

"So, do you come here often?" Lydia asked him.

"No."

"This your first time?"

"No, third."

"Are you from around here?"

"No. New Orleans."

"What brings you to St. Louis?" she asked.

"The *Josephine*."

Some time later, she figured out that he worked on board the steamboat named the *Josephine*. During the day, he was a part-time waiter and croupier in the gambling room. Some evenings, he worked as a security guard, and he sometimes did duty on the bridge with the captain.

Because he was on duty that night, he left early, but before he did, he excused himself and delivered a parting comment to

Lydia. "Miss Pearlman, perhaps I'll see you again when I pass through."

When he was gone, Selma asked her, "Got something working for you, honey?"

"If I do, I think it's going to be an annual event."

Lydia did attend a few more dances over the next few months, but the only steady partner she had was Judge Featherstone. On one of those nights, she had managed to get in two or three dances before he fell down drunk, and, like Selma had once said, she could smell puke on him. Occasionally, a few younger fellows would ask her to dance, but she was sure the other girls had lined them up for her.

In time, she gave up on Saturday nights, even though the girls always invited her. "I'm just not a dancer, I guess," she said. She could indeed dance by now, but it was painful always to sit so long before someone asked her onto the floor. More than anything, she simply felt uncomfortable and out of place.

She began spending more free time in the library, and if she wasn't reading there, she was always taking reading material home.

"How's Almetta getting along?" Bertha from the library once asked her.

"Not very well," Lydia answered.

"You tell her we miss her at the temperance meetings. You do that, now, will you?"

"I will," Lydia promised, but she was not sure Almetta would even remember that she was a member of the league. Almetta did not get out much anymore, and not at all during the winter months. She chose to remain in her room most of the day, where she would sit at a window and stare out at the street for hours at a time, hardly saying a word.

One afternoon, on a day that offered a bright sun even though the temperature outside was near freezing, Lydia was brushing

Almetta's hair near the window.

"You have such pretty hair, Aunt Almetta. Do you like it when I brush it for you?"

A half minute passed before she answered. "Despicable! My God, you are so despicable!"

Lydia stopped brushing, sure that her aunt was off in a different world.

"I can never forgive you! Get out! Get out!"

After a long silence, Lydia again raised the brush, and in a soft voice, Almetta said, "Yes I do." A moment later, she said, "My medicine. I need my medicine."

"You don't require medicine anymore, Aunt Almetta. You gave it up at the same time you gave up cigar smoking."

"Did I give up my tea?" she asked.

"No. Would you like some?"

She was again silent for the longest time, and then out of nowhere she asked, "How come you have this obsession with reading?"

Lydia humored her. "I like to read. It helps me with my writing, too."

"Go see Bertha at the library. Tell her I sent you."

Lydia made tea for both of them, and afterward, when her aunt dozed off in her chair, Lydia found a book and spent the rest of the afternoon reading.

Later that evening, she decided to pen another letter to Eugenia.

March 11, 1874

Dear Grandmamma Eugenia,

Forgive me I have not written in some time. Sins I did not hear from you I assum you moved to Filadelthia. I hope to hear from you soon. St. Louis has been a good move for me. I study and read often, in hopes my writing improvs. Many of us girls from the stashun restarant go to a dance on Saturday nights. I met a young man who said he wants to see me again. His name is Matthew. I even danced with Gerard Featherstone a few times. He is a circut judge, an important man in the comunity. My friend, Colleen, I think has a gentleman friend she met at the dance, and I think it is serius.

I bot a horse for the buggy, and Calvin taut me how to harnes it. His name is Jake. It saves me some money because of the streetcar, but he eats. Soon it will be garden time for planting. Aunt Almetta is fine. I offen look at the pictur of momma and daddy, but I don't think of them that much any more.

I hope you are well. Please greet Jonathan for me and hope he is better.

Love, Lydia

Lydia reread the letter. It was not entirely true what she said about Matty, the fellow who worked onboard the *Josephine*, but a relationship between them would be something her Grand-mamma Eugenia would like to hear. Lydia wished she could find a beau, someone who took a genuine interest in her, but so far that had not happened.

She had endured crying spells over the issue, but that was not something Eugenia would want to hear. Life had become somewhat lonely, but that, too, was not a topic she wanted to discuss.

Calvin had been very consoling, and she liked him, since he was so good to her. It was the only good relationship she had with a man, but he was a colored man, and that was not something to write about in a letter.

Even though Judge Featherstone was a drunk, he still was an important man in the community, so her statement about him was basically true.

There was also no way she could divulge how she came into the money that bought Old Jake. Eugenia would not understand her taking a forty-dollar tip from two train robbers.

Since she had not heard from Eugenia in some time, she was certain she must have returned to Philadelphia, and she had no good reason to ask her to greet Jonathan Girt. He had more than likely forgotten about her.

SEVEN

Late in March, on a warm afternoon, Calvin was digging with a hoe, planting a garden for Lydia. Almetta, draped under a quilt and sitting in a chair on the veranda, appeared as stoic as ever, facing the warmth of the sun. In the past few years, this, as well as the window in her bedroom, had been one of her favorite spots.

When Calvin heard the clatter of a wagon, he looked up to see Amos drive in with another load of wood and stop near the cellar door.

"Hello, son," he greeted Calvin as he stepped down. "Ain't this a beautiful day?" He noticed Almetta in her chair. "Missus Almetta," he greeted as he removed his hat. He grinned and waited for a response.

"She don't hear or see nothin' much anymore," said Calvin as he began unloading the wood.

"That's a crying shame," said Amos. "She was a real good lady one time. She still is, but she just don't know it anymore. Lydia around?"

"No," answered Calvin. "She rode off this morning in the buggy. Shoppin' I guess."

"How is Miss Lydia nowadays?" Amos asked.

"Daddy, she's a troubled woman. She treats me good as gold, but she's unhappy."

Amos grunted as he pulled on his gloves. "How can that be?

She's got this old plantation place, a horse and buggy, a job . . ."

"Yeah," Calvin interrupted. "But she's lonely. She ain't got no man, and she ain't got no family like you got momma and me and the girls."

Amos shrugged. "Calvin, she's young yet. Your momma and I didn't even settle on family matters till we was in our twenties." He thought a moment. " 'Course, we already had you by then." He grabbed for some more wood. "Time will take care of everything."

Calvin shook his head. "I don't know. Miss Lydia's a bit on the skinny side, and I know she hasn't attracted anybody. At least, she don't dance no more. All she does is read in her spare time. What I sees is what I know."

"Calvin," Amos said as he wiped his brow. "You's a romantic. That's what you are, a romantic."

Just as they finished unloading the wood, Lydia drove in with the horse and buggy, stopped before the carriage house and greeted the two men.

"I've got all kinds of seeds," she said, while Calvin helped her down. "Cucumbers, squash, radishes, onions and carrots and lots of flower seeds." She opened a bag and doled out the packets. "Potatoes are in the cellar."

She looked at Amos, her face shining underneath a wide, brimmed bonnet. "You raised a fine boy, Amos. Anybody that's willing to help a woman plant flowers must be something special."

Amos chuckled. "He's my flower child, I guess."

Lydia gave a warm smile. "Calvin, as soon as I change my clothes, I'll come out and help you." She skipped up the few steps to the veranda, where she greeted Almetta.

After she went inside, Amos remarked. "She looks happy to me, son."

Calvin nodded. "There's times when she's happier than others."

Amos was gone by the time Lydia came out of the house wearing a different set of clothes. She walked briskly to the garden carrying a hand tool. "Well, let's get to it."

That evening, after Calvin, Almetta and Lydia had eaten, Calvin retired to the carriage house. He made sure old Jake had plenty of hay before he headed up the stairs to his quarters. He stoked the stove to take the chill off the room, then settled down next to a lamp to read.

An hour later, he closed the book, shucked his clothes and put out the lamp. As he had done so many times before, he sat on a chair near the window that offered a view to the back of the plantation home.

A half hour passed until he saw the light on the lower level dimmed, which meant Lydia was now climbing the stairs. When the light on the second floor appeared, he stiffened, his eyes focused on her bedroom window.

Moments later, he saw her silhouette pass by, and seconds later she passed by again. A light-colored curtain covered the window, but through it he watched intently as Lydia slipped off her clothes, one article at a time. She moved out of view, and then she came back into it, and as she pulled the final undergarment over her head, he could see the form of her bare breasts through the curtain.

"Oh, Lord," he whispered to himself. "She is a beauty."

For the next few minutes, he could only see the burning light of the lamp, and when that went out, he breathed heavily and slipped into his bed.

The first week in April, Calvin was back at work in the fields at the Wilkinson's, breaking ground for corn. The summers always kept him busy, and his course was set. By mid-April, the ground would be seeded, and for the next sixty days, Calvin and his father and numerous other field hands would be hoeing through the fields, cleaning out the weeds and cockleburs. In May, the hands would start groundbreaking in the cotton fields.

There was very little respite for Calvin, Lydia knew. As soon as the corn was harvested, he would be involved in shelling and bagging it and then hauling it to the levee for distribution by steamer or rail.

About the time he finished with that, September would roll around, when the cotton fields were in full bloom, and he would be off again with dozens of other workers, dragging the long sacks through the fields, picking the heads one by one.

Lydia sat on the veranda, distraught over her situation. "Dear Lord," she mused. "Where is my life taking me?"

Luckily, for the first few weeks of summer, Almetta took a slight turn for the better. It was simply impossible for Lydia to make a trip home at midday from the restaurant, and so she always kept something on hand for Almetta to eat. It could be as simple as sandwiches, sauce and fresh vegetables when they were in season, or leftovers from the night before. Even though Lydia's best intentions lay with Almetta, her aunt still managed to snap at her.

"I can make my own meals!" she barked. "Done it all my life!"

On the positive side, Lydia wanted to believe that she was coming back to her senses and that perhaps she could actually take care of herself. But too many times when Lydia returned from work in the evening, she discovered that Almetta had not eaten anything during the day.

Over the next several days, Lydia would often catch Almetta staring off into space, and ever so softly she would say, "Elmore should be here soon," or, "Tell Calvin I need my medicine."

A visit by Doctor Regenfeld didn't produce much comfort. "She's become feeble-minded," he said. "Not much you can do but keep her comfortable."

That was the problem: keeping her comfortable. Almetta had opened her home to Lydia and given her shelter, and as a result, Lydia felt a strong obligation to care for her as best she could. For Lydia, living here initially had been fairly comfortable, but now Almetta had become a burden, and life wasn't as easy. The best solution would be to have someone remain with her and care for her daily, but Lydia couldn't afford that.

She did the next best thing. Cass, the iceman was still making deliveries three times a week, and so Lydia asked if he would check on her periodically.

"Yes, ma'am. That would be no problem," he told her.

Even Curly, when he passed by, agreed to look in on her if he didn't have any passengers on board his streetcar, and whenever Amos or Calvin happened to be in the neighborhood, they would stop to check on her, but that wasn't very often.

The summer kept everybody too busy. The only comfort Lydia found at home was in her garden, where she could hoe out weeds and watch the flowers and vegetables grow.

The tulips were the first to bloom. She cut them and placed them in vases throughout the house, and as soon as other flowers blossomed, they followed suit.

Almetta seemed to sleep away most of the days, and even when she was awake, Lydia could barely carry on a conversation with her. The boredom of each day being the same as the day before was taking its toll. It was as if loneliness was seeking a partner, and the only one available was Lydia. The familiar phrase *Where is my life taking me?* kept coming back to her.

Evenings, she would read beside her two lamps, but her concentration wouldn't hold. Her mind would wander, reflecting into the past, searching for something good to dwell on. Her best thoughts usually focused on the girls at the restaurant. If there was any place she could laugh, it was with them, and without them, she wouldn't have any social life at all.

It was always a joy to talk to Amos whenever he stopped in, but most of all, she missed Calvin.

One morning when she had a day off from work, she rose early, and after fixing a quick breakfast, she helped Almetta into a comfortable chair on the veranda, where she enjoyed the warmth of the rising sun.

Wearing an old dress, and with her hair tied up with a ribbon, Lydia proceeded to clean the kitchen area, and afterward moved from room to room downstairs, mainly dusting and utilizing the carpet sweeper. The day flew by, and by late afternoon, she had worked herself up to Almetta's bedroom. It had been some time since Lydia had cleaned it, and in fact, dusting off the furniture was about all she really had to do. She worked for several minutes and then realized that not once had she ever cleaned out Almetta's wardrobe closet.

She removed old dresses and coats that Almetta had not worn since Lydia arrived. In doing so, she opened up some space, and at the back of the wardrobe she discovered several small canisters. Curious, she opened one of them only to find needles and spools of thread.

A second canister contained some letters and postcards, and while sorting through them, Lydia discovered a photo of Almetta and a man, whom she presumed was Almetta's husband, Elmore. The two did not appear at all young, so Lydia guessed it was not a wedding photo, unless Almetta had married late in life.

When she opened the third canister, she gasped when a roll of bills fell out. With nervous fingers, she counted out nearly three hundred dollars.

A rush of energy came over her as she searched the back of

the wardrobe for more boxes and containers. In a small jewelry box, she discovered another small stack of bills. It was clear to her that Almetta had stashed away the money and more than likely forgot about it.

Lydia searched through some remaining boxes and a chest of drawers, but she did not find any more money.

Back downstairs, she made sure Almetta was comfortable in a chair in the den before she went to the carriage house livery, where she harnessed up Old Jake to the buggy.

The Wilkinson plantation was three miles away. She traveled the first few miles on Clayton Avenue past the last home at the extreme edge of town. The road now narrowed to wagon ruts, and somewhere along this road, Calvin was supposed to be working in one of the fields.

In a short time, she spotted the field hands, and at a cross-section, she turned and moved on at a rapid clip another half mile. Before she even began to slow, Calvin saw her, put down his hoe and hurried toward the road.

She stopped beside some water jugs.

"Miss Lydia," Calvin said as he neared and removed his hat. "What brings you out here this late in the day? I hope it doesn't concern Missus Almetta."

Lydia couldn't have had a bigger smile on her face. "It does, but in a good way. I need to speak with one of your sisters."

Calvin drank from one of the water jugs, corked it and smiled. "That can be arranged. Might I ask what about?"

"I need the services of a maid for Aunt Almetta." She saw Calvin cringe a bit. "You do have a sister who could provide that service, don't you?"

Calvin still seemed confused. "Oh, yes, but my daddy would have to make that decision."

"That's fair enough. Any more water left in that jug?"

Calvin held up the jug. "This is the worker's water. Most all of us have been drinking from it."

"Well, I'm a worker, too," she said, as she reached out a hand. Calvin handed over the jug and watched her take several mouthfuls. His heart jumped a beat to think that she had placed her lips on the same spot where he drank.

"Your home out here somewhere?" she asked him.

Calvin anxiously spun around and pointed across the field. "That's it over there."

All she could see were three small shacks nestled in a row among some trees.

"The first one," Calvin said.

"Are you finished working for the day?" she asked him.

He glanced at the sun. "It's about that time."

"Come on," she said, as she handed him the reins.

He was hesitant. "Miss Lydia, I don't know that this is a good idea. We don't got near the nice home you have, and momma . . ."

"I don't put that much value on property," she interrupted. "And it's about time I met your momma."

Calvin displayed his white teeth with a wide grin as he climbed into the seat. "Momma would be proud to meet you."

By the time they reached the dwelling that Calvin called home, Mrs. Jefferson and three of her daughters were lined up on the porch underneath an overhang held up by two flimsy poles. It looked as if it would come down any minute. Lydia had considered her home back in Virginia dilapidated by any conditions, but this house, at least from the outside, appeared to be a shack in shambles. Beyond the house, four poles supported a rickety roof of boards and tarpaper—an open livery, she guessed. Inside it was Amos' mule and wagon. Several pieces of clothing hung on a line strung from the house to the livery, and beyond the livery, two milk cows grazed in a pasture.

Nearby, chickens pecked away at bits on the ground, most of them in a garden plot. Lydia forced a smile as they rode up.

"Momma, that's Calvin!" she heard one of the girls shout.

Calvin was smiling. "That's Jocelyn, Tildie and Delia," and as he pulled on the reins, he let out a "Whoa, Jake." When they stopped, he was every bit the gentleman as he helped Lydia down. "Momma, this is Miss Lydia."

Calvin's mother was a good-sized woman with a perfect set of teeth shining brightly, like Amos' and Calvin's, and her face, like the faces of the three girls, was the color of a ripe chestnut.

"Miss Lydia," Mrs. Jefferson began, "we've heard lots of good things about you." She stuck out her hand. "Welcome to our home."

She introduced each of the girls, and as she did so, each gave a curtsy. The girls were like three peas in a pod, all with curly hair, all with pigtails tied up in ribbons. Their dresses were made out of flour-sack material, Lydia knew for certain, since she had worn something similar back in Grundy.

"You girls get some chairs out here," Mrs. Jefferson commanded, and immediately the three scooted inside. She turned to Lydia. "Can I offer you some lemonade on a hot day like this?"

"That would be fine."

In seconds, each of the girls came out carrying a wooden chair and plunked them on the porch.

"Jossi," she said to the oldest of the three, "go find your daddy and tell him we have some special company." Immediately, Jocelyn hurried down the steps and ran off.

The porch was on the shady side, perfect to avoid the low rays of the sun, and with a nice breeze coming across the field and blowing against Lydia's face, she felt refreshed. As she looked down the way toward the other two homes, a few coloreds were on the porch of each, looking back. Obviously, these other two homes housed field hands, just like the Jeffersons.

"Ain't this a beautiful day?" Calvin's mother said as she came out with a tray loaded with glasses and a huge pitcher. "Yes, sir, the Lord made this day special."

She poured the glasses full.

Their conversation for the next several minutes came easy. The corn was growing, but rain would help. The girls were good helpers around the house, one of the cows wasn't giving much milk anymore, and Amos and Calvin were putting in full days from daybreak to dusk.

"And my day never ends," she said.

When Jocelyn returned with Amos, he removed his hat as he came up the steps. "What a surprise," he said. "Miss Lydia, it is always nice to see you."

As soon as he had a glass of lemonade in hand and had settled back in a chair, their conversation eventually came around to Lydia's task at hand. "I need someone to help out with Aunt Almetta," she began. "Since Calvin can't help during the summer months, I was hoping maybe one of your daughters would be willing to take on some responsibility."

Amos and his wife eyed each other.

"I can pay," said Lydia. "I came in to some unexpected money." The two were still silent, mulling over the offer. Lydia thought her proposition would be easily accepted, but the two still eyed each other, as if her offer wasn't reasonable.

"Jossi's only thirteen," Amos said, as if her young age might be a factor.

Lydia smiled and turned on some charm. "Just like the Lord made this beautiful day, He provided me with the means to take care of Aunt Almetta. And if the good Lord is willing, maybe He will find a solution right here at the Jefferson home."

Mrs. Jefferson beamed and obviously loved the way Lydia had phrased her needs. She looked at Jocelyn and grinned "It'd have to be Jossi, here. These other two are too young to go off."

Amos nodded his approval. "She can cook and sew and wash clothes and run errands, and she don't eat much."

Lydia laughed. "She'll have her own room next to me, and she can eat as much as she wants." She turned to the young lady. "I hope you like gardening, because I have a garden that needs tending."

Jocelyn couldn't have delivered a bigger smile. "Yes'm, I do like working in the garden."

"Jossi?" her momma asked. "That sound like something you can handle?"

Jocelyn couldn't take the grin off her face as she nodded.

"I can pay twenty dollars a month," Lydia added. "Would that be appropriate?"

The eyes on all of the Jeffersons grew to the size of chicken eggs.

Amos threw an arm around Jocelyn. "That would be very fine, Miss Lydia."

Mrs. Jefferson was ecstatic. "We've got fried chicken, grits and rhubarb pie for supper, Miss Lydia, and you are welcome to share it with us."

"I'd be happy to."

"Calvin, go kill me a couple chickens," she said, as she grabbed the pitcher of lemonade and refilled Lydia's glass. "Yes, indeed. The Lord has brung us a real nice day."

The sun was dipping beyond the horizon by the time they finished their meal.

"I'll be happy to escort you home, Miss Lydia," Calvin offered.

"That would be nice, but how will you get back?"

"I'll take Babe along." Babe was Amos' mule.

With Babe tied on behind the buggy, the two headed back to

town. "That's so nice of you to take Jocelyn on as a helper," Calvin said. "It's difficult to find work for a thirteen-year-old, and worse if you're colored. My momma and daddy very much appreciate the offer, and so do I."

When they rolled into the yard, a light was on in the house upstairs, which told Lydia that Almetta was in her bedroom.

In the livery, Calvin lit a few lamps and removed the harness from old Jake, and when he finished, he walked Lydia back to the house.

"Thank you for everything, Calvin," she said, and then, to Calvin's surprise, she rose up on her toes and kissed him on the cheek. For a few seconds he simply stared at her, his face displaying his surprise.

Finally he said, "I s'pose I better be gettin' on. Good night, Miss Lydia."

He swung up onto his mule and started off. As he headed up Market Street, he turned and looked back at the house one more time and felt a surge of excitement charge inside him.

For the entire ride back, he could not get Lydia out of his mind, and when he reached home, a mild fear overtook him. During the many months he had come to know her, he'd felt the pangs of love slowly creep into his heart. No matter how hard he tried to repress his feelings for her, a deep hurt inside him kept coming back like an unrelenting plague.

"Oh, Lydia," he moaned. "Why couldn't you be colored like me?"

EIGHT

The following Sunday, Calvin brought Jocelyn by wagon to the plantation home, and when Jossi, as she preferred to be called, saw the size of the home, and in particular, when she entered her room, she cried a load of tears. "Miss Lydia, I never believed I would have my own room, and in such a nice home. I won't disappoint you."

Lydia could easily understand. She gave her a gentle hug, remembering that she had experienced similar emotions when she first arrived. Jocelyn brought only a few items with her, mostly personal things and only one additional dress, which suffered greatly from style. Though it was patched in several places, at least it was clean. Her underclothes were not much more than rags, so Lydia donated a set of her own. Though Jocelyn was six years younger than Lydia, she was only a few inches shorter. In spite of the fact that she had larger breasts than Lydia, the underclothes fit rather well.

Over the next few days, Jocelyn took to her duties with fervor—cooking for Almetta, constantly cleaning anything and everything, and on an afternoon when Lydia arrived home early from work, Jocelyn had already washed clothes and had them hanging on a line.

"Mostly Missus Almetta's things," she said.

"How are you and Almetta getting along?" Lydia asked. From the first few days, it appeared they had a rather good relationship going.

"Jes' fine. Whatever she wants, I get it. She loves being waited on, and she sure 'nuff likes corn cake."

"Corn cake?"

"I baked it this morning, jes' like momma taught me."

The days came and went, and summer was slipping by quickly. Whenever Jocelyn wasn't busy attending Almetta, she was working the garden. She always had fresh flowers in the house, and every day, fresh vegetables were on the menu.

One day Lydia brought a box from town and handed it over to Jocelyn. Her face blossomed when she opened it. Inside was a long blue dress with white lace. "Oh, my!" Jocelyn exclaimed. "Help me put it on!"

In her room, she stood before a mirror as Lydia helped her into it, and when all the buttons were fastened, Jocelyn swirled around and watched her reflection in the mirror. "Do you think I'm pretty, Lydia?" she asked.

The question stunned Lydia. "Yes," she said. "You're very pretty." She definitely was. Her chestnut-colored skin was smooth and without any blemishes, and her big eyes danced with excitement every second of the day. And her hips filled out the dress like it had been tailor-made.

"Yes, you sure are pretty," Lydia repeated.

"Thank you for this gift, Lydia. It's beautiful!" She spun around again and gave Lydia a bear hug.

"How would you like to show it off at the July Fourth parade?"

Jocelyn shook with excitement. "I ain't never been to a parade."

"Well, we're going."

"Miss Lydia, we'll be the two prettiest girls there."

Lydia nodded and gave a faint smile. "Yes, won't we."

As the parade unfolded, thousands of people lined Market

Street. Lydia and Jocelyn, stood elbow to elbow in the crowd as the string of unending floats and wagons streamed by. Among them was the fire engine, which Lydia had seen in the previous two years.

The five men from the Irish band that had performed at the Planter Hotel came by on a flatbed, blasting their strange assortment of instruments. The eerie sound of the bagpipe especially thrilled the crowd.

"I ain't never heard such a noise," said Jocelyn.

Wagon after wagon passed by with long canvas signs hanging on their sides, either advertising a place of business or depicting an Independence Day slogan.

Two columns of cavalry soldiers rode by on their horses, their blue uniforms shining in the hot sun, and right behind them rode several Indians on their mustangs. Their bright buckskin regalia and eagle-feather bonnets drew huge applause from the crowd.

"I ain't never seen Indians before," remarked Jocelyn. "Are they dangerous?"

"I don't think these are," Lydia answered.

The Women's Temperance League was well represented, and as they marched by waving their signs, they hollered out in loud voices how the evils of drinking were the downfall of humankind.

More wagons, stagecoaches, Conestogas, buggies of every kind and a half dozen bands from surrounding communities made their presence known. Clowns with funny faces skipped along, and generals in fancy uniforms representing both the Union and Confederacy gave a stately appearance on their horses.

After an hour and a half, the parade ended with over a hundred men from the Masonic Lodge passing by and waving their flags. And finally, the city workers with their brooms and brushes cleaned the horse manure left on the street.

When the crowd began to disperse, Lydia and Jocelyn hurried to the park, where Lydia had made arrangements to meet some of the girls from the restaurant.

They soon found Colleen and Selma and were greeted heartily by the two. However, Hattie Boyle, a recent employee of the restaurant and two of her friends, whom Lydia didn't know, looked Jocelyn up and down with peculiar faces. Obviously, they were not pleased to have a colored girl among them.

Lydia overlooked their snobbery, but Jocelyn, who was prone to jabbering at length, said barely a word. Before Lydia had even been able to spread out the food from her basket, she spotted Calvin and a few other field workers walking by.

"Calvin!" Lydia beckoned to him, but he just waved and kept on walking. "Calvin!" she shouted again.

"Miss Lydia," Jocelyn quietly cautioned. "It ain't proper to invite a colored man into a white crowd."

Hattie Boyle, having overheard the comment, said, "She's right. Blacks belong with blacks and whites belong with whites." The smug look on Hattie's face matched those of her two friends.

"Hattie Boyle." Lydia glared at her. "Calvin works for me during the winter, and he's also a dear friend, and Jocelyn is his sister."

Hattie's face was unchanged. "You should pick your friends more carefully."

Lydia pointed a finger at her. "You are, without a doubt, a bigot."

"A what?" asked Hattie.

Lydia grunted. "You don't even know what bigot means."

"Well, I know it don't mean nigger lover."

Jocelyn shrank back when she heard that.

Hattie stood up and motioned for her two friends. "I believe it's time we leave."

119

"I believe it is," Lydia retorted. When they were gone, she turned to Colleen and Selma. "I thought we fought a war over this?"

"We did," said Selma. "But for some, the war isn't over yet."

Colleen patted Jocelyn's hand. "Don't you worry none. Selma and I accepted the peace."

"We've got fried chicken in our basket," said Selma. "What have you got in yours?"

"Fried chicken, corn cake and rhubarb pie," Lydia answered.

"Corn cake?" asked Selma. "What the hell's that?" Before their picnic was over, Selma knew well what corn cake was, since she had two pieces.

The Jefferson family was a stone's throw away, where the black populace had congregated. "Come on, Jossi," Lydia said as she got to her feet. "Let's go visit your family." She turned to Colleen and Selma. "I don't understand. It's okay if black people work for whites, but it's not okay to associate with them publicly."

As Lydia and Jocelyn walked off, Selma mused, "She doesn't understand, does she?"

"No," said Colleen. "She's too naïve to see the difference."

Selma nodded. "I just hope her relationship with the Jeffersons doesn't get her into trouble."

"I don't think she cares," Colleen said. "After all, the Jeffersons are the only family she has."

When Lydia and Jocelyn reached the Jefferson family, Amos had his hat off. "Miss Lydia," he greeted.

"I saw Calvin here earlier," Lydia said as she looked around.

"Calvin, he done run off with some others," said Mrs. Jefferson. "He's somewheres here in the park. You get plenty to eat?"

"We did."

"I got more corn cake in my basket here," she said.

Lydia laughed heartily. Corn cake was definitely a Jefferson delight. After a few minutes of conversation, she left Jossi with her family, excused herself and headed off toward the bandstand. She hoped to spot Calvin, but he was nowhere to be found.

Some distance away from where the band was playing, she picked a shady spot under a tree and spread out a blanket. The music was barely audible from this far away, but she did not mind. She found it refreshing to let her thoughts drift on this sunny day, happy that she had found Jocelyn to care for Almetta, but unhappy that she had not been able to spot Calvin.

"Miss Lydia, I believe?" came a voice from behind her.

She looked up into a vaguely familiar face.

"I'm Matt McGrath."

Lydia squinted, examined the ruddy-faced man with the few big freckles. He was wearing a dapper gray suit and had removed his hat.

"You don't remember me? We danced once at the Planter Hotel some time back."

Lydia smiled. "Matthew, yes, I do remember. Forgive me. The lighting on the floor was not very bright that night."

"It never has been. May I?" he asked as he motioned to the blanket.

"Of course," she said, charmed that he had spotted her and even more charmed that he remembered her name.

"You were the quiet one, if I remember correctly," she said.

He shrugged. "I suppose."

"Are you still working on that steamer, the *Josephine?*"

"No, I'm not."

She waited for him to go on. "Which means . . . ?"

"I have changed professions." He gazed off at the band.

"Which means . . . ?"

He acted as if he didn't hear her. "May I say you look very smart in your attire. The crimson color brings out the brightness of your eyes."

Lydia was flattered.

"And I see that a compliment brings a smile to your blushing face."

Lydia felt a warmth crawl up around her neck. She guessed she might be blushing, although never before had she ever been given an opportunity to do so.

"I see you are still working at the railroad restaurant."

"Yes. How did you know?"

He smiled. "I have spies."

Lydia did not know exactly where this conversation was leading, but she was taken by his easy manner. He was not the most handsome man she had met, but he was friendly enough, and he possessed a pleasant mystery about himself that intrigued her.

"There's a dance at the outdoor pavilion tonight."

The smile on her face was permanent as she grabbed at her bonnet when a mild wind whipped through. She held the hat firmly, waiting for him to go on.

"I'd be honored if you would attend with me."

Lydia's face froze. Somehow she was sure that he might ask, but now that he actually did, she choked up, unable to respond.

Matthew made a face. "Did I hear an answer?"

"Forgive me! Yes. I'd be happy to attend with you. But . . ." She was now thinking about Jocelyn and Almetta.

"But what?"

"Yes. I'd be delighted, but I have a few things to take care of. Some arrangements, you understand."

"Of course. Shall we meet at the pavilion, say eight or so?"

"That would be fine."

He slipped his derby back in place, then rose and offered to help her to her feet. "Tonight at eight," he said with a warm smile.

As he walked off, she watched him for the longest time,

expecting that he might meet some other friends, but after a while, he simply disappeared into the crowd.

Lydia examined her hands. They were sweating and still warm from his touch. She gathered up her blanket and basket, and with the excitement of a young miss being invited on her first social engagement with a fellow, she trotted off to find Jocelyn.

Shortly before eight, Lydia was strolling across the grass toward the pavilion, her eyes searching for Matt McGrath. The sun was still full on the horizon, but the air had cooled considerably. She had made arrangements for Amos to drive Jocelyn home, for which she was thankful, and which would free her up for the night.

Several tables and chairs were scattered around the wooden dance floor that had been set up in front of the bandstand. She had no idea who was playing, and she didn't care.

As the crowd gathered, the tables were quickly occupied. She scanned the area, but she still did not see Matt. After a few minutes, she felt her heartbeat increase, concerned that she was about to be abandoned.

A warm hand suddenly grabbed hers from behind, and when she turned, Matt was grinning at her. "I've been watching you for the past five minutes. You're blushing again, aren't you, and I love it!"

She was blushing.

"Come on," he said. "Let's get us a table before they're all gone."

They took one on the fringe of the dance floor, and he ordered drinks for the two of them. For the longest time, they talked about everything and nothing, and after a half hour, if anyone had come by and asked what their conversation entailed, Lydia was sure she wouldn't be able to remember a thing.

They danced well into the night, and before it was over, they joined Colleen and her beau, Joseph Blacksmith. Selma eventually showed up without an escort, but not at all short of partners. Though her language was often crude and her face was splotchy from red freckles, she was a dancing fool. Any man on the floor who loved to dance kept her busy.

At a moment when Matt and Joseph were off to purchase more refreshments, Colleen leaned in on Lydia. "Is this a serious thing with your fellow?"

She smiled. "I've only seen him twice. How serious can that be?"

"Could be enough," said Selma. "I once married a man after knowing him two hours. 'Course, we were both drunk at the time."

That drew some curious looks. When Colleen asked how long the marriage lasted, she said, "Till the next day. We ran down the justice of the peace, gave him ten dollars and he tore up the marriage certificate."

"Good for you," said Lydia.

"Wasn't good for me. Couple days later I learned he was a cattleman worth thousands. I should have never divorced the bastard. I could have been rich."

All three girls laughed hard. They were still laughing when the music started up again and a fellow whisked Selma onto the floor.

"I love that lady," said Lydia.

Colleen shook her head in disbelief. "We all do."

Matt McGrath summoned a cab when the dance was over and quietly told the driver to take his time on the way to Lydia's home.

It was a comfortable evening and not at all cool as the two sat side by side behind the driver, but when Matt asked if she was cold, she responded, "A little."

She guessed that he would put his arm around her if she said she was, and when he did, she felt her heart pounding. She could have ridden around town like that for hours, but eventually the cabbie pulled up at her home. Like the gentleman he was, Matt helped her down and held her arm as he escorted her to the door. "I'll be leaving by steamer in the morning," he said, "but I'd like to see you again, if I may."

"You may," she said as she turned to him.

"Would it be too presumptuous of me if I kissed you good night?"

"Not at all," she said.

He removed his hat and kissed her lightly on the lips. Seeing her warm response, he wrapped his arms around her and kissed her for the longest time.

Without another word, he smiled, put on his derby and walked back to the buggy. Inside the house, Lydia pulled a curtain aside and watched the buggy wheel around and head back toward the city.

"Lydia?" came a voice from behind her.

Lydia turned to see Jocelyn standing in her nightclothes and holding a lamp.

"Did you have a nice evening?" she asked.

Lydia's heart was still racing. "I had a wonderful night!"

NINE

July 6, 1874

Dear Grandmama Eugenia,

On July 4th, the Eads Bridge across the Mississippi off-
ishally opened. It is hugh. Two trains can cross at one time,
and above the tracks, wagons can cross. The town had a
big celebrashun, and so many people attended. But best of
all, Matt McGrath asked me to a danse. He was the fellow
I dansed with long ago. He is tall and has some frekles and
curly brown hair. He wants to see me again!

I higherd Jossi to take care of Aunt Almetta. She is
Calvin's sister. They get along real well and Jossi can cook
almost anything, but best of all Corn Cake. It is delishus
and dosn't even taste like corn.

Jossi and I saw the Parade again and Indians and the
same fire engin as last year, but differnt horses.

I am looking forward to seeing Matt soon. He even
kissed me. Next month I will be 18. I think he is much
older, maybe 30. He has a new profeshun, but I don't
know what it is.

The garden is growing with lots of flowers and vetchta-
bels. I still read and study, but for two days my hart is not
in it, and you can tell why. I hope you are well.

Love, Lydia

Lydia's eighteenth birthday passed by uneventfully, as did the entire month of August. By mid-September, Calvin's job delivering cotton had slowed down, and he was once again in need of work for the winter.

Jocelyn was good at some of the easier tasks around the house, but during the winter months, simply keeping the home warm would be a chore. This year, Lydia decided to keep both the upstairs and downstairs warm. Jocelyn needed a bedroom, and Lydia had plenty of the money she had discovered in Almetta's wardrobe left. She also approached Calvin to ask if he would consent to another winter of work, and he gladly accepted.

September remained unusually warm, and to keep Calvin busy, Lydia instructed him to make any repairs necessary on the exterior of the home.

"We're going to paint this house and give it the fine look it deserves."

"Yes'm, that's a good idea."

"Buy us a quarter of beef and half a hog. This winter, we're going to eat a lot of steak and boiled ham."

"Yes'm."

"And see if you can get some fresh catfish."

Inside of three weeks, and before the cold weather set in, Calvin had the house painted and a good supply of wood and coal on hand. He habitually drove Lydia into town in the morning for work and picked her up in the evening, but on one cold morning when he dropped her off at the station restaurant, she gave him different instructions.

"Calvin, no need to pick me up tonight. I'm staying at a friend's house. Pick me up tomorrow night at the regular time."

"Yes'm."

That evening after work, Lydia left the restaurant dressed in her heavy coat and wearing gloves and a fur hat to protect her against a biting wind. She crossed to Fourth Street and headed up the block, tucking in her chin against the cold. By the time she reached the library, snow was swirling about her. She kept her head down and turned the corner, thankful to be on the lee side of the wind. At Sixth Street the wind tore at her again as she headed for Washington.

The street was practically devoid of traffic and pedestrians, and as she neared the Lindell Hotel, she looked up and saw him standing at the entrance. She hurried her pace across the street, her heart beating from excitement.

"Lydia," Matt said as he grasped her hands and pulled her toward him. He gave her a light kiss, then took her by the arm and escorted her into the lobby of the hotel. A host seated them in the elegant dining room where they ordered a meal, and an hour and a half later, after finishing the last of a bottle of red wine, the two left the table, passed through a few rooms at the rear of the hotel and climbed the back stairs to the third floor.

When she entered his room, a lamp was burning on a desk next to a four-poster bed. He removed his coat and helped her remove her wraps, and after hanging them up, he took her in his arms and kissed her ever so gently.

He was holding her so closely that he could feel her heart beat, and when he saw the nervous look on her face, he said, "If you like, I'll turn down the lamp."

She was slow to respond, and then, "Yes, if you don't mind."

He turned down the wick until the flame was extinguished, but through the window curtain, a dim ray of light from a street lantern offered some illumination in the room.

She sat on the bed, her whole body trembling lightly, and then, slowly, she began unfastening the buttons on the front of her dress.

Matt McGrath had fought for the Confederacy, but he did not have what Lydia considered a Southern accent. While working onboard the *Josephine* steamship, he'd had many varied duties, among them, working the casino and card tables. "I've been traveling up and down the Mississippi and Missouri ever since the war," he told her. "If you can read a man's face, you can read his cards."

Having gained knowledge of card playing, he left the *Josephine* and became a professional gambler, but he continued to travel the waterway, switching from one steamship to another, always searching out the most likely crowd where money was to be won.

Lydia never thought about gambling as a decent profession, but Matt McGrath seemed to have money all the time, and he treated her well when he was in St. Louis.

She met with him secretly two more times, each about a month apart, and two days before Christmas day, she received a package postmarked from Bismarck, Dakotah Territory. She knew that Bismarck was a city somewhere far north on the Missouri. Inside the package was a short note and a pearl necklace. *A pearl for a pearl,* the note said, and it was signed, *Love, Matt.*

Lydia was all smiles as Jocelyn placed it around her neck, and as she turned her head a few times to examine it in a mirror, Jocelyn exclaimed, "My, my. That is the most beautiful necklace I ever seen. Your man must think you're something special."

Calvin was present and forced a smile, having known for some time now that this man, Matthew McGrath, had entered her life. Calvin had figured it out when he was asked not to pick her up at the restaurant on certain occasions. Though he did fantasize about having a relationship with Lydia, he knew that he had absolutely no chance with her. He could only guess that she had made love to this man, but that was her affair, and he understood her motives and desires. She deserved a good man, yet to see her so happy over the gift that this white man had given her hurt him terribly.

"It is beautiful, Lydia," Calvin finally said. She was so busy admiring the necklace that she did not even notice the constrained look on his face.

For Christmas Day, Calvin and Jocelyn returned to their own home, and although they invited Lydia to have Christmas dinner with them, she declined. "I think it best that I spend the day with Aunt Almetta."

Almetta had hardly spoken a word in the past few months, and simply sitting in a chair near the fireplace to keep warm would occasionally bring a slight smile from her. She could still walk with help, but every morning and evening, Lydia or Jocelyn would aid her up or down the staircase. When Lydia offered to make up a bed downstairs for her, she managed to grunt out, "No, no," as she pointed upwards with a finger, indicating she wanted to sleep in her own bedroom.

Nearly three months had passed since Lydia last heard from Matthew. Somehow, she believed he wasn't coming back, but one evening at the restaurant, just as she changed out of her uniform and into her street clothes, Colleen sought her out.

"Lydia, there's someone in the office waiting to see you."

"Who is it?" she inquired.

Colleen's broad smile answered Lydia's question.

Lydia hurried out of the changing room and went directly to the office. He was standing next to Mr. Longhorn's desk when she entered, and as soon as she closed the door, he wrapped her in his arms and kissed her firmly. "I missed you, darling," he said.

She drew back. "Your face?"

"It's nothing." He touched the nasty scar over his eye and shrugged it off. "A big loser tried to get his money back."

"When did this happen?" she asked.

"Couple months ago." He quickly changed the subject. "Did you receive the gift I sent?"

She nodded, the joy filling her face. "It's a wonderful gift. I never thought I'd ever have a pearl necklace."

He grinned. "A pearl for a pearl." He motioned outside. "I noticed your ride is here."

"Calvin?" she asked. "Shall I tell him to head back home?"

"That would be nice."

They made love in the same hotel and in the same room as before, and after their lovemaking, they lay quietly in the dark. She felt so at ease and was so in love with this man. To think that she had for the most part forgotten about him after that first night they danced.

"Would you consider traveling with me?" he asked abruptly.

"Where?" she asked.

"On the river. There are many nice cities to visit."

"You would continue gambling?"

"Of course."

"And what would I do?"

He was silent for a moment, and then ever so nonchalantly, he said, "Oh, you could spot the high rollers, maybe search out the ones who would be more receptive to losing at the card table." She did not respond. "There are a lot of men out there who can't wait to give away their fortunes. For some, gambling at cards is an obsession. Those that don't know when to quit usually become the losers."

"And you take their money?"

"They're after mine. It's just that I'm better at cards than most. I think you'd find this life exciting."

"What about Aunt Almetta?"

"Jocelyn could take care of her. If it's a matter of money . . ."

"No, that's not it," she said.

The conversation wasn't leading in the direction Lydia anticipated. When he first mentioned traveling, she jumped to the conclusion that he might have been indicating marriage, but at the moment, he seemed to imply that she should become a traveling companion.

She could not leave her aunt under these circumstances, not after Almetta had taken her in, given her a home and shelter and a place in society. To many, these acts of compassion may not have been considered any great sacrifices, but they were very important to Lydia.

"I . . . I'll have to think about it." She was cautious and feared her answer would be found unacceptable to him.

"Of course," he said as he hugged her and stroked her face. "I didn't expect you to give an immediate answer."

Matt McGrath remained in town for another day, and Lydia once again spent the evening with him. She was apprehensive that he might press her to break her ties with her aunt and join him on his gambling escapade on the river, but during that second evening, he did not even bring up the subject.

The next morning when she went to work, he left on a steamer headed for New Orleans. While she was changing into her work clothes, Colleen saw the sad face she was wearing. "Lydia, you look like you just lost your best friend."

"I might have." Lydia covered her mouth with one hand, and no matter how hard she tried, she could not hold back the tears.

Colleen put an arm around her. "Come on, honey. Tell me about it."

June 4, 1875
Dear Grandmama Eugenia,

I have not heard from you in so long. I hope nothing has happened to you. It has been over a year since I last wrote, but so much has happened.

I still see Matt McGrath. He has a very good position

with the steamship line here in St. Louis, but he travels considerably, therefore I do not see him as often as I like. But when we do meet, we often spend an evening dining at one of the fancy restaurants, and then he escorts me home. Sometimes we go on picnics in the countryside, but not in the winter, of course.

My best friend, Colleen, was married a week ago today. She has a wonderful husband, Joe Blacksmith, whose father owns a drygoods store, which he hopes to inherit some day. Colleen now works at the store, so she is no longer here at the restaurant. I miss her, but we still see each other once in a while. My best friend at the restaurant is now Selma Ritter. She is a rare individual. I don't think she will ever marry, because she always says what she thinks, and men don't necessarily like that trait in a woman. She is twenty-eight years old and says she will be an old maid. She was married once, but just for a day.

Jocelyn treats Almetta very well. Auntie has not said a word for at least two months. She has become frail, and I fear she may not be with us much longer. Calvin painted the house last fall and Jocelyn and I canned a lot of vegetables. Calvin's daddy, Amos, brought us many sacks of corn, so we canned that, too. He also brought us watermelons and cantaloupe when they were in season.

Calvin is back at work at the Wilkinson plantation. The only time I see him is when he picks up Jocelyn once in a while so she can visit her folks. Sometimes I drive her out there with the horse and buggy. The Jeffersons are a very nice family and have been good to Almetta and me.

I bought a dictionary a few months ago. It took me a long time to write this letter, so I hope you find every word spelled correktly. I hope you are in good health.

Love, Lydia

Lydia reread her letter. Almost all of it was true. She didn't want to tell Eugenia that she had been sleeping with Matt McGrath. What she wrote, she considered fairly correct, since Matt had, on occasion, escorted her home.

She had not heard from him in months, which was something else she did not care to impart in the letter. Because of his long absence, she initially feared he had been hurt, or worse, maybe even killed. She did not at all discount the possibility that since she had refused to travel with him, he may have given up on her and would never return.

She didn't want to believe that, since he was the only man who had taken an interest in her, and making love to him was thrilling, an experience beyond explanation.

Yet what he had requested of her, if she were to join him, was to be a lookout, so to speak. She was to seek out gamblers who were vulnerable, those who were more apt than others to lose their money at a card table. She surmised that such card players were those who had had too much to drink and could not think clearly.

She did not inquire exactly how she was to carry out this deception, but she knew she could not in good conscience entertain such a scheme. If Matt McGrath couldn't accept her as Lydia Pearlman—citizen of St. Louis and love of his life, then he would have to find a partner elsewhere.

Three days after she mailed the letter, she returned home with Calvin after work only to discover Doctor Regenfeld's buggy out front. When she and Calvin entered the house, Jocelyn beckoned them from the top of the staircase. They hurried up the stairs to Almetta's bedroom. Her aunt's face was as white as the sheets she was lying in.

"I'm sorry, Lydia," Doctor Regenfeld said. "She just took her last breath a few minutes ago."

"It was a blessing," said Lydia as she sat next to her aunt.

"Yes, it was," he responded. "The symptoms were slowly coming on. It was inevitable."

"I never even knew how old she was," Lydia said.

"Sixty-three," he said. "Before she died, she mentioned Elmore's name a few times." He shrugged. "I don't know why. Delirious, I suppose, to the last minute."

He packed his bags and stood. "She was a good woman. Never had any children of her own, but she took in a lot of orphans over the years and found homes for most of them. That's what I'll remember her for." This was the most the doctor had ever said about Almetta's contribution to society.

"Did her husband ever help her with these orphan kids?" Lydia asked.

"No, he didn't. He, ah . . ." He stopped, and then repeated, "No, he didn't." Without any further elaboration, he recommended that she contact Harrison's Funeral Parlor. "Mr. Harrison's wife is a member of the Temperance League and was one of Almetta's good friends."

When the doctor was gone, Lydia touched the cold hands of her aunt and sat for the longest time, reflecting back on the first day they had met.

That twitching eye of hers would be still forever.

Two days later, the Harrison's hearse brought Almetta's body to the Wesleyan Cemetery, which was located no more than a hundred yards north of her home. A pastor, whom Lydia did not even know, said a few words to a crowd of about forty people. Most of the ladies were from the Women's Temperance League, but only a few brought their husbands.

Amos, Calvin and Jocelyn represented the Jefferson family, and two young ladies about Lydia's age also came to pay their respects. She wondered who they were, and afterward they introduced themselves. Both had been taken in by Almetta when they lost their parents.

"I'll always remember her kindness," said one of them.

"Almetta had a heart of gold," said the other. "She was so good to all of us. You must be very proud of her."

It was strange, thought Lydia. Why did not more people mention that Almetta had at one time taken in orphans? She without a doubt was well known for her active support of the Temperance League, but very few ever praised her efforts to provide a home for youngsters. Doctor Regenfeld spoke of it briefly, and Amos knew about it, as did these two young ladies, but it was not a subject Lydia heard discussed in social circles.

Two weeks later, Lydia penned another note to Eugenia.

June 21, 1875

Dear Grandmama Eugenia,

I am sad to tell you that Aunt Almetta died a few weeks ago. She had a wonderful funeral. For many years she took in orphans but she is best remembered for her work in the Women's Temperance League. I have gone through her things and donated most of her clothes to the needy. She really did not have much. I have found a few photos and some personal items but do not know what to do with them. I am not sure what I will do with the house, since it is so big and so far from work. Perhaps time will tell.

Jocelyn has agreed to stay on for a few more months until I decide, and Calvin or Amos stop in every other day just to see how we are doing, and that is very comforting.

Independence Day celebration is soon, but I don't know if I will attend. The parade is always the same, but don't worry about me. I am okay. Please write.

Love, Lydia

A few days later, on a hot afternoon, Lydia and Jocelyn were working in the garden when they heard a buggy pull up on the street. They did not pay attention to the arrival, and it was not until they heard the back door of the house open that they noticed a man standing on the porch. He had obviously come through the house from the front. He was dressed in a dark frock coat that reached to his knees, and underneath it, he wore a white shirt covered with a gray vest. Although his pants matched the coat, his clothes were not new, and his shoes showed signs of heavy wear. He did not bother to remove the derby on his head when he addressed her.

"Are you Lydia Pearlman?"

"I am," she answered. "And what are you doing walking through my home without permission?"

His face contorted in anger. "I don't require permission to step onto my property."

She shook when she realized to whom she was speaking.

"I'm Elmore Boggs, and this is my home." He walked down the few steps closer to her. "Of course, you probably didn't realize that, so I can understand your confusion."

The stern look and wavy hair were reminiscent of the photo she had once seen. His hair was gray now, and deep lines covered his face, but there was no doubt that he was Almetta's husband.

"Who's this nigger girl, your maid?"

When he said that, Jocelyn closed in next to Lydia. "She happens to live here with me."

He looked Jocelyn up and down and forced a smile. "Well, I want to be fair about this. I'll give you two a few days to vacate the premises. That should be adequate time."

Lydia held her ground. "And if we don't vacate the premises?"

He stiffened. "Then I shall have to take legal action. I have the law on my side."

As he was about to leave, Amos and Calvin appeared from

near the house. Elmore Boggs eyed the two and then turned to Lydia. "I want you and all your nigger friends out of here. Two days and not a second more."

When he was gone, Amos saw the distraught look on Lydia's face. "That's Elmore Boggs," he said.

"I know," Lydia answered. "He wants us out of the house. Obviously, he must have heard that Almetta died." She hung her head. "Does he have any legal claim to this home?"

Amos' face went blank. "Miss Lydia, I ain't familiar with the white man's law, but it might could be that he does."

"What are we going to do?" asked Jocelyn.

Lydia squared her shoulders, and with a defiant look, she said, "Well, first we'll find out if he has any claim."

The next morning, Lydia pulled up outside the courthouse in her buggy, where she tied the reins of Old Jake to a post ring. She entered the building, and after inquiring if Judge Featherstone was in, the secretary asked if she had an appointment.

"No, I don't, but the judge will see me."

"The judge doesn't see anyone without an appointment."

At that moment, Judge Featherstone appeared in the doorway of his office, and seeing Lydia, he nodded to his secretary. "It's all right. Please, Miss Pearlman," he said as he motioned for her to enter his room.

The secretary had a most curious look on his face as Lydia passed by.

"My dear," said Judge Featherstone as he closed the door. "We haven't danced in some time, have we?" He offered her a seat. "To what do I owe the pleasure of your company?"

She was only mildly surprised with the comment, since this was the first time she had seen him when he wasn't drunk. She came directly to the point. "Elmore Boggs showed up yesterday."

Judge Featherstone sank back in his chair and clasped his hands over his fat belly. "I was afraid this might happen."

"He wants me out of the house in two days."

The judge shook his head. "I was hoping he'd be dead by now." He produced a document from a drawer. "That man," he said as he picked up a pen and began writing.

The fact that Elmore Boggs showed up at her home upset Lydia enough that she asked for a few days off at work. After two days had passed, she wondered if she had made the right decision, since there was not much to do at the home except work in the garden.

She was hoeing with Jocelyn, when once again Elmore Boggs appeared from out of nowhere. "You damned bitch!" he yelled.

When Lydia whirled around, Boggs was standing defiantly, his face distorted with anger. He held up a piece of paper in his fist and shook it at her. "You did this!"

She knew what the document was. "Yes, I did," she answered. It was an order from Judge Featherstone that granted Lydia two months to remain in the home until the settlement could be probated. According to the judge, the long absence of Elmore Boggs could legally be construed as abandonment. Under such circumstances, Elmore Boggs might not have had any legal claim to ownership of the home.

Elmore Boggs wadded up the document and threw it at her feet. "What did you have to do to get this judgment against me, sleep with him?"

The wrath in Lydia erupted fully. She gritted her teeth and swung the hoe with the fury of someone gone mad. The steel blade ripped into the side of his face, knocking off his hat. He screamed out, and before he remotely knew how profusely he was bleeding, she wielded the hoe again and again. He threw up his hands to protect himself, and as he moved back, he stumbled and fell to the ground. She was relentless as she continued to wield the hoe.

"God damn you woman!" he shouted as he struggled to scramble out of her reach. She whacked him again and again until he was screaming so loud that the cabbie who had driven him up suddenly ran onto the scene.

Jocelyn grabbed Lydia's hand just as the cabbie bent over to render aid to Elmore.

"Good Lord!" the cabbie shrieked, his face ridden with fear. "What's going on here?"

"I'm giving this bastard what he deserves!" Lydia shot back as she raised the hoe again. "Get him out of here or I'll thrash the hide right off of him!"

As the cabbie pulled Elmore to his feet, blood was running down over his eyes, and his ear was half torn away. He limped off, swearing as he went. "By God in heaven, you'll pay for this, you bitch!"

Lydia was so livid that she was shaking. "How dare you invoke the Lord's name!" she shouted as she raised the hoe again. Now the cabbie threw his hands up for protection, thinking she would thrash him as well. Lydia and Jocelyn followed them out to the street and watched while the cabbie helped Elmore into the buggy. As they drove off, Elmore was pressing a blood-drenched handkerchief against his face.

It was then Lydia and Jocelyn noticed Curly in his streetcar. He, along with a few passengers, gawked at Lydia for the longest time, and then he snapped the reins to his horse and continued on down the street.

"My, Miss Lydia!" Jocelyn exclaimed, still shaking and nervous from the encounter. "You sure 'nuff get mad when you get mad!"

Lydia looked over the blade end of her hoe that was bent and covered with blood. "Looks like I'll need a new one in case he comes back." She delivered the comment in all seriousness, but as they walked back to the garden, they both started laughing.

"Lucky thing you didn't have no shotgun," Jocelyn quipped. "Otherwise Mr. Boggs be sure 'nuff dead by now."

They returned to their work in the garden, but the adrenaline was still racing through Lydia. After two altercations with the man, she now had a clear understanding why Almetta rarely spoke about him.

According to Judge Featherstone, Elmore had disappeared from St. Louis some seven or eight years earlier. The judge was unable to ascertain whether a deed existed that indicated Elmore Boggs was the official owner of the property, and as far as he was concerned, Lydia was free to do with the plantation home as she desired, since she was Almetta's only remaining kin.

Jocelyn read the concern in her face. "Lydia, if'n you'd feel better, I could get Calvin to come over and spend the nights here."

"No," she said. "I can take care of myself." She looked up and smiled. "I meant, we can take care of ourselves."

"Yes'm, we sure can."

On Independence Day, the town was filled with the traditional crowd watching the annual parade. Jocelyn was off with her parents somewhere, and Lydia was asked to work at the restaurant. She did not mind, since her thoughts were too occupied with the house and what to do about it, and she had no special plans for the celebration anyway.

She and Selma Ritter were standing outside the restaurant now, taking a break and able to catch a glimpse of the activities as the trail of parade marchers turned the corner near Broadway.

As they were watching, Selma puffed on a cigarette and said, "You ever catch sight of that son of a bitch again?"

Lydia knew she was talking about Elmore Boggs. "No. He hasn't come back."

"I wouldn't, either, if you took half my face off with a hoe. What are you going to do with the house?"

"I haven't decided."

"If you want to rent out a room, let me know. The building I live in is being torn down to make space for a lumberyard."

"Hey, girls." Mr. Longhorn was at the door motioning for them. "Got a few hungry customers just walked in."

When he closed the door, Selma made a face. "Shit. Can't even finish a cigarette."

By the time Lydia arrived home, it was near eight. She unharnessed Old Jake, fed him and headed for the house. A wind had picked up out of the north, and as she looked skyward, it appeared as if it might rain. She hurried inside just as a layer of dark clouds rolled across the sky.

She thought Jocelyn had already returned from the city celebration, but the house was vacant. Either Calvin or Amos was to bring her home, but if they didn't hurry, she was sure they would get caught in a rainstorm.

Inside the house it was already dark, so she lit a lamp and left it burning in the kitchen for Jocelyn. After she washed up, she ascended the stairs to her room, where she lit another lamp and set it on the dresser in front of a mirror. While she was brushing her hair, a gust of wind blew so hard that she felt the house shake, and from somewhere in the house she heard a door slam.

"Jocelyn?" she called out, sure she had just returned and entered downstairs. "I'm up here, honey."

Not hearing anything more, Lydia went to the balcony and peered down. "Jocelyn?" she asked again.

She looked around and noticed the door to Almetta's room was closed. She guessed that a window in her room must have been open and the sudden wind more than likely slammed the door shut.

When she opened the door, she gasped at the interior. The wardrobe doors were wide open, and the contents from all of the boxes and containers that Lydia had once searched through were strewn about the room. At first she thought the wind had whipped the doors open and scattered everything, yet every drawer from the dresser was pulled open. The wind wouldn't do that. Even the mattress and bedding had been dragged off the bed frame.

"What on earth?" she said as she stared at the mess.

The door suddenly banged shut behind her, and when she spun around, she shuddered at the shadow standing in front of the door. She knew it was Elmore Boggs.

"She signed the house over to ya, didn't she?" he said. "Where you got the deed hid?"

His voice was slurred, and he was weaving slightly.

"You get out, you filthy scoundrel!"

His snide laugh drowned out her voice. "Ain't got yer hoe with ya this time, ya little bitch." He stepped from the shadows and whipped back his hair to show half of his ear was missing. A deep gash ran across his forehead where she had struck him. "You done this, and I tol' ya I'd get even."

Ever so quickly, he grabbed the front of her dress, and as she pulled away, the buttons on her bodice tore loose, exposing her underclothes.

She struggled, but he grabbed her shoulders and wrenched her to the side. Caught off balance, she dropped to the floor. He was on top of her, his face so close that she could smell the foul whiskey on his breath.

She wanted to scream, but he snapped her head sideways with a fierce blow. Adrenalin charged inside her as she raked his face with her fingernails. He cursed and reached for her hand, but she twisted away and groped for anything her fingers could touch. Somehow she grasped the handle of a hand mirror, and she swung it fiercely at the side of his head. It shattered, driving shards into his flesh. When he yelled in pain, she scrambled out from underneath him and swung the mirror again. The edge of it caught him on the raw flesh where his ear had been torn away causing him to scream in agony.

She was on her feet and charged for the door. She whipped it open, but then he tripped her, and she went down again. She kicked back, and on all fours, she quickly crawled out of his reach. She got to her feet, but he jumped in front of the staircase, barricading her escape.

Frantic, she turned and ran to her room and slammed the door. With nervous fingers, she locked it. Her heart was pounding as she heard his voice screaming from the other side.

"God damn you!" he hollered. He was kicking at the door, and with each blow, the jamb loosened. Knowing the door wouldn't hold, and with her nerves still shaking, she scanned the room for anything she could use to defend herself.

She picked up the small sitting chair from her dresser just as the doorframe broke through with a horrendous crack. He stood in the doorway with blood streaming down his face, and although she swung the chair at him, he threw up an arm, taking only a glancing blow.

Like a madman, he tore at her clothing. "God damn you, woman! God damn you!" A hard fist to her face flopped her backward onto the bed. With blood leaking from the edges of her mouth, she lay with her breasts exposed, her breath pumping hard as he clawed to tear the rest of her dress from her.

Half conscious, she moaned, wanting to scream, but the pain in her face wouldn't let her. He grunted and ripped at her underclothes, and she knew he was about to violate her.

"No, no," she moaned.

He was on top of her now and fumbling with his belt and pants when he heard the footsteps outside on the balcony.

"Lydia!" a voice called.

"In here, Calvin!" she screamed back.

Elmore Boggs raised himself up when he saw the black figure in the doorway, his face a mask of confusion. He was barely on his feet when Calvin swung a poker at him. Elmore shoved an arm up for protection and gave a hellish scream when the bone in his forearm cracked.

A second blow split his forehead wide open. Even then, Elmore managed to stay on his feet, but he was no match for Calvin's strength. Another blow to the head elicited a final grunt from Elmore. He fell backward against a chest, and as he slumped to the floor, his arm whipped against the oil lamp on the bureau. In seconds, oil poured from the glass bowl and flames surged across the floor.

Jocelyn was in the doorway now and screamed out for Calvin to stop, but her voice went unheard. Calvin swung the poker again and again, smashing in Elmore's face.

"Stop, Calvin, stop!" Jocelyn screamed over and over.

Elmore's limp body was lying in the oil, and now his clothing caught fire. "Get help!" Calvin shouted at Jocelyn, and as she ran off, he wrapped Lydia's partially nude body in a blanket. By the time he picked her up, the fire had already reached the curtain, sending a rush of flames spiraling upwards to the ceiling. Calvin carried Lydia's limp body down the staircase, and when he reached the outside, flames were shooting out of the bedroom window.

A few people had gathered on the street, and now, with the wind whipping and the upper story of the mansion a brilliant glow from the spreading flames, sparks and hot debris flew across the yard to the carriage house. In no time, the roof sparked into flames.

With Lydia in safe hands, Calvin gathered a few men and ran for the stable. Some men pushed out the buggy while Calvin loosed Old Jake from a stall and ran him outside.

It was futile even to think about putting out the fire. The flames whipped fiercely in the wind, and now the upper half of the home roared as smoke billowed away. The fire on the roof of the carriage house and livery crackled and timbers collapsed. Flames engulfed the structure.

A half hour later, the fire engine pulled up with its small crew, but battling the blaze was beyond hope. Both the home and the carriage house were in full flame, and although several firemen worked the pumps on the fire engine, the heat from the fire was so intense, they could not even get close. The ferocious wind was making its claim on the old plantation.

Many thought the one saving grace would be the oncoming rainstorm, and although the evening was filled with a driving wind out of the north and a sky free from stars, not one raindrop fell.

The crowd that gathered could do nothing more than watch sadly as both structures burned to the ground.

TEN

Doctor Regenfeld sat across from Judge Featherstone in his office, a newspaper draped in his hands. He had just reread the headlines of the catastrophic fire that had consumed the Boggs home and carriage house two days before.

"It was Elmore Boggs for sure?" the judge asked.

Doctor Regenfeld put down the paper. "She said it was. I have no reason to doubt her. Of course, he was charred beyond recognition."

At that moment, the judge's secretary opened the door to the judge's chambers and announced that Police Chief O'Fallon had just arrived. He entered wearing his traditional dark blue uniform with the markings of his rank on his epaulettes. His uniform was always spotless, and his hair was immaculately trimmed, as was his gray beard and mustache. He usually wore a jovial look on his face, but today, his solemn look matched the occasion.

"Michael," the judge said to O'Fallon. "I believe you know Doctor Herman Regenfeld."

"Indeed," the police chief said as he shook his hand. He assumed a chair and came directly to the point. "We have a predicament with this Elmore Boggs fellow. Because of the condition of the body, we really can't be sure it was him."

Judge Featherstone nodded. "The doc here thinks so. Miss Lydia Pearlman said it was Boggs, and Calvin and Jocelyn verified it."

"Ah, yes, Amos Jefferson's family members, I believe." The chief twirled one end of his mustache. "However, these two Jeffersons were in her employ, were they not?"

"What are you getting at, Michael?" asked the judge.

"It appears that Boggs had several fractures on his skull, as if he may have been struck with a heavy object."

Neither the judge nor the doc said anything.

"It could well be a case of murder," the chief suggested. "Have you considered that?"

"Or self-defense," the judge added.

"Possibly," the chief agreed. "But is it not also possible that Boggs might have been killed so this Miss Lydia Pearlman could inherit the house? I understand there was some question as to who was rightful owner after Almetta's death."

Doc Regenfeld shifted uneasily in his chair. "Let me understand you correctly. She kills Elmore and then burns down the house that she is supposed to inherit? I'm afraid I can't go along with that scenario."

The chief hunched his shoulders. "The fire may have been accidental, but it's obvious it was not the fire that killed Boggs."

"What are you suggesting?" asked the doctor. "That Calvin and Jocelyn were accomplices to a murder plot?"

"Our department considers every possibility," the chief answered. "After all, that's our duty."

"That's absurd," said the doc. "She's not capable of such a deed."

"Well, someone was."

Again, the judge's secretary interrupted with a light knock on the door. "Miss Pearlman is here."

"Send her in," the judge said.

When Lydia entered, she had a slight bruise over one eye and a small cut on her lip. She hesitated when she saw the three men. She had expected her arranged meeting to be a private one with only the judge present.

"Please," the judge said, as he motioned Lydia to a chair. "You know Doctor Regenfeld, and may I present Chief O'Fallon, from our police department."

Regenfeld simply nodded. The police chief gave her a courteous bow and an extended look. "Miss Pearlman," he addressed her.

"Please, don't be alarmed," the judge told her. "Chief O'Fallon has a few questions he'd like to ask about the night the fire consumed your home."

"Almetta's home," she corrected him. She felt some apprehension in coming to see the judge, and although she knew and trusted the doctor, she was uncertain about the police officer before her.

"I believe we met once before," O'Fallon said as he sat. "During the investigation of Mr. Devon's demise some time back."

She easily remembered, but said nothing. He was one of the policemen who had interviewed all the girls at the restaurant concerning Devon's murder.

Chief O'Fallon took in a deep breath. "Miss Pearlman, on the night of the fire, I understand Mr. Boggs entered your home unannounced."

"Almetta's home," she again corrected.

"Yes, of course. Could you tell us briefly, the circumstances under which, ah . . ."

"How Elmore Boggs died?" she finished. "That's what you want to know, isn't it?"

The chief was taken back with her straightforwardness. "Yes, if you would be so kind."

"I discovered him in Almetta's bedroom. He was ransacking it, searching for something, which he said would prove that he owned the home."

"A deed, perhaps?" the chief asked.

"Yes. We quarreled, he attacked me and I fought back. I managed to get into my bedroom and lock the door. When he broke through the door, I struck him with a poker."

All three men were astounded at her admission.

The chief was especially surprised. "Do you usually keep a poker in your bedroom for protection?"

"I did ever since Elmore first came to the house and threatened me. That was a few weeks earlier."

"And did you quarrel at that time?" he asked.

"Yes. I hit him with a hoe several times and took off half of his ear. He said he would get even with me."

Doctor Regenfeld exchanged glances with the chief. "That's correct. I know that Elmore suffered several cuts and bruises."

"What did he do at that time to provoke you?" the chief questioned.

Lydia eyed the judge before she answered. "He made some accusations that were untrue."

Not expecting to hear all these statements, the police chief produced a pad and pencil and began taking notes. He directed another question at Lydia. "When Elmore Boggs entered your bedroom, you immediately struck him with the poker?"

"Yes."

"How many times, would you say?"

Regenfeld and the judge leaned in, curious to hear her response.

"I . . . don't know for sure. I can't remember exactly."

The chief noted her hesitance and pressed for an answer. "Would you say two or three times?"

"She said she can't remember," Doc Regenfeld said.

Chief O'Fallon gave the doctor a stern look, which implied that he was asking the questions.

"I hit him until he fell to the floor."

The chief wrote something in his pad. "I see. And how and

when, exactly, did the fire start?"

She hesitated again.

The police chief saw her nervousness. "You said Elmore Boggs fell to the floor. Again I ask, how did the fire start?"

Lydia paled and dropped her face into her hands. After a few seconds, she looked up, her eyes wet with tears. "He . . ."

"He what?" the chief asked.

Regenfeld jumped up from his chair. "For chrissake, Herman, haven't you figured it out yet?"

The chief's words softened a bit as he answered the doc. "There were those witnesses at the scene, who maintained Calvin Jefferson carried Lydia out of the house in a blanket, and that she was unconscious, or nearly so. And if she was nearly unconscious, then my question remains, who struck Elmore Boggs with the poker?"

"I did!" Lydia screamed out. "I killed him! I killed him!"

Lydia broke into heavy sobs, and at that moment, Selma Ritter threw open the door. "What the hell's going on here?" She hurried to Lydia and threw her arms around her, and then cast a look of disgust at the three men. "I heard everything in the other room! For chrissake, the son of a bitch tried to rape her. What are you three? The judge, jury and executioner?"

Affronted by her tone, Chief O'Fallon drew in a deep breath and turned to the judge. "Why is this woman here?"

"You can ask me why!" Selma shot back at him. "I can speak!" The chief's mouth dropped open in disbelief. "Lydia asked me to come along. She needs a friend at a time like this, and by God, she doesn't deserve to be harassed by the police!"

O'Fallon opened his mouth, but Selma cut him off. "You ought to be ashamed of yourself!"

"Miss Pearlman," the judge consoled in a soft voice. "You are free to go."

"You're damn right she's free to go!" Selma chided.

As soon as they were out of the room, the chief mused, "I remember her now. God, that woman's got a wicked tongue."

"Quite," said the judge. "I've never known Selma to hold anything back." He stood and paced to the front of his desk. "Gentlemen, we need to take a lesson here." He looked at the police chief. "You weren't in St. Louis when Almetta Boggs ran an orphanage out of her home."

"No, I wasn't, but I heard that she did so," the chief answered.

"And you never knew why her husband, Elmore, left St. Louis?"

"Rumor had it that he simply abandoned his wife."

Doctor Regenfeld continued. "It was more than that. Elmore Boggs assaulted several of the orphans, and it didn't make any difference if they were boys or girls. When Almetta learned about it, she pushed him down the staircase and nearly killed him. After that, he disappeared."

"She never pressed charges?"

"No. The embarrassment was too much for her."

The chief's face went blank. "So Lydia didn't kill Boggs."

"No," Regenfeld said. "It's obvious Calvin did. She was just protecting him."

"Then Calvin must be held accountable," the chief dared to say.

"No!" Judge Featherstone cut in. "It makes no difference who killed him. The man deserved to die. As far as I'm concerned, Elmore Boggs entered her home drunk, threatened her, fell down and knocked over the lamp, which started the fire."

Doc Regenfeld grunted. "I cared for Lydia after the ordeal. Her clothes were torn from her body, and she had numerous bruises on her hands and feet. If you were to drag this woman into court, she will still maintain she killed Boggs. She would never admit Calvin did it."

"But why?" O'Fallon asked. "He's a colored man."

"But he's a good colored man, and he was in love with her. I saw it in his face many times. He's one of the few real friends Lydia has ever had. In the name of humanity, let this woman be. She's gone through enough."

The police chief slowly rose to his feet, put away his pad and nodded at the two men.

When he was gone, Doc Regenfeld sat again. "Do you think he'll press charges against Lydia or Calvin?"

"No," the judge answered.

"How can you be so sure?"

"Because I'm the one who got Michael elected."

Doc Regenfeld rubbed his eyes and made a face. "If anyone ever learns Calvin killed Boggs, nobody's going to care who he was protecting. You know he'll hang, just as sure as we're sitting here."

The judge smiled defiantly as he offered the doc a cigar. "You take care of your patients and I'll take care of the police force."

After both lit up, the judge swiveled back in his chair and blew out a puff of smoke. "Every now and then I feel like I actually earn what the city pays me."

ELEVEN

The fire took everything. Lydia lost all her personal belongings and money she had stashed away, although most of the cash originally belonged to Almetta. For safekeeping, Calvin kept Old Jake and the buggy at his home. Jocelyn returned to the Jefferson household, and Lydia moved in temporarily with Selma Ritter.

"Everything's gone," Lydia lamented to Selma. What clothes she now possessed had been donated by Selma and Colleen. A few girls at work gave her some personal items, like a comb and mirror and a purse and even a few dollars to help her get by.

Sharing the apartment with Selma was a good arrangement, but within another week, even this accommodation would no longer be a safe haven for the two of them, since the building was soon to be torn down to make way for a new lumberyard.

"Cheer up, honey," Selma said in a consoling voice. "We've both been down and out before. Ain't nothing we can't overcome."

Her words were encouraging, but Lydia's head was filled with too many distractions. She did not like the way the meeting in the judge's chambers was handled, and she was not sure that she wouldn't be summoned again. From what she had learned of Police Chief O'Fallon, he was well liked by the city and had a good reputation for following through on his cases.

Of course, she alone realized that the policeman had never solved Devon's murder, and since so many months had gone by, she was reasonably sure he never would. Colleen, so happily married, had, for all practical purposes, cast the event aside. If she had any remorse about killing Devon, she never showed it. And she needn't worry about Lydia; it was a secret that she would carry to her grave.

That Calvin had killed Elmore Boggs was a second secret she would hold forever. Selma guessed that Calvin was responsible for the deed, but Lydia staunchly maintained that she had killed him, so Selma, being the good friend that she was, dropped the issue entirely by saying, "Makes no difference who killed him. The son of a bitch got what he deserved."

With all these thoughts running through her head, it was impossible for Lydia even to think about working, so when Selma left for the restaurant, she remained in the apartment.

A few days later toward evening, she heard a knock at the door, and when she opened it, Amos stood before her. He removed his hat, his eyes on the verge of tears. "Miss Lydia, he's gone."

"What? Who?" she asked, as she ushered him in.

"My boy, Calvin. He done run off last night. Oh, Lord, I don't know what to do."

Lydia felt her heart flutter, having feared this might happen.

"I know what he done, Miss Lydia. Jocelyn told me. I's so sorry for all this trouble I's causing you."

She put an arm around him. "Amos, this isn't any of your doing. You should be proud of Calvin. He was protecting me."

"I know, I know, but his runnin' off an all ain't good. For sure the white folk are gonna think he done Mr. Boggs in, and if'n he's caught . . ."

"Amos," she consoled him, "Jocelyn and I are the only ones who know what happened, and we aren't going to tell a soul, so you don't have to worry about the police coming around."

"How can you be so sure?"

"Because I told them I killed him."

Amos' eyes grew as big as saucers. "Miss Lydia, you can't take the blame for what my boy done. Oh, Lordy." He sat and buried his face in his hands.

Lydia could do nothing more than reassure him that Calvin would be all right and that he had nothing to fear from the police. When Amos left, he seemed a little calmer, and so did she. At that moment, she decided that in the morning, she would return to work. Getting her life back in order was now a priority, and sitting around the apartment and feeling sorry for herself wasn't helping matters any.

The next day, she worked the morning and noon shifts, busy and happy to be back among her friends. In mid-afternoon, while Lydia and a few girls were taking a break, Mr. Longhorn summoned her and said a gentleman was waiting for her in the office.

Her curiosity was piqued as she hurried to the back of the restaurant. When she entered, Judge Featherstone was sitting at Longhorn's desk. By the rather forlorn look on his face, she feared something was amiss.

"Miss Pearlman," he greeted as he motioned for her to sit down. He took in a deep breath setting his thoughts in order. "As you may know, Calvin has disappeared."

She threw a hand up to her lips.

"No, no, nothing to worry about," he calmed her. "But Chief O'Fallon was informed by one of his men that Calvin suddenly left St. Louis, and as you can imagine, rumor is floating around down at the police station that he is mixed up in this, ah . . ."

"They think he killed Elmore Boggs," she finished.

"Unfortunately," he said, his face filled with regret.

"I killed him with the poker!" she said sternly. "You can't hold Calvin responsible for an act I committed!"

The judge was quiet for a few moments. "Miss Pearlman, we both know you didn't kill him. Doc Regenfeld knew your condition when Calvin carried you out onto the street. You couldn't have killed him."

Lydia's gaze fell and she lowered her head.

"But I have a way out of this situation that is best for all of us, and in particular, it will keep your friend, Calvin, out of harm's way."

He presented a document on which was written a confession of her guilt. She read through the paragraph, which the judge had composed.

"It basically says what we would all like to have happened. It states that Elmore Boggs tried to rape you, and that you simply defended yourself. Would you agree that the statement is as you would have it appear?"

"Yes," she said.

"Will you sign it?"

"Yes."

"There is one stipulation, however," the judge said. "Once you sign, it would be best if you leave St. Louis."

Her mouth dropped open, a reaction he expected, since he knew she would not understand. "I'll hold this sworn affidavit for a few days before I submit it. That should give you time to disappear in any direction. With a sworn affidavit in the hands of the police chief and you gone, he won't be able to follow up on the matter, and I'll make sure he doesn't. The case will easily be settled, and no one needs to know what really happened. That will protect you and Jocelyn and Calvin, and no matter where he is, he won't be the object of a manhunt."

She stared at the document, her mind running so fast she could hardly think. The admission of guilt would keep Calvin out of harm's way, and she certainly owed that much to him.

The judge laid fifty dollars in cash in front of her. "It isn't much, but it will give you a start."

He set a pen and ink bottle in front of her, and after she signed, she reached for the money, hesitated, then slowly picked it up and left the room.

The next night, without telling anyone, not even Selma, Lydia slipped onto a steamer headed north. All she carried with her was a small valise that contained an extra set of clothes.

Unknown to her, she was being followed by a gentleman dressed in a dapper gray outfit and wearing a top hat to match, and this same gentleman made sure he acquired a cabin on the same deck as she had.

That first night on the steamer Lydia tossed and turned, her mind unraveling what had transpired in the past few days. After three years of living in St. Louis, everything she once knew— her home, work and friends, were suddenly gone. She grieved mostly for Calvin and the situation in which she had placed him. She could not rid herself of the fear that the police might still pursue him. She could only hope that the affidavit she had signed would exonerate him. Unfortunately, he didn't know about the affidavit, thus he might spend the rest of his life running from something that no longer mattered. There was the possibility that the newspaper would eventually clarify everything, and if so, Amos might, in due time, be able to inform him.

Several times during the night, she jerked awake, shaking, tears streaming down her face, afraid and unsure of what her own fate was to be. When morning finally came, she woke tired from the fitful night of unrest.

Matthew McGrath sat at a table by himself in the dining room of the steamship, his breakfast already finished, only a coffee cup at his elbow. He glanced up from a newspaper every time someone entered the dining area. Dressed in the same gray suit as the night before and wearing a fresh shirt, he presented a figure of wealth.

He was sure Lydia would eventually show up, and near ten o'clock, she arrived and was escorted to a table some distance away at the far end of the room. Though she was seated facing away from him, he did not mind. He had no intention of approaching her; rather, he wanted her to notice him first.

Occasionally, he caught her profile when she turned her head to the side, and he could see the distraught look on her face. He had read the most recent newspapers from St. Louis and knew about the devastating fire that had demolished her home. He had also read about the body that had been discovered afterward.

For the past few days in St. Louis, he had kept a close watch on her. He knew that she had visited the courthouse on at least one occasion, and that Judge Featherstone had made a trip to the railroad restaurant. Though it was purely conjecture on his part, he guessed that the judge made the visit specifically to see Lydia.

The fact that she was on this steamer now, coupled with the discontented look on her face, indicated to him that she might have had something to do with the death of the individual found in the charred remains of the plantation home.

Lydia was not on a pleasure trip, he was sure. In fact, he would bet a thousand dollars that she was on the run. He laughed silently, knowing this was a sure bet. After all, he was a gambling man.

He maintained a steady vigilance on her. She ordered a simple breakfast of toast and marmalade along with a carafe of apple cider, and fifteen minutes later, she got up from the table and abruptly left the dining hall.

Surprisingly, she passed within ten feet of him on the way out, and although Matthew purposely lowered his newspaper enough for her to notice him, she walked right past, looking neither right nor left.

She appeared tired, and the certain vibrancy that normally sparkled in her eyes was missing. Matthew had never considered her to be a beauty, but she was exactly the type of woman he could use on his gambling trips. He had discovered that a woman of extraordinary beauty attracted too much attention around the tables. Lydia was the type who would not turn the heads of onlookers, especially those concentrating on their cards. In a crowd, she would be a perfect candidate for him.

Though she had not noticed him when she left the dining area, he was not at all disappointed. That meant she had a great deal on her mind, which would make her vulnerable, and that is exactly the way he wanted her.

Matthew McGrath left the dining room, and upon ascending the stairs to the upper deck, he was not at all surprised to discover Lydia sitting on a bench near the rail. Her gaze was fixed on the shoreline, as still as the calm river water below, her eyes unwavering.

He occupied a seat on a bench some distance away, opened his newspaper and pretended to be reading.

Lydia sat for the longest time, staring across the water, her mind unaware of what she was gazing at. She was not at all sure she had made the best decision in leaving St. Louis, but she'd done it, and now she had to live with it.

With the fifty dollars the judge had given her, she'd purchased a ticket for Kansas City, which exhausted a third of the money. She guessed the city would be large enough so that she could hide. Once there, she hoped she could find work of some sort, but she cringed, knowing that she would be starting all over. It seemed more and more likely that she might well be spending the rest of her life as a single person—an old maid, as Selma had once called it. God forbid that she should end up like her aunt Almetta, old and feeble-minded, or like her mother, unaware of the world around her.

The thought shook her to the bone. With a feeling of hopelessness, she stared down at the churning water trailing behind the steamer, and for a brief moment she imagined herself floundering in the river, helpless, ending a life that seemed destined to reap nothing but despair.

Abruptly, the horn on the steamship blew, and upriver a southbound steamship answered with a lonesome blast. As the two ships passed, passengers from the other steamship waved and shouted greetings.

As she turned her head to follow the ship on its passage, her eyes stopped on the man in the gray suit behind the newspaper. She blinked, not sure she recognized him, and when he lowered his paper a bit, she gasped in astonishment.

"Matthew!" she shouted as she jumped up from her seat. She stood motionless, her gaze frozen on him as he approached her.

He removed his hat and gave her a warm smile. "Lydia!" he exclaimed. "What brings you onto this river means of travel?"

She stood motionless, so happy to see a familiar face, and then, unable to hold back her sorrow, she burst into tears. He drew her into his arms, and for the longest time, she pressed herself against him, letting her stress drain away.

"Lydia, my dear," he consoled her. "You're safe here with me." He produced a handkerchief and wiped away her tears.

"Matt, I'm so happy to see you," she blurted out.

He was still smiling, his face glowing. "Come," he said as he led her to the staircase. "Tell me what this is all about."

They found two comfortable chairs in the corner of the lounge where they could share some privacy. Lydia, so overjoyed to have found Matthew on the same steamship, did not even ponder why they had not seen each other for the past year.

She poured her heart out, retelling the events that had led to her sudden departure from St. Louis. Matthew listened intently, taking in the loose ends that rounded out his understanding of the scenario of events.

"You signed an affidavit saying you killed him?" Matt asked in a low voice.

"Yes. I had to in order to protect Calvin."

Matt nodded. "How very noble of you. You have my complete respect."

"Do you think I did the right thing?" she asked.

"Of course. You've always done the right thing. I don't believe I've ever met a woman who possesses such a high regard for integrity as you do."

She genuinely smiled for the first time since they met. She needed such reassuring words, something positive in her life.

"Where are you headed?" he asked.

"Kansas City."

He raised an eyebrow. "That town can be a challenge. It's big, different from St. Louis."

"In what way?" she asked curiously.

Matt thought a moment. "It's a cow town, lots of transients passing through and a lot of saloons. Not the best place for a lady to be setting up a new home."

Lydia lowered her head. "I don't know what I want for sure. I just know I can't go back to St. Louis."

"And why should you?" He brushed back the curls over her forehead and gave her a big smile. "There are a lot of places out there to see, a lot of excitement just waiting for you." He let a moment pass. "For both of us, if you wish."

She could easily read the offer in his words. She'd turned him down once, and now she was again facing the same choice. "I'd like to think about it, if you don't mind." She recollected that she had given him that exact phrase before.

"Of course," he said. He straightened up and smiled. "I'd very much appreciate it if you would have dinner with me tonight."

"I'd love to."

"Good. In a few days, we'll be reaching Boonville. Almost nightly, the Thespian Hall has a dance. That would bring back some memories, would it not?"

Her face lit up with the suggestion, but then she spread her hands out to display her dress. "I don't have a set of respectable clothes to wear to a dance."

He grunted. "That's not a problem. When we dock, the first thing we'll do is go shopping."

She touched his hand and felt the warmth of it. "Matt, I'm so very happy I found you." With a wonderful sense of euphoria overcoming her, she leaned across and kissed him on the lips.

That evening they dined on roast pig, the suggested entrée, and during the course of the meal, she drank almost as much wine as he did. Afterward, he did not hesitate to ask if she would spend the night in his cabin, and she willingly accepted.

Lydia woke late the next morning to find a message from Matthew that he was off to challenge his luck in the casino. She couldn't believe how relaxed she felt, and how good it was to bounce out of bed looking forward to the day.

At noon, Matthew located her on the upper deck and had a quick lunch with her, and that evening she once again dined with him. She surmised that he was doing well at cards, since he was as jovial as she had ever seen him. For the next two days, Lydia did nothing but bask in the sun on the upper deck, a scenario that wouldn't have seemed possible a few stressful days earlier. Discovering Matthew onboard the same steamer had provided her with an unimaginable sense of relief.

On the upper deck, she was in a dream world, content to simply watch the landscape skip by. On the west bank, a train paralleling the river quickly caught up with the steamer and moved on. When she inquired from a fellow passenger what line it was, the man simply answered, "The Pacific. Runs from St. Louis to Sedalia."

She had never heard of Sedalia, but she assumed it was a town at the end of the track. Later, Matt confirmed it, saying he had once visited the town.

"Is there anyplace you haven't visited along the Missouri?" she asked him.

"Fort Leavenworth," he answered with a huge laugh.

"Why do you laugh?" she asked curiously.

"Well, besides being an army fort, it's a prison for some and a cemetery for the rest, and I don't want any part of either."

When he laughed for the second time, she laughed along with him.

The steamship made a few stops at docks where only a few buildings were located, towns in the making, she guessed. In the early afternoon on the third day, they docked at Boonville, a small town with the hustle and bustle on the dock of a developing city.

"Very quaint," she told Matthew as they departed the ship carrying their bags.

"Nothing like St. Louis, but it has its charm."

Matt hired a taxi that took them through the center of the city to a hotel off of Main Street. Later in the day he escorted her past the Thespian Hall, a massive Greek-structured building. He informed her that the main floor was the ballroom and theatre, that the Masons had the upper floor, and strangely enough, the basement was used for roller skating.

"Have you ever roller skated?" he asked her.

"No. But I'd like to try."

"That's Saturday night only. Looks like we'll have to go dancing after all."

Lydia was hanging on to Matt's arm like a school kid holds on to a candy stick. As they walked along Vine Street, she was very much impressed with the cleanliness of the city and surprised that such a small city had lampposts.

He escorted her into a cove that led to a dress shop, where a young woman about her age approached them.

"Matthew," she greeted him as if they were old friends. Her hair was done up in fancy swirls around a tiny face. She wore simple makeup, and silver rings dangled from her earlobes. Her dress was mauve and pale green, a combination that Lydia never thought would blend so fashionably together, but she looked elegant as she turned to Lydia and gave a warm smile.

"Miss Lydia Pearlman," Matt said introducing her. "This is Madame La Font, an old acquaintance of mine."

French, Lydia was thinking, and at the same time, she wondered how this young lady could be considered an old acquaintance of Matt's, since she couldn't have been more than thirty years of age.

Matt seemed very much at home in this dress shop. "Madame La Font has very good taste. She will do you well." With that, he excused himself and said he would return within the hour.

When he was gone, Madame La Font set herself to work. "I think I have fine dress for you," she said with a sweet French accent.

Lydia's wardrobe at its finest had mainly consisted of three different dresses, almost all three alike, and none of them expensive. As she looked about the room, and in particular at the lovely dress that Madame La Font was pointing to on a manikin, she knew she could never afford anything so nice.

"Tres élégant, n'est ce pas?"

Lydia guessed at what she said. "Yes, it's lovely."

"You know Matthew for long time?" the woman inquired suddenly.

The question took Lydia by surprise. "Over a year."

"Ah. So long as that," she answered with a surprised look on her face. "You like?" she asked as she pointed out the features of the dress.

What she meant by *so long as that,* Lydia did not understand, but Madame La Font, with the charm of a lady about to make a sale, escorted Lydia to a back room where she tried on the dress. When she returned to the front to examine herself in a mirror, she happened to glance across the street just as Matthew appeared with another man on the front steps of a bank. The two were engaged in a short conversation, and when Matt departed down the street, the other man retired inside.

"Exquisite, no?" Madame La Font said as she turned Lydia around.

"Yes, very," Lydia answered.

"I have another selection to suit you quite well," she said as she escorted Lydia to the back room again. "Perhaps you also need some personal items?"

She was definitely a saleslady. Lydia had left St. Louis with the bare essentials in her bag, and there were many other items she could use. While Madame La Font made suggestions, among them underclothes and perfume, Lydia was suddenly feeling very comfortable. Never before had she been treated like a celebrity of sorts, and although she assumed Matthew was going to pay for all this, she did not want to total up a huge sum of money; thus, she was selective with her choices.

When Matthew returned, Madame La Font displayed the apparel and personal items she had picked out for Lydia. After giving her a look of great satisfaction, Matthew retrieved several bills from his wallet and paid the amount.

That night they danced for hours in the elegant ballroom of

the Thespian Hall. All night long, she felt like a queen and believed she looked like one as well.

TWELVE

The new clothes necessitated a small trunk, which Matthew procured before they departed from Boonville early the next morning. Onboard a different steamer named the *Josephine,* a steamer on which Matthew had worked earlier, they rented a single cabin.

After they settled in, Matthew opened a small case which contained a pearl set in a gold band. "Try this on," he said. Lydia's eyes widened, not at all sure how to react to the offer. She was sure he was going to propose to her, but then he quickly added, "It would be more convenient if those around us believed we were man and wife."

Any thoughts she'd had of this ring representing an engagement disappeared immediately. She kept a smile on her face, holding back her disappointment, yet in the back of her mind she wanted to believe that his intentions were good, and that he would, in a matter of time, propose to her. After all, their renewed relationship had been underway for only a few days, and a commitment like marriage did require time.

"It's lovely," she said as he slipped the ring on her finger.

"A pearl for a pearl," he said as he kissed her. She remembered that was what he had written on the note when he sent her the pearl necklace for Christmas over a year ago. She had already told him that the necklace, along with everything else she possessed, had been lost in the fire, and now she firmly wanted to believe that this ring was a gift to heal the loss.

After a quick breakfast, she thought sure Matthew would be off to play cards once again, but instead, they returned to their cabin, where he produced a deck of cards.

"How would you like to learn this game of poker?" he asked. "I believe it would be good for you to have some idea of how I earn a living."

At first she hesitated, and then said, "Why not? Maybe I can teach you a thing or two along the way."

He shuffled the cards quickly, fanned them out, whirled them back together again, and then spread them in long row, facedown. With a flip of the end card, all the cards moved like a wave until they were faceup. Her eyes were as big as saucers, she was so taken in with the dexterity of his hands.

He gave a laugh of appreciation as he systematically selected cards from the deck. He put together the lowest winning hand, which was any pair, and then made up all possible hands up to a royal flush.

"One pair is the lowest hand you can be dealt," he said. He pointed to the various hands, and as he did so, he informed her that two pairs would beat a pair, that three of a kind would beat two pairs and so on.

When he worked his way through all the possibilities and thought she understood the essence of the game, he produced a small card from his pocket, on which the same hands were labeled in the order of the lowest hand to the highest, and gave it to her for reference.

For the remainder of the morning, he dealt out one hand after another, and within a few hours, she gained the gist of the game. Matthew knew the exact odds of drawing a card to fill out a full house or a flush. The odds, of course, changed according to how many players were at a table. He could recite the odds of drawing to a better hand like Lydia could recite the Lord's Prayer. It seemed simple at first, but it was becoming more complicated all the time.

"Cards are just half of it," he explained as he winked at her. "You have to learn to read a man's face, his body actions, his quirks when he has a good hand. Sometimes it's just a faint twitch of the eye, or a flat face. Everybody's different."

"What am I holding at the moment?" she asked as she looked over the cards in her hand.

"Three of a kind, maybe face cards, or two high pairs."

She laid down a pair of tens and a pair of kings. "How did you know?"

He laughed. "Well, in your case, and since you're new at this, it was just a lucky guess. But if you were a regular player, I'd read something on you. That's what it's all about. That's what sets apart the winners from the losers.

" 'Course, the real good card players usually give off wrong signals. Those are the ones you have to watch. You have to determine if they're for real or they're bluffing, and some bluff real good."

She wasn't sure she understood all of what he was saying, but she was at least entertained by the morning's lessons.

After lunch, she thought she might just lounge on the upper deck, since the days of nice sunshine and a glorious temperature were holding, but Matthew asked her back to the cabin, where they spent the rest of the afternoon playing five card draw until supper.

After they ate, Matthew headed for the casino, and she, thankful she had been granted a reprieve, retired to the cabin with a book that she borrowed from the ship's library.

For the next few days, Lydia was back in the cabin, spending most of the daylight hours playing poker and learning which cards to throw and which to keep. "Gotta make the best draw possible," he said.

After she had played enough hands to understand the

methodology of the game, Matthew gave her a hundred dollars and told her she could keep what she won at the end of two hours of poker.

The offer intrigued her.

"Nothing to lose," he told her.

She couldn't think of a better challenge. "Deal the cards," she said.

They played one session after another, but she was unable to keep any of the hundred dollars, since he won each time and usually long before the two hours was over.

Every hand dealt was slowly becoming a bigger challenge, and slowly she began to grasp the spirit of the game and especially the excitement that came with winning a hand.

On one hand, he said, "I think you're bluffing."

She was.

"I'm guessing you're drawing to a full house," he told her on another, and she was.

But he would always nod his approval and compliment her on her decisions. "You're catching on real fast," he told her as he patted her hand.

"You think so?"

He laughed. "I think you're betting more conservatively, just so you can keep some of that hundred."

She laughed along with him. She was holding out, now realizing that if the money was hers to start with, she would have to be a little sharper with her decisions.

"What does a good night of cards bring you?" she asked.

He shrugged. "Couple hundred. A real good night hits a thousand."

She studied his face. "Did you ever lose a thousand in one night?"

The smile on his face slowly faded. "On occasion. Can't win all the time."

"Winning is everything, isn't it?" she asked.

He dealt out another hand. "Winning's the only thing."

If she had heard one line repeated in the past few days, that was it.

August 12, 1875

Dear Grandmama Eugenia,

I am writing to you from Kansas City. So much has happened in the past few weeks and I must bring you up to date. Elmore, Almetta's husband, returned after a long absence and I decided to let him have his home back, since it was really not mine.

As luck would have it, oppertunity presented itself. Can you believe it! I am engaged to be married! I renewed my relationship with Matthew McGrath and we are presently traveling by steamship, headed toward Bismarck, Dakotah Territory. I have no idea what Bismarck is like, but everything is so exciting!

Kansas City is a cattle town and very small compared to St. Louis. We are staying in a hotel across from the Coates Opera House. Matt has treated me well. I have some new clothes, and I am learning about his profession so I can help him in his work.

I miss St. Louis and all the friends I left behind, but someday I will return. I hope your health is good. I do not have a permanent address, since we are on the move, so please wait until I have one. I will write again within a few weeks.

Love, Lydia

She read over the letter and all its lies. She could not tell Eugenia that the house burned down and that Calvin had killed Elmore Boggs, nor did she dare write that Elmore had degraded the orphan children under the care of her aunt Almetta. The statement about being engaged to Matthew was sort of an exaggeration, but the fact that they were headed for Bismarck was basically true, since the city was located somewhere to the north on the Missouri River.

She was actually learning the profession of card playing, and she did miss Colleen and Selma and the Jefferson family, and maybe someday she would return to St. Louis. Her mind wandered, and she wondered where Calvin was at the moment and whether he was safe. With him still in mind, she sealed the letter in an envelope and descended the staircase to the lobby, where she purchased a stamp from the clerk and left the letter to be mailed. The clerk, erroneously believing that Lydia was Matthew's wife, handed over an envelope that was addressed to him. She returned to their room, and for the longest time, she sat at the window overlooking the town of Kansas City. This town was a railroad center, the main line of the Kansas Pacific, and its stockyard was filled with cattle. Her view reached across a huge yard of cattle pens to the Plankington and Armour Packing House, where wagons and railroad cars were constantly being loaded. Below on the street, the trail of wagons rumbling back and forth was unending.

The only reason the two of them had decided to remain here for a few days was because Matthew had some business to attend to. What his business was, she didn't know, but tonight they were to attend the opera, something she was very much looking forward to. While she was looking down on the street, she happened to see Matthew as he entered the hotel, and a short time later, he entered the room.

"How's my darling this morning?" he asked. He removed his hat and kissed her.

"Your darling is fine," she answered. "What have you been up to today?"

"Oh, just catching up on some incidental matters." He

reached into his pocket and held up two tickets. "The opera," he said. "Are you still for it?"

"Of course."

"It's by Mozart, and it's in German."

She laughed. "Do you speak German?"

"No, but prior to the opera, we've been invited to a banquet where you'll have a chance to meet Mayor Woods and his wife. They speak English."

She laughed again. "How did you arrange all this?"

He removed his coat and sat at a small desk. "I have friends in the right places."

She remembered the envelope. "The clerk downstairs gave me this," she said as she handed it over. "It's addressed to you."

He tore open the envelope and read the short note. If Lydia had learned anything about reading faces while playing cards, the frown that Matthew put on said everything. He sat up stiffly, folded the note and placed it in his pocket.

"Anything wrong?" she asked.

He took in a deep breath. "Well, a change of plans. I have some urgent business up north. We're going to have to check out early. I'm afraid we won't make the opera." Her face went blank. "I'm sorry I have to disappoint you."

"No," she said. "Business comes first. I understand."

"I knew you would." He gave her a hug and kissed her. "Let's get our things together."

But she did not understand. Within an hour they were on the levee with their bags, waiting for the next available passage. After purchasing tickets, they boarded and found their cabin, and as the steamship pulled away from the dock, she could see the stress drain away from Matthew's face. It was obvious that the reason for their sudden departure had something to do with the note he'd received. From whom it was and what its contents were, she did not know, but her curiosity gnawed at her.

Matthew did not go directly to the gambling casino as he usually did. Rather, he hung around the upper deck sipping at tea or coffee most of the day. That evening, after dinner, he eventually headed for the casino area, leaving her alone in the lounge.

He was wearing a different jacket this evening, and with her curiosity still at a peak, Lydia returned to their cabin and searched through the pockets of his gray coat, where she discovered the note that had so disturbed him.

It was handwritten. *Matt, I want your debt resolved before you leave Kansas City.* It was signed, *John.*

She had no idea who John was, but Matt, without a doubt, owed money to the man. And since the note was addressed to Matt and not Matthew, she assumed it was from a known acquaintance. She searched through some more pockets in the same coat and discovered a letter of credit from the Boonville Bank, where they had docked just a few days ago. The letter of credit was good for two thousand dollars, payable back in six months at an interest rate of four percent.

She recollected seeing Matt and another individual speaking with each other on the bank steps in the small town. At the time, she assumed he had withdrawn money from the bank, but obviously, he had taken out a loan.

For the better part of the evening, Lydia sat contemplating what sort of fate awaited her with this information she now possessed. She resolved herself to reading in order to clear her mind and was engrossed in a book when, near midnight, Matthew returned to the cabin.

"You're up late." He didn't bother to smile as he removed his coat and sat at the small table across from her.

"I couldn't sleep," she said as she folded the book shut. She shoved the envelope and bank letter of credit across the table top at him. "What sort of trouble are you in?"

His face suddenly flushed with embarrassment. "These are my personal affairs. You had no right to search through my coat pockets."

Lydia challenged him with a look. "If we're going to travel together and live in the same compartment all the way to wherever we're headed, you're going to have to confide in me."

He stood and paced a bit. "I've had some bad luck over the past few months."

"How much bad luck?" she asked.

"I owe a few creditors."

"This John fellow from Kansas City is one of them?" she asked as she tapped the note with her finger.

"Yes."

"And the banker in Boonville?"

"Yes."

"Who else?"

He jammed his hands in his pockets and shrugged. "Suffice it to say there are a few more."

"How much do you owe?"

He hesitated. "A little over six thousand."

She shrank back, unable to imagine such a sum. "How do you ever expect to pay back that much money?"

He walked about the room, his head down, his face as solemn as she had ever seen it. "I had a plan."

"What sort of plan?"

"We could do it together. You know the way the game goes."

"So?" She had a good idea where he was headed with his reasoning, but she wanted to hear it from him directly.

"All you would have to do is wander by the tables and occasionally signal what a man is holding."

"And how do I do that?" she asked.

He saw a spark of relief in his dilemma as he sat down across from her. "I have a way." His voice was charged. "Lydia, darling, if you help me out of this mess, I'll get a respectable job and give up gambling."

"How can I trust you?" she asked.

The smile hung on his face. "You take charge of the winnings and pay off the creditors. I'll give you a list, and when everything's paid off, then . . ."

"Then what?"

"We'll settle down."

"Together?"

He was smiling from ear to ear. "As husband and wife." He took his hand in hers and held it ever so gently. "I promise."

This was a promise she would hold him to. An encouraging smile covered her face. "What would I have to do?"

It was a thirty-hour ride to St. Joseph, and most of the time Matthew drilled Lydia on a methodology of passing information. Learning the various card hands had been a long and tedious process for her, but now that she could recognize them, giving a signal to Matthew had become an easy task. If a hand showed two pairs, she spread her ring and middle finger apart. If the highest pair was tens or better, she held her hand vertical. If the man had two pairs below tens, she held her fingers apart and leveled her hand.

Three nines or below was signified by spreading the index finger away from the other three. If the three of a kind were tens or above, she would spread the little finger away from the remaining three. If the man had a full house, she touched her thumb and forefinger together.

Matthew presented hand after hand to her, until she could manipulate her fingers with ease, each signal indicating what cards he presented. It was far from an exact science, but a signal would grant enough of a hint to give Matthew an edge, especially if he held a decent hand.

It was not necessary to beat every hand. If the odds were against him, he simply would fold his cards. Not betting a losing hand was every bit as good as betting a winning hand, and under those circumstances the odds would slowly shift in his favor.

At St. Joseph, Missouri, the steamer docked to unload some cargo and pick up new passengers. Inside of a few hours, the ship was once again headed north toward Nebraska City, their next stop.

That evening, Matthew and Lydia headed for the casino. "You need to be discreet about your movements," he cautioned her. "You can't be at my table all the time. Move about like other men and women, and engage in conversation if need be, even while at my table. You need to be as unassuming as possible."

"I understand," she said, and she also understood the price she was paying. She was becoming a cheat like he was, but he was the only friend she had right now, and he was also the only man who'd ever promised to marry her, and she was not going to let him get away.

She had visited the casino before, but this was the first time she intended to spend any extended time inside the large room. Tables were scattered here and there, some with gamblers around them, others empty. Nearby, a faro dealer was plying his trade against a small crowd, and at the far end of the room, a half dozen men stood around a roulette table. Plush and comfortable leather chairs and couches were set in circles where one could simply lounge.

Barely audible above the rhythmic churning of the paddlewheel, a low chatter of voices carried throughout the room. Chips jingled. Cards shuffled. Wheels spun.

"There's a fat gentleman in a frock coat at that corner table,"

Matthew said to her. "He's the one I want. A few days ago he took over three hundred from me.

"Be discreet," he reminded her as he let go of her arm and went to the table. She watched as he was introduced around. He specifically spent a few moments talking with the fat man, a smile on his face all the time.

When Matthew sat down, he produced a wad of bills from his inside coat pocket and placed them in front of him. In seconds, cards were dealt and the betting started.

Lydia sat in one of the leather chairs not too far away from the table and ordered a soft drink when a waiter approached her. She eyed the table at which Matthew was sitting and watched him take in a winning hand. Cards were dealt around again.

"Do you mind if I sit here?" A rather stout lady dressed in a green gown was addressing her. A set of heavy stones ringed her neck on a chain, matching her bracelet and a large ring on her finger.

"No, not at all," Lydia replied. The lady plopped in the chair as if she had been on her feet all day, and when the waiter returned, she ordered a whiskey.

"Harold plays cards," she said. "I drink." She pointed to the fat man at Matthew's table. "That's him over there."

Their conversation did not amount to much. She was the mother of five grown children. Harold, her husband, owned a mercantile store in Omaha, and his two sons worked for him.

"Are you traveling alone?" she asked.

"No. That's my husband next to your husband at the table."

"Ah," she said with a broad smile. "And you are headed to . . . ?"

"Back home to Bismarck," she answered, and then she regretted she had mentioned Bismarck, hoping that the lady was not familiar with the town.

When she answered, "Never been there," Lydia held back an urge to laugh.

In a short time, a few more ladies joined them and Lydia found herself engaged in a conversation that centered mostly on children and families.

After a half hour, Lydia, like some of the other ladies, got up and moved about the casino. She ambled along with others and eventually made her way to where Matthew was gambling.

It was a simple thing to glance at cards, not only those in the fat man's hand, but others as well, and after giving the signals she had so conveniently memorized, she moved on.

The night passed slowly for her, but she was not at a loss for conversation. Before midnight, she had become acquainted with several women, some married to gamblers, and some who obviously were ladies of the night. With painted faces and dresses hiked almost to their knees, they set themselves off as a separate entity. They were young, like herself, and the way they flitted with ease from one gentleman to the next made them appear very much at home.

Lydia periodically made her way back to Matthew's card game, but shortly after midnight when Matthew was quite a few dollars ahead, she retired to the cabin. She was already in bed but not asleep when he returned. He whipped off his coat, sat down next to her and flopped a pile of bills on the bed.

"Four hundred ninety dollars," he said with a grin. "After you left, I stuck around long enough to let old Harold win back a hundred." He laughed lightly. "He wants his revenge tomorrow, so we'll give it to him." Matt pulled off his boots and began removing his shirt and pants. "He owns a saddle shop in Omaha."

"He also owns a cattle ranch a few miles south of there," Lydia added.

Matt pulled a face. "Oh?"

She thought he'd like to know that, and she added one more bit of information. "That fellow at the next table to your left— the cigar smoker. Do you know who I'm talking about?"

"I remember him."

"Beringer is his name. He owns a hotel in Nebraska City. His wife said he's a good poker player until he starts drinking."

Matthew slipped into bed beside her. "Very interesting." He studied her with a huge grin. "You were good tonight." He kissed her and gently began slipping her nightgown upward over her head.

She shook with excitement. "Is this my payment for being good?"

"That and four hundred ninety dollars toward my debt."

She smiled. "You love me, don't you, Matt?"

"How could I not love you?"

After they made love, he fell asleep almost immediately, but she lay awake for some time, calculating how many four-hundred-ninety-dollar winnings would be required to pay off the six-thousand-dollar debt.

By the time they reached Nebraska City, Matthew had won over nine hundred dollars. He won some more from Harold, the fat merchant and cattle owner, and stripped a few hundred from the cigar-smoking hotel owner named Beringer. The man was indeed a good poker player, but after a few drinks, Matthew was beating him without Lydia's help.

Lydia's ability to sit in a crowd where she could glean simple gossip or tips about other players was invaluable, and she knew it. It surprised her that Matthew seldom needed her to signal what cards a man was holding. She wondered if her mere presence might have contributed to the confidence he was displaying at the tables. He was very good at reading the faces of his opponents and their cards, and now he seemed to be betting much more conservatively.

If he was winning, he didn't count on Lydia to help him along, but whenever he hit a losing streak, she recognized it and came to the rescue. A quick pass by the table and equally quick gestures with her hand told him what he wanted to know.

The process seemed risky at first, but now it was almost too easy. Yet she kept reminding herself that within a few months—if their luck held—the debt would be paid off, and the two of them could get on with their lives. To cheat men out of their money was far from honorable, but it was the price she was willing to pay. Some day she would require forgiveness from the Almighty, she was sure, but that day would have to be put off for a while.

THIRTEEN

The city of Omaha sprawled away from the river into hills laden with trees. To Lydia, the business district was not much different from St. Louis, though smaller. The city boasted the largest stockyard west of the Missouri, but whether that fact was true or not, she did not know.

The Paxton Hotel, where she and Matthew were now staying, exuded elegance. Fancy colored carpeting rolled throughout the lobby and dining room. Red, plush leather chairs were settled around tables covered with red satin cloth, and all plates, saucers and cups possessed swirling red rose designs that matched the porcelain handles of the silverware.

This was a luxury Lydia had never experienced. She could not imagine anything more decadent, yet she was enjoying every minute.

"You would think this hotel catered only to the rich," she mentioned to Matthew as they ate their noon meal. "But look around."

The dining room was nearly full. Those dressed in suits and ties were obviously the bankers and merchants, and those in dusty clothing and worn boots were the cowboys, she guessed. Strangely enough, at the table next to them, a young, good-looking lady with long golden hair sat across from a fellow with a face leathered from the sun. He was wearing a tattered shirt and canvas pants, but she was dressed in a fancy buckskin coat. Her tight pants were brown with a black stripe running down each pant leg, and she, too, like the fellow across from her, was wearing western boots.

"I've never seen a lady dressed like that," she whispered to Matthew. "Do you suppose they're ranchers?"

Matthew just shrugged and cut off another piece of steak.

Outside on the street, a small crowd of men had gathered, and through the window, Lydia noticed that two of the men had pencils and pads, evidently reporters of some sort. They were interviewing a tall, lanky man, but from where she sat, she could not get a good look at him.

Moments later, the tall man left the others on the street and entered the lobby of the hotel. He gave off an imposing appearance with his long, curly locks and pointed mustache. His hat was flat-topped with a wide brim, and underneath a long, frocked coat, he wore two pearl-handled guns on his hips, both with the butts facing out. The clerk at the counter pointed him in the direction of the dining room, and the man marched in with long strides.

Matthew sat with his face glued on the man, a piece of steak stuck on his fork.

"Do you know him?" Lydia asked.

Matthew gasped, and under his breath, he whispered, "That's Wild Bill Hickock!"

"So who's Wild Bill Hickock?" she whispered back.

"He's a marshal with a reputation. He's well known in Nebraska and Kansas."

"Do you know him personally?"

"No. But I saw him once. I wonder what he's doing in Omaha?"

The tall man slipped his hat off as he approached the two at the table nearby. Caught up in his black attire and with the two fancy pistols at his side, Lydia could not help but eavesdrop on their conversation.

During the next few minutes, she learned the man across from Wild Bill was Jesse DuRoche, and the lady's name was Katrina. What their connection was with each other, she had no idea, but they seemed to be having a friendly conversation and laughed a lot.

When the name Buffalo Bill came up, Matthew had his ear cocked. He had heard of the frontier scout whose reputation was based on the record number of buffalo he had shot in one day. Evidently Hickock and Buffalo Bill had some ties with each other, something to do with a failed venture in the East, but all of this was new to Lydia, and bits and pieces of their conversation were drowned out by the chatter in the room. Before the three left the table, she heard Hickock say he was headed for Cheyenne, wherever that was.

That evening, in the casino, Lydia had the opportunity to observe this fellow named Wild Bill lose some money at the tables. His reputation as a marshal and gunfighter must have far surpassed his ability to win at cards. Even though Matthew did not play cards at the same table with him, he heard that the former lawman had lost well over a hundred dollars, and Jesse DuRoche, his friend, did not fare well, either.

Those two left the casino long before Matthew, and when Matthew finished for the night, he had won over two hundred dollars, but not without the help of Lydia.

They remained in Omaha for a few more days, and after summing up Matthew's total winnings over the past week, which amounted to nearly sixteen hundred dollars, Lydia, with the bulk of the money and a list of debtors Matthew had provided, walked up the street to the Mercantile Bank. There she wrote out three letters of credit and handed over the cash to pay for them. Interestingly enough, seven hundred of the debt was with a bank in St. Louis.

The president of the bank, a robust man, who introduced

himself as Pierce Dennison, and who handled the transactions for her, was most cordial. "I hope to see you more often, Miss Pearlman," he said as he thanked her and escorted her to the door.

As she was leaving the bank, the lady in the buckskin clothing, known as Katrina, was just entering. Although Lydia recognized her, this lady did not know Lydia, and they simply passed each other without saying a word.

"What a pleasant surprise, Miss Dvorak," Lydia heard the president say to the lady. The greeting grabbed Lydia's curiosity. This lady, dressed in buckskin, obviously was on good terms with the bank president. On the way back to the hotel, she could not help but wonder what sort of role this woman played in society. There was no doubt in her mind that she more than likely lived somewhere near this community.

Later that same day, Matthew McGrath entered the same bank and addressed a teller at the counter.

"This morning, my wife made a deposit with your bank," he told the clerk. "We've had a change of plans, and I'd like to withdraw the money."

"Your name, sir?" he asked.

"McGrath."

The man searched down a list of transactions. "I'm sorry, sir, but I do not find that name on the list."

"It would be Lydia McGrath. She's a rather small lady, black hair, wearing a crimson dress. She wrote out some letters of credit, I believe. I would like to cancel those, if I may."

"I do recollect seeing a lady with that description, sir," the clerk said politely as he examined the entries on the list for a second time. "I do have an entry for three letters of credit, but the name is Pearlman, not McGrath." He looked up, seeking a response from Matthew.

Matthew cringed, angry at his own stupidity. It had not occurred to him that Lydia would use her own name and not his. "I, ah . . ." He stopped, searching for some solution.

"I can summon Mr. Dennison, our president, if you like?" the clerk offered.

Matthew twisted his face. "Damn! Damn!" he cursed.

The clerk's eyes widened, not sure what the reaction meant. "Shall I summon Mr. Dennison, sir?" he again asked.

"No!" Matthew McGrath spun on his heels and stormed out of the bank, cursing under his breath as he went.

Two days later, they left by steamship once again, traveling on the *Far West*. Sioux City was the next major town on the Missouri, and a town with which Matthew was very familiar. He had spent many gambling days in this area and had run up a few debts that Lydia did not know about. Well over a year ago, he had taken a severe beating because he did not pay his losses. That's where he obtained the scar across his forehead—the one Lydia had inquired about. It was just by luck that he had managed to get out of town before the same two men paid him a second visit.

"We have almost a whole day layover," Lydia said to him. "Would you like to take an excursion through the city?"

"No," he said, feigning illness. "I don't feel well today. I think it was something I ate. I'd just like to remain in the cabin and rest. You go, Lydia," he suggested.

She questioned his excuse. "You were fine this morning before we docked."

He couldn't have placed a meaner scowl on his face. "That was this morning, this is now. This town is nothing but one big stockyard from one end to the other, and I've seen enough cattle to last a lifetime. If you want to see cattle, then go see them!"

She narrowed her eyes. "Matthew, I don't deserve to be talked to like that."

"You're right." His attitude softened as he put an arm around her. "I'm sorry. I . . . just don't feel well."

"I'm sorry, too," she said. "I had no reason to doubt you."

Later in the afternoon, the *Far West* steamer left the levee of Sioux City and headed upriver toward the next town, Yankton, the capital city of Dakotah Territory. Interestingly enough, once the steamship was underway, the sickness that Matthew had been experiencing seemed to disappear. In fact, less than an hour out of port, he suggested they attend the dining room. Lydia chose an elaborate pink dress trimmed with silver lace and a lace shawl to match. While she dressed, Matthew stood in front of a mirror.

"I'm famished," he said as he donned his gray jacket. He adjusted his tie and brushed the sleeves, making sure he was presentable. "I feel lucky tonight," he told her. "We'll get this debt paid off in no time."

He ran a brush through his hair and turned to her. "Ready?"

After dinner, Matthew went directly to the casino. Within an hour, heavy bets were filling the table—so much money that several people gathered to watch the stakes. Lydia was among them. She slowly moved from man to man, signaling what each person held. When cards were dealt, two men folded. However, the man betting the big money did not draw a good card, yet he shoved a stack of bills on the table as if he had a good hand.

Matthew kept up with him, matching the bets, and when it came to showing their cards, Matthew's two pairs took the pot. As he reached for the money, the man across from him, known as Big Jim Curry, grabbed Matthew's hand and said with a snarl, "You bet two small pairs when twelve hundred dollars are on the table? Mister, you've been eyeing this lady behind me for some time. You two have been cheating this table all night long."

Lydia's face went white as she eyed Matthew. He froze in place, and then he panicked and reached for a derringer inside his coat. Big Jim Curry whipped a handgun from his shoulder holster and fired two shots across the table. Matthew flew backwards off his chair when the .45 slugs smashed into his chest. He was dead before he hit the floor. Two men grabbed Big Jim from behind to restrain him, and someone amid the scuffling hollered for a doctor. Almost immediately, the captain of the ship was on the scene.

"He was cheating!" Big Jim complained to the captain. "And this little bitch was giving him the signals!" He wrestled himself away from the two men and, as roughly as possible, slapped Lydia across the face. Blood spurted from her lip, and when she wiped at it, she was shaking so fiercely that she could hardly speak. No one seemed remotely inclined to come to her rescue when he slapped her again. Then a lady stepped in front of him to ward off another blow. Lydia stared incredulously at her rescuer. She was the lady from Omaha, who wore the buckskin clothes! Lydia hardly recognized her in a dress.

"You keep out of this!" the irate man screamed at Katrina, and as he tried to force her aside, she pulled a Colt pistol from her handbag and stuck it in his face.

"Since when do men slap ladies around?" she asked in a deadly voice.

Big Jim jumped back, not expecting to find a gun pointed at him, especially by a woman. Others looked on with amazement, but Katrina cocked the hammer back and held the Colt steady.

"She's a cheat just like he is!" Big Jim complained as he pointed to the man on the floor.

"Well, now he's a dead cheat, and you can collect your money," Katrina retorted. "But act like a gentleman."

"Come on, Jim," someone cautioned. "Enough's enough."

A few others helped calm the man down, and Captain Marsh, who knew Katrina, backed her up. "Katrina, take this woman to your cabin and keep her there." He eyed Big Jim Curry. "You and these other fellows collect what you got coming and call it a night." He commanded some other men to pick up Matthew McGrath and take him to the forward quarters.

When everyone seemed to calm down, Katrina put an arm around Lydia. She was still shaking, and tears rained out of her eyes. As they were leaving, one of the men carrying Matthew's body said, "Got both shots right in the heart."

Inside the cabin, Lydia was still sobbing, and in spite of Katrina's consoling efforts, it was several minutes before she was able to gain some composure.

"What's your name, darling?" Katrina asked her.

"Lydia Pearlman."

"Was that man your husband?"

Lydia hesitated. "No." She expected Katrina to question her response, but she didn't. Lydia dabbed her eyes with a handkerchief. "I saw you at the Paxton Hotel in Omaha. Was that your husband with the scrubby beard?"

She laughed. "No, I'm not married. That was Jesse DuRoche. He used to drive the stage out of Yankton. Some time back, he was one of Wild Bill's deputies in Abilene."

Lydia knew whom she was talking about.

"He and Jesse lost all their money playing poker, so I had to lend them a hundred dollars for a train ride to Cheyenne.

"Frank's my man," Katrina went on. "He's a cowboy and works on a ranch west of Omaha."

"Is that where you're from?"

"No, my roots are in Yankton."

"You live in Yankton and have a man in Omaha?" Lydia asked. "You must not see him very often."

Katrina laughed. "Not now, but I will. 'Course, he doesn't know that yet."

Lydia had a hard time figuring this woman out. She wore buckskin clothes and had a cowboy for a lover, yet now, she was dressed in an extravagant blue and cream satin dress. She was a good-looking lady, in Lydia's opinion, with curves that Lydia would never possess. Lydia guessed she was in her late twenties or early thirties.

Katrina sat at a dresser, pulled a ribbon off her hair and swirled her golden locks around. "Tell me about this fellow you were traveling with. Were you cheating at the tables?"

Lydia lowered her head. "Yes."

"At least you're honest." Katrina rolled her eyes when she realized what she had just said. "Were you in love with the man?"

"Matt was his name." Lydia made a face. "I'm not sure."

"If you're not sure, you weren't. What are you running from, honey?"

The question took Lydia by surprise. This lady, Katrina, was very perceptive, as if she knew Lydia had left a great deal of trouble behind her. Before Lydia could decide on an answer, Captain Marsh knocked on the door and looked in.

"Katrina, this girl can remain with you," he said, "but when we reach Yankton, I want her turned over to the authorities. I've talked to a few witnesses to the incident. This McGrath fellow reached for his gun first and Big Jim shot him in self-defense." He looked at Lydia. "I don't mean no offense, but it does appear you and your partner were cheating somehow."

When he closed the door, Lydia buried her head in her hands, her crying spell coming on again. "What will they do to me?"

Katrina put an arm around Lydia. "I know Sheriff Conway. Don't worry, darling, everything's going to be all right."

FOURTEEN

Yankton was not a large city by any means, compared to Omaha or St. Louis, but it was busy. Drays and wagons were loading and unloading from a half dozen steamships. A few warehouses stuck out in huge blocks, and like every other river city, most small businesses that lined the waterfront were saloons and brothels.

Yankton was definitely Katrina's town. When she and Lydia stepped off the steamship, waiting for the authorities to show up, a half dozen people passed by who knew Katrina. Some just waved, others stopped for a short conversation.

As young as Katrina looked, Lydia would have never guessed she had three children. The oldest, John, who was sixteen, worked at the Greenwood Indian Agency upriver, and the two younger children, a boy and a girl, lived with friends of Katrina on a farm near a small town west of Yankton, called Tabor. Lydia had never heard of Tabor, but then, she had never heard of Yankton until a few days ago.

While they were standing on the levee, two men wheeled a cart onto the steamship, a pine box its only cargo. They disappeared into the hold of the steamship, and minutes later, they emerged and pushed the cart past Lydia and Katrina. Lydia knew that Matt McGrath's body was inside. A few tears rolled down her face as she watched the two men load the box onto the back of a wagon and drive off.

"Miss Lydia?" Captain Marsh was suddenly alongside her.

"I'm sorry about the death of your friend. I've been running the *Far West* from Bismarck to New Orleans for several years now, and word gets around." He was silent for a moment, but when he wrinkled his face, Lydia knew he had something more to say. "It may not be my place to say this, but you weren't the first person to be in partnership with McGrath."

Lydia shrank back. "What do you mean?"

Captain Marsh looked off for a moment, then brought his eyes back to hers. "There have been other ladies." He touched the bill of his hat. "If you'll excuse me, I have duties to attend to." He gave a graceful bow and walked across the gangplank back to his steamer.

Katrina was nodding her head. "Well, honey, there comes a time when you just have to get on with your life, and this is as good of a time as any."

Lydia's face was drenched with tears, but now they were not over the death of Matt McGrath. Rather, she was thankful that Katrina had befriended her. "You've been very good to me and you don't even know me."

Katrina smiled. "Sometimes people need help, sometimes they just need a friend." She shrugged, and then added, "There are a few exceptions, however. Now and then you run across a mean son of a bitch, and you've got to treat him like one."

The comment forced a slight smile from Lydia. It reminded her of Selma Ritter and how crass she could be at times. However, Lydia did not at all consider Katrina to be a crass person. A wagon pulled up, and sitting behind the reins was a man wearing a badge on his vest.

"Hi, Sheriff," Katrina greeted.

"Howdy, Katrina. I'm supposed to pick up a couple people. Know who they are?"

"You're talking to them. Get down off that wagon and help us up like a real gentleman."

Sheriff Conway threw her a surprised look, pulled the brake on the wagon and crawled down. He offered an arm to Katrina first. "What'd you do? Shoot somebody?"

"Somebody did," Katrina said as she sat on the bench seat.

The sheriff offered Lydia an arm. "I hope you didn't shoot nobody."

"No, I didn't," Lydia said. "But somebody did."

The sheriff climbed up next to the ladies, and as he swung onto Broadway in the direction of the jail, he directed his comment at Katrina, "I don't know which one of you's in trouble, but the judge is out of town for a week, and you know I don't lock up no ladies."

"Then just take us to my house," Katrina suggested. "And let me know when the judge gets back."

"Right," he said. "Come on, Molly," he hollered as he snapped the reins on his horse.

Lydia was impressed with Katrina Dvorak's home. Though it was a two-story affair, it wasn't nearly as large as the plantation home that burned down in St. Louis. A large living room, den, bedroom and kitchen made up the main level. The upstairs boasted four small bedrooms. Unlike her home in St. Louis, this house was located in a neighborhood of homes a few blocks off of Broadway.

"I haven't even been here an hour, and I like this town already," Lydia said as she sat down to a cup of tea.

Katrina chuckled. "Lydia, darling, any town would appeal to you after what you've been through."

She was so very right, Lydia admitted to herself as she reflected on Matt McGrath. She should have learned a lesson the first time around with him.

"One day in a park, Matt simply swept me off my feet," she told Katrina.

"Apparently for the wrong reasons," Katrina said. "You don't strike me as the kind of girl who would like to spend a lifetime traveling up and down the river."

"I didn't intend to. We were going to pay off his debts and then settle down."

"Honey, gambling with love is tough enough. Gambling on love with a gambler is worse. You never come out a winner."

What Katrina said hurt her deeply, but it was true. She cursed herself for being so gullible. About all she could do now was let the matter slip into the past, which wasn't all that easy, since she still had to face the authorities. A man was dead and she was as much at fault as anyone.

Lydia again looked Katrina over critically. She was a striking woman, beautiful in Lydia's estimation. "I'm surprised you aren't married," Lydia said.

Katrina refilled Lydia's teacup. "My first husband was struck by lightning while plowing a field. My second husband died at sea on the way to America, and Albert died of a burst appendix three days before our wedding. Marriage doesn't seem to be in my cards."

Lydia was dumbfounded with her explanation. "You . . . lost a husband on your way to America? You're a foreigner?"

"An immigrant, but now I'm an American. Just got my citizenship papers a few weeks ago."

"Where did you come from?"

"Prague was my home for many years."

"Your English is very good," Lydia said. "I don't even detect an accent."

Katrina gave her a huge smile. "I've been told that before, but I thought people were just being polite. But when you say it, I believe you, because you're honest."

It was strange to hear that statement, especially since she was now awaiting an arraignment as a cheat. "So, you've given up on marriage?"

Katrina shrugged. "I don't think about marriage so much anymore. I think more about compatibility."

"And this Frank fellow, this cowboy friend of yours . . ."

"Frank's wonderful," she finished. "He's fun and daring and doesn't have a care in the world. And he loves me just as much as he loves his horse."

Lydia held a hand up to her lips and snickered.

Katrina went on, "That's a compliment coming from a cowboy." Lydia's smiling face suddenly sagged. "Marriage is important to you, isn't it?"

Lydia nodded. "If only I had your beauty."

"Honey," Katrina said, as she put an arm around her. "Beauty isn't on the outside. It's on the inside." Katrina poked her on her heart. "It comes from here, and someday someone will discover your heart and all the beauty inside of it."

Lydia's eyes were still welling up with tears. "Do you really think so?"

"I know so," said Katrina. To her, the frailty in Lydia was apparent. She was not a beauty and not shapely, but Katrina had a strong feeling that inside this young lady was a heart of gold.

Five days later, the new territorial judge, Judge Rossteuscher, returned, and Lydia's arraignment was scheduled. Katrina accompanied her to the court hearing, where five men were ahead of her, all waiting to be tried for various misdemeanors they had committed in the city, mainly being drunk and disorderly. For expedience, the judge lined them up all at once and fined each ten dollars or ten days. None of them could pay the fine, so they were all hauled back to the jail.

A half dozen ladies from the Women's Temperance League were the only others present at the proceedings, and when they badgered the judge for not fining the drunks more, he slapped the gavel and cautioned them to remain in their place.

If Lydia weren't being tried, she would have laughed. Lydia could well imagine that at one time or another, her aunt Almetta had sat in on meetings like this.

Judge Rossteuscher looked over what little documentation he had regarding Lydia's situation, which was nothing more than a written affidavit from Captain Marsh stating the charge against her, and that the shooting of Mr. McGrath, the deceased gambler, was warranted.

Judge Rossteuscher looked into the somber faces of the temperance group. "Are there any witnesses present who can testify that this lady in any way aided the deceased Mr. McGrath in the act of cheating?"

The six temperance ladies eyed each other but said nothing.

"Since we have no witnesses, I can see no reason to . . ."

"I heard she was a cheat," Mrs. Sanborn said as she stood among the ladies. She was a huge-shouldered lady with dark, piercing eyes and more wrinkles than a prune. Whenever these ladies appeared in court, which was often, she was always the spokesperson.

The judge raised an eyebrow. "Mrs. Sanborn, this courtroom does not find people guilty by hearsay."

"This city should not tolerate her kind of ilk," the matron retorted with spunk.

Katrina spun around and faced her. "What kind of ilk is that, Mrs. Sanborn?"

The lady shoved her nose in the air as she replied. "You know what I mean. All these reprobates that hang around down by the pier. And you with them! You don't fool us none wearing that dress today in the courtroom. We know what you are."

Judge Rossteuscher slapped his gavel a few times. "Ladies, ladies!"

Lydia could hardly believe what she was witnessing. These temperance ladies were directing their accusation as much at Katrina as her!

Katrina was on her feet. "And what am I, Mrs. Sanborn?"

"Dressing like a man, riding horses, hanging out with those cowboys and all that other riffraff down on the levee."

"Well," said Katrina. "How I dress and where I hang out is my business. If you prefer to waste away your day in courtrooms, or have tea at three every afternoon with your snooty friends, or wash your husband's underwear and can't wait to carry out his chamber pot every morning, that's your business."

Mrs. Sandborn grunted. "Well, I never!"

One of the other ladies jumped up. "Who are you calling snooty?" Now, all the ladies were on their feet, and the bailiff and the judge were beside themselves, not knowing how to respond.

Mrs. Sanborn, smug and with her nose still in the air, abruptly switched subjects as she pointed a finger at Lydia. "Katrina is sticking up for that lady, who is just as big of a cheat as that dead gambler. I insist she be fined!"

The other ladies were still on her feet, mumbling and grumbling.

"All right," said the judge as he brought down the gavel. "One dollar fine. Case closed."

"I'll pay the fine, Judge," said Katrina as she reached into her purse. She looked at the faces of the defiant temperance group of ladies. "I'll also pay the fines for the other men you sentenced."

"That'll be fifty-one dollars," said the judge, "payable to the court, and the court will accept an I.O.U."

The ladies, eyeballing the judge with faces full of contempt, traipsed out of the courtroom, grumbling as they went.

When they were gone, the judge remarked, "Miss Dvorak,

your comments were rather refreshing. This group of ladies has always been a . . . ah . . ."

"A pain in the ass?" Katrina finished.

He smiled. "Fifty dollars will be sufficient."

Katrina paid the fine, which released all the drunks from jail.

"What about me?" Lydia inquired.

The judge just smiled. "You have been exonerated." Lydia didn't know what the term meant, and he read her concern. "You are free to go," he clarified. "You have been found not guilty."

She could hardly believe his words. On the way out of the courtroom, Katrina explained, "Captain Marsh and the *Far West* left three days ago, and all the gamblers involved went with him. I knew they wouldn't hang around for a trial, especially since they got their money back."

"And now I'm free?" Lydia asked.

Katrina laughed. "You sure are. What do you say we go down to the stables and check out Barker?"

"Who's Barker?"

"My horse. Ever ridden one?"

"No."

As they drove to the stables in Katrina's buckboard, Lydia could not help but admire her newfound friend. "One moment I'm on trial, the next moment you're rescuing me from the temperance ladies, and now we're off to see a horse."

Katrina chuckled. "Isn't life grand?"

Over the next week, Lydia came to know and respect Katrina as a close friend. Katrina Dvorak had a reputation for helping immigrants get settled in and around Yankton, and it made no difference if they were from Bohemia, as she was. She aided anyone who was in need of help. At one of the hotels, those who were destitute could acquire a meal that Katrina paid for. She also financed those who wished to open small businesses after they had been turned down by banks.

Obviously Katrina had money, but where it came from Lydia did not know, and she did not ask. It amazed her that after only five years in America, Katrina had done so well for herself.

However, Katrina's relationship with her children plagued Lydia. The oldest was working, but why her two youngest were not living with their mother was a mystery. Lydia did not remotely think it was her place to question the arrangement, and she assumed that if Katrina wanted to clarify further, she would. She was a lady who didn't hold back, as evidenced by her performance in the courtroom.

Almost every day, Katrina spent some time at an office in downtown Yankton. She referred to her "confidant" as she called him, as C.J. Lydia guessed he was a lawyer or somehow connected with real estate, since Katrina mentioned in passing that she had business in Sioux City and Omaha that dealt with property. Some days she wore a dress, other days she put on her buckskin attire.

Lydia, as appreciative as she was for all that Katrina had done for her, still wished to seek employment and be on her own. It was not in her nature to live off another.

"I need to go back to work," Lydia told Katrina.

"I was expecting to hear that from you. If I can help you find a job, I will."

"I was a waitress at a railroad restaurant. I can do that sort of work again."

Katrina wrote two names on a piece of paper and handed it over. "I don't know if these hotels are seeking help, but you can try them."

That afternoon, after receiving directions, she walked to the St. Charles Hotel and asked for the manager.

"We don't have any openings at the moment," he told her,

"but if you'd like to leave your name, we'll get in contact with you."

Lydia wrote her name on a slip of paper and told the man that she could be reached at Katrina's residence. He looked suspiciously at her name and simply nodded. After she left, he summoned another man from his staff and inquired, "Does this name mean anything to you?"

His second in charge read the name. "She's the one that was involved in that shooting on the *Far West*. I heard the judge let her off."

The manager again glanced at the name on the paper. "Can't have that kind of woman working in a respectable establishment. The judge can do what he wants and so can I." He wadded up the paper and tossed it into a wastebasket.

At the Colson Hotel, the owner inquired what her name was, and when she answered, he scrutinized her for a moment and simply said, "Sorry. I don't have any openings and I don't anticipate any."

By the end of the day, Lydia had walked from business to business, now willing to take on any menial job. Disgruntled and with no results, she ended up on the wharf, and after wandering into and out of a half dozen places, she returned late in the day to Katrina's home.

"Any luck?" Katrina asked.

"Yes," Lydia responded without cracking a smile. "I got a job as a waitress at the Steamers Inn."

"Who hired you?"

"Her name was Mrs. Briggs. She was very cordial."

Katrina raised an eyebrow. "Nothing at the hotels?"

"No. Not at the hotels, not at Excelsior Drug Store, nothing on Center Street, nothing on Walnut, nothing anywhere." She was silent for a moment. "Wherever I went, they asked my name. My reputation as a thief has gotten around."

"You're not a thief!" Katrina chided her, yet she'd suspected something like this might happen. The newspaper had published the shooting of Matt McGrath, and Lydia's name was now public record.

"The Steamers Inn is not quite what you think it is," Katrina cautioned.

Lydia's eyes dipped. "I know what it is, but it's a job. As soon as I earn enough money, I'll move on to a town where my reputation isn't known."

"I admire your courage," Katrina answered. She had eaten in the Steamers Inn as well as a few other questionable houses on the waterfront, but Katrina could take care of herself. Whenever she frequented such places, she always wore her buckskin clothes, and underneath her jacket, she wore her shoulder holster with the nickel-plated Colt. She knew very well the sort of clientele that hung out on the wharf. Although Lydia was young and naïve, she did have determination, so Katrina decided to let that quality run its course.

Waitress work was routine for Lydia, and within a week's time, she was reaching a tolerable level of comfort. However, the men who frequented the Steamers Inn were a rowdy bunch, mainly roosters, as those who worked the docks were called.

Cuss words at the table were commonplace, and the phrase that recurred most was, "Where's my goddamn food!"

One balmy day, Lydia was busy in the kitchen when she heard a gunshot. By the time she reached the eating area, blue smoke was curling up around a burly man in frontier clothing. "How about some service?" he hollered.

It couldn't have been quieter in the room when Lydia approached the man. All eyes were on her as she watched the man shove the pistol back in his belt, the barrel pointed down at his groin. "If that gun of yours goes off again," she said, "you won't be needing any service."

Those nearby that heard the comment burst out laughing.

The squatty heavyset man held a blank face for a moment, and then a smile slowly emerged. "What's good on the menu?" he asked.

"For you, big boy, raw chicken."

More chuckles came from the tables nearby, and the frontier man broke out laughing from deep down in his belly. "Well, bring it on, and it better be a fat one."

For the next few days, the frontier man showed up religiously for lunch and dinner. His name was Abraham Calder, but most called him Ham. Every year about this time, he passed through Yankton on a steamship headed upriver.

"I'm a trapper," he told her one day. " 'Course, ain't much'ta trap these days. Getting slimmer all the time."

Ham was almost as wide as he was tall. A curly brown beard layered his face, and full locks rolled down over his shoulders. Someone in the restaurant had heard that a few years back in the Montana wilds, a hunter had taken a shot at Ham. Dressed in his frontier clothing, someone had mistaken him for a bear. Underneath all the clothes and head and face of bushy hair, Lydia guessed that he might be a rather good-looking fellow.

A few days later at a dinner meal, Ham arrived with his beard clipped and his hair cropped, and although he wore the same buckskin attire, he appeared a bit slimmer to her. She found herself taken with him. Without a doubt, he had become somewhat enamored with her, so she looked forward to his visits.

Life for Lydia had taken a turn for the better. A week earlier, Madame Briggs had offered to rent her a room above the inn where some of the other girls who worked stayed, and Lydia decided to take up the offer.

Katrina wasn't too thrilled about her moving to the Steamers

Inn, yet, she realized that Lydia was a woman with a set mind, and Lydia had told her earlier that she did not intend to remain at Katrina's permanently.

"We're not severing ties," Lydia had told her. "It's just more convenient. You know I appreciate everything you've done for me."

"I do," Katrina answered. "You just be careful. The wharf area can be rough sometimes. If you ever need help, you call me."

Lydia had had her share of rough times. Everything since St. Louis had been proof of that.

Moving into the Steamers Inn was more than convenient. Lydia now had a room on the upper level, which could be reached from the interior of the inn or by a back staircase from an alley. The room was small but clean, yet far from private. Usually at night, the bar girls downstairs would drag clients up to their rooms. When Lydia heard laughter or stumbling in the hall, she knew the clients were either cowboys, soldiers, roosters or other riffraff. When she heard soft footsteps in the hallway, the clients were usually local businessmen, merchants or other prominent individuals who wished to be discreet about their escapades.

Over the next few weeks, Katrina would drop in occasionally for lunch, and quite often she sat with a few of the cowboys who worked the stockyards. "You look healthy and happy," Katrina told her.

She was, but what Katrina did not know was that for almost a week, Ham, the frontier man, had been climbing the back stairs and spending the nights with her.

September 1, 1875

Dear Grandmama Eugenia,

I've had some tragedy enter my life. A few weeks ago, while traveling up river from St. Louis, my fiancé Matt had an accident and fell overboard. We presumed he drownd, since his body was never found. I have endured this tragedy through the strength of God and am so fortunate, that Matt left me a handsome amount of money, so that I am not in need.

In Yankton, Dakotah Territory, I met this wonderful lady, Katrina Dvorak, who introduced me to the owner of a prominent eating establishment, where I am presently employed. I really don't need to work, but I find it necessary to keep busy, and this oppertunity appears to be a blessing in disskys.

In so short of a time, I have also had the pleasure of being introduced to Mr. Abraham Calder, a merchant involved in the fur trade. I do fear that soon he will ask me to become involved with his business in some manner, and although he appears to have captured my heart, I am loath to accept any proposal of engagement, especially so soon after the death of my beloved Matt McGrath. Time may tell.

Life has been very good to me, and as well, I hope you are in good health. Don't worry about me. I will be all right.

Love, Lydia

About the only truth to the letter was that Ham treated Lydia well.

One evening after Ham silently made his way up the back stairs to her room, he surprised Lydia with a bouquet of wildflowers. "I think them's brown-eyed susans," he clarified. "Find 'em lots up Montana way. Them 'n some other purple flowers."

Ham ambled on about trapping on the Powder, Tongue and Big Horn rivers, but she was not familiar with any of them. "Colter Creek 'n Clark Crossin' produce some'a the best beaver 'n mink," he told her. "They's far down off the Yellerstone." She had heard of the Yellowstone River, but exactly where it was, she didn't know. "Once't I shot a buffalo 'n left him lay fer a day. When I come'd back, a big ol' grizzly done took him over. Had to shoot 'em three times a'fore he'd give up on the hindquarters.

"Had so much meat, had'ta share both the bear and the buffalo with the Injuns. I get along with the Injuns good," he bragged. "They's good people and 'preciative'a what one does fer 'em. Once't ya make a friend of a Injun, you gots a friend ferever. That's what I like 'bout 'em."

She loved his stories, and though he was a bit crude with his language and often clumsy in bed, at least by her standards, he was a lovable fellow, always cheerful, seemingly happy every minute of the day, and best of all, he was always charged with excitement every time he came to see her.

During the day, she would spend her off time just thinking about him and all the places he had traveled to, and she wondered whether she could adapt to his kind of lifestyle. After a few days of daydreaming, she decided that she would take a chance on him if he ever asked her.

It was strange. Three days slipped by without Ham calling on her. He hadn't even dropped in for a meal, and now she feared some tragic event had befallen him.

"Madge," she finally asked Madame Briggs. "I haven't seen or heard from Ham for some time."

"He headed out a few days back," Madge answered.

Lydia's face went blank. "For where?"

"His usual haunts, Montana or Wyoming. He's got a half dozen squaws out in the wilds waiting for him."

"He's married?"

"I don't know as marriage is a factor," Madge said. Then she saw the distraught look on Lydia's face. "Honey, you didn't think he'd stick around, did you? He's a trapper—a frontiersman. Just be happy you made a few bucks off of him while he was here."

Madge retired to a back room leaving Lydia gaping, on the verge of tears. It was bad enough that Ham had left her, and that he had Indian women waiting for him. What was worse, was that Madge Briggs thought that she had been sleeping with him to earn money!

She cupped the sides of her face with her hands and stared at the floor.

"Are you okay?" one of the girls asked her.

"Yes, yes," she answered, and then she ran up the stairs to her room. She was so angry, she couldn't think clearly. She pulled a small can from the depths of her closet in which she had been saving some money. She had less than eight dollars, and another week's rent for the room was coming up.

She sat on the edge of her bed, weeping bitterly. "Oh God, oh God, how will I ever earn enough money to get out of this hellhole?" After a few minutes, she slowly gained her composure and wiped away the tears with a handkerchief. She primped her hair, and after the redness in her eyes subsided, she descended the staircase to the back room where Madge Briggs had her office.

"I wonder if we could talk for a minute," she asked Madge.

FIFTEEN

Katrina's business ventures kept her busy for the better part of two weeks. She just finished instigating an investment opportunity with a brick mill west along the river and learned that Josie Kern had recently opened his locksmith business with a small loan he had acquired from her. Within the next few days, she would have funds available for a gunsmith and a general store that concentrated mostly on clothing and footwear.

Katrina did not expect all of the businesses that she invested in to flourish, but anyone who came to her with a sound plan and a lot of determination received a contract and sufficient funds to get the business off the ground.

Most recently, she was so involved in her business dealings that she rarely found time to ride, so on this sunny afternoon, she dressed in her riding clothes, saddled up Barker and headed off to the stockyards where she often met with some of the boys.

When she rode up to the bunkhouse, several of the young cowboys gathered around to greet her.

"Where you been hanging out?" one asked.

" 'Bout time you came to visit," said another.

They all knew Frank, her newfound cowboy friend, and joked with her, asking if he was still alive.

"Well, he's got a broken nose," she remarked, "and a few cracked ribs from bronc busting, but he was still kicking the last time I saw him." That brought some laughter. Her conversation with the boys took several turns until Lydia Pearlman's name came up.

"Everybody's calling her Pearl now," one of them said, and with the comment, all the cowboys suddenly became silent.

"Go on," she prodded the cowboy.

He was reluctant at first, but he added, "Rumor is, you throwed her out, and that's why she ended up doin' what she's doin'."

"And what might that be?" Katrina asked.

The cowboy could not look Katrina in the eyes. "Well, you know, sportin' with the cowboys and such."

Katrina did not want to believe what she heard, but she feared the worst. She climbed on Barker and rode to the docks, where she tied her horse outside of the Steamers Inn. When she entered, Norma was cooking, but Lydia was nowhere around.

"In her room," was all Norma said, as she pointed upward.

Katrina wandered to the back and climbed the steps. At the top, four doors lined a corridor, two to each side. She stood for a moment and heard sobbing coming from behind the first door.

She knocked lightly and recognized Lydia's voice. "Go away!"

Katrina slowly pushed the door open to see Lydia on a bed curled up in a fetal position, wearing only her nightclothes. Other clothes were strewn about the room, and a strange, pungent odor permeated the air.

"Katrina!" Lydia exclaimed as she crawled from the bed and wiped at her red and swollen eyes.

"What happened, darling?" Katrina asked, even though she knew this young girl had become a fallen angel.

Lydia fought to contain her crying. "I'm so ashamed," she began. "I don't know how it happened, but I'm nothing but a damn whore now."

"It was the money, wasn't it?" said Katrina as she sat and

wrapped an arm around her. "Well, I understand. It might be easy money, but this kind of business can be hard on the soul."

"I had sixty dollars saved," Lydia blurted out in between sobs, "enough to buy my way out of here, but this morning when I checked, somebody'd stole it all." She broke into heavy sobs, practically choking, unable to hold back her tears.

"You cry it out, baby, and get it out of your system."

Katrina held on to her and gently rocked her back and forth on the bed, tears coming into her own eyes. She had misjudged this young lady and should never have allowed her to get in with this crowd. She couldn't blame any of the men that slept with her, since this was their domain, and this sort of behavior was expected of them.

But what a price to pay just to get out of town.

"I should have been looking out for you," Katrina said. "This is my fault."

"No!" Lydia said as she pulled away from her. "This is not your fault! It was my decision to become a whore. This is not your fault!" Lydia buried her face into Katrina's arms once again. "I'll never get out of here now."

"Oh, yes you will. Come on, darling, I'll help you pack."

Lydia returned with Katrina to her home. If nothing else, she needed to rest, and during her waking hours over the next few days she talked at length with Katrina about how and why she had taken the path she did. Although Katrina tried to dissuade Lydia from leaving Yankton, she was adamant. "No. I've made up my mind. I can't live here anymore."

With the decision firmly fixed in Lydia's mind, Katrina knew there was no dissuading her, so the next day, Katrina made arrangements with Gerhard Bahn, who was headed for Sioux Falls with a load of freight. The following morning, a half hour after sunup, Gerhard drove up with his freight wagon pulled by six mules.

"Gerhard's my best friend," Katrina told Lydia. "He'll take good care of you."

"*Ya*, you don't worry," Gerhard said in his German accent. He loaded what little baggage Lydia had behind the seat and waited while the two, wrapped in each other's arms, shed tears of good-bye.

As soon as Gerhard helped Lydia up onto the seat, Katrina put a hundred dollars into her hand. When she saw the wad of bills, the tears flowed again. "How can I ever repay you?" she asked.

For Katrina, this was nothing more than payment in kind. "Honey, you just send me a letter when you get settled."

Lydia leaned over the seat and gave Katrina a final hug. When Gerhard yelled at his nearly deaf mules, the wagon lurched and headed toward town and the road that would take them to Sioux Falls. Two blocks away, Lydia turned and waved, and at that moment, she wondered if she would ever see Katrina again.

When the wagon was out of sight, Katrina felt her heart sink for Lydia. This dear, young, fallen angel needed company along the way, someone to talk to, someone who could console her.

Gerhard was exactly what she needed.

Gerhard Bahn reminded Lydia of Ham—short and wide, like a big block of wood. An hour outside of Yankton, they crossed the James River by ferry and angled north onto the Yankton-Sioux Falls Trail. The morning began with a warm and inviting sun, but by noon, the two of them had drunk up Gerhard's jug of water.

Lydia had not said much during most of the trip. As the mules labored along the rise of the trail, she could see a small village down below, across from a stream.

Lydia gave a huge sigh. "I was afraid we might run out of water."

Gerhard gave a weak laugh. "*Es gibt Wasser ueberall.* Mile that way," he pointed to his left, "mile *da drueben,*" he pointed in the other direction. "*Kein* problem. Winter is big problem."

Whenever Gerhard spoke, his words came out half in German and half in English. She was confused. "Water in the winter?"

"*Nein.* Ice, snow, cold. *Letztes Jahr,* I have big blizzard. Three days later, help come." He stomped his foot. "Three toes frostbite. One for each day." He laughed heartily at his little joke.

"*Ya, das war ein* big storm." He looked at her with his blue sparkling eyes. "You have good smile. You smile more often. Good for you."

She remembered Matt McGrath had once told her something similar. Where that was and when, she had already forgotten.

"How do you know Katrina?" she asked him after a while.

The question caused him to give a broad smile. "*Das ist eine interessante Frage. Ya,* we go back long time. I give her first ride to Tabor in wagon. Katrina *und drei Kinder.* John, he's big now, good job at Greenwood. Joseph and Josephine live in Tabor with the Rehureks."

She didn't need to prod further. Gerhard went on freely how he had come to know Katrina over the years, and that she was his best friend.

"She give me money to start freight line. *Wir sind* partners. Soon I send for my brothers to come to America. Bahn Brothers Freight Line. I like that."

"Katrina helps a lot of people, doesn't she?"

"*Ya, immer.* She help you," he said with a big smile. "She help me, she help anybody who need help. *Sie ist eine gute Frau.*" He smiled again underneath his grubby beard, which caused her to wonder whether there had been more to their relationship at one time than just being business partners.

"I understand she has a man friend in Omaha."

"*Ya*, Frank. He is cowboy, cattleman. *Ya, der is gut fuer sie.* Good for her. She like cowboys and cattle. I think she buy cattle company in Omaha." He thought a moment. "*Aber, Ich bin nicht dazu sicher.* Don't know for sure," he clarified.

"She's very well off, isn't she?"

"Oh, *ya*, she is very well, healthy. Good, strong woman."

"I mean, she has money."

Gerhard laughed. "Oh, *ya*, but you don't know by her clothes."

"How did she acquire her wealth?"

Gerhard paused with the question, not understanding.

Lydia rephrased the question. "Where did she get her money?"

"When Judge Tuman died, he give her house and some money. Inheritance, I think you call it."

"She was married to a judge?"

"No. Just live with him. Katrina does not marry. Not anymore. Too many problems."

Lydia sat back, reviewing. Katrina had two dead husbands and a third man died before they were married. A judge left her some money after he died, and now she had a fifth friend, a cowboy from Omaha. She wondered if there were any others.

"She has had many men in her life," Lydia said.

Gerhard had the strangest look on his face. He bobbed his head and said, "*Ya*, but only one at a time." And then he chuckled, as if something in the back of his mind triggered a devilish thought.

As the wagon slowly made its way down a steep hill to the village below, Lydia reflected on her own experiences with men. She had had an interest in only three over the past few years, if she counted Calvin. McGrath had been a no-good, and Ham was nothing more than a fleeting affair. Of the three, Calvin was the one who had treated her with the utmost respect. If he had been a white man, she could have easily married him.

In Yankton, she had slept with a dozen or more different men within the past few weeks, some two or three times. But not one of them had taken an interest in her beyond fifteen minutes of pleasure and a three-dollar fee.

She wondered which one of them stole her money.

The village turned out to be nothing more than a general store along a slow-running creek. An attached corral, an outhouse and two other small buildings made up this out-of-the-way store called Saybrook Station, as Gerhard labeled it. Someday, it might become a real town, but that seemed a long way off.

While Gerhard and the owner of the store unloaded some supplies from his wagon, she entered the store and looked around. The interior was much smaller than she imagined, but it was jammed with clothing, tools, harnesses and anything else one might need in this wide-open country.

She entered a second small room, in which a makeshift bar, built from rough-hewn wood, occupied a corner. No more than nine or ten liquor bottles sat on a shelf behind it. On the bar, a barrel with a spigot held beer, she was sure.

She heard hoofbeats from outside and saw two men on horses ride up and tie their reins to a post. She heard some conversation between them and the proprietor, and almost immediately, the two entered the small barroom. Both were bearded and wearing dusty, shabby clothes. One of the men was wearing a pistol belt.

"Well, by Jesus," said the shorter of the two when he saw Lydia sitting at the bar. Both men ogled her as if she were the last woman on earth.

"Name's Percy," the short man said. "This's Jeb, my little brother." He motioned to him. "Beer," he commanded. While Jeb poured two mugs of beer, the man named Percy sat down next to Lydia. "Could we buy you a refreshment?" he asked.

Both were close enough for her to smell the heavy stink coming off of them. "No, thank you," she said.

"Don't get many purdy ladies around these parts," Percy said. "Plannin' on stayin' here 'bouts?"

"No."

"Where ya headed?"

"I don't believe that's any of your business."

The short man stood and stiffened with the comment. "Well, ya don't gots to get snooty. We's just bein' friendly."

The proprietor came in and looked at the two men. "Percy, Jeb, you two behave yourselves."

"We's just being friendly," said Percy.

"Yeah, friendly," repeated Jeb, his brother.

Percy sat down next to her again. "Any chance'a the two of us sneakin' off to the back room fer a few minutes? I gots a dollar."

Lydia's face flushed at the suggestion. She reared back and smacked him hard across the face, knocking his hat to the floor.

"By God!" Percy yelled as he grabbed her by the shoulders. "Ain't nobody gonna . . ."

He went down like a piece of lead when Gerhard thumped him over the head with the barrel of his revolver.

"This's a real lady," Gerhard said as he pointed the revolver at Jeb. He motioned to the man on the floor. "You pick up him and get out."

"Yessir! Yessir!" Jeb said as he hauled Percy to his feet and slapped his hat in place. The two made their way outside, and moments later, they rode off on their horses.

"I'm sorry ma'am," the proprietor said to Lydia. "They really don't mean no harm. Just that they don't know how to act around a lady. I do apologize for their behavior."

Lydia was taken aback with the man's sincerity. "Thank you," she said. "Thank you, Mr. . . ."

"Prentice," he answered. "Edgar Prentice."

"Thank you, Mr. Prentice. And thank you, Gerhard," she said as she smiled at the bushy-faced German.

Gerhard and Mr. Prentice finished up their business, and after a quick sandwich and a glass of lemonade with ice, Lydia and Gerhard were on their way again. As the wagon labored up the long hill back to the Yankton-Sioux Falls trail, Gerhard was whistling.

"You seem in a happy mood," she said.

"*Ya.* Is good to have a nice lady along. *Ya, sehr gut.*"

"You hit that man good," she said.

"*Ya.* He have bad manners."

She was quiet for some time. "Do you really think I'm a nice lady?"

"*Sicher. Ya,* of course."

"I don't think you know me that well."

"I know you," he said. "Katrina tell me about you. Some cowboys tell me about you. They say you good woman."

"Did they tell you I was a whore?"

Gerhard seemed to let the comment go by. She thought it was perhaps because he didn't know what the word meant.

"For young woman who not married, this frontier difficult," he said at last. "Sometimes whore is necessary."

He did know what the word meant.

"It is job," he said. "You alone, like many other young woman. What other job is for young woman, if not married?" He looked at her and smiled. "*Meiner Meinung nach, du bist ein schoenes Maedchen.*"

She had no idea what he said. He realized that he had made

the statement in German, so he clarified. "You nice lady." And then he added, "Katrina nice lady, too."

Once again he was whistling. It seemed whenever he mentioned Katrina's name, his fuzzy face lit up as if he was the happiest man in the world.

She set her eyes straight ahead. She could not get it out of her head that the two men back at the Saybrook Station addressed her as if they thought she was a whore, and for the longest time she could not shake the thought that maybe she looked like one.

Later that day, they crossed the Vermillion River, and a few miles beyond that, they spent the night at the Turner Way Station, a general store not unlike the store that Prentice owned.

She learned from Gerhard that both of these roadside inns at which they had stopped were crossroads for traffic moving from east to west. Part of the Sioux Falls-Yankton Trail they were traveling on paralleled the Vermillion River north and it eventually met up with the Mitchell Trail.

She had no idea where Mitchell was or how far, but at the end of the day, she was so tired from riding that sleep came easily in spite of the fact that the mattress on her bunk was about as hard as the ground outside.

From a high hill near noon the next day, the small village of Sioux Falls came into view. It lay a few miles away beyond the mighty Sioux River, and as they headed down to ford it, she wondered how deep it was.

"Water low now," Gerhard said. "Sometimes big and high and I wait whole week to cross."

He plunged in without any thought, and as they crossed, she could see heavy shale rocks barely a foot and a half underwater.

Another fifteen minutes passed before they reached the outskirts of the village. She had thought Sioux Falls would be much larger than the few short streets that ran along the front of the river, and she was very surprised to learn that it was comprised of no more than 1,500 residents. As soon as a post office was approved by the government, it hoped to be a viable town on the map.

Gerhard stopped outside a general store with a large sign above its front that said Ziegenfuss Mercantile.

Gerhard couldn't have been more at home. He and Herman, the proprietor, were constantly jabbering in German. Herman and his wife, Gretta, had two boys and two girls, ages four to fourteen. The oldest son, Wolfgang, was helping the two men unload the wagon while Lydia relaxed inside the store. When they finished, Gretta served a heavy meal of pork chops and sauerkraut with boiled potatoes and onions. Afterward, she dished up rhubarb pie for dessert.

"Delicious, absolutely delicious," Lydia complimented Gretta.

"Sank you," Gretta answered with her limited vocabulary. She seemed to understand what Lydia was saying, and if there was any question about the conversation at the table, either Herman or Gerhard interpreted. The four children were all fairly fluent in English, and surprisingly, the youngest, Agnetha, seemed to take to Lydia. She sat on her lap, showed Lydia her favorite doll, and when Lydia retired outside to the fresh air on a porch, young Agnetha was constantly at her side.

That night, Lydia spent the night at the Ziegenfuss residence, and Gerhard slept in the livery, which was but a few buildings away.

Early the next morning, Gerhard showed up for breakfast at the Ziegenfusses', and afterward, he escorted her outside. As they walked along the street, she asked, "And who is this man, Mr. Pettigrew?"

"He sells land. *Ist'n Rechtsanvalt.* Lawyer. Big man in Sioux

Falls," Gerhard answered.

"And why are we going to see him?"

"Katrina, she make arrange."

The Pettigrew firm was one block over and a few doors down from the Ziegenfuss Mercantile. A placard with *Attorney at Law* lettered on it hung outside the office. Gerhard escorted her inside to where Mr. Pettigrew was sitting behind a desk.

"Gerhard," he greeted as he stuck out a hand. "Good to see you again." He turned to Lydia. "And who is this charming lady?"

Lydia was sure she turned a light shade of red when he asked. Gerhard introduced her as he handed over an envelope to Mr. Pettigrew. "From Katrina," was all he said. He left and headed back to the Ziegenfuss store.

Though Mr. Pettigrew wore a mustache and a nicely trimmed beard, his broad smile was evident as he opened the envelope and retrieved a letter.

"Please, have a chair," he told her, and while he read over the short letter, she kept her eyes on this tall, handsome man. He was dressed fashionably in a silk shirt and string tie, and the dark blue vest under his suit coat gave off some sort of glitter as if spattered with tiny ice particles. Her eyes wandered to a photo of a young woman on the corner of his desk. Lydia assumed it was his wife.

"You must have made an impression on Katrina," he said, keeping his eyes on the letter.

She was curious what Katrina had written, and curious to know what her connection was with Mr. Pettigrew. "If I did, I'm very grateful," she finally said. "She's a very kind person."

He smiled as he folded up the letter. "That she is. And a very good businessman." He chuckled. "Rather, business lady."

"May I inquire how you know her?" Lydia asked.

"She has various business dealings, real estate holdings, property. I've been in communication with Mr. Shipley, her business partner, most of the time, but I have met Miss Dvorak on a few occasions. I understand she recently entered the cattle business with someone in Omaha."

"That must be Frank," Lydia answered.

"Yes, Frank McCann. I'm not sure it's purely a business relationship."

Lydia smiled. "I believe you're right in your assumption."

Mr. Pettigrew leaned back in his chair, and for a few seconds his gaze seemed to drift off into a different world. "Yes, yes." He came out of his dream world and swiveled his chair around. "You're seeking employment, I understand."

She figured that might have been part of the contents of the letter. "Yes."

"Your background?"

She thought a moment. "I worked at a railroad restaurant in St. Louis for a few years."

His eyes brightened. "St. Louis. I'm impressed. That's a big city. Have you had any accounting experience?"

"Sir?"

"How are your skills at keeping books?"

"I can add and subtract, if that's what you mean."

He faced the outside. "You're staying with the Ziegenfusses, I presume?"

"For the moment, but I don't wish that to be permanent."

"Understandable. Yes, yes. Give me a day or so and I'll see what I can do for you."

She assumed the interview was over and stood. "Thank you, Mr. Pettigrew."

He took her hand and delicately kissed the top of it. "Richard," he said.

★　★　★　★　★

November 5, 1875

Dear Grandmama Eugenia,

I am writing to you from a small village called Sioux Falls. It is located about 80 miles northeast of Yankton on the Sioux River. Many exciting things have happened to me since my last letter. I wrote that I met this wonderful lady, Katrina Dvorak. She discovered my talent for book-keeping and sent me here to work at the Cataract Hotel. I also work closely with a lawyer and real estate agent, who has an office here. Katrina owns property in this area and occasionaly makes a trip here, so I hope to see her soon.

This is a growing community, and I am fortunate to have met some very prominent members. This village is located on a river with several cascades. It's a beautiful area with shores of red rock. It is called quartsite, I am told. I learned that this rock is being used for buildings instead of lumber, and in fact, several men work daily to retreve the stone. It looks like hard work to me, but these people don't seem to mind. The Indians used to live here.

I have not heard from you in so long. I am also boarding at the Cataract Hotel, where I work. It was part of the ar-rangement. Sioux Falls does not have a post office yet, so when you write, address the letter to Katrina Dvorak in Yankton. She will forward the letter with a friend.

I am in good health and hope you are the same.

Love, Lydia

Lydia put away her pen and leaned back in her chair. A fresh sense of nausea overcame her as she eyed the bucket by her bed. "Oh, God, oh, God," she moaned as she gripped her stomach, bent over and held her head in her hands. Within a minute or so, the rush of nausea passed.

Her quarters were a small room in the hotel on the second floor, simply furnished with a bed, mirror, a cabinet for her clothes and a writing table. A pitcher of water and a basin were always at the ready, especially now, when she was on the verge of gagging.

Her job was twofold; she often worked in the kitchen or waited on customers in the adjoining dining room. During off hours, and when convenient, she handled the front desk where overnight guests signed in.

Her hours were flexible, arranged by the manager, Iver Bjornson, which was very good, since for the past few days, she had acquired some sort of sickness and was vomiting periodically throughout the day.

She felt her forehead now, thinking she had a fever, and though her skin was a bit warm, she did not think her state was critical. A simple flu, she was sure; something that would pass.

She returned her thoughts to the letter she had just written. Sioux Falls was not at all the exciting community that she'd believed it would be. It was small with few people—so few, that whenever someone spat in the street, everyone knew who had done it by the end of the day.

There were no secrets in this village. John Barda, who ran the local brewery, was building a house on Minnesota Hill and had a squabble with his wife on the design. Although he made an attempt to beat her, she wielded a knife in response and left four ugly scars across his chest and belly. Doctor Phillips, who was a regular dining customer at the Cataract Hotel, patched him up, and later the same day, John and his wife reconciled.

Bill Moen, the saddler on Main, shot himself in the foot while trying to roust a badger out of his chicken coop, and Homer Putnam nearly drowned below the falls.

The most devastating information Lydia learned was that Mr. Pettigrew, whom she'd had her eye on for a few weeks, was seeing a young miss by the name of Bessie Pittar. In fact, they were engaged to be married, although no date had been set. It saddened Lydia that Miss Pittar was his choice. Of course, he never knew Lydia had an interest in him, nor did she have the faintest idea whether he had an interest in her. It was necessary to keep one's personal problems to oneself, since any kind of gossip traveled like wildfire in this community that suffered from the lack of a newspaper.

Reflecting on her letter once again, Lydia had very few dealings with Pettigrew, other than to wait on him in the dining hall, but it seemed a good thing to at least mention him in the letter. Why bother Eugenia with incidentals? It was also, of course, a lie that Katrina had sent Lydia to Sioux Falls specifically to work in the Cataract Hotel. That just happened. But again, the truth of her situation was more painful than a lie.

She was, however, grateful that Katrina had whisked her away from Yankton, where her reputation as a whore was on the lips of everybody. At least here in Sioux Falls, no one knew about her past.

It was difficult to fathom how anybody could live in this little dirt town that lacked any sense of culture. No large buildings, no pavilion, no park, other than the area at the falls, which seemed to be the gathering place for picnics.

No place to dance, since the village did not have a band, and even if it did, she was not sure she would attend anyway, especially now, feeling as poorly as she did.

She had met some prominent members of the town, of course, such as Dr. Phillips, the local physician and, like Mr. Pettigrew, a land developer. In fact, the main street was named Phillips, since it was the doctor who had platted out the original streets of the town. She had also been introduced to a younger man named Melvin Grigsby, who was in the banking business and who also dabbled in real estate. Phillips, Pettigrew and

Grigsby often frequented the dining hall for lunch or dinner at the same time. On several occasions, Lydia had reserved a back room in the hotel where the three often held conferences.

The Ziegenfusses, though on a different level, were as prominent as anyone, so, really, the statement that she had met some prominent people in the community was quite valid.

It wasn't, however, as though she was well acquainted with any of these people, like the friends she had made in St. Louis. In fact, the town did not have a judge or even a police department, and in that sense it had no law other than the few city locals who took it upon themselves to hand out vigilante justice when necessary. If Sioux Falls was representative of the edge of the Western frontier, Lydia could not remotely conceive what kind of civilization lay further west in Dakotah Territory. People here eked out a living by working long, hard hours throughout the day. Yankton, as small as it was, possessed some sense of culture, but Sioux Falls, for lack of a better description, appeared to be nothing more than an anthill on the prairie. It didn't even have a railroad running through it, let alone a stagecoach.

When she thought about it, this village wasn't much different from Grundy, her hometown. Most folks dressed in drab, black clothing with no sense of style. The simple dresses she had brought with her were just as stylish as those other women in town wore, and the one dress that she had acquired from the French lady in Kansas certainly was as colorful and stylish as any woman might wear, but, of course, Lydia had no occasion to wear it.

There was no doubt that women tended to appear a little more tidy than men. The men working along the river mining quartzite wore the same clothes day in and day out, and hardly any of them shaved. It was obvious that bathing regularly, and hygiene in general, was overlooked by most.

There were exceptions, of course. Those who ran businesses and had gained some prominence in the town, such as Mr. Pettigrew, dressed a little more respectably. Dr. Phillips always appeared well dressed, as did his wife, Hattie.

Lydia glanced out the window of her second-floor room, from which she could see the activity along the river just a few blocks away. It was a beautiful area, a spot where she often went just to sit and meditate. Gerhard had told her that the grassy shoreline, now used for picnics, once was a meeting place for fur traders and Indians. That made sense, since this was the location of the falls, where fishing also was plentiful.

On a high bluff to the north that overlooked the valley, the Sioux Indians had killed a man and his son by the name of Amidon. That had been some thirteen years ago during an Indian uprising that began in southern Minnesota. She knew nothing more about the killings other than that the Indians had long since moved westward and were not considered a threat in this area.

Lydia turned suddenly, the queasiness back. She lunged for the bucket near her bed, and after retching several times, she puked up some phlegm and bile. Feeling somewhat better, she quickly dressed and went downstairs.

Sixteen

To reach the kitchen Lydia had to walk through the lobby where Iver Bjornson, the hotel manager, greeted her. "Good morning, Lydia," he said. Iver, as short and wiry as he was, had muscles on his arms the size of Lydia's thighs. Somehow, he had picked up the nickname Stubby, but the moniker didn't at all fit his strength and power. He at one time worked at a warehouse, where it was maintained that he could load a flatbed wagon with fifty-pound sacks of flour by himself in less than a half hour. He had endured a heart attack some time back and was forced to rely on work that didn't tax him. He was grateful to be running the hotel now.

"Got a small pack train coming through from St. Paul today," Stubby said. "Sighted last night just this side of Beaver Creek. Should be here some time this afternoon, I'm told. My missus and two younguns are down with the grippe and I'm about to head out. Can you take care of the army boys when they arrive?"

"How many will there be?"

"I'm guessing just a few of the officers. I'm sure the enlisted men will camp along the falls. Can you handle it while I'm gone?"

"I'll be happy to," said Lydia. "Don't you never mind, and I hope your family gets over their sickness soon."

Stubby examined her critically. "You all right?" he asked. "You still look a little peaked this morning."

"Probably the same thing your family has. I'm sure we'll all get over it in time."

Later that afternoon, the pack train from St. Paul arrived. The train wasn't at all as large as she expected. It consisted of eight wagons and perhaps thirty or forty soldiers. The command settled on the river as Iver said they would, and by late afternoon tents sprang up and campfires were giving off wisps of gray smoke.

To have a better view of the activity, Lydia ran up the stairs to her room. From her window she could easily see the encampment. While she was observing things unfolding down below, she saw two soldiers on horses riding up from the river. She guessed they were officers, so she quickly returned to the front desk.

Moments later, the same two men tied their horses outside and entered the hotel. One was an officer, she was sure, since he had a yellow stripe running down the sides of his pants. The other had chevrons on his uniform: a sergeant, she guessed. The young officer looked around the lobby and seeing only Lydia, he finally asked, "Are you in charge here?"

"Iver Bjornson usually is, but his family is ill and he left this morning. Can I help you?"

The officer promptly removed his hat. "Well, ah . . ." When the officer noticed the man next to him had not removed his hat, he nudged him, forcing him to do so.

"Are you Captain Gates?" she asked.

He seemed surprised that she knew his name. "Yes, I am."

She produced a ledger and drew some paperwork from it. "We didn't know how many of you would be spending the night as guests."

"There'll be only two, myself and Colonel Holz. And you are Miss . . ."

"Lydia Pearlman."

"It is my extreme pleasure, Miss Pearlman," he said with a slight bow. He motioned to his companion. "This is Sergeant O'Mallory."

She nodded as he greeted her. The sergeant was a stocky, sturdy-looking man with a full beard. Unlike the sergeant, the captain stood tall and lean. A jagged scar ran from his hairline to his cheek, cutting across his eye and leaving a battered eyelid that drooped, as if that eye were half asleep.

"Captain," she said. "It says here you'll be needing supplies."

When he retrieved a paper from inside his tunic, she noticed he strained his eyes in order to read the equipment list. "Siggenfoot, or something like that," he said.

"Ziegenfuss?" she asked.

"Yes, that's it."

She turned the ledger for him to sign in, and after he did so he put his hat back on and turned to leave.

"You passed the Ziegenfusses' store on the way up from the river," she said to be helpful. "Just off to your left on the way back."

He smiled. "Thank you, Miss . . ."

"Pearlman," she replied.

The sergeant abruptly inquired, "I'm a guessin' there's a bar or two in town, mum?"

"Yes," she answered. "I'm sure your boys will find them. Sioux Falls isn't that big."

"My boys'll smell 'em out," the sergeant quipped.

The two tipped their hats and left the office. Lydia watched them as they crawled on their horses and ambled back toward the river.

Lydia remained at the desk for the remainder of the day. That evening, Captain Gates returned with Colonel Holz, a big man with thick gray hair and a heavy beard to match.

"We meet again," the captain said. He introduced the colonel, who didn't bother to remove his hat. He just grunted a barely audible "Ma'am." Taking what few personal items they had with them, they retired to their room, but less than a half hour later, both entered the dining room and ordered a meal. Though Lydia remained on duty in the lobby, she could easily view the table where the two officers sat. Surprisingly, they spent a few hours at the table, and when they finally got up, the captain had to help the colonel to his feet. As they passed through the lobby, the captain had an arm around the colonel, practically dragging him to the back where their room was located.

Lydia felt sympathy for Captain Gates, having to cater to a superior officer who was definitely drunk. She heard their door slam, and suddenly her thoughts reflected on her aunt Almetta and her role in the Women's Temperance League. Her mind was fully back in St. Louis now, and she wondered what happened to Calvin. She sorely missed her two best friends, Selma and Colleen.

Shortly, and to her surprise, the captain returned to the lobby. "I wish to apologize for the behavior of the colonel," he said to Lydia.

"I imagine it's been a long trip for you boys from St. Paul."

"That's no excuse for his behavior."

Suddenly a gunshot sounded from somewhere down the block, and shouts broke the quiet of the night. The captain quickly crossed the lobby and threw open the door. He peered down the block and then stepped back in.

"Just some of the boys." He saw the concerned look on her face. "Sergeant O'Mallory's with them. He'll keep them under control. They're sort of like his family." He took a seat in a leather chair in front of the desk and adjusted the pistol holster at his side as he did so. She came around the desk and sat across from him.

"It's a little brisk tonight," he said.

"It's November. Up here it gets brisk this time of year."

He smiled. "Of course, I'm sure you're used to it."

He obviously thought she had lived here for some time. "Have you been with the military long?" she inquired.

"Ever since the war."

"Where are you boys headed?"

"To Fort Sully on the Missouri, just the other side of Pierre. Must be about another six or seven days' journey."

She had heard of Pierre.

"I've never been this far west," he said. "The falls here are about as nice of a site as I've ever seen. With that much water flowing by, I'm surprised I didn't see a mill."

"There are some people in town considering building one, but I don't know when." She expected that he might comment, and when he didn't, she went on, "Most folks around here picnic down by the falls."

She saw his eyes lift and watched a warm smile form on his face. "It's been a while since I've had the pleasure of a picnic." His eyes dropped and then he looked up again. "I wonder if . . ."

She was reading him perfectly. "If what?"

"I hope it wouldn't be too forward of me, if, maybe tomorrow, if you happen to be free, maybe we could . . ."

"I'd love to," she finished.

His face lit up with the sudden response, and when he stood, the smile stayed on his face. "That would be just fine." He remained still for several seconds, as if he did not know what else to say, and then he put on his hat. "I suppose I better check on those boys."

"Better check on that sergeant, too," she said as he headed out the door. He still had the smile on his face when he left.

If Captain Gates returned that night, Lydia didn't know, since she retired about ten. For the first hour, as she lay awake in bed, her thoughts remained on him. She assumed he had received his scarred face in battle, but his looks didn't at all detract from her interest in him. Underneath those scars, she could see a man of compassion. After all, he had aided his drunken colonel to bed and apologized for his behavior, and he was concerned about his soldiers who were raising hell earlier, and above all, he was polite, a man of easy manners.

In the month and a half since she arrived in Sioux Falls, he was the only one who showed some interest in her. It was hard to forget what Selma had told her so long ago, that the two of them didn't have to worry about being violated by the manager of the railroad restaurant, since neither of them were beauties.

Yet Katrina had told her that her own beauty lay within her heart, and that someday, someone would recognize that beauty.

She fell asleep wondering if Captain Gates might be that person.

Iver Bjornson was back at the desk in the morning, and when Lydia came down the stairs, he handed her a note. She quickly read it and squeezed it against her breast. The message was from the captain, and it said he would be by to pick her up around two o'clock that afternoon.

"Good news?" Iver inquired when he saw the state of ecstasy she appeared to be in.

"Yes!" she answered as she headed for the kitchen.

That afternoon, Captain Gates pulled up in front of the Cataract Hotel driving a buckboard. When he entered the lobby, Lydia was waiting for him wearing the fine dress she had procured several months ago from Madame La Font in Boonville. She'd also packed a picnic basket full of food earlier that morning in the kitchen.

Captain Gates, his uniform much cleaner than it had been the day before, removed his hat and looked her over. "That's a very pretty dress," he said, "and if you don't mind my saying so, you look lovely in it."

The comment made her heart flutter. She had been told that before by a few men, but only when such men were seeking pleasures from her. She sincerely believed this officer meant it.

Like a gentleman, he escorted her to the buckboard and helped her up onto the seat. As they started off down the street, Sergeant O'Mallory and two soldiers stood on the side gawking as they passed, but Captain Gates kept his gaze forward, as if he did not even recognize them.

They turned at the corner and followed the street toward the river. Ahead, the encampment of soldiers had bivouacked below the falls. As they drove along the river, a few soldiers were bathing in the water, naked as jaybirds. A few jeered when they saw the captain and Lydia drive by in the buckboard.

The captain just smiled.

"My," said Lydia. "That water has got to be cold this time of year."

"It is," he answered. "But these boys are used to it. Got to wash the grime off whenever you can."

For an early November afternoon, the sun was beating down warmly. Instead of remaining at the falls where the soldier camp was located, Captain Gates headed south along a path paralleling the river. In a short time, the road veered away from the river, and after another quarter hour the captain turned off and headed up over a low rise. Below, trees were thick along both sides of the Big Sioux. The captain maneuvered the buggy through the trees to the river's edge, where he stopped and helped her down.

"This is beautiful," she said as she looked around.

"Yesterday when we passed by here on the other side, I was thinking the same thing."

She had brought along a blanket, which they spread on the grass along the bank. He removed his pistol and belt before he settled beside her. The only sound they could hear was the gurgling water as it flowed over a trail of jutting rocks.

"I don't even know your first name," she said, "or where you come from."

"Most people just call me Gates. I never did like my first name."

She probed some more. "So what is it?"

"Kellem."

"I think that's a pretty name."

He chuckled. "I never thought of Kellem as being pretty. Pretty is a word that belongs to a girl like you."

A sudden rush of warmth charged across her face.

He nodded, his smile warm. "I do believe you're blushing, Miss Lydia."

"I do believe I am," she responded. She let a few seconds lapse, and then, "Tell me a little something about you."

He picked a long stem of grass, peeled off the end and began winding it through his teeth. "Not much to tell. I was a farm boy outside of Philadelphia. Went to war when I was sixteen, got a battlefield commission when I was nineteen and just stayed in the military after the war. Never did like farming."

"Do you like being a soldier?"

"It's all right. Lot of inept people. Lot of hurry up and wait. Lot of boredom. And sometimes I'm not sure where I'm being sent and why."

"You said you were headed for Fort Sully."

"Yes. But who knows? I've heard we're all bound for Fort Lincoln eventually, to join up with Custer's Seventh Calvary. I served under him in the war."

"I've never heard of him."

He grunted. "You're not missing much. The man was crazy. Tried to whip the enemy all by himself, and strangely enough, he often did. I saw a half dozen horses shot out from underneath him. The man was just plain lucky, but someday his luck will run out.

"What about you?" he asked. "What brings you to this little village on the plains?"

That was a loaded question for her. She was careful with her answer. "I lost my parents when I was sixteen and spent the next few years living with my aunt in St. Louis."

He kept his eyes on her. "St. Louis is quite a city. What got you up here on the edge of the frontier?"

She dropped her gaze. "Well, I guess I came upon hard times." She looked directly at him, frowning. "I had . . . some . . . hard times."

He saw she was struggling with her words. "You don't need to tell me anything more." He was silent for some time, and then, feeling a passion overcome him, he leaned across and kissed her ever so delicately. She wrapped her arms around him, never wanting to let him go, so he kissed her again and again and again. Just being with him thrilled her, filled her with an excitement she had never before encountered.

The day was slipping by too quickly. They nibbled at the fried chicken she had brought along and ate cream-covered rolls for dessert. Since the sun remained warm and brilliant, she shucked her shoes and he removed his boots. Holding her skirt up, she waded into the cold water after him, and for the longest while, they simply traipsed along the shoreline, picking up stones, giggling, talking about nothing in particular; just enjoying each other and the moment.

Toward evening as they headed back to Sioux Falls, a chill

crept in on them. Captain Gates removed his tunic, draped it around her and held her close to him.

"This has been the most wonderful day of my life," she said. "I wish it would never end."

"We were supposed to leave tomorrow, but I'm guessing we might be able to extend our stay another day or two."

"Will the colonel go along with that?"

"He will if I keep him drunk. Like I said, there are a lot of inept people in the military. He earned his rank working behind a desk and hanging around the politicians, while most of us boys went out and did the fighting. He's already in a sad state, and when he reaches Fort Sully, he'll be worse. He'll never adjust to this kind of life."

"Will you be coming back through Sioux Falls again sometime?"

"It's possible." He kissed her. "Would you like that?"

She smiled and kissed him back. "What do you think?"

That evening, the two dined at the Cataract Hotel. Colonel Holz made a brief appearance when Sergeant O'Mallory and another lieutenant escorted him through the lobby to his room. He was obviously drunk again, and although the sight was repugnant to Lydia, it confirmed what Captain Gates said earlier: if the colonel remained drunk, the column might well extend its stay for another few days.

That night in bed, Lydia once again spent a few hours reminiscing about the day and her newfound captain. He was a gentleman in every respect. If she'd learned anything about his background, it was that he'd never really had a relationship with another girl. He had received the battle scars on his face early in the war, and after a lengthy stay in an army hospital, he went back to the front. Returning to farm life didn't appeal to him, although he did take leave from the military for a month to pay a visit home. "It only confirmed what I always knew," he told her. "That I never wanted to be a farmer."

He hadn't paid a visit to the farm in the past four years, and he didn't know when his next visit would be. "We've got this Indian problem in the West," he told her. "I don't really want to be involved in it, but you go where the generals send you."

She could only surmise that he had taken an interest in her because his face was horribly scarred. She knew she was not a pretty woman, and in that sense, she felt the two were a perfect match for each other. Her only regret was that he would be moving on to Fort Sully in the next few days. The more she thought about his leaving, the more despondent she became. How she could fall in love with this man in one day was more than an idle question, and the mere thought of losing him crushed inside her.

She fought to hold back her tears, but eventually cried herself to sleep.

The first thing she did in the morning was to check with Iver at the desk. "Is Captain Gates here, yet?" she inquired.

"No, Lydia. He left early this morning." Iver saw the distraught look sweep over her. "But the colonel is still here."

"In the dining room?" she asked.

"No. He ain't up yet."

She pressed a hand to her breast and sighed a breath of relief. "Did the captain, by chance, leave a note?"

"He did," Iver said as he playfully pulled an envelope from underneath the desk. He was smiling as he handed it over. "You must have made quite an impression on this officer."

"Iver, I'd appreciate it if you and I kept this to ourselves."

"Yes, ma'am. You can trust me to keep quiet."

When Lydia left for the kitchen, Iver smiled inwardly. She was fooling no one. All the kitchen help knew she had made an excursion the day before with the captain. Sergeant O'Mallory had stopped in while they were gone and inquired about the captain's whereabouts, and anyone who had dined the night before in the Cataract could not have missed how the two sat across from each other for nearly two hours. Their conversation was hushed, their hands often touched, and their faces were aglow with the sort of look that signified love was on the horizon.

That afternoon, Captain Gates showed up with the same horse and buckboard. With another picnic lunch packed the two headed off, this time to the north, up the Minnesota Hill. Once at the top, they followed the bluff eastward to a point that overlooked the valley below.

All along this bluff, a panoramic view of the valley offered a majestic and calming appearance. The cascades were prominent on the winding Sioux River, with sprays jutting upwards as if a whale had surfaced in an ocean to blow. At the base of the falls, smoke from the army-encampment fires curled up in strings of gray. Intermittently, trees lined the sides of the river, and to the west beyond lay the few streets of the city. The buildings, so distant and so tiny, appeared like rows of posts sticking up in the air. When the two of them stopped and found a spot to light, it was easy to pick out the Cataract Hotel, one of the tallest buildings.

The sun was bright in the sky as it had been the day before, but the temperature had cooled. On this high bluff, the wind whipped briskly, sending a chill through Lydia. The heavy shawl draped on her shoulders and Kellem's arm wrapped around her gave her warmth and comfort.

"I can't imagine what it's like farther west," Lydia said as she gazed over the valley.

"Mostly rolling plains, I'm told," Kellem answered. "All along the Missouri forts are lined up every so many miles from here to Montana."

"What do soldiers do at these godforsaken places?"

"Mostly they guard the settlers from the Indians."

"I've heard that they are savages, that they kill and plunder and steal."

Kellem nodded and let a few seconds go by while he formulated a response. It came, slowly and methodically. "Well, I guess if a bunch of foreigners came into Sioux Falls and told everybody to move out, you'd be angry, too. No telling what you might do to keep your home and defend your family. That's what the Indians are doing. We're constantly pushing them westward out of their homelands, so what else would you expect?"

Lydia sat quietly, taking in what he was saying.

"They don't understand our mentality. We call it progress. They call it an encroachment upon their land. We tell them our president is their great white father, and they say they have their own great Indian chiefs." Kellem shook his head. "We whites try to buy the land from them, but they don't understand ownership. They don't understand how one can own the grass and trees and rivers, when all these elements have always been open to the Indians. It's sad. It's really sad."

"And you are going to Fort Sully to protect the settlers when you just said it shouldn't be that way?"

Kellem dipped his head. "I'm not educated. I'm just another soldier. I go where they tell me to go, I do what they tell me to do."

"If you don't like the military, why don't you leave?"

He chuckled and shook his head. "It is strange, isn't it? The problem is I like traveling this land. I've ridden over all the eastern half of this great country and love the freedom of moving around. I volunteered to come out West. I hope someday I make it all the way to California. There's a whole lot of excitement out there just waiting for me." He was silent for the longest time. "There's a lot to see yet before I die."

"Is there no room for anyone else in your life?"

He pulled her closer and pressed his cheek against hers. "I've been struggling with that ever since yesterday, ever since . . ."

"Since we met?"

"Yes. I've spent the last ten years or so pretty much on my own. There really wasn't anyone else that interfered with my independence until I met you."

"I didn't mean to interfere," she said.

He straightened up and cupped his hands around her face. "That was a poor choice of words. What I meant was, since you've entered my life, I have to rethink everything. It's taking time to sort this out, and I haven't got much time left before our pack train moves on."

"I think I could love you," she said. Her eyes welled up. "Could you love me?"

He grimaced, as if he had been struck over the head with a club. "This sort of love is all new to me. I love this country, I love meeting each day with a new challenge, I love traveling from place to place, and I love my parents and my five brothers and sisters. But," he brushed a hand over his scarred face, "I have never loved a woman because of this. And because of this, I've never found a woman who loved me."

She stared incredulously at him. Then, remembering what Katrina had once told her, she bravely dared to say, "Kellem, real love comes from the heart. I can find it in my heart to love you. Can you not do the same?"

He was at a loss for words. "I . . . I think I can. It's just that I'm not sure I know how. It . . . It's all so new to me."

It was awkward, their conversation, for both of them. He seemed as vulnerable to love as she. The two let the afternoon slowly meander by as they delved into each other's past. He talked freely about his travels, about the war and the battles he had fought, and the incessant killing on both sides. Near the end of the war, he faced starvation and months of misery in a Southern prison camp, and along the way, many of his fellow soldiers had died in his arms. Since the war, he had been stationed in three different forts, and St. Paul was his last assignment.

For all practical purposes, he had experienced only military life and nothing else since he left home. The life of soldiering had become his only comfort.

Lydia, on the other hand, had lived a very different life. She explained how she came to live in St. Louis, and as carefully as she could, she skirted the issue that had forced her to leave. She mentioned the Jefferson family, but she did not mention that she had very much loved Calvin, a black man, at one time. She talked of the friends she left behind, again careful not to mention the circumstances that forced her to move on.

Nor did she mention her involvement with Matthew and her short gambling career, or her affair with Abraham. Worst of all, she had become a whore and slept with numerous men, but in reality, she had never loved any of them. She didn't tell him that, either.

It was all too painful to tell him the truth. She had come to lie so easily in her letters to Eugenia that even now, as she explained away her short life, it was easy to leave out the bad parts. Not confessing everything was a big lie in itself, but Kellem was special. He did not deserve to hear all of the rot that had infested her over the years.

By the time they returned to the hotel, the wind was even more brisk, and the temperature had dropped considerably. As he helped her down and escorted her to the door, he excused himself, saying, "I think I better check on the boys. I've been delinquent in my duties."

He glanced around, and when he saw no one close by, he removed his hat, embraced Lydia and gave her a firm kiss.

She watched as he drove off in the buggy, and when he was out of sight, she stepped inside out of the wind.

"Miss Lydia," Iver greeted. "The girls are setting up the backroom for a conference dinner. I think they're expecting you to help them."

"I will," she said as she headed for the staircase. "Just as soon as I change my clothes."

A half hour later she entered the kitchen where she helped prepare food for the conference dinner, but her mind was not on her work. She could only think of Kellem and this second wonderful day they had spent together. In so short of a time, she had learned so much about him, and she was sure she was in love with him. She had never felt this way about anyone—not Matthew, not Ham, not Calvin. This feeling she carried for him lay deep in her heart. She tried to remain optimistic about their relationship, but he was a soldier, and soon he would be off on assignment. She dreaded the thought of his leaving, yet she knew it was inevitable.

She hoped she would see Kellem some time during the evening, but he did not return. It did not really surprise her, since she knew she had selfishly taken him away from his duties.

That evening, she helped cater the meal to Pettigrew, Phillips, Grigsby and four other gentlemen, none of whom she knew. The wives of those who were married were present, and Betty Pittar, Richard Pettigrew's betrothed, was at his side.

Bits and pieces of conversation that she heard mostly centered around real estate and property. The group was celebrating a land deal that had been made. As Lydia came and went, on more than one occasion she overheard comments about the military column that had stormed over the village.

"The colonel is nothing but a drunk," she heard one of the men say.

"Well," another commented. "Maybe the soldiers are a little hotheaded and a bit crude, but they're spending money."

One of the ladies added, "Yes, but it's all on liquor and women."

"Well," responded Mr. Pettigrew, "we all need to make a living."

It was near ten-thirty when Lydia finally retired to her room. She had given herself a sponge bath, and now, sitting on the edge of her bed and clad only in a light nightgown, she hummed almost silently as she combed her hair.

A light knock on her door turned her head. "Yes?" she said.

"Lydia?" When she cracked the door, Kellem stood before her, his face clean-shaven, his hair combed back, wavy and brown. He had shucked his pistol belt and tunic and was wearing a loose-fitting white shirt.

She knew why he had come, and as soon as he entered, he closed the door quietly and took her in his arms. For the longest time, he held her close to him, his cheek pressed against hers.

"Kellem," she whispered. "Forgive me for loving you."

He smiled and kissed her.

He remained the entire night, making love to her, and the next evening, they met again and made love all through the night.

The following morning the column left for Fort Sully. Lydia watched from her window as the wagons formed a line, every soldier in his place, the colonel in the lead, followed by Kellem riding on his dark sorrel. As the wagons rolled off along the river, she saw Kellem turn in the saddle, and even from this distance, she was sure he was looking back at her hotel window. She waved, knowing there was no way he could see the gesture, but at that very moment, he removed his hat and held it up for a few seconds, as if he had.

When the last of the wagons was out of sight, she broke into sobs.

Seventeen

A month slipped by, and though the weather held for most of the time, an occasional flurry of snow pressed its way into the valley. Today, such a flurry was whirling around giving the outdoors a miserable, cold feeling. Hardly anyone was on the street.

As Lydia sat at a window observing the developing storm, young Wolfgang Ziegenfuss, dressed in warm clothes and mittens, came running from across the way. Snow swirled around him as he shoved the door open to the lobby.

"Miss Lydia," he said, almost out of breath. "Mr. Bahn just arrived with a load of freight. Momma says you should come for supper."

"I'd love to. What time?"

He put on the strangest look. "At supper time." He turned, bounded out the door and ran back down the street.

When it stormed, few guests frequented the hotel, so she easily made arrangements to be away. Shortly after five, she dressed in a warm coat and pulled a fur cap over her head. The snow was coming down more fiercely now and the wind whipped at her as she walked briskly into the cold. For a moment, she recollected a night like this in St. Louis, when she had walked along a street headed for the Lindell Hotel, but almost as quickly the thought disappeared.

When she turned the corner, Gerhard's mules and wagon were in front of the store. At that moment, Gerhard, dressed in a heavy fur coat and hat came out of the store with Herman.

He spotted her. "Lydia," he said as he opened up his arms and gave her a heavy bear hug. "*Es ist gut dich wiederzusehen.* Good to see you again." He stood back, a wide smile cutting across his red and windburned face. "You go inside, we unload. Too cold for you."

Inside the store, she stomped the snow off of her feet, and as she began removing her coat, she gasped. "Katrina!" she cried as she threw her arms around her. "I had no idea you were coming!"

"Thought I'd surprise you," Katrina answered. She was dressed in her buckskin clothes and wearing fur boots. The two simply stared at each other for a few moments, their faces radiant.

"You picked a cold day to come to Sioux Falls," Lydia said.

"It was nice when we left," she answered. "I was worried the last ten miles, but Gerhard has made this trip often enough, and I trusted his judgment."

Gretta worked in the kitchen while the two women sat for almost an hour, chatting about anything and everything. When Herman and Gerhard returned from outside the table was set, and after Herman delivered a short prayer in German, Gretta served up a dinner of pork sausage with a combination of potatoes, carrots and onions all mixed together in a huge bowl.

"Farmer's dinner," she said with a jovial smile. She produced a bowl of dark gravy, put a jar of canned pickles on the table and sliced up a fresh, hot loaf of wheat bread. It was almost embarrassing. Gretta had spent most of the afternoon preparing the meal, and inside of twenty minutes, almost everything was consumed.

The sudden change in weather stopped the commerce of the entire village. Not knowing how long the early winter blast would remain, Gerhard settled in at the Ziegenfusses, and Katrina took a room at the Cataract Hotel, where she intended to meet with Richard Pettigrew some time within the next few days.

The next morning, Katrina woke from a comfortable sleep to hear the silence that signified snow. Outside, drifts were already piling up against the storefronts.

She washed quickly in cold water, brushed her hair and threw on her buckskin clothes. She thought she might find Lydia in the kitchen, but she had not yet come down from her room.

"Could I get a teapot and a couple cups?" she inquired from one of the ladies in the kitchen. In a short time, she headed up the staircase to Lydia's room carrying a tray. She knocked lightly on the door.

"Yes?" she heard a weak voice respond.

When Katrina entered, Lydia was sitting on the edge of her bed holding a bucket she had just puked into. "This damn flu," she cursed. "I had it last month for a few days, and now it's back." She set the bucket aside and sat up straight, dressed in her nightgown.

"How about some hot tea?" Katrina said.

"That sounds good," Lydia responded. Katrina poured for both of them, and after a few sips of the tea, Lydia seemed totally refreshed, her rosy cheeks proof of it. "I don't understand," Lydia went on. "I can't seem to shake this. Every morning, the same nausea strikes me."

Katrina smiled. "You're feeling good now, are you?"

"Yes."

Katrina felt Lydia's forehead. "You don't have the flu, darling." Lydia's eyes widened. "Have you had your monthly curse?"

Lydia's face paled. "Not yet."

Katrina smiled wryly. "Well, I've been through this three

times myself, so I wouldn't count on it showing up."

Lydia stared ahead, stunned. The realization that she might be pregnant caused her to choke. "Katrina, I haven't been whoring around, believe me."

"I didn't say you were."

Lydia dropped her head in her hands.

"Lydia, honey, your life is your business and nobody else's, so if you don't want to talk about it . . ."

"I intended to write to you about this soldier I met."

"But you didn't."

"No . . . I didn't." She looked down at her stomach, as if one month of pregnancy would show. When she looked up, Katrina held up a large, brown envelope and handed it over.

"It's from a Reverend Stilter in Virginia," Katrina explained. "I read the letter, since it was addressed to me personally, but the message is for you."

Lydia curiously opened the envelope and unfolded the letter. The date at the top indicated it had been written four months earlier.

August 4, 1875
My dear Miss Dvorak,

Your name and town is the most recent knowledge I have of Lydia Pearlman's whereabouts, thus, I have forwarded this information in hopes that you may have contact with her and will convey the following sad news.

Eugenia Calhoun, to whom Lydia has sent many letters, left our community of Grundy in December of '72. We did not hear from Eugenia since that date, and it is only recently that we discovered she suffered a heart attack en route and died before she reached Philadelphia. I opened the most recent letter from Lydia in which I discovered your name. I have enclosed that letter as well as those that were never opened. I realize the arrival of this sadness is an imposition upon you and do beg your forgiveness.

Should you have knowledge of Lydia's whereabouts, please forward this information and convey our sympathies to her. She is in our prayers.

Affectionately,
Reverend Everett Stilter
Grundy, Virginia

Lydia looked up, her eyes watery. "I always called her Grandmama, but she wasn't my real Grandmama." She counted six unopened letters alongside the opened one. The most recent letter she had written to Eugenia was not among them. It probably hadn't arrived before Reverend Stilter sent this correspondence.

"It's sad that your Grandmama didn't have the opportunity to read your letters," Katrina said.

"No, it's not," Lydia responded. "They were all lies anyway."

She had barely blurted out the word lies when she broke into tears. Katrina patiently watched the poor girl, her tears flowing, her shoulders shaking with every sob. Katrina could do nothing except imagine her pain and let her cry it out. Over the next few minutes, her weeping slowly subsided.

Lydia looked at Katrina through red, swollen eyes. "He's a captain. His name is Kellem Gates. I only knew him for a few days, but I so love him." She blew her nose on a handkerchief. "Is that crazy? To fall in love with a man in just a few days?"

Katrina nodded. "Not at all. I met my first husband three times in as many years for no more than a few hours each time. I knew I wanted to marry my second husband after an afternoon chat and a dinner. A week after I met Albert, I was sleeping with him. I would have slept with him earlier, except we were seventeen miles apart. He proposed and I accepted, but he died two days before our wedding.

"And the judge? Well, he hired me on to look after his invalid wife. Three years later, she died, and I'll admit it was a few months before I even considered sleeping with him. I think it was because he was twenty years older and didn't think I had any interest in him."

"Did you sleep with him?"

"Just a few times. He had a hard time peeing, let alone making love."

A slight smile broke on Lydia's face. "What about Frank McCann?"

"I met him while I was living with the judge. A month after the judge died, I went to Omaha on business. I knew Frank was working nearby on a ranch, so I looked him up, dragged him back to the Paxton Hotel in Omaha and slept with him that very night."

Lydia took in a deep breath. "You did?"

"He bought the wine, I paid for the room." She let a few seconds pass. "Cowboys never have much change in their pockets."

Lydia laughed out loud.

Her laughter brought a chuckle to Katrina. "Feeling better?" Lydia nodded and Katrina went on. "So, what's your next move with this captain friend of yours?"

There was no easy answer to that. Lydia planned to write to him, especially now that she was carrying his child, yet she was skeptical about maintaining a relationship with him. "He's a soldier," Lydia said glumly. "I don't know if he would give up soldiering to marry me."

"You never know," Katrina said. "Maybe having a son is all the coaxing he needs. After all, sons grow up to be soldiers. And besides, soldiers have wives."

That was a positive notion for Lydia, and she brightened even more with the suggestion. "But I'm going to have a child,"

Lydia said as she ran her hands over her stomach. "What will people around here think of me?"

"You sure as hell are not the first woman it's happened to. I used to wonder what people would say if they knew how many affairs I've had, but my life is my business, and the way I live is the way I choose to live. It may be unconventional, but that's never bothered me. Life's too short. If I spent a year mourning every man that died on me, I wouldn't have time to do any living."

Lydia took in everything Katrina said. "It all seems so simple for you."

"Life is as simple as you make it." Katrina stood up. "I'm getting hungry. If you don't mind having breakfast with a lady dressed in smelly buckskin clothes, I'll be downstairs."

Lydia's lips curved upward. "Give me ten minutes."

As soon as Katrina left, Lydia dashed some cold water on her face, whipped a comb quickly through her hair and pulled a dress from her closet.

Over the next few days, time played into Lydia's hands. She cried a few silent moments over the death of Grandmama Calhoun, yet she was relieved that none of her most recent letters had reached her. She burned the unopened letters in the stove in her room. As she sat watching the flames rise up from them, a renewed sense of vigor charged her. It was as if all the lies she had written in those letters no longer existed, and that she had been given a reprieve from her past life.

Katrina kept busy over those few days with real estate dealings. Exactly what they were, Lydia did not know, but Katrina was well acquainted with Richard Pettigrew and Josiah Phillips, and in fact, held meetings with them in their homes.

Such information provided unfounded gossip for the townsfolk. Still, from what Lydia could glean from table conversation in the dining room, Katrina was well respected as a business person in spite of the fact that she wore buckskin clothes and, more importantly, that she was a single lady. Lydia had no idea whether any of the Sioux Falls populace knew about Katrina's personal affairs. She guessed they didn't, but if they should ever learn of them, it certainly wouldn't be from her lips. Though Katrina's business dealings required a lot of time, she and Lydia still spent many hours together either at the hotel or at the Ziegenfusses'.

On the third morning of Katrina's visit, when Lydia awoke she glanced out the window to see a brilliant sun. If there hadn't been snow on the ground, one would have thought it was a spring day. Outside, though the sun was bright, the air was brisk and cold.

That morning at the Ziegenfuss Mercantile, a clammy calmness swept the air as Katrina crawled up into the wagon seat next to Gerhard. Both were bundled warmly, ready for the return trip to Yankton.

"I wish you would stay," Lydia told Katrina.

Katrina hunched her shoulders under a heavy fur coat. "I promised to spend Christmas with my children," she answered, as she leaned down and gave Lydia a kiss on the forehead. "You take care. We'll see each other in the spring."

As Gerhard drove off, his mules were puffing heavily, and frost was already forming around their noses. In the quiet of the morning, the creaking harnesses and crunch of packed snow beneath the wheels sounded across the open ground. Lydia watched for the longest time until the wagon disappeared into a haze of white.

She pulled her shawl tightly around her and quickly walked back to the warmth of the hotel. In her room she sat at her table, pulled a sheet of paper and pencil from a drawer and began writing.

December 10, 1875

My Dearest Kellem,

Hardly a month has passed since your column left for Fort Sully. That morning from my window, I saw you wave your hat and knew it was meant for me. I do not hesitate to tell you I cried as you rode out of sight.

Every hour of every day, I relive the fond memories of the short time we spent together. Falling in love with you was so easy, that I cannot help but believe fate brought us together. My days are long without you, and I miss you. I am so happy to tell you that I am carrying our child, and even now as I write, my hand is on my stomach, so close to this little one. I cannot yet feel it move, but it is there, growing every second. I do not wish this situation to be a burden to you, but it is proper that you know we will be father and mother of this child next July. I spend the mornings with the stomach sickness, but it is worth every moment. Katrina, my very good friend from Yankton, visited recently and only left for her return trip an hour ago. It was she who recognized my condition. She is my mentor and benefactor. One could not ask for a better friend.

On a sad note, my Grandmama Eugenia from Virginia died. It has taken more than two years for the news to reach me. I can only hope that this letter to you does not befall similar circumstances.

The winter has come upon us with a vengeance and has shut us in like hermits, bringing the town almost to a standstill. I hope the winter treats you kindly. I can only guess that this same storm swept its way across the prairie from the west. With each breath of fresh air I take, I shall imagine that you breathed the same air only a few days earlier. My dearest Kellem, I send my love.

Yours with affection,

Lydia

Every day, Lydia checked with Iver in the hotel lobby. Anyone who was sending correspondence in any direction normally left it at the Cataract. Word would get around when someone was traveling through, and in Lydia's case, she was waiting for word from someone headed west. The weather, so unpredictable at this time of year, was the main obstacle to mail delivery, but she was informed that eventually some hardy traveler would brave the winter and take a letter or letters, if not to the exact destination, then at least partway where the letter would be placed in another's hands to be forwarded. Such was the means of mail travel for this part of the territory. It was not at all convenient, but then, there were not that many persons intent upon sending mail, especially westward, where very little territory was open to settlement.

It was not until after Christmas that two heavily bearded frontiersmen spent a few nights at the Cataract and agreed to carry her letter as far as Pierre, their destination. Although they offered to deliver her letter for free, she insisted upon paying each of them two dollars, which they reluctantly accepted. However, before they left, they drank up the money in the Cataract bar.

Thus, eighteen days passed before her letter even left Sioux Falls. In the interim, she thought of many other things she wanted to say, but she decided to send this one letter first. She would wait for a favorable response to the news that she was carrying Captain Gates' child before she would send another.

She spent Christmas with the Ziegenfusses and joined several of the townspeople for a New Year's celebration in the hotel. On both days, a storm blew in from the northwest, piling up snow to an unfathomable degree. On those days when it didn't storm, it seemed a heavy cloud layer would move in and hover for days on end, preventing the sun from making even a meek appearance.

The month of January dragged on, long, cold and dreary. If Lydia gained any respite during this time, it was near the first of February, when she was able to crawl out of bed without the fear of having to puke in a bucket. Her stomach had not swelled to any noticeable degree, so no one, not even those nearest to her, knew that she was pregnant. In any case, she was certain that in the coming few months, she would be able to conceal her pregnancy by wearing a billowing skirt.

And so Lydia waited, day after day, wondering when her letter would reach Kellem. There always remained the possibility that it might not, and even if it did, she was not so much curious as she was fearful of what his reaction might be.

In her free time, she would sit in her room and read to pass the hours, but hardly an hour would pass without her constantly fighting off the thought that she might never receive an answer from him.

EIGHTEEN

Snow whipped fiercely at the column of men, eighteen in all, as they urged their horses along the bank of the Missouri led by Captain Gates.

The column had spent the past two weeks at the Cheyenne Agency, some thirty miles north of Fort Sully, and was now on the third day of a journey that should have been made within fifteen hours. Shortly after leaving the agency, a fierce norther blew in across the bluffs. They could have turned back at that point, but no one expected the onslaught to be so bitterly cold and long. By the time they had covered ten miles, half the men were frozen stiff in spite of the warm winter gear they had donned.

Luckily, they camped in a dense copse of trees, where hastily made campfires provided enough warmth for them to weather the night. They set off on the second day with the winds at their backs, only to be bogged down in the deep snow that had accumulated along the river bottom. For most of the day, the column meandered, unable to find the trail, and in time, their horses, thick-haired and wheezing from the cold, were quickly wearing out.

"For chrissake sake," Captain Gates fumed at his sergeant as he strained into the blowing white. "Where the hell are we?"

"I'm a guessin' nigh on to four or five miles from the fort," he answered.

"We should have brought along an Indian. I never heard of

an Indian getting lost."

"Oh, I dunna think we're lost, sir," Sergeant O'Mallory retorted good-naturedly. "It's more that we ain't quite sure where we are."

Captain Gates chuckled along with the sergeant, as he squinted into the vast white expanse ahead. "Let's set up camp here and wait it out. Send a couple men out hunting. I don't care what they shoot. I'm so hungry I could eat crow."

"Aye, sir. A fat crow would taste mighty good about now."

The command to camp spread quickly, and while most of the soldiers remained behind to build fires among the trees, a few sharpshooters left in search of game. To a hail of cheers, the two returned within a few hours with a buck deer hanging across one of their saddles.

That night the men ate heartily, consuming every morsel of meat. As Captain Gates and his sergeant sat on a blanket near their fire, the old soldier swallowed his last bit of venison and looked up. He was estimating the weight of the deer and running some figures through his head.

"Cap'n," he said. "I figger each trooper ate near five pounds." Captain Gates grunted and lit up a thin cigar. The sergeant went on, " 'Twould be nice if'n we could top this meal off with a shot of rum."

The captain eyed the sergeant as he pulled a flask from inside his tunic. "That's against regulations."

The sergeant's bushy mustache bounced as he cackled, "Only if we get caught."

The two each had a swig from the flask, careful that none of the other men saw them, and when the sergeant tucked the canister away, the captain said, "Better post a couple guards on the horses."

"Are ya thinkin' a coupl'a Injuns might be prowlin' on a night like this?"

"If I wake up in the morning and find my horse gone, I'm going to have you carry me the rest of the way to the fort."

Sergeant O'Mallory cackled again as he rose to his feet. "Aye, sir."

When the sergeant left, Captain Gates edged himself closer to the fire and pulled a blanket over him. The men were out of the wind for the most part, but the temperature was still below freezing. As cold as it was, the captain let his mind drift back to those few nights he had spent in Sioux Falls so many days ago. Such warm thoughts of Lydia finally let him doze off.

Late the next morning, with the sun shining brilliantly on their backs and nearly blinding them from the reflection on the snow, the column of men rode through the gates of Fort Sully. Captain Gates reported in to the colonel, dropped off some correspondence from the fort at the Cheyenne Agency and then retired to his quarters.

As he removed his heavy coat and hat, he spotted the envelope on his bunk. *To Captain Gates at Fort Sully* was all that was written on the front. Curiously, he opened the envelope and began reading the letter within.

Just as he was finishing, Lieutenant Bennet, a fellow officer and friend, entered and came over to him. "You and your boys got caught up in that storm, I see."

"Yeah," Captain Gates answered. "I'm still half froze to death."

"Ain't we all." The lieutenant laughed as he eyed the letter in Gates' hands. "That arrived a few days after you left. Fellow from Pierre driving some horses this way brought it up." The officer waited a few seconds. "Good news?"

A slow smile crept into Captain Gates' face as he folded up

the letter and stuck it back in the envelope. "Yes, very good news."

The first three days in March brought on mild weather, with the sun shining strong every day. It shone so strong, in fact, that the winter's snow began melting with a rapid fury. With each melting day, the streets of Sioux Falls became gouged with deep wheel ruts where wagons passed by. Lydia was hurrying along the boardwalk from Ziegenfusses', headed back to the hotel. She had just gotten word that an officer was looking for her.

It was impossible to cross a street without mud filling one's shoes. When Lydia reached the corner, her heart fluttered. Tied to a post in front of the hotel stood a lone horse dressed with the traditional McClellan saddle on a blue and yellow blanket.

She charged across the street, not at all careful where she was stepping, and when she reached the hotel front, the soles of her shoes were covered with muck. She threw open the door and slid in on her feet.

"Kellem!" she cried out as she eyed the officer. When he turned, her face went blank.

"Miss Pearlman?" he said to her. He was as tall as Kellem, but slighter in build. "I'm Lieutenant Bennet."

She stood silently, pressing a hand to her breast.

He reached inside his tunic. "I have a letter for you from Captain Gates."

"Is he all right?" she questioned.

"Oh, yes, ma'am. He just asked me to deliver this."

She accepted the letter and stared at it with wide eyes.

"I'm passing through with a few men," the lieutenant went on. "We're headed for St. Paul, but will be coming back through here within a few weeks. If you'd care to send a letter back, I'll be happy to deliver it for you on our return trip."

Her heart was still beating heavily as her eyes held fast on the letter. "I'm sure I will!"

He slipped his hat in place and headed for the door and was already mounted when Lydia ran out onto the boardwalk.

"Thank you, Lieutenant!"

He touched the bill of his hat with his glove and rode off. Lydia returned to the hotel lobby and quickly ran up the stairs to her room, where she tore open the envelope.

February 26, 1876
My darling Lydia,

Your letter has brought me the most exciting news. Forgive me for not being able to respond immediately, but it has taken me some time to digest all of what has transpired between us. To know that I am to be the father of your child pleases me to the extreme, but all of this, as I am sure you are aware, is quite a revelation. I have not, as of yet, shared any of this news with my fellow officers, as I am still in a state of shock and joy.

Of course, I wish for you to be my bride, and it is with all humbleness that I ask your hand in marriage. My deepest regret is that I am unable to propose to you in person.

As you indicated in your letter, fate has definitely brought us together. Who would imagine that a simple stopover in Sioux Falls could bring me such joy and excitement. This has caused me to reevaluate my military career, and as such, I must carefully consider my immediate future, or shall I say our immediate future.

You are steadfastly in my thoughts. I, as well as several others here at Fort Sully, am being transferred to Fort Lincoln in Bismarck. Before Lieutenant Bennet returns with your response, I shall already be underway, however, your letter will be forwarded to me. Please understand that although I have made a commitment to join you in marriage, and should you accept, I at the same time have obligations to the military. An officer cannot simply leave the service at a moment's notice. It is my intention to honor this move to Bismarck, but if you find it in your heart to accept me as your husband, I wish for you to join me as soon as possible, and if your answer is yes, I ask that you seek passage to Fort Lincoln by the best means possible. I wish heartily that I personally could escort you, but such a decision does not lie in my hands. I realize that to travel this enormous distance will be a discomfort for you, especially since you carry our child, but every minute of my day without you is equally a discomfort, a heavy burden on my heart and soul.

The military has been my life, and therefore, we must consider whether it will be frugal to remain in the military as husband and wife, or whether other challenges shall present themselves and send us in a new direction. These are thoughts I wish you to carefully think over before we meet again.

This winter has been long and hard, not only on me, but on all of the soldiers at the fort. It can be lonely here on the prairie, but I shall be in a state of heaven when we are once again brought together.

I shall spend my days in devotion to my duties as an officer, but I shall spend my nights dreaming of the moment when I once again hold you in my loving arms.

Loving you always,
Kellem

Inside the envelope was sixty dollars in cash. As she counted it out, she could only believe that Kellem was certain she would accept his proposal of marriage. Why otherwise would he forward the money? She laid the letter aside and let her thoughts wander. She could not believe how eloquently the letter was written. As far as she knew, Kellem had no formal education, but his words were almost poetic.

She held up the letter and reread a phrase out loud. "Of course, I wish for you to be my bride, and it is with all humbleness that I ask your hand in marriage."

Tears filled her eyes as she whispered, "I accept." Her thoughts suddenly jumped a hundred directions at once. She stood and paced the room, then sat again, then rose and walked giddily about the room some more.

"My God!" She placed her hands on her stomach and practically screamed out, "He wants to marry me! He proposed to me! I accept! I accept!"

She immediately sat down and grabbed a pen.

March 18, 1876

My dearest Kellem,

I love you so much! And yes, I accept your proposal of marriage! My regret is that I cannot accept in person. However, I can tell you that our little one is doing fine inside me. He is about four months along the way.

Did I say he? It looks more like an August baby. Would it not be spectacular if it were born on my birthday?

I think about you every minute. I must be in a dream world, because it is impossible to carry out my duties downstairs in the hotel, and I'm sure Iver suspects something. I know the kitchen staff will soon notice how my stomach has grown. Some have already cast it a wary glance. I have remained silent, but when it comes time, I shall announce to the world that I'm going to have your baby!

I promise to be a loving wife, and I know you will be a loving husband. I have no regrets. Should you choose to remain in the military, I shall be proud to become an officer's wife.

I shall devise some way to find passage to Fort Lincoln, and I thank you for the means to do so. I must close, my darling, for if I should write more, it would be the same as what I have already penned. Take care of yourself, and I shall do the same. Until we meet again, carry my love with you.

Love always,
Lydia

Two weeks later, almost to the day, Lieutenant Bennet, along with a dozen soldiers and two wagonloads of supplies, returned to Sioux Falls on their way back to Fort Sully. The lieutenant removed his hat when he entered the hotel. "Miss Pearlman," he greeted.

She was expecting him and came around the desk. "Lieutenant," she responded. "You're headed back to Fort Sully immediately?"

"At daybreak."

Lydia looked down, her mind unraveling. "Is there any way that I . . ."

"No," the Lieutenant answered, anticipating her question. "You cannot travel with us to the fort."

"To Pierre, at least?" she asked.

"I'm afraid not, Miss Pearlman." He smiled. "Captain Gates assumed you might ask that."

A blank look remained on her face. "Then you know our situation?"

"I believe I'm the only one at the post who knows. Kellem pretty much keeps things to himself. But I do know that he is deeply in love with you."

The comment brought a huge smile to her face. "Yet there is

no way that you could find it in your heart to allow me to . . ."

"Ma'am, with all due respect, my heart is willing, but it's not an easy journey across the plains, and March can still deliver some severe weather."

"I've endured severe weather before."

"Sometimes the Sioux tend to harass a small column."

"Indians?" she asked. "I thought they were not a threat in these parts."

The lieutenant twirled his hat. "Well, no, not always, but I'm not willing to take that chance, and neither is Kellem. He made that clear to me. And besides, I'd have to have orders to escort you. I don't have that authority on my own."

She unwillingly gave in. "I see."

"I do hope you understand," he said apologetically.

She nodded. "Why is Kellem being sent to Fort Lincoln?"

He drew in a deep breath. "Well, the Indian situation out West is a concern to the military. I'm guessing it's just routine, sort of, to get the Indians back on the reservation."

"I don't understand," she said.

"Ma'am, I don't understand, either. I'm a soldier. I just do what the generals tell me to do."

"That's what Kellem once told me."

He smiled. "We're both soldiers, and we're good ones, if I may be so bold to say so."

"I believe you are," she said. "If you should see Kellem, tell him . . . I miss him very much."

"I doubt I'll see him, since I will remain at Fort Sully. But I'll be sure the message is passed on."

With that, he tucked the envelope inside his coat and slipped his hat in place. "It has been a pleasure making your acquaintance, Miss Pearlman, and I do wish you a safe journey."

He was suddenly gone.

She remained in the center of the lobby for the longest time.

Eventually she returned to the desk where she sat, her thoughts whirling. She was angry that the lieutenant would not consider taking her along, but he was a military man to the hilt, and, like Kellem, he took his work seriously. She could respect the officer for his position, but that did not relieve her of her desire to be underway as soon as possible.

After Iver returned and relieved her of duty, she wrapped a shawl around herself and walked to the Ziegenfusses' store.

Herman was behind a counter doing some paperwork and greeted her when she approached, "Miss Pearlman, good to see you."

"Herman," she said, coming directly to the point. "Do you know of anyone headed west toward Pierre?"

"The soldiers. They go west tomorrow."

"Other than them?"

He flipped a calendar and scrutinized some scribbling he had made. "Nothing. But you at hotel, you know if people travel, no?"

She made a face. "We don't have anybody."

He was back at the calendar again. "Only Gerhard. He come in middle of May, but he go back south."

She made a face as she headed for the door. "Thank you, Herman."

If she could somehow reach the Missouri River at Fort Pierre, she could find passage on a steamer going upriver. It seemed so simple, but over the next few days, even with some serious inquiry, she could not locate anyone headed west. Perhaps Lieutenant Bennet was right. March could still deliver some cold and miserable snowstorms, so it was not at all unusual that anyone going in that direction might hold off until warmer weather arrived.

As a last result she sought out Coleridge Abbott who ran the livery stable, and asked that if he should learn of a wagon heading west, he was to inform her. Even if he knew of a lone traveler or two passing through, she would acquire a horse and ride along. She had saved up some money of her own, and with the sixty dollars that Kellem had sent to her, she had enough to purchase one.

She could always wait for Gerhard and head back to Yankton, where she could catch a steamship, but he wasn't expected for at least six weeks. She wished she could at least send her intentions to Katrina by letter, but even that wasn't possible. If anyone were headed toward Yankton, she would, of course, have traveled there herself.

"Good Lord," she said to herself. "Why doesn't this town have a stage line?"

Every night as Lydia lay in bed, her head was filled with thoughts of Kellem. In this very bed, he had made love to her those few times, but she could hardly pull the covers over her without wishing he were by her side. Often enough, she would drift off to sleep with tears in her eyes, and every morning she would wake with the same longing for him, longing for the day they would once again be together.

However, it was good that she did not depart with Lieutenant Bennet. As if the officer were clairvoyant, a snowstorm struck the little community of Sioux Falls hardly a week later, shutting everyone in for a few days. No sooner had that storm broken then another whirlwind blizzard stopped the town in its tracks. It would have been nasty if she had been on her way to Pierre, she silently agreed, but all the while she kept thinking she would also have been a few weeks closer to Kellem.

It was not until late April that the mud and muck trails leading out of Sioux Falls were once again fairly dry and passable, and as she had done several times before, she checked with Coleridge Abbott at the livery.

"Sorry, Miss Lydia," he reported. "No one headed west."

She put on a glum face, as she had so many times earlier.

"What fer, anyway?" Coleridge asked her. "Nothin' out there but grass and some buffalo."

"I have business to attend to," was her simple answer. Coleridge cracked an eye shut when he heard that. He could not remotely believe that her intentions were business related, but he said nothing.

Disgruntled, she left. On the way back to the hotel, she was passing the Pettigrew Law office when two men in a covered wagon pulled up front. Since she was but a few feet away on the boardwalk both of them tipped their hats as she walked by, so she returned the gesture with a smile. Why this huge Conestoga was in Sioux Falls aroused her curiosity, but the brass plate on the side of the wagon answered her query. It read, *Manson Surveyors, St. Paul, Minn.*

As she hurried on to the hotel, she thought nothing more of the unusual appearance of the wagon or the fact that these men were surveyors. Before she entered the hotel, she glanced down the street where the two men were just entering Pettigrew's office. For all she knew, it was very well possible that they had been hired by Richard Pettigrew, since he, like Josiah Phillips, was involved in land investments. She had heard that more land to the south of Sioux Falls was being developed.

Later in the afternoon, the same two men walked into the Cataract Hotel and registered. Lydia was at the desk as they signed in.

"Mr. John Grinnel," she repeated as she read his name. She looked up and studied the tall, lanky man, whom she guessed to be in his mid-thirties. He wore a beard cropped tightly around a warm face, and though he wore spectacles, they hung far too low on his nose.

"Yes," he said. "You're the lady we greeted at Pettigrew's office, are you not?"

"Indeed," she said with a huge smile.

"This is my co-worker, John Heiter," he said as he introduced his friend.

Heiter was shorter, well-built, sturdy-looking, with a brick-red face. She guessed him to be about the same age as Grinnel.

"The two Johns," she quipped.

The taller John grinned. "We get called that all the time."

The shorter John didn't seem entertained by the comment.

"How long will you be staying?" she inquired.

"Until the day after tomorrow. We have some business here in your community."

"Oh," she said with renewed interest. "Then you're not remaining in Sioux Falls."

"No, ma'am. We're headed for the town of Prairie."

"I see," she said, although she had no idea where Prairie was located. "And while in Prairie you'll be . . ."

"Surveying for the railroad."

"I see," she answered again. "Your rooms are at the back, down the hall. Dinner is served from seven on."

"Do we require reservations?" the taller John inquired.

She wanted to laugh. "No. This town is too small for reservations."

As soon as they were off to their rooms with their baggage, Lydia turned her attention to a wall map. She scanned it for the longest time searching for the city of Prairie, and then, realizing that they had mentioned they were working for a railroad, she located the nearest line, and directly on it was the town of Prairie.

"The Chicago and Northwestern," she said out loud as she read the name of the railroad. She pressed a finger to the map and ran her eyes upward, and then she said in a whisper,

"They're going north."

That evening, the two Johns were finishing up their meal in the dining room when Lydia approached them. "Mr. Grinnel, Mr. Heiter," she greeted. "I don't mean to intrude, but could I have a minute of your time?"

"Of course," the taller John said. The other John kept a scowl on his red face and held it there while she sat.

She was straightforward. "I'd be interested in taking passage with you as far as Prairie."

Both men raised their eyebrows.

"I'll pay my way."

John Grinnel cocked his head. "That's over a hundred miles, ma'am. That's four or five days of travel."

"I'm aware of that."

John Grinnel gave the offer some thought. "John?" he asked his co-worker.

"No," the short man grunted.

The answer punched hard at Lydia. "Do you have something against traveling with a lady?" she asked.

"Ain't no place out there for a lady," he scowled. "Besides, it's against company policy."

"I can assure you I will not be a bother," she charged.

"No," he said again.

"I can cook. Surely you'd have nothing against fresh biscuits and cakes every morning. I can get jelly and syrup. And a nice ham that will last us through the trip."

John Grinnel's eyes lit up.

"No," said the shorter John. "We got a wagon full of equipment, so there ain't enough room."

She tried again, harder. "That wagon of yours will carry over twelve hundred pounds. It'll hold six sacks of flour, two barrels of molasses, a chest of drawers and an upright piano. And it will sleep a family of ten, so don't tell me you don't have enough room!"

John Grinnel sat back, startled by the verbal thrashing, but his partner just grunted.

When Lydia left, John Grinnel began cleaning his glasses with a napkin. "That woman's got spirit."

"Too much," the short man answered. "Reminds me of my former wife."

Two mornings later, the surveyors, with their covered wagon and equipment, left the town of Sioux Falls. The trail out of town took them past the cascades of the Sioux River and up a long sloping hill. At the top of the bluff the dirt path meandered in a northerly direction.

The morning began with a chill and heavy dew, but by midday the sun was shining brightly. The trees, most which stood along the river in the distance, had not yet leafed out, and the rolling hills, barren with nothing more than short brown grass from the winter season, offered a bleak landscape.

"Jesus," remarked John Grinnel to his partner. "Ain't a hell of a lot out here." They had seen a few sod houses in the distance, and by the end of the day they passed the small town of Dell, which was nothing more than a way station near the river. As the sun began to set they were still short of Flandreau, the first major community of sorts, they had been told back in Sioux Falls. To their amazement, they had not once passed another wagon or even seen a rider on horseback.

With dusk coming on, they were about to camp for the night, when they spotted something ahead. "What the hell's that?" John Heiter remarked.

John Grinnel adjusted his glasses and squinted at the dark hump sitting against the trunk of a lone tree.

As they neared the figure came into focus, and they pulled to a stop.

"Hello, boys," Lydia greeted.

"My God!" John Grinnel blurted out. "Miss Pearlman! What are you doing out here in the middle of nowhere?"

Both men dropped to the ground, amazed to find her here.

"I had almost given up hope you two would show up," she said in a weak voice. She rose stiffly to her feet, feeling a fainting spell coming over her. Just as her knees buckled, both men rushed to her and held her from falling to the ground.

"I told you she'd be trouble," John Heiter scolded his comrade.

NINETEEN

It was pitch dark when Lydia stirred. She was lying near a fire covered with a blanket. In the flickering flames, she caught sight of the two men across from her but quickly shut her eyes and listened in on their conversation.

"I can't believe she walked this far and just waited for us," John Grinnel was saying. "What if we had decided to leave later?"

"I think she's crazy," Heiter said. "Where do you suppose she's headed?"

"I don't know, but she's desperate to get somewhere. In her state, she shouldn't be traveling at all."

Lydia heard their hushed comments and realized that they must now know she was pregnant.

"She needs a doctor."

"Where the hell do we find a doctor out here? Shit. I knew this woman was going to be trouble."

"You don't know nothing!" John Grinnel shot back. He was silent for a moment and then reprimanded his partner in a hushed voice. "Goddammit, get over this thing with your wife. Just because she left you doesn't mean every woman is like her. This woman needs help."

"She's crazy."

"She's not crazy. She's just determined."

A long silence followed until Heiter's response came. "Maybe you're right. What do we do? Take her back to Sioux Falls?"

"Gotta be a doctor in Flandreau. That can't be more than a few hours ahead."

Lydia opened her eyes and looked about.

"Miss Pearlman, are you all right?" John Grinnel asked.

She appeared as if in a daze. "Yes."

"We brewed some tea. Would you like some?"

"Yes."

John Grinnel poured tea into a metal cup, propped her up, placed the cup in her hands and helped her sip at it. "Thank you," she said. "Thank you both."

"We were worried about you," John Grinnel said. "How on earth did you get this far?"

"I walked," she answered. "I knew you were leaving at daybreak, so I left at midnight and walked as far as I could."

"Figuring that we would pick you up," he said.

"Of course."

John Grinnel shook his head in disbelief. Overnight, the temperatures most assuredly had dropped close to freezing. She wore a bonnet, but her only other protection was a shawl she'd wrapped about her. "You must have walked twenty miles, and you don't even have extra clothes."

"Oh, yes, I do," she finished. "I have a bag and some personal things."

"Where?"

"In the back of your wagon. I stashed it there last night before I left town. No sense carrying it."

John Heiter, the shorter of the two, grunted, "Jesus! She is determined!" And then his voice softened. "Where are you bound for?"

"Fort Lincoln." She thought a moment. "That's where my husband is stationed. He's an officer."

Both knew Fort Lincoln was near Bismarck, hundreds of

miles away, an incredible journey for a woman to be making alone. "Incredible," John Heiter said.

Over the next hour, she sipped more tea and ate some bread and salt pork that the men had brought along. That night she slept inside the Conestoga, where, according to what John Heiter had said the day before, there was not room for her. The men unfolded their bedrolls outside on the ground. In the morning, Lydia rose at the same time the other two did and, discreetly, she wandered off toward the river to find a place to relieve herself.

While she was gone, the two Johns discussed their wayward lady. "She looks pretty spry this morning for feeling so poorly last night," John Heiter remarked.

John Grinnel agreed. "Yes, she does. I ain't so sure she was even weak last night."

"You think she feigned it? If that's the case, I'd bet she ain't got no husband in Fort Lincoln, either."

"She's not wearing a wedding ring," John Grinnel answered. "Not that that means anything."

"But she's with child," Heiter said.

"Yes. I don't know what kind of game she's playing, but she's hell-bent on getting to Bismarck, and I don't think there's any stopping her, so it's probably best we help her get to Prairie. From there, she's on her own."

At the river, Lydia had washed her face and combed her hair, and when she returned, she looked refreshed and her cheeks were rosy. "You boys got a frying pan?"

"Yes, ma'am," Grinnel answered.

"If you'll get that fire built up, I'll have pancakes ready in twenty minutes." The two stared after her as she headed for the back of the wagon. "I got some nice ham, too. You boys like ham, don't you?"

★ ★ ★ ★ ★

May 2, 1876

To my dear Katrina,

I hope this letter reaches you in short time. I am told the mail path to Yankton is by means of the railroad to Minneapolis, and thence to you by the same means. I am presently in the town of Prairie, about 120 miles north of Sioux Falls. I regret that I was unable to send a letter before I left, but no one was headed your direction.

So much good fortune has befallen me. I cannot thank you enough for introducing me to this community. Often, I wondered what this small town had to offer, but in time, providence brought me Kellem Gates. I am so in love with this man. He asked me to marry him and asked that I seek passage to Fort Lincoln at my earliest convenience, which is the reason for this correspondence.

I considered waiting for you and Gerhard to arrive in the spring and hoped to ride back with you and find my way to Fort Lincoln by ferry. According to Herman Ziegenfuss, you were not due to arrive until mid-May, thus it might have been another month before I would be able to reach Fort Lincoln.

I am in a frenzy, so happy, and cannot wait to be in the loving arms of Kellem. Surely, you must know how I feel, as I am certain your feelings for Frank McCann must be very similar.

I managed to find travel with two survayors this far. They are both named John, but they are not at all two peas from the same pod. However, for the past four days, I cooked them biscuits or pancakes for breakfast. I even brought along a ham, ten eggs, a can of peaches and a pie, all which I procured from the hotel kitchen. Though these two may have been reluctant to take me on as a passenger,

I believe I queled their concerns by filling their stomachs.

Before I left, I did, however leave a note for Iver at the hotel indicating my intentions, thus I'm sure word will soon reach the ears of those who care and halt any gossip that I may have been kidnapped and left for dead somewhere on the prairie.

My intentions at this point are to continue northward until I reach the Northern Pacific railroad, which will convey me to my final destination. How I do that exactly is yet a mystery, but I shall find means.

Please convey my greetings to Gerhard, and don't worry about me. The Lord seems to provide. Should you write, please forward your letter to Fort Lincoln in care of Captain Kellem Gates. I shall write further whenever possible as I continue my journey. Thank you for all you have done for me.

With affection, Lydia

Outside the depot, and hanging from a chain on a post, a wood placard had Prairie Junction printed on it in elaborate black letters. A few hours earlier, Lydia had watched the two Johns and a railroad representative head west on the track, pumping a handcar. The Chicago and Northwestern track was nothing more than a spur line that ended fifteen miles away at a place called Lake Kampeska Station. Lydia surmised that the two Johns were probably going to survey the land to continue the line.

She had already posted her letter and left it in the depot, which was nothing more than a log hut along the tracks. A handful of small buildings made up this tiny jerkwater town of Prairie, and some hundred yards away, a railroad car on a side track depicted the only sign of life. A half dozen men were unloading lumber, most of it being stacked into a small warehouse, some of it being loaded into the back of a huge dray.

From a distance, it appeared all of the men were dressed in dark uniforms, as if they might have been railroad men, but, as she neared, she realized their jackets were just similar.

The men saw her coming, and for the last several of her steps, they all stopped working and fixed their eyes on her like a pack of wolves eyeing a lone sheep.

She felt a bit apprehensive. "Who's in charge here?"

One of the men stepped forward and removed his hat. "I might could help you."

"I'm looking for means of travel to Fort Lincoln."

The man stared back at her. "Ah, ma'am, afraid I don't know where Fort Lincoln is."

"Near Bismarck."

"Oh. I know where that is, but ain't nobody goin' there that I know of."

"I wouldn't expect to travel all the way," she clarified. "I'm just looking for passage in that direction."

The man glanced at the wagon. "Wilbur Cruzatte is headed north with this load of lumber." Lydia looked over the men, expecting that one of them was the man he was talking about, but none of them moved. "As far as Big Stone Lake," he added.

When she pulled a map from her bag and unfolded it, the head man poked a finger on a spot. "That there's Big Stone."

The map depicted where Big Stone led into Lake Traverse farther north. "Where will I find this Mr. Cruzatte?"

"At his usual place when he's in Prairie." She heard some chuckles from the other men when he said that. "He'd be at Carrie's Palace," the man said as he pointed toward a few buildings.

"Thank you," she said, as she walked off.

A rough sign hanging at a slant indicated the saloon. When

she entered, the man behind the bar put down the paper he was reading and fixed his eyes on her. She looked about. *Palace* was a misnomer for this clapboard-sided saloon. The bar was nothing more than a few planks above a kickboard, and the only place to sit was two small tables and a few chairs off to the side against a wall. A staircase led upward to a single door on the second floor.

"Ma'am?" the bartender asked with a strange look at her.

"I'm looking for Wilbur Cruzatte."

He nodded toward the corner. "That's him." The man at the table with a gray, grizzled beard was the only person in the place. His head was lying flat on the tabletop as if someone had slammed it there with a hammer, and his mouth was wide open. Boney fingers were wrapped tightly around an empty bottle.

She sat at the table. "Mr. Cruzatte?" she asked, but he didn't stir.

"Mr. Cruzatte?" she said again. When no response came, she looked over at the bartender. "When does this man wake up?"

"When he has good reason."

She looked over his crumpled figure and jiggled him. His floppy leather hat was worn beyond wearing, and although he had on a canvas jacket, most of it was patched.

"Have you any water?" she asked the bartender.

The bartender hesitated, knowing what her intention was, and then brought up a small pitcher from underneath the counter. "I don't know as I'd wake him that way."

"Well, I've got good reason." She returned to the drunken figure at the table and asked one more time. "Mr. Cruzatte?" She waited a few seconds and then poured the water over his head.

The old fellow abruptly jerked up, instinctively drew a pistol from his belt and blasted a shot upward. Inside the small room, the shot resounded like a cannon, and the recoil from the old dragoon revolver rocked him backward off his chair.

As he thumped against the floor, Lydia jumped back, startled by the reaction she had caused. Above her, heavy, acrid blue smoke from the weapon hung in air. Seconds later, the door to the bar flew open, and the same men who had been unloading the lumber charged in.

"Ain't nothin'," the bartender told the men. "Just Wilbur waking up with good reason."

Everyone was laughing except for Lydia and Wilbur.

"I don't believe this is at all funny," Lydia scolded them.

Their laughter subsided, but only momentarily. As the workers went out the door, she could hear them chuckling. When Wilbur's pistol fired, a young girl had come through the door at the top of the stairs. She was clad scantily in pantaloons, and after a short surveillance of the floor below, she turned and slammed the door shut.

The bartender was back at his paper, but he was cackling more than he was reading. Lydia guessed the event with the old man was all in fun. Obviously, this had happened before, and for a moment, she too, cracked a smile.

"He could have shot me," she said to the bartender.

"Shouldn't have waked him."

"I had good reason."

She waited patiently while the old man set his chair upright. He looked about with narrow, searching eyes, then shoved the pistol back in his belt and sat down across from her.

"Wilbur Cruzatte?" she inquired.

His eyes flicked from left to right. "Depends."

"On what?" she asked.

His voice was wary. "On what fer you want Wilbur."

"I need a ride to Big Stone Lake, and I understand you're taking a load of lumber that direction."

The old man licked his lips and stroked his beard. "What yer askin' fer is scout p'rtektion." His eyes opened wider, showing some interest.

She analyzed what he just said. "Yes, scout protection. And I'm willing to pay for such services."

His eyes widened even more. "In that case, I'm Wilbur."

"Can you escort me that far?" she asked.

"I could."

"How soon can we leave?"

"Soon's I get paid."

"How much would that be?"

Wilbur licked his lips again as he gave the question some real thought. "Four dollars flat."

As soon as she laid the money down, he scraped it up, stumbled to the bar and slapped it on the counter in exchange for two full bottles of whiskey. He turned to Lydia. "Got baggage?"

"At the depot."

"Got any grub? Scout p'rtection don't come without fixins."

"I've got some."

"Good 'nuff," he said as he stumbled out the door carrying a bottle in each hand. She followed him out.

As soon as the men finished loading the lumber in Wilbur's dray, he drove the four-mule wagon to the depot, where he stuck Lydia's bags behind the seat and helped her up.

She had no idea how far it was to Big Stone Lake, but she did know they were following a trail that kept the Manka River in sight most of the time.

"When do you expect us to arrive at Big Stone," she inquired.

"It's thirty-five miles. Late t'morrow night, if'n we don't get rain drenched."

"Rain drenched?" she inquired.

"Yep. Storm's a'brewin ahead o' us."

She looked where he was pointing and guessed he might be a little off in his weather forecasting. She couldn't see any clouds. However, when they came over the next high rise, she saw the dark haze on the horizon, and it did appear menacing.

"Rain ain't so bad long's it don't come in heaps."

She was paying attention. "And if it comes in heaps?"

"River swells. Got one river to cross a'fore we reach the south end of Big Stone. Gets messy with setch a heavy load."

Late in the afternoon, and even though they had another few hours of daylight left, Wilbur eyed the oncoming clouds and took precautions. He parked the wagon on a high rise among some trees, rolled a canvas off the top of the wagon and staked the ends to the ground. Although he unhitched the mules, he left the riggings on them and tied them to a picket line, which allowed them to graze. Back at the wagon, he dug a shallow pit. Lydia helped by gathering up some wood while he worked away, and in no time, Wilbur had a small fire going. He laid out another canvas on the ground and procured two blankets from his wagon. With canvas underneath her and another wrapped around three sides of the wagon, Lydia was surprised how warm and comfortable she was. When the first wave of rain hit, the two of them were protected fully from the onslaught.

Wilbur shared some beef jerky and hard biscuits with her, and after they ate, he whipped out the bottle of whiskey, uncorked it and threw down a heavy swallow.

He smacked his lips and shoved the cork in place. "Shore do thank you fer the four dollars fer the whiskey," he cackled. "Always like t' carry a bottle, though I never drink on the job."

"You're drinking now," she said.

He cackled, "Ain't on the job now."

He uncorked the bottle again and offered it to her, but she declined.

She never dreamed she would be riding out a rainstorm

underneath a wagon with an old-timer like Wilbur Cruzatte, but she did not worry. He was very gentlemanly and unusually quiet, at least initially.

Thunder cracked only yards away as a flash of lightning ripped along the hillside. Wilbur glanced out at his mules. "They're still there."

As he took another shot from the bottle, she pulled the blanket up about her neck and inquired when they would be underway again. Wilbur shrugged and said he wouldn't consider hitching up the wagon until the road dried out.

"Grounds too soft. Mules couldn't pull her," he complained.

There was no doubt he was right. Sitting under the wagon watching the relentless rain pouring down gave her time to think about her task at hand. Wilbur took advantage of her mood and asked where she was headed. When she told him Fort Lincoln to join her captain, his face shined. He had spent twelve years in the military as a cavalryman, and he knew where many of the forts throughout the Dakotah Territory were located.

When she produced her map, he pointed a finger at a spot on the Missouri. "That there's where an Injun got the best of me. Thought I kilt him dead, but he rosed up and smacked me good with a stone mallet. Some thought I'd never recover." He pulled off his hat and showed her a knob half the size of an egg, where the mallet had split his head open. " 'Course, he thunked he kilt me dead, too, but I fooled 'im.

"Spent a half year recuperatin' in Bismarck till the army booted me out." His mind wandered off. "Damn, them was good days."

She wondered how those could be good days, especially after he had spent six months recovering from a wound, but something he said must have triggered a pleasant memory, since a smile remained on his face for the longest time.

They pulled out on the third day with the morning sun hard in their eyes, and later that day, they left the dirt road where the Manka River swung to the east. Inside of an hour they reached another small river that had swelled far beyond its banks.

Wilbur looked over the area. "That's what I was a'feared a'. Gonna be another three or four days a'fore we c'n ford this overgrown creek."

He poked in the back of his wagon bed. "Ain't much left back here t' eat. Looks like I'm gonna need to shoot somethin' fer our next meal." He pulled a carbine from behind the seat. "Hope you ain't got nothin' agin eatin' skunk or badger."

She made a face that gave him a hearty laugh.

While he was gone, she bathed in the cold rushing water of the stream, and as she sat on a rock shivering and waiting to dry off, she ran her hands over her protruding stomach, thinking up names.

If it was a boy, she liked the name Caleb, since it began with the same initial sound as Kellem, and if it was a girl, she had already picked out Katrina.

She had dressed and had a fire going when Wilbur returned with a small deer, already gutted. She had a voracious appetite, and Wilbur could not believe how much she was eating.

She noted his curious look. "I'm eating for two," she said as she patted her stomach.

As she bit into some more meat, he cackled, "Judging by the way you're chomping that tender loin, I'd guess you was eatin' fer three or four."

She loved the way he laughed.

A few days later when the water receded, they crossed the small creek and finally reached the south shore of Big Stone Lake. It had taken them eight days to cover thirty-five miles.

TWENTY

Gerhard and Katrina arrived in Sioux Falls with the first spring freight load of supplies and stopped in front of the Ziegenfuss Mercantile just as Herman came out to greet them.

"I know you come this week," Herman said as he pointed a finger at his temple. "I feel it up here."

After a few handshakes and greetings for the rest of the family, Katrina singled out Wolfgang. "Wolf, run up to the hotel and tell Lydia we've arrived."

"She's not here, Miss Katrina. She left about a month ago."

The news stunned Katrina. "For where?"

Wolfgang shrugged. "I think for Fort Lincoln. I know Mr. Bjornson at the hotel has a letter for you."

Katrina wasted no time getting to the hotel, and when she entered, Iver was behind the counter and knew why she had come. He pulled a letter from underneath his desk and handed it over. "Miss Dvorak," he greeted.

She tore open the envelope and pulled the letter from within.

Dearest Katrina,

I penned this letter on April 29th, knowing that this news will fall into your hands at a much later date. I know you will rejoice along with me to learn that Kellem has asked me to marry him. He sent money and requested that I find passage to Fort Lincoln at my earliest convenience. Herman informed me that you would be arriving perhaps in mid May, but my heart lies with Kellem, and I simply could not wait that long.

Please don't be angry with me. I had no way of informing you of my intentions. God willing, I will find safe passage northward with two surveyors as far as Prairie. From there I hope to find means of travel to the railroad, which will take me to Bismarck.

Along the way, I shall write whenever means of posting a letter is possible. If all goes well, I should reach Fort Lincoln by early June.

I ask you not to worry about me. I shall endure this long journey, no matter what hardships may lie ahead.

> With affection, Lydia

When Katrina finished reading, she looked up at Iver. "She said she found passage northward with two surveyors."

Iver grimaced in thought. "There were two surveyors here at the hotel some time back."

"And you didn't try to stop her?"

"Miss Dvorak," he said apologetically. "One morning, she simply was gone. There were a few items in her room, but her traveling bag was gone. No one in town knows what happened to her. I discovered the letter inside my desktop a few days after she disappeared, and it was mixed in with some other letters, as if she didn't want me to find it immediately. And since it was addressed to you, I certainly had no right to open it."

"You are perfectly right, Iver," Katrina admitted.

"We're all worried about her. What shall I tell everyone?"

Katrina felt the same apprehension Iver was experiencing. "If anyone inquires, simply tell them she found passage to Fort Lincoln."

"But did she really?" Iver asked.

"I wish I knew."

★ ★ ★ ★ ★

That evening Katrina and Gerhard finished up their meal in the Cataract Hotel dining room. Gerhard had already read the letter from Lydia. He sat back in his chair with a glum face, staring down at his wineglass. "I don't understand, Katya," he said, using her familiar name. "What you think? Iver say the two surveyors leave town without her. But she say she travel with them."

"I don't understand, either, Gerhard. All I know is that love is powerful and on occasion it causes one to do crazy things."

They both laughed, both reminiscing. A few years back, Katrina had found passage with Gerhard to the Greenwood Indian Agency to visit her son. On the way back to Yankton in a wagon, a sudden thunderstorm forced them into a wayside inn. It was a moment in time when a streak of passion sprang into Katrina's life, and Gerhard just happened to be the lucky bystander. It was a one-night affair, never to be repeated, but the two had remained friends after the incident.

Katrina saw that strange gleam in his eye. "I know what you're thinking," she said to him.

Gerhard chuckled. "You see. That is what Lydia was thinking."

Katrina smiled. "She's pregnant. What a brave, stupid girl to travel in her condition." She opened a small pad in which she maintained notes and thumbed through a few pages. "Today's the fifteenth," she said. "I wonder where Lydia is right now." She paused. "I hope she's safe."

"Mr. Reed," Lydia summoned the man at the wheel of the paddleboat. "I have to relieve myself again."

Leonard Reed frowned, and when he did so, the seven teeth he possessed showed yellow and jagged. A bushy gray and red speckled beard almost hid his face, and a mop of tangled hair poked out from underneath an old seaman's cap. He was dressed somewhat like Wilbur: shaggy jacket, patched pants and high knee boots worn beyond normal use.

Leonard looked over at Wilbur. "Woman's gotta pee ever' hour."

"Can we please go to shore, Mr. Reed?"

"Ain't no more goin' ashore," Leonard said. "Got time to make up fer. You gotta pee, pee off the side like us men."

"I'm not equipped to pee like you men," she shot back.

"She's pregnant," Wilbur interjected. "Pregnant women pee mor'n unpregnant women. Leonard, you gotta have some compassion."

"Shee-it," Leonard said as he spat out some brown goo. Most of it hung on his beard as he handed her a gallon can. "If'n you gotta pee, take this and squat yerself behind the lumber."

She looked at the lumber wagon. There was no way she could hide on this small paddleboat. "I require privacy," she said.

"Shee-it," Leonard relented. "Okay, we'll give you privacy."

He and Wilbur turned their backs and stared off at the shore.

Lydia had no other choice. She hoisted her skirt, sneaked the bucket underneath and commenced to let her water run.

At that moment, the engine coughed again, and with a final blast of black smoke, it stopped.

"Shee-it," said Leonard as he released a valve that sent hot steam shooting upwards like a daytime firework display. He frantically whirled some wheels and opened a spigot that blew out more steam.

He gave a terse look at Lydia, who was still squatting over the bucket.

"I know, shee-it," she said mimicking Leonard's tone. Wilbur cackled for the longest time, but Leonard didn't think it was funny.

He opened the fire door to let the boiler cool down and

waited a half hour, cussing every minute before he even entertained putting a wrench to the engine. They spent most of the day floating on the Big Stone before Leonard was once again able to stoke the boiler with wood and get the steam engine running.

That evening, they reached the narrow channel that ran between Big Stone and Lake Traverse. Wilbur was to deliver the lumber to a fellow named Martin Jonason, who had a small sod house at the north end of this channel. At this time of the year, the channel was scarcely over two feet deep, barely deep enough to allow Leonard's paddleboat passage. Leonard confessed that on more than one occasion, he had been stranded in one lake or the other and had to wait for rain before he could cross.

"Yessir," he said. "This channel's usually dryer than a one-hump camel what sprunged a leak." Lydia burst out laughing at the comment, and Leonard, as stoic as he usually was, smiled, happy with his own little joke.

Unable to maneuver in the dark, Leonard halted the boat along the shore, where they planned to spend the night. He ran a plank from the bow to solid ground, and as Lydia carefully made her way along it, Leonard graciously removed his hat and bowed. "Hope you have a comfortable pee, Miss Lydia."

Wilbur followed behind, holding Lydia's hand, cackling as he went.

May 18th, 1876

My dearest Katrina,

This letter comes to you from a paddleboat somewhere on Lake Traverse. There is no way to forward mail in this godforsaken area, but I shall pen my thoughts to wile away the boredom I am experiencing and post this letter later on.

I am now thinking I should have waited in Sioux Falls

and traveled back to Yankton with you and Gerhard. But of course, I could not have known that at the time. I managed to seek passage with a wagonload of lumber from Prairie to Big Stone Lake. Wilbur Cruzatte is the driver. If a heavy rain hadn't hampered our travel, he might have remained sober for most of the trip.

Somewhere short of Big Stone, we bogged the lumber wagon down while crossing a creek. Wilbur had to transfer the lumber one board at a time to the opposite shore in order to lessen the load. I helped until I felt a terrible cramp. While I rested Wilbur unhitched the mules, and from shore, the mules pulled the wagon over with a corral rope. That night I noticed I passed some blood.

Along the way, I learned that Wilbur is delivering this lumber further north by way of Big Stone Lake, which I was excited to hear. We waited another two days on shore until a paddleboat showed up. Wilbur ran the entire lumber wagon onto the boat and then left his mules to graze freely until he returns. Traveling on the river is comfortable, but the engine breaks down quite often, and now we have been moored on shore for the past three days. I would make better time if I walked, but if I exert myself, quite often I feel almost faint. I am sure it is because I'm carrying this child, still it is a joy to feel my stomach roll when this little one inside decides to exercise.

Leonard Reed is the owner of this paddleboat but it is nothing more than a flat raft with no sides. His clothes should have been burned a year ago, and he obviously has not bathed for several months. He has bad teeth and bad breath and his favorite word is shee-it, which is quite adequate, since that is how he smells. He's an older fellow, like Wilbur. As crude as both seem in appearance, they treat me well, and they can be so funny at times. Wilbur shoots game, so we do not fret for meat. Leonard has makings for pancakes, but I make sure he at least washes his hands before he starts cooking.

We were supposed to deliver the lumber at the entrance to Lake Traverse at a sod house that belongs to a man named Martin Jonason, but when we arrived, a note said Wilbur was to deliver it to the north end of the lake instead. I worried that his mules would be gone when he returned, but he didn't seem concerned. Time doesn't mean much around here.

I now hear the engine running once again. I shall continue this letter at a later date.

May 20th

We managed to cover about two miles and the engine quit again. As a result, Leonard's cussing vocabulary has increased considerably. Something on the paddle wheel broke which was good, because Leonard had to strip down and crawl into the water to fix it. I have never seen such white skin on a man. He has a big belly and a tiny butt, and he was so hairy I could not see anything else. Wilbur asked him if an Indian had scalped him of his private parts. I laughed so hard I almost wet myself. Wilbur says if the engine isn't working by tomorrow, he will go across country and borrow a team of horses from somewhere and we will drive the lumber wagon the rest of the way. Leonard is taking this boat on to the Bois de Sioux River which leads to the Red. From there, he says I can take a steamboat to Fargo. I hope he is right.

Wilbur fished for part of the day and caught some purches, or something like that and a good sized pike. They are very tasty and a welcome change in food.

This is not a godforsaken country, like I penned before. It is my impatience that occasionally blinds me to the surrounding beauty. This lakeshore is laden with reeds and flowers from lilly pads that are starting to bloom and the water is so blue. We drink out of it daily. A slight breeze over the water cools me when it is hot. The sun is so grandiose and so orange in the early morning, and from a nearby hill, I can see for miles. There is a freshness and beauty about this country that is enticing. I have seen no farms or any other signs of life, which is very strange. Wilbur and Leonard said they would live nowhere else, and I am beginning to understand why. One needs to experience the solitude of this land to really enjoy it. It takes very little imagination to visualize teepees here where Indians must have once lived.

Time goes by slowly for me, but Wilbur and Leonard are never in a hurry to go anywhere. It is a lonely time, but I tolerate it by thinking of Kellem and knowing that this journey will eventually bring me to him. Though he is hundreds of miles away, he invades my thoughts so easily.

Last night I woke to hear wolves howling and an owl was somewhere nearby. Every time I heard a fish jump in the water, I nearly came out of my skin. I don't think either Wilbur or Leonard heard any of it. If I slept enough nights in the open, perhaps I would get used to the night sounds too.

It is pleasing to write about that which surrounds me. It is like a remedy of sorts, a kind of freedom I've never experienced before, and it helps me pass the time. I must be starting to sound syrupy. I miss you. I miss a lot of things.

In the early morning, Leonard filled the boiler with wood, fired up the engine, and they continued northward. By late morning, Lydia felt lazy from the warm sun and slipped under the shade of the wagon to rest. The constant thumping of the paddlewheel had a mesmerizing effect on her, a soothing rhythm that allowed her to easily doze off.

She had no idea how long she had been sleeping, but suddenly she heard a voice saying something like, "Waschichu . . . Waschichu squaw. Waschichu . . ."

Hearing this strange voice so near her, she woke to be staring into the face of an Indian.

She shrieked a godawful scream, and in return, the Indian let out a war cry as shrill as hers. As she jerked up, she realized the Indian was in a canoe alongside the paddleboat, and now he was laughing loudly.

She looked into the faces of Wilbur and Leonard, who were bent over in hysterics.

"My God!" she yelled as she jumped to her feet. "You are the rotten scum of the earth. You two are nothing more than . . ." She stopped, unable to interrupt the laughing spell of the three men. Tears were rolling out of their eyes.

A few minutes passed before they finally contained themselves. Leonard and Wilbur both spoke the Indian's language and conversed for some time, until Leonard eventually made some sort of trade with the Indian. They were still laughing when the Indian pushed off in his canoe and headed back to shore.

Lydia was surprised to see several teepees spread out in some trees. More canoes lined the shoreline and beyond them, a few Indian women sat on the ground near fires. From somewhere, she could hear youngsters yelling, and then she saw them chasing after a dog.

"They're Sioux," said Wilbur as he saw her steady stare at the camp. "Sisseton Sioux. That buck what come up was Red Bear, one of the head warriors."

"What did he want?" she asked.

"Tobacco."

"What for?" she inquired.

"T' smoke," Wilbur answered. He looked after the Indian, who was now reaching shore. " 'Course, it helps get us through their territory without losing our scalps."

He wandered over to Leonard, and as the two waved at some youngsters, she wondered if Wilbur really meant what he said about scalps.

May 23

I feel as though I am writing a journal. I had my first Indian scare a few days ago. Wilbur and Leonard had an Indian wake me up from a deep sleep. I know I screamed, but it was all in fun, as everyone laughed except me.

I have had some good fortune. Wilbur expected to leave the lumber here at the north shore of Lake Traverse, but another message said that the recipient had decided to move to Breckenridge on the Red River, so we are presently moving up the Bois de Sioux. That message was stuck on a willow branch. Can you imagine such a way to communicate?

Wilbur said this fellow named Jonason could have sent the lumber by the St. Paul railroad, which would have taken the load directly to Breckenridge, but of course, no one knew that at the time. It is lucky for me, though, since I have a smooth ride the entire distance.

This is such flat country. How anybody can live off of it is a mystery to me. Whenever we stop for whatever reason, I can walk up a bank and see for miles in every direction. I can't believe how treeless the plains are. Once a few Indian boys on horseback spotted us and followed along the shoreline shouting. They wanted to trade for guns, but Wilbur and Leonard wouldn't do it, so the youngsters shook their lances and bows and shouted something that made Wilbur mad. He drew his pistol and fired it in the air and they rode off. I worried that we might be attacked later, but my two brave escorts assured me we would not have trouble.

The Bois de Sioux and the lesser Ottertail River formed the headwaters of the Red. The size of the town of Breckenridge surprised Lydia. Several city blocks extended east into Minnesota, and a few main thoroughfares ran roughly north–south. As the raft moved effortlessly along, she was amazed by the number of small businesses she could see. Harness shops, boots and shoemakers, meat markets, hardware, lumber yards, farm machinery, and numerous hotels and restaurants dotted the landscape. This town was a metropolis compared to Sioux Falls, but as Wilbur explained, five years earlier, this had become the western-most point of the St. Paul and Pacific Railroad, which made Breckenridge a major distribution center for goods in many directions.

"Lucky it's spring," Wilbur informed her. "Water's up. Sometimes the river's so low, ain't no steamer c'n make the journey." As soon as they docked, Wilbur escorted her to the Hyser Hotel near the railroad yards, where she took a room. No one knew for sure when the next steamboat from downriver was due, so she had no choice but to lay over until it arrived.

Her hotel room was rather good-sized, and recognizing that Lydia was pregnant, the proprietor was every bit a gentleman. He arranged to have a bathtub brought to her room and filled it with hot water. It was the first decent bath she'd had since she left Sioux Falls. She sank into the tub and soaked until the water turned lukewarm. Afterward, she washed what few dresses and underclothes she had in the tub's tepid water and hung her belongings to dry on wooden wall pegs. That night, she slept as soundly as she could remember.

Morning came quickly, and as she was finishing up her breakfast, Wilbur and Leonard entered the dining area.

"We found Jonason and we's all unloaded," Wilbur said. He stood next to her, his hat in his hand, an almost forlorn look on his face. "Well, I s'pect we'll be heading back. My mules prob'ly runned off to Minneapolis by now."

"I want to thank you boys for all your help," she said as she rose from the table. The glum look remained on Wilbur's face, and then to her surprise, he threw his arms arm around her and hugged her.

"We's gonna miss you, Miss Lydia," he said. He seemed on the verge of tears as he stepped back.

Leonard pulled off his cap, opened his arms and delivered a big bear hug. When the two left the hotel, Lydia stood at the window, watching as they ambled toward the river where the raft was moored. When they pushed off from shore, she stepped outside onto the boardwalk, gave a wave and saw them raise their caps in return.

The proprietor was standing behind her. "You must'a made an impression on them two. Ain't never seen 'em so sentimental."

It struck Lydia that she would probably never see either one again. In the distance, the raft moved along at an easy pace, the empty lumber wagon on board, the shuffling sound of the paddlewheel now almost inaudible. She'd had no idea that the short time she spent with them must have created a lasting memory.

The hugs she had received from each suddenly took on more meaning.

"I'll miss you boys, too," she whispered.

Three days passed before a small steamboat arrived from Fargo.

Lydia packed what few belongings she possessed. She had
acquired some food to take along. When she approached the
desk to pay her bill, the proprietor greeted her with a huge
smile.

"Your bill's been taken care of," he said.

She was stunned. "By who?"

"Wilbur and Leonard."

Her mouth hung open. "But they're gone, and they had no
idea how many days I'd be here."

He was still smiling. "Makes no difference. Next time they
show up, they'll take care of it."

"I can't let them do that."

"They can be ornery cusses. If I let you pay, they'd be all
over me next time I see 'em. I'll help you with your bags, if you
like."

The proprietor placed her bags in a wagon and helped her up
on the seat. A driver whisked her off to the Red, some distance
away, and the boat that she boarded was first class compared to
Leonard's raft. It was thirty feet long and ten feet wide, with a
roof for protection and a stack that bellowed black smoke like a
railroad engine. This boat did not haul much freight by any
means, but it was easy transportation, and it only made the
round trip from Breckenridge to Fargo about four months out
of the year, and only when the area enjoyed a wet season. As the
boat left Breckenridge, she learned that the Red was one of the
few rivers that flowed north, and that it snaked its way all the
way to Winnipeg, Canada.

Less than an hour away from the city, the boat passed Fort
Abercrombie. She could see nothing more than a high wall of
posts circling the compound, but as the boat slid beneath a high
bank on which the blockhouse stood, several soldiers were
splashing in the river, naked to the waist. Spotting Lydia, they
whistled and waved, and she heard one of them holler out,

"Take me with you!"

It was then she realized that she was the only lady on the boat, and she suddenly felt special. Seeing these soldiers reminded her of Kellem, and over the next few miles, she remained teary-eyed.

June 1, 1876

Dearest Katrina,

I have reached Fargo safe and sound by steamboat and am staying at the Headquarters Hotel, a huge three story building. I shall be leaving tomorrow by train for Fort Lincoln, but first I must bring you up to date. I reached Breckenridge where I had my first warm bath in a month. I'm surprised I did not have any fleas or lice on me.

Wilbur and Leonard paid my hotel bill! They must have discovered something in me that I wasn't even aware of. When I reached my room, I honestly cried I was so happy. Those two were so genuine and so good to me in spite of the jokes and fun they played on me, and I shall miss them.

Tomorrow begins the final leg of my journey. I can hardly wait to see Kellem. I have inquired from those here at the hotel on Front Street what the landscape is like near Bismarck. I understand the Missouri River bottom is filled with lush trees and that the fort itself lies on the west bank of the river among rolling hills. Hills will be a welcome change from this flat landscape I have traveled for the past several weeks. I heard that I probably will see buffalo as I travel west.

I am excited and at the same time somewhat apprehensive. I'm sure military life will offer a challenge but I'm looking forward to it. I know I speak for Kellem as well when I say we would be delighted to have you visit us in our new home should your travel schedule allow.

I sometimes feel faint which I am sure is typical for a woman with child. I know once I get settled, I will regain some strength. Fargo is so flat and without trees like Yankton, and from my third floor hotel room I can see all around, but there is not much to see. The businesses are to the north and I can see one church steepal. Moorhead is across the river, but I am told it is mostly saloons.

I hope someday to meet your friend Frank. Be sure to greet him and Gerhard. I hope all is well with you. As soon as I post this letter and the many pages that preceded it, I shall look forward to another good night's rest. I shall write again when I reach Bismarck.

Affectionately yours,
Lydia

TWENTY-ONE

Although Bismarck was less than two hundred miles from Fargo, and though the train moved at a moderate pace, it stopped every few miles to take on water and fuel. The stops became monotonous with sometimes twenty to thirty minutes spent standing still. It was not until the train reached Jamestown that Lydia bothered to depart, mainly to stretch and find a good meal.

The depot contained a dining area that was not unlike the railroad restaurant in which Lydia used to work, and as she sat waiting for her meal, she saw two men at a table, both wearing long coats. Her mind wandered back to the time when the two train robbers had entered to eat a steak dinner at the restaurant station in St. Louis. She recollected their names were Jesse and Frank Woodson—or so they said.

Good thoughts of her best friends, Colleen and Selma, remained in her memory for the longest time. She now wondered if Selma was still working in the station, and if Colleen still helped her husband in the dry-goods store. She decided that when she reached Bismarck, she would send a letter to them.

Her mind skipped to Calvin Jefferson and his family. She had no way of knowing where Calvin had escaped to and whether he was safe or not.

For the next few minutes, she sat unmoving, recollecting

those years in St. Louis, focusing on the good times rather than the worst.

"Ma'am?" the lady serving the food said.

Lydia snapped out of her daydream and picked up a fork. She ate a few bites, but then suddenly, her appetite was gone. She set the plate aside and sipped at the tea until she figured it was time to return to the train.

As she stood, she felt a charge of liquid between her thighs and quickly made her way to a toilet, where she examined herself. Finding spots of blood on her underclothes, she cleaned herself up as best she could, and then made her way back to the train and entered the passenger car.

For the next several hours, the train continued its rhythmic motion, stopping at the various sidings. She was told the train would require about seventeen stops, and as they pulled into Crystal Springs, well over half the distance, she peered outside onto a bleak setting. As far as she could see, the plains spread out in a vast empty expanse. She had expected to see some buffalo by now, but someone had remarked that the great herds were far to the north at this time. She could not remotely guess what a great herd count might mean, but she assumed maybe in the thousands.

After a few more stops, she summoned the conductor and asked how many more fuel stops the train needed to make until they reached Bismarck.

"This is our fourteenth siding. Only three more," he answered. He leaned over and noticed that her eyes had momentarily slipped shut. "Are you feeling all right, ma'am? You look kinda pale."

"I do feel a bit faint."

He left and a short time later returned with a younger lady, who brought some water for her. "Drink this," the lady said. "You'll feel better."

Lydia brought the glass to her lips and sighed as she nodded. The cold water did feel refreshing. "What's your name?" she asked.

"Halona."

"I'm Lydia."

Halona placed her hand on Lydia's forehead and felt her cheeks. "I think you have a slight fever."

Lydia stiffened and pressed herself back into the seat, working hard to get her breath. "I was unable to eat at our last stop. Perhaps that's why I feel so weak." She arched her back and held her stomach, and then she groaned a long, heavy breath.

Halona saw the torment in her face and smelled the discharge. She slid her hand under Lydia's dress, and when she drew it back, it was covered with blood.

"Sir!" she beckoned to the conductor. "I need warm water and towels! This lady is going to have a baby!"

Halona scooted Lydia down on the seat to make her more comfortable and lifted her skirt. As she did so, others in the passenger car stood up to see what the sudden attention was.

Halona glared back at them. "In the name of courtesy, please give this lady some privacy!"

An older lady suddenly was at Halona's side. "I can help, dearie," she said. "I've delivered many a little one into this world."

As the train moved on, Lydia's screams drowned out the metallic clank of the wheels against the track. The car swayed rhythmically back and forth, and throughout the car, one could hear her screams interspersed with "Kellem, Kellem, Kellem!"

"What's she saying?" inquired the older lady.

"I don't know," Halona responded. She carefully eased her hands under Lydia's dress and pulled at her underclothes. "Just lie easy," Halona soothed her. "Take deep breaths and just lie easy and everything will be all right."

The older lady gave Halona a questioning look, and in return, Halona simply dipped her eyes and shook her head.

When Lydia awoke, her vision was blurred. She saw nothing more than a white haze. She turned her head slowly, somehow thinking she would be glancing out of the train window, but then she realized she was in a room somewhere. She could hear voices, murmurs, from some distance away.

Moments later, her eyes began to focus, and she was staring up at a white ceiling.

In front of her, a face appeared, a lady with red hair. "Selma?" Lydia inquired.

The face stared back, having heard the name. "Lydia, I'm Halona, remember? Halona. We met on the train."

"Where am I?" Lydia asked, her voice trailing off as if a wind had whisked it away.

"You're in a hospital," Halona answered. Lydia's eyes slipped shut momentarily and they slowly opened again.

"Do you know who I am?" Halona asked.

"You're Selma," came the weak answer.

"You've lost a lot of blood, but you're in good care now. Do you understand?"

Lydia's eyes opened fully as she tried to raise herself up, but the weakness pulled her back down. "My baby?"

Halona looked at her with sorrow and slowly shook her head from side to side. "I'm sorry, darling."

Halona expected that Lydia would break into tears, but her eyes remained wide open, her face now placid and white, as if her entire life had drained away. She choked as if to cry, and her lips quivered, but no tears formed in her eyes. And then her eyes slipped shut again.

A doctor was suddenly at Halona's side and saw that Lydia had fallen back into unconsciousness. Halona had tried to save the baby, but the train was still a few hours away from Bismarck, and keeping the little one warm had presented a problem. Even if Lydia had been awake and alert after the baby came into the world, her milk had not dropped, and there was no way the baby could acquire any nourishment.

From the very onset, it was a bad scene. Halona knew it, since she herself was a nurse. She guessed the baby was born a few months prematurely, and even under the best circumstances, the chance of it surviving would have been very slim.

"Not much we can do," said the doctor to Halona. "What do you know about her?"

"Nothing," Halona answered. "She thinks I'm Selma, whoever that is. All I know is she was traveling alone. The conductor on the train said Bismarck was her destination."

"When she wakes again, she may still be delirious, but see what you can learn. There must be somebody she was coming to see."

Another day and a half passed before Lydia stirred again. Halona, along with her other duties in the hospital, had been constantly checking on her. It might well be, she was thinking, that Lydia had relatives or friends in Bismarck, but for now, the girl was all alone. It was innate in Halona's nature for her to pay particular attention to those patients who seemed to have nowhere else to turn.

"Feeling better?" Halona asked Lydia as she grasped her hand.

Lydia, her face yet pale, seemed to be staring off into nowhere, and then she said, "You're Halona."

"Yes. You were calling me Selma for some reason. Who's Selma?"

Lydia forced a slight smile. "I worked with Selma in St. Louis. You have beautiful red hair just like her. Your face is a bit thinner, but your eyes are the same. You could easily pass for her sister.

"But you're prettier," she added.

The compliment did not cause Halona to blush in the least. She wasn't sure that the young girl before her was totally grasping reality.

"Do you know where you are?" Halona asked.

"Yes. In a hospital."

"And you remember what happened?"

"Yes. I lost the baby. Was it a boy?"

"Yes."

"I thought so."

Halona knew Lydia was now living in the real world. "We've got to get some nourishment into you. Do you think you could take some warm soup?"

"I'll try."

Halona patted her hand as she stood up. She disappeared for some time and returned with a tray, and after propping Lydia up, she began to spoon-feed her. While Lydia ate, Halona was running things through her mind. She noticed that Lydia did not have a ring on her finger, yet she did not want to probe into her life. She was sure that in due time, Lydia would open up, but even after taking nearly a bowl full of chicken soup, mostly broth, Lydia simply pushed herself back against the pillow and let her eyes gaze upward.

As Halona took away the tray, Lydia looked about the room. A few other women occupied beds, none of them stirring at the moment. A window was across from her, but all she could see were leaves from a tree. She was in Bismarck, she knew, which meant she was near Kellem. The thought of him sent tears rushing to her eyes. She kept from sobbing, but internally she felt her heart break. Without a child, she wondered if his affection for her would change.

In due time, Halona returned to the open bay, and after assisting some of the other women, she made her way to Lydia's bedside.

"You're looking so much better," Halona said.

"My hair must be a mess," Lydia responded.

Halona smiled. "I just happen to have a comb with me. Would you like me to comb your hair?"

"I would."

Halona propped her up, and with her soft hands, she began running a comb through her hair.

Lydia closed her eyes and savored the moment. "You've been good to me. I have a favor of you, if you will?"

"Of course."

"Captain Kellem Gates is stationed at Fort Lincoln. Could you get word to him that I am here?"

"I heard you say that name on the train. Is he your husband?"

"No," Lydia instinctively answered. She hesitated. "Yes," then said, "No."

The warm smile in Halona's face was comforting for Lydia. "I understand," Halona whispered. "Your secret is my secret."

Relief flooded Lydia. "Thank you. And thank you for combing my hair. It reminds me of the many times I combed my auntie's hair back in St. Louis." For the next several minutes, Lydia rambled on about the friends she had left behind in that river city, of her travels up the Missouri and her eventually reaching Yankton and Sioux Falls. She discreetly left out all the reasons that had forced her to move from one place to another. If Halona was able to fill in the answers, Lydia did not care. She had come through a lot in the past year, and now all she could think about was Kellem.

"I can't believe you traveled all the way here from Sioux Falls by yourself," Halona remarked. "Especially under the circumstances."

"I probably shouldn't have," Lydia said. "My baby might still be alive."

"We'll leave that to God's judgment," Halona comforted. "There are some things in our lives we have no control of."

"And you believe that's God's judgment?" Lydia asked.

"It's as good a place as any to leave unanswered questions. Some things good happen to us as we go through life, and some things bad happen. Living with the good memories is easy, but dragging all the unfortunate events along with us until we die is a heavy burden."

When Halona left, Lydia pondered her words. They were reflective, to an extent, of the same kind words and philosophy that Katrina had instilled within her. She was indeed fortunate to have run across Halona.

She wondered if she was married.

Across from Lydia, a strong ray of inviting sunshine beamed through a window. She sat up as high as she could in hopes that she might be able to see outside, but she couldn't. She swung her feet off the bed to the floor and intended to walk across to the window, but as she tried to stand, she felt her legs wobble. A shooting sensation whirled in her head, a dizziness she could not control.

She eased herself down on the bed, lay back against the pillow, and as soon as the spinning in her head settled, she closed her eyes and welcomed the sleep that awaited her.

During the next two days, Lydia's condition improved considerably. Though still weak, she was able to get up and walk about the hospital for short periods of time. The balcony, where she would sit and stare off across the Missouri at the fresh green countryside, had become her favorite resting place. The days were warm, the sun pleasant, and the air fresh with the aroma of flowers from somewhere nearby. She was told that Fort

Lincoln lay beyond the river in and among some rolling hills that were dotted with thickets of trees. Though she could not see any of the buildings, she knew that somewhere beyond the rising hills was where her Kellem was stationed.

Halona had made contact with an officer at the fort and assured Lydia that information regarding Captain Gates would be forthcoming. As Lydia sat on the balcony, she caught sight of Halona down below, and for just a second she glimpsed a soldier walking beside her, but before Lydia could get a good look, the two had already entered the front door below her.

Her heart pounded for the next minute until Halona appeared from behind her, but the officer who accompanied her was not Kellem. He was a young-looking man with a clean-shaven face and thick blond hair, a handsome fellow.

Halona introduced him as Major Hodges. He had already removed his hat and gloves and offered a hand to Lydia.

"Miss Pearlman, I am pleased to make your acquaintance." His voice was soft and pleasing, and now, up close, she could see that his eyes were deep gray, like Kellem's. "I know Captain Gates personally, and in fact, he gave me this letter to present to you upon your arrival."

He handed her a sealed envelope. Lydia let her gaze drop to the envelope and she shuddered involuntarily. Her mind reflected on Kellem and the wonderful few days they had spent together. It had been over seven months since they had shared their private moments together, and not an hour passed by when she didn't think of him. After traveling several hundred miles to reach him, all she had was this letter. She had so counted on gazing upon his face by this time.

The major saw the sorrow that came over her and was most cordial as he spoke. "It is unfortunate that we must meet here in a hospital. Your friend, Miss Halona, informed me that you had a severe case of the grippe while en route, but I trust you are feeling much better?"

Lydia eyed Halona, pleased with the reason she had given the officer for her hospital stay. "Yes, I'm convalescing very well, thank you. Is Kellem all right?"

"Yes, but he is off on assignment and regrets that he was not here to personally meet you. Of course, he had no knowledge when you would arrive. I can only assume that his letter will provide you with more details."

Lydia was torn with frustration. "When you say 'off on assignment,' what does that mean?"

"He was assigned to the Seventh Cavalry under General Custer. The troops left Fort Lincoln about three weeks ago."

"For where?" she inquired.

"Ma'am, I don't exactly have an answer to that. Their mission is to return the Indians to their reservations."

"I don't understand," Lydia said. She realized that was the same phrase she had delivered to Kellem so many months ago, when she inquired about the Indian settlement problem.

Major Hodges, his forehead deeply wrinkled, was about to answer, but before he could even utter a word, Lydia interrupted, "I know, you don't quite understand, either."

He seemed amused. "Strangely enough, those are my exact sentiments. Miss Lydia, if I can be of any assistance in your comfort, you are free to call on me. I shall be at your disposal."

"Thank you, and thank you for delivering this letter."

The major gave a gracious bow, and as Halona escorted him back to the interior of the hospital, Lydia opened the envelope and retrieved the letter. Along with it was a small sum of money.

May 16, 1876

My dearest Lydia,

By the time this letter is in your hands, you obviously will have reached Fort Lincoln. I know that my good friend and confidant, Major Tom Hodges, will make every endeavor to see that this message arrives safely. Our cavalry unit leaves tomorrow, and even as you read this letter, we will be perhaps days or weeks underway. Though I shall be miles from you, my thoughts shall remain with you with every minute that passes. It is with deep regret that I could not be present to greet you upon your arrival, for if I had, I most assuredly would have held you in my arms and kissed you over and over, once for every day we were apart. I shall hold such thoughts in my dreams.

I do not know how long we shall be in the field, but be assured, I shall return to you and our unborn little one as soon as duty permits.

I ask that you do not worry about me, for such thoughts are burdensome, and I want your arrival and stay to be as comfortable as possible. You may count on Major Hodges to aid and help you to become established in Bismarck until I return. Since we are not yet married, it is impossible to arrange for means of settlement on the grounds of the fort. I know you will understand, as you are a strong woman, worthy perhaps of even more praise than I can offer.

My love for you cannot be any stronger. I long for the day that we are once again together.

With all my precious love,
Kellem

Lydia pocketed the dollars Kellem had included, money she could certainly use. She slowly folded the letter and replaced it in the envelope, and as she did so, tears streamed from her eyes. She could not have been happier to read such words. Though she had lost their son, at least she still had Kellem.

Halona soon returned and saw Lydia's face wet with tears. Lydia smiled and said, "Under this wet and dreary face, these are tears of happiness, not sorrow."

"I'm so glad to hear that," Halona responded. She helped Lydia up and began walking her back to the interior of the hospital. "Are you about ready to leave this place?" she asked.

"I believe so, but I don't have a place to stay until Kellem returns."

"I just happen to know a single nurse who has a spare room."

Lydia did not expect such an offer. "I don't even know your last name."

"Tibbs."

"Halona Tibbs," Lydia repeated. "I like that."

Twenty-Two

June 10, 1876

Dearest Katrina,

The train trip from Fargo to Bismarck did not end with the happiness I envisioned. Shortly before my arrival, I experienced a miscarriage and lost the baby. He was a boy, and is laid to rest here in Bismarck not far from the local hospital.

I have shed tears over this loss, but I seem to find fortune at the most opportune times. I have met a wonderful friend, Halona Tibbs, who is a nurse and who brought me through this ordeal. I presently am staying at her residence, but it is a temporary address, I am sure. Should you send a letter, address it to the Bismarck Hospital in care of Halona, or else to Major Tom Hodges at Fort Lincoln, a friend of Kellem.

Kellem was unable to meet me, since he is on assignment in the field attached to the 7th Cavalry. His troop is somewhere in the west involved in the settlement of the Indians to bring them back to their reservations. I do not understand what this settlement means, but I am optimistic that Kellem will return within a month or two, or so I am informed by what little news appears in the paper. I am not at all sure that even the newspaper has accurate reports of the movement of such troops.

Kellem addressed a letter to me before he left with most

reassuring words of encouragement. My heart is saddened of course, since he is not here, but I shall remain optimistic and look forward to the day when he returns.

I hope this letter finds you in good health. I am gaining strength every day and Halona is a godsend, since she is so sweet and generous, and gives me encouragement. I am truly blessed to have met her.

This city is much larger than what I can see from my view, and the fort is so distant across the river that I cannot see it. But I shall in due time make a trip there to see Major Hodges. Perhaps he can give me more information about Kellem's whereabouts and his eventual return.

I remain in debt to you for the generous time you afford me with your sound advice and friendship. Please write.

Love, Lydia

Halona's residence consisted of half of a little two-story home no more than a fifteen-minute walk from the hospital. Lydia easily adapted to the small quarters in which she was now staying. She had considered looking for work, but was satisfied to simply convalesce during this time. Though her room was small, she had access to a small parlor and an adjoining kitchen, and a veranda on the second floor offered a majestic view of the city to the south. The majority of the businesses were down below, and beyond, a line of cottonwoods, box elder and aspens outlined the meandering path of the Missouri.

Fort Lincoln lay somewhere to the southwest, obscured by trees and small hills. Lydia had anticipated visiting the fort, if for no other reason than to see where her living quarters would eventually be once Kellem returned. However, the fort was nearly ten miles away, and an opportunity to make the short trip had not yet presented itself.

Halona spent her days at the hospital, and on occasion, she

worked evenings. Whenever she returned, Lydia would have meals prepared for her. In their free time, the two girls talked at length about everything and anything. They giggled and laughed incessantly, it seemed.

Lydia could not have found a better friend than Halona. She was single, had aspirations of marriage, like Lydia, but on more than one occasion, she stated that nobody had taken any interest in her yet.

Lydia understood that very well. Halona was twenty-three years old and feared if she didn't marry soon, she would end up an old maid. Lydia felt lucky. She would be twenty next August and had already found her man. Of course, the search hadn't been easy. In fact, her chance meeting with Kellem was as close to a miracle as she could imagine.

A small collection of books remained on hand in Halona's library, and with so much free time on her hands, Lydia spent her days reading, which she always enjoyed. Since a small kiosk was no more than a block away, Lydia would venture down every few days to purchase a paper. The recent money that Kellem had given her was sufficient to last another month or two, and she felt secure here with Halona. If need be, she would seek employment, which in itself would be good therapy, since it would help her days pass by more quickly.

A week later, Lydia happened to be reading a small article in the *Tribune* prefaced with an almost nondescript headline that mentioned the Seventh Cavalry.

She read the article with extreme interest, and when Halona returned that evening after work, Lydia had a map laid out on a table and the newspaper folded to the page of the article.

"What is it?" Halona inquired when she saw Lydia sitting so still.

Lydia showed the article to Halona, and after Halona read it, she looked up, seemingly not understanding Lydia's concern.

Lydia explained, "It's a telegraph message from a reporter who is with the Seventh Cavalry. That's where Kellem is. They are to overtake the Indians with the help of another army."

Halona was not following her reasoning.

"Don't you see?" Lydia went on. "Two separate armies are converging on the Indians at a place called the Big Horn Valley." Lydia pointed out the location on the map.

"Lydia," Halona implored. "This is nothing more than a maneuver to bring the Indians back to their reservation."

"But it says here, General Gibbon's forces are to intercept the Indians from the south to prevent their escape."

Halona sat and hunched her shoulders. "Lydia, I believe you're making more out of this than it really is."

Lydia sat silently for the longest time, then noticed the date that the telegram was sent. A few days had already passed.

Captain Gates led his company along the lower side of the bluffs. Ahead of him, no more than a hundred yards away, rode Major Reno with two other officers. Captain Benteen and three companies had divided and headed off to the south some time earlier, and Custer had already left the main body with three companies and was skirting the hills to his right. The men and horses were already out of sight.

The sun bore down with menacing heat. As Captain Gates turned to look back at his men, he could see by their faces that they were beat from riding nearly seventy-five miles in the last twenty-four hours.

Captain Gates cast a gaze to his left, then to the right. No Indians were in sight, but some of the scouts had reported that a huge camp lay ahead. In fact, a runner had come by with a message to bring up the packs from the train left behind. Gates had been in battle before, but he did not like the maneuver in progress. He spurred his horse and rode on to catch up with Major Reno.

"Major," he addressed the officer as he slowed alongside. "What does this son of a bitch think we are?"

Reno cast a wary glance at Gates and shrugged. "I trust by your choice of words, you are referring to our illustrious commander, his highness, Custer?"

"You're damn right. He's divided us into three battle commands and left the pack train behind. Look at our men," Gates implored as he pointed behind him. "They're worn out. Half are ready to fall out of their saddles and the other half are scared shitless. They're green. And the bunch with Custer isn't any better. Most have never even seen an Indian!"

"You should have voiced your concerns to Custer earlier," Reno said.

"I did. But the son of a bitch doesn't listen to anybody."

"That's the second time you have alluded to our leader by that title," Reno mused.

Gates went on, his voice louder, "Even his scouts told him there are too many Indians. We don't even know what we're up against. And why isn't he waiting for Gibbon? And where's General Terry's army? That was the plan! He was to wait for support!"

Reno abruptly stopped his horse, turned in his saddle and said in a most disquieting voice, "Custer thinks the Indians will get away, and that's why we're not waiting for Gibbon or Terry. If you want my opinion, I agree he is not only a son of a bitch, but a goddamn stupid son of a bitch. Before the day's over, a lot of us are going to be dead. And if we disobey his orders, before the day's out we'll be dead anyway, so get back to your company. As soon as we cross that creek ahead, the bugler is going to sound the charge."

Captain Gates rode back quickly and joined his lieutenants.

"What happened?" one of the lieutenants inquired.

"Not much," Gates said, "other than we all seem to agree he's a son of a bitch." They enjoyed a short chuckle, and then Gates commanded his lieutenants, "Ready your men. In about five minutes, we're all headed for hell."

In a short time, their companies crossed the Little Big Horn. When the bugle sounded, Gates drew his pistol and urged his horse into a lope. His mind flashed to Lydia for a few seconds. Then, as he gazed across the open ground, he saw the huge number of Indians riding directly at them.

The pounding of hoofbeats thundered like a gigantic herd of buffalo. As the soldiers neared the enemy, shots rang out from everywhere. And now, all Kellem could hear were the fierce war cries as the Indians rode at him—hundreds and hundreds of them!

"My God!" he heard Major Reno exclaim, and at that moment, Captain Gates saw the first few soldiers shot out of their saddles.

The news of the massacre at the Little Big Horn shocked the entire nation, and especially the populace in the city of Bismarck. The daily reports in the newspaper were unclear, since it was not yet confirmed how many soldiers had been killed, nor did anyone possess any details of the battle.

Lydia's heart raced at every piece of information she read. Two full days after the battle and wrought with fear of the unknown, she hired a buggy and driver to deliver her to the Missouri levee.

As she crossed the river on a ferry, the faces of the individuals around her depicted the sorrow they felt. If any of the passengers on board had loved ones who were lost at the Little Big Horn, she did not know. It was all she could do to hold back her tears, since she did not know if Kellem was safe or not, and no one had yet seen a casualty list. With every passing second, she felt a shudder run through her body. She feared the worst, but prayed for the best.

On the opposite shore, the fort was within easy walking distance. Several soldiers were on horseback. To the south of the fort grounds, a huge herd of cattle mingled, grazing on the rich grass of the hills. Strangely enough, many of the men on horseback tending the herd appeared to be cowboys rather than soldiers.

At the gates of the fort, a young soldier knew who Major Hodges was and pointed out the building in which he had his office.

She hurried along the gravel walkway and entered the charge of quarters with the same anxiety she'd experienced since early morning. Major Hodges, his face tired and filled with remorse, rose from behind his desk.

He forced a smile as he offered a hand. "Miss Pearlman, you have been in my thoughts for the past forty-eight hours."

"Do you have any news of Kellem?" she asked. Her eyes were searching his. He appeared saddened beyond description.

"No, I don't. Unfortunately, we don't have much information."

"What do you know?"

He seemed reluctant to answer her, but went on, "For some reason, Custer divided his forces. All of those men who were directly with him were killed."

Lydia's whole being sank as wetness filled her eyes.

"But we do not know for certain that Captain Gates was among these men. It is very possible that he may have been with a separate company."

"When will you know?" she asked.

The major grimaced, unsure of the answer. "We do know that the *Far West* steamship is underway to bring back the wounded. We expect it should arrive here early next week."

The news did not raise her hopes.

"Miss Pearlman," the major went on. "Many soldiers survived the battle. I know of your feelings for Captain Gates, and my sympathies lie with you. I can only hope that he is among the survivors."

He escorted her to a window and pointed across the grounds where several women were sitting beneath a huge shade tree. "Those women already know they lost their loved ones. The lady in the blue dress is Libby, General Custer's wife." The major folded his hands behind him and stared at the ladies for the longest time. "It's a sad day for all of us."

At that moment, a lieutenant entered the building and addressed the major, "Sir, Mr. McCann said he will meet you by the corrals at your convenience."

"Very well," said the major. "Tell Mr. McCann I'll be with him shortly." He turned to Lydia. "I must return to my duties. We have several hundred head of cattle that have just arrived."

Lydia was stricken with a sudden thought. "You said McCann. Would this be Frank McCann, by any chance?"

"That is his name. Do you know him?"

"Frank McCann from Yankton?"

"I wouldn't know that for certain. These cattle come from Texas. However, the original cattle company is located in Omaha."

She had first met Katrina in Omaha. "I know that's him. I know it," she said. "Would you take me to him?" she implored.

The major went to the doorway and summoned the lieutenant back. "Lieutenant, get a wagon up here immediately."

In a short time, with his horse tied on behind, Major Hodges drove Lydia to the sloping banks of the hill where the cattle were held, and where several cowboys and soldiers were cutting out beef for the cattle pens. The major stopped the wagon and waved a hat at one of the closer men.

The cowboy, riding in a saddle of shiny black leather astride a palomino, loped over to the wagon. "Major," he said as he reined up. Seeing Lydia, he removed his hat. "Ma'am," he greeted and then slipped it back on.

The cowboy lived up to the description Katrina had once given her, Lydia was thinking, as she looked him over. His skin was leathered from the sun, yet his face was cheerful in appearance, and he looked stately and muscular in the saddle. He also wore a sidearm.

"You and this young lady may have a similar acquaintance," the major said to the cowboy.

Lydia spoke to him. "Do you by any chance know Katrina from Yankton?"

A huge smile broke out on Frank McCann's face as he once again pulled his hat off. "Who do I have the pleasure of addressing?"

"Lydia Pearlman," she said. "Does that name mean anything to you?"

"Oh, yes, ma'am," he said as he swung out of the saddle, walked up to her and offered his hand. "I know your name very well, and it is an extreme pleasure to finally meet you."

The major dropped from the wagon and untied his horse. "I can see that you two have much to discuss. Miss Lydia, I'll be in contact if I receive word of Captain Gates." He mounted and rode off toward the cattle pens, leaving the two alone.

"This is a real surprise, Miss Lydia," Frank McCann said. "Yet I don't quite understand how it is that you and I have made this chance meeting."

She explained that she intended to marry Captain Gates, who was stationed here at the fort. She also told him that she had traveled from Sioux Falls to Fort Lincoln, but that the battle with the Indians at the Little Big Horn had for the moment interrupted their immediate plans of marriage.

"I only know of you through Katrina's letters," Frank said. "I've been driving cattle since April, and I haven't had much contact with her. As soon as I deliver the final four hundred head to Fort Buford, I'll be heading back to Yankton."

"I've written to Katrina, but you must greet her for me when you return," Lydia said.

"What have you learned about this captain friend of yours?" he asked.

She told him what the major had said, which was very little, and that a steamship was underway to bring back the wounded. If she didn't learn anything prior to the return of the steamship, she intended to visit the wounded and inquire further about Kellem Gates.

As the two conversed, a young rider on a handsome sorrel horse rode up. "Frank," the young man said. "Got 'em counted out. The major said he'll sign off for 'em when you got time."

"Joseph," Frank said. "Come off that horse and meet a friend of your ma's."

The young fellow dropped from his horse and tore his hat off his head. "Lydia," Frank said. "This is Joseph Dvorak."

The name startled Lydia. "Joseph? You're Katrina's youngest son?"

"Yes'm."

"How old are you?"

"Fifteen, ma'am, soon to be sixteen."

He, too, was wearing a sidearm, Lydia noticed, a silver-plated pistol in a shiny black belt. He had been working on a ranch in Texas. When he finished delivering a herd to a Nebraska railhead, he met Frank McCann in Ogallala and was moving north with the consignment herds.

"I'm sorry I don't know you," Joseph said.

Lydia smiled. "That's all right." She studied his face. "You have your ma's eyes and her smile, did you know that?"

"People tell me that."

It was a strange turn of events for Lydia that afternoon. She had only intended to visit Major Hodges, but to discover Frank McCann, Katrina's lover, and young Joseph at the same time seemed to be a good omen. Just talking to the two made her forget about Kellem, at least for a moment.

Later in the afternoon, Frank escorted her to the corrals, where she met the rest of the cowboys. Most had been hired in Texas and didn't know Katrina personally. However, she met Rick, Frank's long-time friend, and Peg Washington, a black man, who ran Katrina's ranch west of Omaha.

"She done got me this leg of mine," Peg confided in her as he rolled up his pant leg to display a wooden leg that fitted into his boot. He displayed a set of big, white teeth behind a wide smile. "Yessuh, she's one fine woman."

That evening, Major Hodges arranged for a wagon in which Frank McCann escorted Lydia onto the ferry and back to her home near the hospital. After he delivered the remaining cattle to a northern fort, Frank said he would be passing through Bismarck again within a few weeks, and he promised to look her up on his return trip.

Halona was waiting for Lydia when she entered the house, and after a long and lengthy talk and much crying over the day's events, Lydia finally turned in. She spent a fitful night, which became the norm over the next several days.

Twenty-Three

Independence Day was not marked as a glorious day of celebration. Bismarck had planned a parade long before the incident at the Little Big Horn. The city delegates decided to go on with it in spite of the gloom that hung not only over Fort Lincoln, but over the entire nation.

Everyone anxiously awaited the news of the aftermath of the battle. More reports came out in the newspaper daily, detailing the events, until finally, a list of the known dead appeared.

Everyone lamented over the huge number that had died, but to Lydia's relief, Kellem Gates' name was not among them.

A report in the *Tribune* stated that some time on July sixth, the *Far West* steamship would arrive at Fort Lincoln with men wounded in the battle.

That morning, Lydia paid her fare to cross to the west side of the Missouri. On the levee, preparations were already set up with a line of hospital wagons and several medics who would transport the wounded to the fort infirmary. In the early afternoon, the steamer made its appearance to throngs of onlookers standing en masse on both sides of the river. On the west side, a few reporters from the *Bismarck Tribune* were on hand to write up their accounts of the arrival, as well as any other information they could glean about the massacre. A crowd made up mostly of women and children stood motionless to the side waiting to discover, like Lydia, whether their men were among the living.

At a small building near the river, several high-ranking officers had made their presence known. They would welcome the men back, if indeed *welcome* was the correct word. These officers would eventually interview the wounded soldiers and deliver the necessary reports to Washington.

As soon as the steamer docked, several officers boarded, among them Major Hodges. Lydia stood alongside the crowd, waiting, her heart a lump in her chest. In a short time, several soldiers carrying gurneys entered the steamer, and within a few minutes, some of the wounded were being brought out. The first few were the most seriously hurt. They had severe wounds in their chests and legs; some had limbs missing; others were unrecognizable, since their faces were wrapped in bandages.

The parade of the battle-weary and wounded seemed unending. Whenever a woman recognized her man, the wailing began, and soon a murmur rang from the crowd as more and more women ran to their husbands or loved ones.

Lydia had been looking on, hoping that at any moment she might spot Kellem. As each wounded soldier passed or was carried by, she held her breath until Major Hodges was suddenly at her side. With him was a man in a black uniform with a black naval cap.

"Lydia, this is Grant Marsh, the captain of the *Far West*."

She gasped, recognizing him as the same captain who had been aboard the steamer when Matthew McGrath was shot at the card game!

Marsh removed his hat and held her hand gently, giving no indication that he knew her. "Ma'am, Major Hodges told me who you are. I met your friend Frank McCann hardly twenty-four hours ago at Fort Buford. He indicated you were seeking out a Captain Gates, I believe?"

She threw her hand up to her mouth, her heart fearful. "Yes."

"Captain Gates is not among the wounded on this steamer.

He and a half dozen others are listed as missing. I wish I had more positive information on this man. A few stragglers have appeared even five days after the battle. Some remained hidden, others were wounded and were not found until recently, so I would not give up hope."

She wasn't reassured. She answered with barely a whisper, "Thank you."

Captain Marsh lifted his hat back in place, bowed slightly and hesitated. "Have we met before?" he asked.

"I don't believe so," she said.

He nodded, touched the bill of his hat and headed back to the riverboat.

Major Hodges watched the captain for a few moments, his thoughts a jumble of confusion, and then he looked back at Lydia. "I'm sorry," he said.

Lydia looked over the casualties who were being loaded into the hospital wagons. "Perhaps the infirmary could use some help," she offered. "I would be glad to give assistance."

Major Hodges inclined his head. "Of course. I'll be happy to recommend you."

As they slowly walked to the quarters where the officers were stationed, she held fast to the major's arm, as if to steady herself. Besides administering aid at the infirmary, she hoped to inquire of the wounded whether any of them knew Captain Gates or perhaps served in his company. If one of them remembered seeing him on the battlefield, that would be important to her. Of course, she might also learn that someone might have seen him killed in battle.

Either way, she needed to know.

At the infirmary, Lydia was given a white smock to wear over her dress and a white cap that nurses normally wore. Initially, her duties were simple: to bring water to the wounded and move from individual to individual and fulfill any requests they had.

That chore was simple, and that night she was given quarters where she could sleep with other women who were offering similar help. So that Halona would not worry about her, she sent word back that she had volunteered to help with the wounded, and that she expected to remain at the fort for the next few days.

Her second day began with similar menial duties, but by midday she was summoned to a separate room where she was asked to help clean wounds and apply what medicines and ointments were available. The worst of the men had huge pieces of flesh torn away or deep puncture wounds where either a bullet had struck them or an arrow had been pulled out.

From an adjoining room, she could hear the moans of soldiers who had learned that gangrene was setting in and that an arm or a leg needed to be removed. Some of those who had arrived already were amputees from the battlefield. At least these men who were about to have limbs removed had chloroform available to put them under before the operation.

Lydia could not fathom the horror of being wounded in a battle and having surgery performed while one was still conscious. The mere thought sent a shiver through her. But as the day dragged on, such thoughts diminished considerably. Simply being around the wounded and witnessing the terrible carnage seemed to dull her senses.

Within a few more days, after most of the men had been given the best attention and care they could receive, her main duty had been reduced to making soldiers feel comfortable. Sometimes that meant just touching a hand or patting a face, or offering a smile. As she moved from soldier to soldier, from bed to bed, she offered words of hope. If a soldier requested it, she even said a prayer.

Such requests were easy for her, since she herself was a victim of the same helpless feeling these men were experiencing. Sometimes a soldier would ask her to write a letter, a duty she willingly accepted. Of these, some were illiterate and others, with a hand or arm badly mangled, were unable to perform such a simple task.

With each soldier, she would casually ask whether he knew Captain Gates. There were those who did, but so far no one knew of his fate. The most information she had gained came from a lieutenant who had ridden into battle with Kellem.

"During the initial charge my horse was shot out from underneath me," the lieutenant said as he lifted a bandaged arm. "Broke my arm when I fell. I escaped to a thicket of trees and eventually scrambled to safety a few days later when the Indians suddenly left."

The lieutenant seemed to be in a daze for a few seconds, then looked into Lydia's eyes. "Captain Gates wasn't more'n twenty feet from me when I went down. The last I saw of him, he was still riding towards the encampment."

He offered a strange smile and then said, "I'm guessing your name is Lydia."

Lydia's eyebrows jumped. "Yes, it is."

He gave her a genuine smile. "I thought so. You fit Kellem's description." Then his smile disappeared. "I wish I could be of more help."

A few days later, Lydia was still attending the soldiers in the base infirmary and happened to be outside during a break when she saw a steamer at the docks. She did not think much of the paddleboat, because many had come and gone since the battle, and those paddleboats that docked on this side of the river usually did so because they had goods to deliver to the fort.

She was sitting alone when she saw a cowboy headed her way

on foot. He was coming from the other direction, from the charge of quarters building. She watched him for some time, narrowing her eyes in the beating sun, and now she was sure she knew who he was.

She was on her feet and smiling as Frank McCann approached. He was wearing what looked like a new shirt, but he'd donned the same sweaty hat that she remembered. He removed it and gave a big grin. "Miss Lydia," he greeted. "Major Hodges told me I'd find you here. Good to see you again."

She was somewhat surprised to see him, and yet not really surprised, since he'd said he would look her up on his way back through.

"Kinda dressed like a nurse," he said as he sat down.

"I've been working like one since these wounded soldiers arrived."

Frank nodded, his face solemn. "You must'a heard I saw them up north some time back."

"Yes. Captain Marsh told me he met you."

Frank hung his head. "It ain't good, is it?"

"No, it's not," she said as she drew in a deep breath. Lydia had had enough of wounded soldiers and the sorrow that the massacre had dropped on everyone, so she put on a smile and changed the subject. "Get all your cattle delivered?"

"We did. Some of the boys are sticking around over in Bismarck celebrating. I doubt they'll be back in time to leave, but that's all right. They've got enough pay to grab another steamer back."

"How's Joseph?" she asked.

Frank glanced down toward the river. "Just as peppy as ever. He's hanging around with Peg and Rick. They're all kinda anxious to get back home. I got about an hour before the boat leaves. The captain said he'd give a few horn toots before he departs, so's I know."

"How about you? Are you looking forward to getting back?"

The grin was back on his face. "Katrina's waitin' for me. Can't think of anything better at the moment." He chuckled. "A cowboy can push cattle only so long. Comes a time when a man's got to get back to civilized duties."

He was silent for some time, and she knew his mind was momentarily back in Yankton. "How you doing?" he asked. "Any word on that captain fellow of yours?"

"No," she said. "Nothing." Then, with all the pent up emotions suddenly bursting upon her, she broke into tears.

Before she even realized it, Frank McCann had his arms around her holding her tight. "Darling, I wish I could whisk away all your sorrow." He patted her gently. "Sometimes the trail we're on just ain't goin' in the right direction, and there ain't much we can do but try to get off it."

He held her for some time, and then she sat up and wiped away the tears with a handkerchief. "I guess so," she said, as she fought to regain her composure.

Frank saw all the hurt in her face, but was helpless to do anything about it. He wasn't sure what he should say. "I'll be seeing Katrina in a few days. Anything you want me to pass on to her?"

"Tell her I miss her and I wish she was here."

"I wish she was, too," Frank said. "Katrina's got that sorta thing about her that makes a person feel good. She's kinda like a ray of sunshine comin' thru a bunch of black clouds."

Lydia listened closely to Frank's words. The mere mention of Katrina's name made her feel better.

Their conversation ambled along, and for the next several minutes they talked about cowboys and cattle and Katrina and Joseph. Frank brought her up to date on John, the oldest, who was set on wedding a young girl who worked with him at the Greenwood Agency. Katrina's daughter, Josephine, was at a school somewhere in St. Paul, getting an education.

"She wants to be a doctor," Frank said. "Kinda hard to imagine a woman doctor, but then, Katrina's into cattle and real estate. And those ain't usually a woman's profession."

"What is?" Lydia asked.

Frank was still for some time, his mind working on the simple question. "Ain't that somethin' to ponder?"

The steamer at the levee gave a couple of shrill whistles that startled them both.

"Reckon we're leaving a bit early," Frank said as he stood.

She stood with him and wiped her eyes. As Frank twirled his hat like some school kid who was guilty of something, Lydia raised herself up and kissed him on the cheek. "Pass that on to Katrina for me," she said.

He nodded and put his hat on. Then, without another word, he headed off for the steamer. Just before he boarded, he gave her a wave. The gesture reminded Lydia of Wilbur and Leonard when they'd departed on their small raft back in Breckenridge.

Five minutes later, she heard some more cutting whistles as the steamer slipped off into the Missouri. In no time at all, trees along the shore obscured it from view.

Lydia could understand why Katrina loved this man. She wondered if all cowboys were so gentle and loving and so easy to talk to.

With her composure back and her courage rising, she returned to the infirmary, where many soldiers still needed her attention.

Twenty-Four

If Lydia had been given a choice, she would have preferred to remain at the base infirmary to attend the wounded, but after another week her duties were reduced to a minimum, and her services were no longer required.

She returned home where she remained with Halona, but Major Hodges vowed to keep her apprised of any news regarding the whereabouts of Kellem. If anything he said reassured her, it was that inquiries were being made regarding a few other missing soldiers who had not been accounted for. Even now, a team of military inspectors was at the battlefield scene, searching for remains of the missing.

Lydia tried to remain optimistic, although even with encouragement from Halona and Major Hodges—who began to show up at their home much more often—her thoughts of ever seeing Kellem alive again seemed more than remote.

Halona, whose expertise was medical rather than mental, began to notice a slow change in Lydia's personality. She had become listless, sitting for hours at a time, sometimes on the veranda staring off to the south, or often just in a chair in the evening, her mind and thoughts seemingly miles away. She retired early and rarely rose before Halona left for work.

In due time and deeply concerned, Halona asked Major Hodges to call on her at the hospital where the two, along with a doctor who had been apprised of Lydia's situation, entered a discussion on Lydia's personality change.

"She refuses to believe that Kellem is dead," Halona said. "Lately she sleeps a lot during the day and has no desire to leave the house. She used to read all the time, but even that's stopped."

Halona explained that Lydia used to talk openly about Kellem and how they had been intimate, and how sorely she missed him.

The doctor just shook his head. "It is necessary for her to realize the reality of her situation."

"I understand that," said Halona. "But what you have to understand is that Lydia is not an attractive girl. She's an orphan, and I think she's had several disappointments in life, especially with men. She eventually found Captain Gates, someone who loved her deeply, but now he's gone."

"We all have disappointments," the doctor retorted.

Halona bit her lip. "Yes, but she thinks about Kellem all the time. He's an obsession with her. She's so deeply troubled."

Major Hodges had been silent for some time listening to the two talk back and forth. "I'm not knowledgeable about all this," he confessed, "but I do know that when Lydia was helping the wounded soldiers she seemed in control of herself in spite of the circumstances. Unfortunately, a military staff at the fort has concluded that Captain Gates and four other missing soldiers are to be declared dead. This will soon be made public, and I'm going to have to inform Lydia. I regret the moment when that time comes."

"She's sunk in melancholy," the doctor said bluntly. "It's a shame. We know so little about melancholia."

"What will happen when I tell her Kellem is declared dead?" the major asked.

The doctor was hesitant to reply, then, "We can only hope she will accept it. If she does, that may turn her around."

A few days later, Halona returned to her home with a letter that had arrived for Lydia at the hospital. It was from Katrina in Yankton. As Lydia opened the envelope and removed the letter, Halona saw a slight smile cross her face, an indication that the letter might have a healing effect. Halona knew how important this woman, whom she didn't remotely know, was to Lydia.

July 26, 1876
My Dear Lydia,

This letter comes to you with great sadness. As you know, Frank returned by steamer. Near the Greenwood Agency, the boat ran aground and he and Joseph and two others saddled their horses to ride the remaining distance to Yankton. Along the way, they stopped at Tackett's Station, a wayside inn with a bad reputation.

Frank had an altercation with a known cattle rustler, and after some gunfire, Frank came home, but was wounded in the abdomen. He died in my arms on the 16th of July and we buried him two days later. It has been a terrible ordeal for me, since I so loved this man.

Though Rick, Peg and my son Joseph were with him when Frank was shot, I thank God that none of them was injured. Before Frank died, he told me he had met with you, and that he shared your sorrow when hearing that your captain was involved in the Little Big Horn battle. I understand Kellem is missing, and I feel a deep sadness in my heart for you.

Is it not strange how we have both endured a similar tragedy at almost the same time? Who can understand why things like this happen?

Unfortunately, life does not present us with guarantees, only choices, so we must both endure these tragedies we have experienced and move on.

I pray that you can come to some resolution with the absence of Kellem, as I must do now that Frank is no longer a part of my life.

With deep affection,
Katrina

Halona could not help but see the extreme sadness in Lydia's face as she read through the letter, and when Lydia finished, she handed it to Halona.

As Halona read the letter Lydia sat still as a stone, her eyes glazed over. She finally spoke. "Katrina writes as if Kellem is already dead."

Halona was about to say that he probably was, thinking that might be the best therapy for her at the moment, but she feared to do so, unsure how Lydia would respond.

"I'm so sorry to hear about Frank," Halona finally said. "I don't even know the man or your friend Katrina, but I can tell that it is a terrible loss for both her and you."

It was as if Lydia hadn't heard a word Halona said. "Her first two husbands died, then a man she wanted to marry died, then the judge, and now Frank." A long silence followed, and then, "How can she do it?"

Halona did not quite understand what Lydia was saying, since she did not know Katrina at all. She could only fill in the words in between, guessing that this lady, Katrina, had also had her share of disappointments in life.

The big difference between the two, as Halona understood it, was that Katrina somehow managed to deal with the tragedies that struck her life, but Lydia simply could not.

As expected, a few days later, Major Tom Hodges arrived at Halona's home, his arrival announced ahead of time so that Halona would be present when he delivered the grim news to Lydia. She read the statement from the military investigation in which Captain Gates, along with a few others, were officially declared dead.

Lydia numbly signed the affidavit, not sure why her signature was required, but when she did so, Major Hodges handed her an envelope, which contained a goodly sum of money. She simply stared at the bills.

"Before Captain Gates left with the Seventh Cavalry, he signed over his pay and all of his personal belongings to you," the major explained. Along with the money from Kellem was an additional sum that the government paid when a soldier lost his life while in the service of his country. Totally, the money would last her several months, but she was not thinking along those terms when she signed her name.

"Captain Gates has an extra uniform and some personal items," the major went on. "What shall we do with them?" he inquired.

Her face remained blank, her eyes steady. "Disburse them as you see fit, Thomas," she said.

The major agreed and noted that this was the first time Lydia had ever addressed him as Thomas and not Major Hodges. At the door, before the major left, he and Halona talked for an unusually long time in voices low enough that Lydia could not hear them. When Halona returned to the parlor Lydia was looking over the few papers that the major had left behind.

"I believe the major is sweet on you," Lydia said.

Halona blushed at the comment and sat across from Lydia, her hands folded together. "What makes you think so?"

"He may be coming to visit me, but he spends most of his time looking at you. I can see the love in his eyes."

"He has inquired whether he may call on me," Halona said.

"And what did you say?"

"I said yes."

Lydia's gaze dropped downward. "Kellem is the only man

who looked at me the way Thomas looks at you. It all seems so easy for you, but then you are a beautiful woman."

"Lydia, what are you saying?"

She looked up, her eyes glassy. "A man like Kellem comes once in a lifetime for me, and now he is no more." She pointed to the money on the table and the paperwork that officially labeled Kellem as deceased. "All I have left is a memory."

As Lydia slowly stood and began climbing the stairs to her bedroom, Halona could not help but feel the deepest sympathy for her, and now she felt her own tears. Without a doubt, Lydia's world had collapsed around her.

For the next several weeks, Lydia's condition did not change much. Halona spent what time she could with her, encouraging her, receiving instructions from doctors at the hospital at what might grant Lydia relief from her melancholy. She didn't notice any particular improvement. On occasion Halona managed to drag Lydia out of the house to small social events, but Lydia was merely complacent and rarely participated in any activities.

Major Hodges continued to call on Halona, and finally the two announced that they would marry. Lydia, still close to Halona in spite of her situation, was asked to be her bridesmaid.

The offer made a noticeable change in Lydia's attitude. She seemed so much livelier and paid more attention to her grooming and appearance. She even volunteered to help prepare the invitations for the event, which was to be a gala affair held at Fort Lincoln. Lydia felt some comfort in that she had come to know a few of the officers when she attended the wounded, and such renewal of acquaintances appealed to her.

It became obvious that when she had a task on hand—something worthwhile to keep her busy—she was most comfortable. Yet, after the passage of a few weeks, Halona realized that once she and Thomas were married, Lydia would be alone in this house, on her own, pretty much as she had been in Sioux Falls.

That same thought struck Lydia like an unforgiving windstorm. Like a moth that remains dormant in a cocoon, she slowly retreated to the confines of the home.

Two days before the wedding, she heard a knock on the door at midday, a strange time for anyone to come calling. When she threw open the door, there stood Katrina with a loving smile on her face and her open arms reaching out.

As the two hugged each other, Lydia burst into tears, her joy overriding her sorrow. A few minutes passed before Lydia could contain herself. Her whole body shook from excitement.

The two women chatted endlessly while Lydia prepared tea. Asked why Katrina had suddenly showed up in Bismarck, she remarked, "I have an invitation to Halona's wedding."

Lydia found that strange. She had helped send out the invitations and knew that Katrina's name was not on the list. It became clear to Lydia that Halona had personally sent the invitation, and although the wedding may have been an initial reason for Katrina's arrival, Lydia knew that Halona had ulterior motives.

"You don't even know Halona," Lydia said.

"I've met her. I just came from the hospital."

Lydia's face sagged. "What did she tell you?"

"That you are not dealing well with Kellem's death."

Lydia frowned, surprised that she was so direct. "There's always the possibility that he's . . ."

"Lydia," Katrina interrupted. "Kellem's not coming back and neither is Frank. They're gone from our lives, just like yesterday's sun."

Lydia looked up into Katrina's face. She was talking about the deaths of two men as though it was an everyday event. "I don't know how you can deal with losing a loved one so easily."

"Lydia," Katrina consoled her. "I've lost five men that I loved. If I spent my time mourning over their deaths, I wouldn't have time to do any living."

"Losing a loved one for you seems so simple," Lydia pouted.

"Not at all," Katrina countered. "It's not simple, it's practical. This is the way life has been dealt out to me. To us. We just have to learn to cope with it. If you choose to spend the rest of your life mourning over Kellem's death, that's your choice. But there are other choices."

"You sound like Halona."

"If I do, I respect her, because she's making sense."

Lydia was once again on the verge of a crying spell. Everything Katrina had just told her did seem reasonable; yet holding back her tears was the hardest thing in the world right then.

Katrina sensed her sorrow. "When was the last time you ate a good meal at a hotel?" she suddenly asked.

Lydia rubbed her eyes as she thought. "I suppose the one I cooked for myself back in Sioux Falls."

The answer forced a chuckle from Katrina. "Honey," she said. "Get your best dress on, 'cause we're going out tonight. Got anything against drinking good wine?"

Lydia wiped a tear from her face. "No, I guess not."

"Good," Katrina said. "The Bison Hotel's got the best there is."

Katrina had a buggy waiting outside, and when they arrived at the Bison Hotel it did not surprise Lydia to find Halona and Major Hodges waiting for them. It had all been arranged by Katrina. After an evening of good food and wine and long conversations, Major Hodges drove Lydia and Halona back home.

That night provided Lydia with the best night's sleep she had

had in weeks. A day later, at Fort Lincoln with nearly a hundred guests present, Halona Tibbs accepted Major Thomas Hodges' hand in marriage. The reception afterward offered fine food, dancing and many glasses of champagne. Before the night was over Lydia had begun to feel like a fairy-tale princess.

The Hodges did not honeymoon at any place in particular, but they also did not let their whereabouts be known for the next few days. Lydia took advantage of the time to spend most of it with Katrina. She shopped and bought herself some new clothes, something she hadn't done in months.

Over the next few days Katrina met with a banker, but what business she transacted Lydia did not know, other than that Katrina had obviously made some business deal involving land speculation.

On the day that Katrina was to leave Bismarck, the two women sat sipping tea in a restaurant along the levee, waiting for the announcement of the steamer's departure. Lydia felt most sorrowful.

"What is this sourpuss face you're putting on?" Katrina asked her. "Bad tea?"

"No," Lydia half smiled. "I wish you would stay longer."

"Darling," Katrina said in her most consoling voice. "I've got a life to get back to. After a few days in Yankton, I'm off to Omaha again."

"For what reason?"

"I've got to figure out what to do with the ranch. I'll need another foreman if I intend to run more cattle. I've got Joseph to look after, and John just got married. My kids, you know."

"You're lucky to have family."

"There's more than family. There's this colonel at the fort in Omaha."

Lydia's eyes went wide. "What colonel? What fort?"

Katrina just smiled. "Someone I know. Someone I'm interested in."

"Is he interested in you?"

"He doesn't know it yet, but he will be."

Lydia could hardly believe what she was hearing. Frank had been gone only about seven or eight weeks, and Katrina was thinking about another man already.

"Eddie set up the deal to deliver cattle to the Indian agencies."

"Who's Eddie?" Lydia challenged.

"The colonel. Colonel Edward Effington."

The door to the restaurant opened and a young man dressed in a black uniform approached their table. "We're ready to board, Miss Dvorak." He returned to the door and held it open for her.

Lydia followed Katrina out of the restaurant and slowly walked to the wharf.

"I'm going to miss you, Katrina," Lydia said, still sad.

"I'd be disappointed if you didn't," Katrina retorted. "Give my best to the newlyweds when you see them."

The two hugged for the longest time, and with a huge smile on her face, Katrina simply said, "Get on with your life, promise me?"

Lydia nodded. "I promise."

As Katrina crossed the gangplank, Lydia hollered after her, "I'll come visit you some time!"

Katrina turned around. "Give me a month's notice so I'm there when you arrive!"

As the steamer delivered a shrill whistle, black smoke belched from the stacks leaving a heavy burned-wood aroma hanging in the air. Less than a mile away the steamer slowly slipped around a bend and disappeared from sight.

★ ★ ★ ★ ★

With each passing day over the next few weeks, Lydia began to feel better about herself. She never did understand how Katrina could so easily accept the death of Frank, and in so short of a time have her eyes on another man. Lydia recollected that after the judge died, in less than a month's time she had discovered romance with Frank McCann.

It was in Katrina's nature to accept whatever life threw at her. The thought was reassuring for Lydia, and she resolved herself to making the same effort.

The newlyweds were in secured quarters on the grounds of Fort Lincoln where Halona managed to gain occasional employment utilizing her nursing skills at the infirmary. Now that Lydia was living alone it soon became apparent that she could not afford to rent this much space. Her money would last a few months, but it was necessary for her to gain employment.

Once again she set out to find work and eventually reverted to the occupation she knew best—working in a restaurant near the levee. The distance from home to work was too great, just as it had been in St. Louis, so she left the house and took a room in a small house just minutes from the restaurant.

Her life quickly fell into a routine. She was at work early and remained there until sometimes seven or eight o'clock. By the time she arrived home she was usually exhausted and sought sleep almost immediately. The clientele was not much different from those men she'd served in Yankton. Many were dockworkers, or roosters, as she remembered them being called, along with a number of people traveling through on the riverboats.

Occasionally soldiers from the fort showed up, but not very often, since they received meals at the base, and what money they did have was usually spent on whiskey and girls from the nearby brothels. While waiting tables, a drunk might on occasion grab Lydia about the waist and get frisky with her, but

Garner Adams, the proprietor, kept a close eye on such rambunctious characters. He was a big man, weighing well over two hundred pounds, and had muscles on his arms the size of Lydia's thighs. If anyone misbehaved, all Garner had to do was make an appearance with a killing look. Even the biggest of such men faltered under the evil eye Garner delivered.

Garner's wife, Gladys, usually ran the place, and she was just as big as her husband. If anyone got out of line while she was in charge, she came out of the kitchen carrying a heavy iron skillet. She was known to have put a few men down with a simple blow to the head. With Garner and Gladys' reputation, they had no trouble hiring waitresses, since word quickly got around that they were good people to work for.

The first snow fell in late October followed by a cold snap that shut down the riverboat traffic in mid-December. With temperatures bitterly cold, workers from the railroad were busy laying ties and rails across the frozen river. Lydia had been watching them work from her window, surprised that they completed the task within a few days. In the summer a train engine and goods, as well as passengers, were ferried across the river where the engine was hooked up to a separate set of cars. How far the rails extended she did not know, but eventually this track was to stretch into the heart of Montana.

She once again was at her window dreaming aimlessly when she decidedly took up a pen and began writing a letter.

January 23, 1877
My Dearest Katrina,

I cannot believe how many months have passed since you last departed Bismarck. I fully expected to write sooner, but my life has kept me busy, for which I am grateful.

You will be pleased to hear that Halona and Thomas are

expecting a baby. I only discovered this last week, and I believe I was the first to know. I know how excited they must be, as I well recall my own excitement when I was once with child.

I could not ask for two better friends than these two. I see Halona more often than Thomas, since his duties periodically take him into the field. What he does exactly, I'm not sure, but it has something to do with courier service between forts. Thus whenever he is away, Halona and I spend time together. We are actually separated by only the river, and it is easy to cross, since boats are always available. Of course, now I can walk across the ice and save a fifteen-cent fare.

I spent Thanksgiving and Christmas with them, and of course, I celebrated the New Year with them also. It seems whenever a special occasion arises, I am always invited. Thomas has received a new duty assignment, which will take him and Halona to Fort Dodge, Nebraska. They will be closer to you, but unfortunately quite distant from me. I shall miss them dearly and dread the day when they must depart. That will be in the spring sometime.

I have taken work as a waitress on the levee and have moved within a few minutes of the restaurant. Mr. Adams, the proprietor, is very good to me and all his help, and his wife Gladys is just as nice, although she is as big as a mountain. We serve good food and do not need to throw anyone out any more than once a week. The police patrol this area quite often, as we have had a few killings recently along the waterfront. In that sense, it is a bit like St. Louis.

Although I am situated in a rather rough part of town, you need not worry about me. I am not at all involved in that unfortunate occupation I held when in Yankton. I have met many people while at the restaurant, but most are transients. I have not been interested in any attachment with anyone yet, as I still think of Kellem often. I am sure that in due time, I may be lucky enough to find someone to take his place. For now I am content to let time be my healer. Thank God I have Halona to lean on. She is so understanding, and so much like you, since she is a very good friend and is concerned about my well-being.

I read an interesting article in the paper a month or so ago. If you recall the Northfield Bank robbery that took place in Minnesota last September, two of the bank robbers were possibly identified as Jesse Woodson James and his brother Frank. I am sure these are the same two who robbed a train I was on when en route to St. Louis some four years ago, and these are the same two men I served in the railroad restaurant in St. Louis a year later. At the time, they said their names were Jesse and Frank Woodson. Is that not a strange coincidence?

I shall close for now and post this letter. I hope these few lines find you in good health. I trust you may have a liaison with your newfound Colonel. I have forgotten his name, but pass on my greetings to him, should a greeting be appropriate. Write and bring me up to date with you and your family.

Affectionately yours,

Lydia

Lydia read over the letter. She considered herself very lucky to have Halona and Thomas for her friends. When she reread what she had written about not having any attachment to anyone, that was the truth. However, the reason was because no one at the restaurant had really paid any attention to her, other than a few drunks. And she did, after all, still think about Kellem quite often.

She folded the letter, placed it in an envelope and laid it on her desk. When she looked outside, clouds had moved in and big snowflakes were falling lazily out of the sky.

March 20, 1877

Dear Lydia,

The past few months found me in Omaha, thus I am remiss in my letter writing. I am so happy to hear you are at work again. I believe work is good therapy. I find that if I am busy, my mind is less encumbered. Please pass on my congratulations to the Hodges. I share their joy in knowing that a child is underway. Should they pass through Yankton on their way to Fort Dodge, ask them to look me up.

I read with interest about your robbery situation. To think that you actually met Jesse and Frank James. Twice! I had something similar happen to me. You too must recall that Wild Bill Hickock was shot in Deadwood last August. He is the man I met in Omaha. His killer, Jack McCall, ended up in our jail here in Yankton. He was tried and found guilty sometime back. Just a few days ago, he was hanged. I had never seen a hanging before. It does give one an eerie feeling to see a man die.

I have not yet cultivated a romance with Colonel Edward Effington, though I still remain optimistic. Recently I discovered that he is still married. I thought they had divorced, but it was only a separation. Evidently she does not enjoy military life.

Joseph is working the ranch west of Omaha and has discovered love, I fear, since he is corresponding with a girl he met in Ogallala. John is happily married and has moved on to a farm. I was informed a week ago that they are expecting a child also, so I will be a grandmother at age thirty-eight. That means new duties for me, but I'm ready.

I hear from Josephine once every few months. Her

schooling is going well, though she finds one of her teachers to be an ogre. Haven't we all discovered an ogre or two during our life times?

I may be traveling to Bismarck toward the end of the summer, or I may send C.J., my consultant and confidant. I will give you advance notice should I make the trip.

Yankton is not much changed, however, the city council was in an uproar over the Little Big Horn massacre and threatened to take out their tempers on the Indians at the Greenwood Agency. By now their tempers have cooled.

I recently bought stock in a railroad that is laying a track to Running Water some forty-five miles to the west from here. The railroads have the advantage of speed and will eventually force the steamships out of business, which means I should soon sell my stock in the Colson Steamship Line.

Yankton is contemplating gas lamplights throughout the downtown, something else I should be investing in.

I still ride Barker at least once a week if the weather cooperates. Without a man on hand to keep me busy, I seem to have more leisure time. I do miss Frank, and I visit his grave once in a while, but I am no longer crying over his death, which probably signifies I am healing. I hope the same is true with you and Kellem. All we can do is take what life hands out and make the best of it.

I wish you every joy and hope your life is finding a happy direction.

Yours with affection,

Katrina

The spring thaw came in late April and brought with it a welcome change. For the next few months the weather remained abnormally warm, and the riverboat traffic once again was in full gear. It seemed that every steamer that passed was laden with military goods bound for forts upriver, reaching as far as Fort Benton, a lonely post somewhere in the middle of Montana Territory.

When Major Thomas Hodges received his orders to relocate to Fort Dodge he was mildly surprised to discover that he had also been granted the rank of lieutenant colonel. It was a sad day when Lydia saw them off on a steamer. To have Katrina return to Yankton was painful enough, and to see her other two best friends leave was a second great loss. The good-bye left Lydia and Halona in tears, much like when Katrina departed, but they vowed to keep in contact with each other by letter and hoped to visit each other in the future.

It was a warm June day when the Hodges left, and that same afternoon Lydia began to reevaluate her situation. The only reason she had come to Bismarck was to wed Kellem, and though she had made a few friends here, none were as precious to her as Halona and Thomas.

She was hard-pressed to find a reason for remaining in Bismarck. It wasn't as if she hadn't been thinking about this situation for months already, and now that Halona and Thomas were gone perhaps a decision would become easier.

She had left Virginia, forced, for the most part, to leave against her will. She had no intention of ever returning there. She had buried that city in her mind years ago, just as she had buried her mother and father.

Since circumstances had compelled her to leave St. Louis, and a bad reputation had driven her out of Yankton, she could not remotely conceive of revisiting these two towns.

Sioux Falls, as small as it was, did not offer any solace either, and unfortunately, Bismarck had become nothing more than a bad memory. Life for Lydia, at least by her reckoning, had been nothing more than overcoming one obstacle after another. But she could make choices, or so she remembered both Katrina and Halona telling her.

"Yes, choices," Lydia repeated to herself. "You've got to move on," Katrina had told her, and so that evening Lydia retrieved a map and began studying it. From all the gossip that she had heard at the restaurant, the town of Miles City in Montana Territory kept recurring. However, she could not find that city on the map. In fact, very few towns were listed in this unsettled land. However, the railroad tracks were being laid in that direction, and boats were constantly traveling upriver.

She wondered who in Bismarck would care whether she left or not, other than Garner and Gladys at the restaurant, but they would have no problem finding help to replace her.

She made up her mind. She quit her job at the restaurant, gave notice to her landlord that she was leaving and packed a trunk.

Two days later she boarded a steamer headed upriver.

TWENTY-FIVE

Miles City—July 9, 1877

Even before the steamship eased up to shore Lydia shrank back after catching a glimpse of the town. In her wildest imagination she had not envisioned Miles City looking anything like this. An unrelenting wind whipped at her, forcing her to hold her hat in place. Ahead of her, a dust devil swirled menacingly on the street. She had only eighteen dollars in her purse, and if she'd had enough money for a return fare she would have turned around and headed back to Bismarck on the next boat.

"Good Lord," she remarked as a worker located her trunk among the baggage and dragged it over to her. "This is Miles City?"

"Yes, ma'am," the man replied. "Fort's down that way a piece," he pointed. "You need a ride somewhere?"

She looked down the dirt street that seemed to be the main thoroughfare. Mostly, she could see canvas tents. Those buildings that held some prominence were built out of logs. At the far end of the street was a larger structure which she guessed might be the hotel she had heard about on the steamer.

"Yes," she finally answered. "The Buffalo Hotel."

He nodded and flagged down a wagon passing by. He loaded her trunk in the back, helped her into the seat, and headed down the street. This was a frontier city with a vengeance. In between the tents other buildings were going up, but almost all were built out of logs, not sawn lumber. She did see one stack of rough-hewn boards which several workers were using to frame up walls.

"Ain't got no sawmill yet," the driver commented. "Cut lumber's precious up here." He pointed to the partially built structure. "That lumber come in on the last steamboat. Soon's the railroad comes through here, gonna be a boom town in the makin'."

"When will that be?" Lydia asked.

"Couple years I 'spect. Don't rightly know how far the tracks is laid this direction."

Dirt swirled up around her again as they continued on. Interspersed with the howling wind, incessant hammering and sawing echoed around her, but as the wagon moved along, men stopped their work momentarily to look up, snatching a glance at her, she was sure. She enjoyed the attention, even though it was brief, but as soon as the wagon passed them by, the men were back at their work.

Near the hotel a man was cussing at a pair of mules as much as he was accomplishing anything. The mules were dragging a heavy iron blade across the ground in an attempt to level it for another structure, but his mules weren't responding to his commands. The man let out another string of foul language, and when he noticed Lydia in the wagon, his face turned red. He sheepishly lifted his hat as if to apologize for such profanity.

At the hotel the driver helped Lydia down and let out a heavy grunt when he lifted her trunk from the back of the wagon. As he began dragging it to the entrance a gun blast echoed from behind them. A man staggered out of a tent just as a second shot tore into his body, and he fell to the ground in a clump.

"My God!" Lydia exclaimed.

"One or two ever' week, ma'am," the driver said, seemingly unconcerned about the shooting.

Two men came out of the tent and stood over the dead man,

one putting his pistol away. A half dozen more men gathered around, and finally two of them grabbed the man by the arms and legs and hauled him off.

Inside the hotel Lydia was still holding her hand against her breast as she approached the counter. The clerk eyed Lydia and her trunk suspiciously. "Can I help you?"

Lydia was still thinking about the dead man on the street. She glanced around to see a few men sitting in wood chairs in the adjoining lobby, all curiously staring back at her.

"I'd like a room," Lydia said.

The clerk hesitated. "Are you sure you're in the right place?"

"This is the Buffalo Hotel, is it not?"

"Yes ma'am, but I thought you might be one of Molly's girls." His face suddenly flushed. "Oh, I beg your pardon. I done misjudged you. A room's fifty cents a day. How long will you be staying, ma'am?"

She had a good idea what the man meant by Molly's girls, but her mind was busy calculating the daily room rate. With the cost of a room and meals she might have enough money for a week and a half.

"A day or two," she finally answered.

"Yes'm," the clerk said. He produced a key and came around the counter. Eyeing the size of the trunk, he hesitated. "I'll get someone to bring your trunk."

She could understand that. He was as thin as a stick of lumber. If he stepped outside into the heavy wind she was sure he would be blown across the prairie.

As the little man led her off to a room she could feel the eyes of the men in the lobby following her as if they had never seen a lady before. Now that she thought back, she didn't recall seeing any other ladies on the street.

She ate in the restaurant hotel that evening, but her meal cost nearly a dollar. That evening she made arrangements for a warm bath which cost another fifty cents. She needed a few personal items as well, and as she lay in bed that night, she calculated that inside of a week, she would be dead broke.

She slept late and did not make an appearance inside the hotel lobby until past ten the next morning. Carrying only her purse, she left the hotel and walked along a boardwalk that fronted some of the establishments. Like the day before, the hustle and bustle of activity in this basically canvas-tent town were nonstop. The wind, still blowing, was at least tolerable.

As she passed one of the tents she read the sign poked into the ground out front that said *John's Bar and Saloon*. She could hear chips clicking and the wheel of a roulette table spinning. A glance inside the open entrance let her catch a glimpse of a lady dressed rather scantily.

She moved on. It seemed every other tent or structure was a saloon. She was not at all certain where she was headed and what she should expect, but she needed work.

She stopped outside a building front that had a huge red-lettered sign that said *Restarant*. She smiled, recognizing that the word was spelled wrong.

She entered a small, dingy room that had no more than a half dozen tables. Only two men were present in a corner. As she sat, a pleasant aroma wafted into her nostrils. She waited patiently until an older man in a white apron finally approached.

She asked for eggs, but he had none. "Flapjacks and ham is all I got this morning. Tomorrow, maybe eggs," he apologized.

"May I ask what the price is?" she inquired.

"Thirty cents," he answered. "And all the coffee you can drink."

He brought a cup of coffee, and the meal followed in record time, with a generous piece of ham. Just as she finished eating the door opened and a lady entered the room and came directly to her table.

"Miss Pearlman?" the lady inquired.

Lydia was surprised. "Yes."

"Do you mind if I sit down?" she asked.

Lydia nodded, curious that this lady, who looked to be in her early thirties, should know her name. The blue satin dress she wore emphasized her tiny waist, and underneath her shoulder straps a long-sleeved white blouse hung loosely, exposing her cleavage. The rouge on her cheeks was a bit more heavily applied than Lydia considered proper, and her eyebrows and eyelashes had obviously been darkened with a pencil of some sort. She appeared stunning, but without the makeup Lydia did not think she would be anything extraordinary.

"Homer told me you took a room in the Buffalo," she said.

"Homer?" Lydia inquired.

"Little, skinny Homer. The clerk. He said you arrived with a large trunk."

Lydia was more than curious now. "Yes, I did. Why?"

"You're about my size. Do you happen to have any extra dresses you'd like to sell?" She noticed the confused look on Lydia's face. "I'm Molly Suggs," she added as she offered a hand. "Perhaps I should explain. There's not a dress shop in this town, so any dresses sell at a premium. Are you interested in selling a dress or two if you have any extras?"

Molly's delivery was straightforward and there wasn't a hint of friendliness in her voice; however, Lydia was taking her offer seriously. She was thinking how far her eighteen dollars would stretch. "I might be," Lydia finally said.

A smile swept over Molly Suggs face like a wave sweeps against the shore. "Looking for work by any chance?" she asked.

"What sort of work?" Lydia inquired, although there was no question in her mind what the lady was about to suggest.

"The only work for ladies like us in this town," Molly said. "The appetites of the men around here are immense, and they don't mind paying for a little fun."

"I don't think I'm interested."

"Honey," Molly said as she stood up. "You can wash clothes, work as a maid or spend sixteen hours a day in a restaurant, but you'll barely make enough money to survive. Believe me. I've been there." She headed for the door, then turned around. "We've all been there. If you decide to sell a dress, you'll find me at the Yellowstone."

Two days later, after making the rounds of the town seeking work and making inquiries, Lydia had no trouble finding the Yellowstone Saloon, a long, narrow, log-house affair. A bar stretched across one entire wall. Small tables and chairs filled the rest of the interior, and at a few of the tables, men were playing cards. In one corner, several men stood around a roulette wheel, trying their luck, and in another corner stood an upright piano, silent at the moment. It surprised Lydia to see so many men in the middle of the day doing basically nothing but spending their money on a no-payback situation.

Just walking into the cigar-and-whiskey-smelling interior brought back some ugly memories of her days in Yankton. As she stood in the doorway, she could feel several pairs of eyes looking her over. Feeling uncomfortable, she was about to leave when Molly suddenly appeared from a back room.

"Lydia." Molly beckoned when she saw her. In no time, Molly ushered her to a back office past a few doorways that obviously led to rooms where some of her girls plied their trade. Once inside the small confines of the office, Molly sat with crossed legs and lit up a thin cigar. Today she was wearing a brilliant green satin affair, short at the knees and exposing considerable skin up around the shoulders.

"Decide to take me up on my offer?" Molly asked.

"Yes."

"Which one?"

The question caught her off guard. "The dresses," she said.

"Find work yet?"

"No."

"I can always use you here," Molly offered. "You choose what you want to do. You can push drinks on the boys and just be nice, or accommodate their biological impulses."

"What do most of the girls do?"

"Little of each. The money's good. I guarantee it. Nobody gets rough, and if they do, Bugger takes care of them."

"Who's Bugger?"

"Two hundred and fifty pounds of muscle. Bugger can drive a post in the ground with his bare fist, and everybody around here knows it."

"No thanks," Lydia said as she stood up. "I'll be in my room all afternoon."

Later that day, Molly Suggs showed up at the hotel and bought two dresses for twenty dollars each. When she left, Lydia sat on her bed looking at the money. If she was frugal this amount might last her another two or three weeks, but it was still short of a ticket back to Bismarck.

The days dragged by for her, and though she sought out work for the next week, the best offer she received was working in a laundry near the Yellowstone River, but the few ladies there seemed to be as dirty as the clothes they were washing, and they were older women. Lydia did not by any means consider herself above them or the work, but she had visions of employment with a bit more class than washing dirty underwear.

Maid work was basically nonexistent. Not one dwelling in the city was of a size to demand a maid in Lydia's estimation. Even if she did find such work she knew the demands would be as Molly said, sixteen hours a day with no time off. Such work might be available within a few years when grandiose homes were built. The trouble with Miles City was that it was still in its infancy.

Near the river and within a few hundred yards of the hotel several men were constructing cattle pens. From her room Lydia could easily see the work in progress. She inquired of Homer, the clerk, what the construction signified. Homer knew the two men responsible for the construction, and seeing as how the two often frequented the hotel restaurant, Lydia had opportunity to meet them.

George Dearing was the younger of the two; William Strong was his stepfather. She discovered that they raised longhorn cattle on a ranch south of Miles City and intended eventually to send their cattle downriver by steamboat.

"Do you need a cook, by any chance?" she asked them.

Both smiled as they ate away at their steaks. "We both got wives that cook when we're at the ranch," George said. He pointed his fork upward with a hunk of beef on it. "In town, this here's our cook."

Lydia found it strange that these men were going to send cattle downriver to markets. Frank McCann had brought cattle all the way from Texas to deliver herds to forts that were within a hundred miles of Miles City. The difference was that Dearing and Strong raised cattle, whereas Frank McCann had brought up fattened cattle.

They were polite gentlemen, but they did not have work for her.

Nor did the livery, not that she had any intention of tending horses.

It made no sense to inquire at the gents' clothing merchant or the cigar and tobacco store or the ammunition and gun shop.

Those stores that sold dry goods were attended by the owners and members of their families, which made sense.

The town of Miles City had barely four hundred residents, not counting the soldiers at the fort, so the number of businesses that could even offer employment was practically negligible. She could, of course, find work easily in any one of the dozen saloons.

Over the next few weeks her money slowly dwindled, and as a last resort, she finally sold her best dress for twenty-five dollars. When that money was gone, she sat for hours, simply running options through her mind. Eventually, she sank to the lowest depth she had reached in months.

She mustered up enough courage and went to see Molly Suggs.

"Got another dress to sell?" Molly asked.

Lydia sank into a chair, her drawn face telling everything. "No."

TWENTY-SIX

December 10, 1877

Dearest Katrina,

Please excuse the lateness of this letter, which comes to you from Miles City, Montana Territory. It may seem strange, but I felt an impulse to move westward after hearing about this town that sprang up on the edge of the frontier. I hope you understand my motive for moving, but I simply could not remain in Bismarck.

Since my arrival, I have had nothing but excitement enter my life. Miles City is small, but a friendly community with much opportunity. After considerable searching and offers of various employment, I sold a few dresses, but realized soon that with so few women in this area, it was not a lucrative business, so I once again am engaged in the restaurant business, the occupation I know best. I am hopeful that this may eventually lead to ownership.

I have a consistent clientele that visits often, which is good for business, and I have gained a reputation for granting good service. I have met several men who seem to have a genuine interest in me, but I have not yet settled on any one in particular. Women are few in these parts, thus I can afford to be careful when choosing a man.

I hope your life beyond business has been rewarding, and I do not hesitate to think for one moment you are without that special leisure which so easily seems to come your way.

I often think of Halona and Thomas Hodges and wonder how well they have adapted to their new assignment in Fort Dodge. They must be expecting their first born very soon. It is terrible that I have not written to them, but I shall endeavor to do so quite soon.

I hope this correspondence finds you in good health. Pass on my greetings to your family. When you write, send the letter to the Buffalo Hotel in Miles City.

Love always,

Lydia

As she walked down to the hotel to mail the letter, Lydia's eyes began to tear. Once again she was writing so many untruths. She did sell dresses, but they were her own. She was somewhat in the restaurant business if one considered getting drunks to buy more drinks to be "in the restaurant business," and her clientele did keep coming back. Whether it was because of good service or not, she wasn't sure, but that was as good a guess as anything. She had actually met several men, in fact had slept with dozens, and there were those who requested her over other girls, so that could be construed as offering good service. In this town being a whore was almost a decent profession, but that was something she didn't dare write in her letter.

Ray Moore was her favorite cowboy. He eventually became a regular, but in the beginning he was as embarrassed as a first-time cowboy could be. He just sat on their first occasion and talked. The second time she managed to get him to remove his pants, and the third time, before he even crawled on, he had squirted all over himself.

She thought he'd never come back, but on his next payday he did, and after some comforting and sweet-talking he was finally able to perform. Though she liked him better than the others, he was still just a cowboy. Ray would spend money on a new bridle or saddlebags for his horse, or a fancy set of spurs before he thought about his inner needs. More than once he was broke a day after payday.

"You couldn't maybe loan me the two bucks, could you, Liddie?" he asked. He called her Liddie instead of Lydia.

She broke down and lent him the two dollars, even though she had to give half to Molly, which meant she was out a dollar until Ray could come back.

He came back a time or two and she even thought he might be the sort of fellow she could settle down with, but cowboys didn't have the means to settle down, let alone have a place to call their own. Their horse and bedroll was their home, and when the winter snows hit Miles City their wrangling came to an abrupt end. Like so many other cowboys, Ray was out of work and headed south to ride out the season.

She hoped he'd be back in the spring, yet she wasn't counting on it. If he didn't return it would be just one more disappointment in her life, and she had already had enough of those.

The worst of her clients were the soldiers from Fort Keogh—rambunctious, uneducated and crude. Half of them couldn't even speak English, and nothing infuriated Lydia more than to have someone shove himself into her and jostle her for five minutes, then get up, buckle his pants and walk out without even saying a word.

For many of them she had become nothing more than a machine, yet she could not blame them for their ill manners. Most had joined the army just to have a place to sleep and something to eat. Fifteen dollars a month in pay didn't go very far, but the girls were happy that the enlisted men so easily squandered their money on girls and whiskey. The trick, of course, was to get them to spend their money on pleasures first before their pay was all gone.

Some of the soldiers treated her with respect. They in general were always fighting among themselves in the bar, but as long as the fighting didn't involve the girls, Bugger would let them pound themselves to death.

Some of the girls refused to entertain the soldiers because of their bad manners, and when asked why Lydia put up with them, she simply shrugged. Inwardly, she could not forget Kellem and how wonderfully gentle and loving he had been. She entertained soldiers only on the off chance that she might meet another like him, but she never did.

The winter snows came on fierce in this open country, and the cold months dragged on. Almost all construction came to a standstill in the little town, which meant the workers weren't earning as much, and that meant business for the girls suffered as well.

With less money coming in, Lydia used up most of her savings. Room rent continued, and wood for heat required a few more dollars. Every day became as monotonous as the day before, and she found herself eating far too much. She even put on weight, which some of the girls said gave her some more curves. That should have been a compliment, but with so much free time on hand, she also began drinking daily. There was a time in late December when she had earned enough money to purchase a ticket on a steamer back to Bismarck, but the river had already frozen up, bringing river traffic to a halt. The stagecoaches quit running, and any freighters that normally passed through, wouldn't be showing up until spring.

There were days when the sun poked through the clouds and it appeared that spring might be on the horizon, and then just as quickly a squall would come through whipping snow into every nook and cranny, obliterating the already drab landscape. She was not alone in the humdrum of melancholy. Everyone, it seemed, turned owly, complaining, griping about the weather.

The girls, especially, were bickering among themselves. When an unsuspecting customer arrived seeking entertainment the girls would line up and those who weren't chosen griped some more.

Lydia was almost always among those not chosen. Melancholia hit her like a freight train. For days on end she sat in her room staring out the window onto a bleak landscape, her thoughts drifting back to similar days in Yankton.

"Oh, my God, my God," she sobbed on more than one occasion. "How did I ever fall back into this?"

From Christmas on, the snows devastated the area, keeping everyone indoors. In early April a bright sun and a three-day thaw brought on the muddy streets, the first sign that spring actually was making an appearance. The ice on the river honeycombed, and a few days later the current broke it up into ice-flows, which was a good sign. Lydia knew that river traffic would once again bring in fresh supplies and her sweet tooth would welcome canned peaches, something she hadn't had in months.

The continued warm days and sun brought out the brilliance of this big-sky country. For most of the girls business began to take on its usual flavor, but Lydia could not come out of her dejection. She was a whore, but she could never be a good one; she had become too selective about whom she would entertain.

It didn't take long before her money once again dwindled to a handful of dollars, and the thought of having to entertain just anybody who came through the door became abhorrent.

"My God," she sobbed again as she sat alone in her room. "Why can't somebody just love me?"

An abrupt knock on the door startled her. "Lydia?" she heard. Molly entered to find Lydia crumpled up on her bed. "You okay?" she asked.

"Yes," said Lydia as she wiped away some tears.

Molly watched her for a few seconds. "Sam at the hotel is asking for you. You feel up to it?"

Lydia pulled herself together. "Yes. I just need a few minutes."

Sam Owens owned the Buffalo Hotel. He had lost his wife to diphtheria some years back, had never remarried and did not have any children. It was not often that he required entertainment of this sort, but when he did, he always asked for Lydia. She didn't know precisely why, and although she enjoyed his company more than most, he never showed or indicated any real affection toward her. He simply did his thing and thanked her for her patience with him, since it seemed to take forever before he could fulfill his needs. And he always gave her an extra dollar.

Sam never came to the Yellowstone Inn, however. He was very discreet about his pleasures and always summoned her to the hotel at night. Of course, every girl in the Yellowstone knew he secretly invited Lydia over, but none of them ever let the information out. Even whores maintained a respectable vigilance about their activities.

As she dressed and brushed some rouge onto her cheeks, she was thinking back on the last time she had met with him. It was at least two months ago.

She threw a shawl about her shoulders and left the inn by a side door. Outside, she realized it was nearly four in the afternoon. She had never been summoned to see him during daylight hours, so the request brought on a deep curiosity.

It was a three-minute walk to the hotel, and as always, she entered through the back door and came into the room behind the counter desk. Little Homer greeted her and ushered her around the counter through the lobby. A few familiar faces were present, most turned aside now. One gentleman whom she knew simply raised his newspaper in front of his face. It was not the normal course for Lydia to be entering the hotel, but she did not care. Over the last several months she had grown accustomed to being shunned by more respectable people in society.

Homer threw open the door for Lydia, and when she entered she was surprised to see Sam sitting on a chair beside the bed. Lying in the bed and fully clothed was a young woman not unlike herself, dark-haired and rather slim of build.

"Lydia," said Sam. "I need your help. This girl just arrived on the stage and she's very sick."

Lydia stood silently for a moment. "Why did you ask for me?"

Sam shrugged. "I sent for Doc Burns, but we can't find him." He grimaced. "I was sure I could count on you." He looked at the girl. "Don't know much about her. We assumed she was going to work either with you girls at the Yellowstone or somewhere else."

"We weren't expecting a new girl."

The young lady on the bed opened her eyes and slowly turned her head toward Lydia. Lydia placed her hand on her forehead and knew she was burning with a fever.

"Get me some cold water, Sam. This girl needs immediate attention." Sam hustled out the door, and as soon as he was gone Lydia rolled the young lady over on her side as gently as she could and began unlacing the back of her dress. The girl needed the comfort of loose-fitting clothes, something that would allow her to breathe more easily. Lydia had already removed her corset when Sam returned with a pitcher of water and filled a washbasin. Lydia drenched a towel and dabbed the girl's forehead, and with another she cooled the skin about her throat.

"Am I going to die?" the young lady asked faintly.

The girl's eyes were glazed, but Lydia calmed her. "No, you're not going to die."

Sam explained that the stagecoach driver said the young lady took ill a few days back, and that he advised her then she should get off the stage and seek a doctor, but she had refused.

Suddenly, Doc Burns entered the room carrying his satchel and came straight to the bedside. He touched the girl's forehead, reached under her dress and felt her legs, then ran his hand along her back.

He looked at Lydia. "Help me get her clothes off." He turned to Sam. "Get me a tub of cold water right now. This lady is burning up."

Lydia and Doc Burns worked furiously to remove her outer clothes and her laced shoes, and when she lay clad only in her undergarment, they continued to soak her with wet towels. Two men came in carrying a tin bathtub and placed it at the head of the bed. Soon more help came through the door and filled the tub with buckets of cold water.

The young lady opened her eyes again, looked at Lydia and mouthed something so quietly that Lydia needed to bend down to hear what she was saying.

"Please . . . tell him . . . I'm sorry," she said weakly.

"Tell who?" asked Lydia. The girl's eyes were now staring, as if unseeing.

"Henry," she answered.

Two more men came in with buckets of cold water and poured them into the tub and ran out for more.

"Let's get her into the tub," Doc Burns instructed. He motioned for Sam and Lydia to help him then suddenly stopped. He leaned down and put his ear on her breast for some time, then looked up and slowly eased himself back with a heavy sigh. "She had the fever for too long." He slowly pulled a sheet up to her neckline and looked at the white, fleshy face. "Young thing, too."

The two men carrying water entered the room again, and

when they saw Doc shake his head they turned around and left.

"Who is she?" asked the doc.

"Don't know," said Sam. "Might be some identification in her bag."

Doc Burns stood up, put his coat back on and picked up his satchel. "I'll get hold of Jacobson and tell him we got a lady over here that needs to be buried." He turned to Sam. "If we can find out who she is and where she came from, I suppose we ought to notify her next of kin.

"Poor thing," Doc Burns said as he again looked into the dead girl's face. "And so young." He left the room.

"Lydia," said Sam. "I'd appreciate it if maybe you'd kind of look through her things. I'll have them brought in."

When Sam was gone, she looked into the face of the girl. There was nothing spectacular about her looks. She had a rather plain face and dark hair, like herself. She was a little slimmer in build than Lydia, but about the same age. Lydia could not help but wonder why she had come to Miles City.

If only there was some way she could learn something from this pale, lifeless face. Lydia's gaze focused on the young girl's dress, now draped over an adjoining chair. She moved the dress aside and saw the small purse.

It contained a mirror and some facial powder along with fourteen dollars and some small change. In a small leather case Lydia discovered a letter of credit from a bank in Chicago. It was made out to the name of Sally Summerfield for the amount of ninety dollars, and had obviously been cashed as indicated by the bank stamp.

Also in the leather case was a series of tickets. Lydia thumbed through them one by one. The girl had come from Chicago to Bismarck, the end of the railroad line, then from Bismarck to Miles City by stagecoach.

However, Miles City was not her final destination. The tickets continued on to Elkhorn Crossing, Montana Territory. Lydia had no idea where that was, or how far.

Sam came into the bedroom carrying a bag, which he set down at the foot of the bed. "Find out anything?"

Lydia began placing the contents back into the purse. "Her name is Sally Summerfield, from Chicago. There's no address, but there's a canceled bank note and fourteen dollars in cash."

Sam shook his head. "Just about enough to bury her and send a wire back to Chicago. Poor girl. I wonder if she had any family."

Lydia was quiet for some time, and then, "I wonder, too."

Less than a half hour later Isaac Jacobson, a man small in stature, entered the room and removed his hat out of respect for the dead girl. As owner of the funeral parlor he was renowned for his promptness and reputation for coming directly to the point.

"I understand she's a newcomer to Miles City," he said.

"Yes," answered Sam.

"Is there money enough to pay for her funeral?"

"There's enough," said Sam.

Satisfied with the answer, Jacobson unraveled a heavy quilt he was carrying under his arm and proceeded to maneuver it under the girl. He wrapped her securely and had Sam help carry her downstairs to his waiting buggy.

By eleven o'clock the next morning Jacobson had already dug a grave and hauled her body to the gravesite. It was a simple funeral. The only people in attendance were Jacobson, Sam, Doc Burns and Lydia. Doc Burns said a few words which didn't amount to much, other than he hoped the Lord would accept her into his arms. He barely had the word "Amen" out of his mouth when Jacobson threw the first shovel full of dirt into the hole.

Ten dollars covered the funeral costs, and the remaining few dollars were enough to send a wire to the bank in Chicago. Sam figured the message of her death would be passed on from there, and really there was not much else anyone could do.

For the next few days Lydia sat in her room, spending most of her hours simply staring out onto the street. She had been asked to entertain clients but refused, easily understood when she simply said that the monthly curse was upon her, which it wasn't.

She could not get her mind off of the young lady, Miss Summerfield. It plagued her that the girl had to die so young. It was so unfair to have been robbed of her lifetime and all that it potentially had to offer. Where was she going, and for what reason? And what did she hope to accomplish?

Another two days passed, and while Lydia was looking out onto the street, the stage from Glendive rolled past, an hour behind schedule. As soon as it was out of sight, Lydia turned to look at the display on her bed. The three dresses that had belonged to Sally Summerfield were neatly laid out along with other wearing apparel. Sam and Doc Burns both agreed that there was no need to send the clothes back, and neither had a problem with Lydia taking over the dresses. Lydia had tried them on. They were plain, but each fit her quite well.

She had thought about selling them to the other girls, yet she could not bring herself to do that. It simply did not seem ethical.

She sat for the longest time staring at them, and as she did so, a hundred things skipped through her mind. Early the next morning, when the stagecoach left for Deadwood, Lydia was on it. Four different stages made the Bismarck-Miles City-Deadwood run, so when Lydia presented the ticket, the driver assumed that he was taking Sally Summerfield on board.

Twenty-Seven

She had no idea where Elkhorn Crossing was, and it made no difference because she had decided that wherever Sally Summerfield's ticket would take her, that's where she would go.

The stage left shortly after daybreak, a time when Sam was at breakfast, as he always was. Hardly anyone else was on the street, and since Lydia took only one bag, her departure was quick and easy. Two other gentlemen from the hotel boarded the stage, both dressed like cattlemen, neither of them Miles City residents. Both nodded to her. They didn't know her or her reputation in Miles City, which gave her some comfort.

She had no remorse about leaving the town, and as she rode along the dusty road bouncing from side to side, she was feeling good. Like all the towns before, Miles City had offered her nothing. Whatever lay ahead of her had to be better than the life she was leaving behind.

Every few hours the stage stopped to change the horse team, and on each occasion one of the two gentlemen travelers would help her down from the coach. When they departed one of them always helped her up. These two were traveling to Deadwood. When they asked what her destination was she simply said, "Elkhorn Crossing." She didn't know where it was, and she was thankful neither of them inquired why she was headed there. Like the gentlemen they were they did not attempt to pry any information from her. She determined it was in her best interest to remain quiet, which she did for the most part.

At one of the change stations a third man entered the coach. He wore a beaten-down hat, and his shirt and pants were worn like his boots. The only baggage this cowboy carried was his saddle, which he threw on top of the stage. When he flopped down beside her she could not help but be reminded of Frank McCann, Katrina's cowboy friend.

At the end of the first day she had traveled some fifty or sixty miles, she guessed. The stage remained for the night at a small station where she slept in a tiny room on a hard cot, far short of comfort, and when morning came she was just as tired as when she went to sleep.

Her meal the night before had cost her two dollars, an exorbitant price for a few biscuits and gravy supposedly chunked with beef, which she couldn't find. Now, as she ate breakfast, she was sure the biscuits she was eating were left over from the night before, except she had jam to spread on them and the cost was a dollar.

"You call this a breakfast?" one of the cattlemen complained to the station proprietor. The cowboy who had spent the night didn't have enough money for either the prior evening's meal or breakfast, so the two cattlemen chipped in and paid for his meal.

On the way out the door the same cattleman took the proprietor aside and grabbed him by the shirtfront. Lydia heard him say in a threatening enough voice, "We'll be coming through here next month, and if your food ain't any better we'll burn this damn place down and you with it!"

As the three men and Lydia walked out to the stagecoach, the cattleman was still complaining. He again turned to the proprietor, his face snarling. "Christ, it don't cost nothing to raise a couple chickens. At least you'd have eggs."

From inside the coach Lydia looked back at the station agent who stood in the doorway like a limp dishrag. The same cattleman hung an arm out the window and shouted at him, "Get some goddamn chickens!"

When the coach lurched he settled back in his seat and tipped his hat at Lydia. "Pardon the excessive language, ma'am."

That morning the coach made two more station changes and by early afternoon was trailing along the Powder River. The expanse on either side of this wide and shallow-running water extended forever, it seemed. As far as Lydia could see, short grass spread across the rolling hills like waves of wheat. Miles away to the west she could perceive a slight rising bank, but in between, not a tree or bush was visible.

The deep blue sky and vast landscape of green belonged to each other. She could not believe how far she could see at any given moment. Then, almost magically, the coach would drop into a shallow valley only to emerge on another ridge from where she again could marvel at the vast open prairie.

She knew they were headed in a southerly direction, and knowing the location of Bismarck and where the Little Big Horn battle took place, she calculated that Kellem must have crossed the Powder River somewhere along here. The thought brought her into a melancholy mood for several minutes.

She glanced across at the two cattlemen who were both dozing from the afternoon heat. The cowboy riding alongside her was constantly looking out at the prairie, like he owned it. It pleased her how polite these three men had been to her. It had been a long time since she had been treated like a lady, and a lot longer since she had felt like one.

She was hesitant to initiate a conversation, but she finally turned to the cowboy next to her. "What do people do for a living around here?"

"Mostly ranch country," he answered. "Used to be some trapping around here, but them days is over."

When he mentioned trapping she thought of Ambrose, or

Ham, as everyone knew him back in Yankton, and then, just as quickly, the thought disappeared.

She felt a real comfort riding with these men. Somehow, she knew, the death of that girl back in Miles City, as morbid as it seemed, had been a moment in time that might well change her destiny. She sat back, not minding the hard bench seat or the bumps and jiggling from side to side.

When the stagecoach began to slow she peered out, expecting to see another change station. Dust swirled around the coach as it jerked to a halt on a high rise. As she looked out she could see the tracks ahead leading down to the Powder River. On the other side, the road continued on.

The driver stepped down from the seat and opened the door. "This is Elkhorn Crossing, ma'am."

She stared incredulously across the plains, her mouth hanging open. Another faint dirt trail led off toward the west and disappeared over a hill. She could see in every direction for several miles, yet there was nothing in sight to indicate that anyone inhabited this land.

"Ma'am?" the driver asked again as he offered her his hand.

She stepped down from the coach to the ground and once again looked about. The other men in the coach also got down simply to stretch their legs. The driver climbed back up to his seat, and then stood on the top of the coach, where he scanned the horizon in all directions.

"You expecting somebody, ma'am?" one of the cattlemen asked her.

Panic struck her, and she was unable to respond. She thought Elkhorn Crossing would be a city. What had Sally Summerfield hoped to do here? Why had a ticket taken her to this destination, a crossroads that seemed to lead to nowhere?

Another few minutes passed as the three men from inside the coach walked about, shaking out their stiff limbs. Lydia could not believe the situation she had put herself in. She was about to tell the driver to move on and drop her off at the next town when he suddenly shouted, "Someone's coming!"

Everyone turned to see where he was pointing. At least three miles away on a long sloping hill, dust swept upwards in the calm of the afternoon. Someone was coming on at a fast pace. Then the figure on the horizon was gone momentarily as it dipped into a valley. They all watched patiently until once again the dark figure slowly formed on the horizon. A buggy drawn by a tall and stout horse continued toward them at a steady clip.

Within a few minutes the buggy pulled to a halt before the stage, and a tall man dressed in a checkered shirt dropped to the ground. His dusty canvas pants were tucked into high stovetop boots, and on his hip he wore a pistol. He came a few steps closer, and when he removed his hat she could see how wavy his hair was—long brown locks that reached almost to his shoulders. A thin brown mustache swept across his leathered face. She thought him to be about forty, and she also thought him to be one of the most ruggedly handsome men she had ever seen.

"Miss Summerfield?" he asked. He was standing about ten feet away.

She stared at him, unable to respond.

"I'm Henry Stouter," he said.

Henry? she thought to herself. That was the name Sally Summerfield had mentioned before she died!

He seemed puzzled. "You are Miss Summerfield, are you not?"

The question stunned her. "Y-yes," she answered. "I am."

When he smiled a few deep wrinkles creased his tanned face. "You are more beautiful than I ever imagined."

She could hardly believe what she just heard. And he had paid the affectionate compliment right here, before this small crowd of onlookers! The passengers, if not stunned, were certainly curious about the drama unfolding before them.

Finally the stage driver broke the silence. "I'll get your bag, ma'am." As soon as he handed it down he hollered out, "Let's go." When the passengers were inside the driver yelled at his horses and slapped his reins. The rumble of the wheels and creaking springs were the only sounds as the coach headed down toward the river. In seconds it splashed its way across to the other side.

Henry Stouter was still holding his hat in his hands and began twirling it. "I'm guessin' this is sort of awkward for both of us."

"Yes," she answered, not sure what exactly she was responding to.

"You had a nice trip? I imagine it was long and you must be tired."

She perceived a Southern drawl in his speech now, maybe Texan. "No. Yes," she said, changing her mind. "That is, the trip was long, but I'm not tired."

He nodded and let out a soft laugh. She liked his laugh, liked his smile. When he offered to help her up onto the buckboard she felt how callused his hands were, but what struck her most was how gentle and polite he appeared. He clicked his tongue and the horse set off at an easy pace.

"We've all been waiting for you," he said as he pointed off to the west. "Every Friday for the past five weeks, one of the boys has been on that hill over there watching through a telescope." He chuckled. "Today the coach stopped so we knew you'd arrived."

He hesitated and hemmed and hawed a bit. "Of course, I want you to be comfortable with everything." She could tell he was searching for words and she gave him all the time he needed.

"Well," he went on. "I want you to meet all the hands and get the feel of the ranch. And then, if you still agree to the arrangement, well, then, maybe in a week or two we can go to Broadus and . . ." He stopped for a moment, and then quickly finished, ". . . and be married proper."

When she turned to look at him she was sure her mouth was gaping.

He went on, "You said in your letter you thought you would like the wide-open country. You still feel that way?"

Her wide eyes and broad smile answered for him as she looked about. This open country was suddenly taking on a new and fascinating beauty for her.

"Can you cook?" he asked.

"Some," she answered.

He laughed. "Anything would be better than what we drum up." He looked at her. "I hope you like it here. The ranch ain't much, but it's growing, and it sure can use a pretty woman's touch."

She loved his chiseled smile, and she loved the long, drawn-out way he spoke. Not hesitating, she edged closer and grabbed him firmly by the arm.

Henry Stouter snapped the reins and set the horse into an easy lope.

Twenty-Eight

The ranch was nearly five miles from where Henry picked her up. As the buggy rolled down a long hill toward the few buildings below, Lydia felt her heart skip a beat or two. A narrow creek wound behind the ranch buildings. Beyond, the prairie stretched on and on, dotted with cattle.

A few huge cottonwood trees along the shoreline of the creek offered the best shade, yet several other smaller trees were growing here and there, some in rows, which indicated that they had been planted and were not volunteers.

Three buildings made up the ranch—the ranch house, a bunkhouse and a large barn. A handful of horses were penned in a nearby corral.

As the buggy rolled to a stop two men came out of the barn and hurried over to them.

"This is Curly," Henry said as he helped Lydia down from the wagon. "Curly does most of the shoeing and blacksmithing." A few gray wisps of hair covered the sides of Curly's head and matched his full beard. His face was wind-weathered like Henry's, but he was much older.

He held out a hand and smiled. When he spoke, a missing front tooth caused him to whistle. "So nice to meet ya's, Miss Summerfield."

The other man was introduced as Andy, a short, stout fellow a bit younger than Curly, she guessed. He carried a constant grin on his face.

"Andy just kind of hangs around with us boys. He don't talk," Henry said.

Andy stuck out a hand and murmured something, but Lydia had no idea what he said. He held up a telescope and pointed to a ridge behind him and mumbled a few sounds. It was obvious to Lydia that he was the one who had been watching for her arrival.

"Chase, Billy and Knute are out on the range," Henry explained. "You'll meet them before the day's over."

The door to the ranch house opened and a squat, heavyset lady waddled out, a limp evident as she did so. She was well into her seventies, Lydia guessed, with a mop of gray hair balled up in the back of her head and a set of yellow teeth showing from her wide smile.

"This is Momma Dee," Henry said. "She's been our cook and momma hen over the years."

"Miss Sally," she said, almost whispering, she was so out of breath. "It sure is nice to have you come all this way, child." She held out a hand twisted from rheumatism. "You come on in, young lady. I've got some cool lemonade made just for your arrival.

"Oh, yes, oh, yes," she said as she took Lydia by the arm and headed back to the ranch house. "Ain't you got the most beautiful eyes I ever seen. Oh, yes, oh, yes. Ain't this a great day the Lord made for us."

Late in the afternoon Lydia met the remaining three ranch hands. Chase, a swarthy, sandy-haired man in his late twenties, was Henry's ranch foreman when Henry wasn't around. Billy and Knute were two young hired hands, smooth-faced and in their late teens.

Momma Dee had a dinner in progress, and Lydia, used to a kitchen setting, jumped in and helped right alongside her. The boys were especially ready for their meal. Upon Sally Summer-field's arrival they had been promised beefsteak with potatoes, wild onions, cinnamon biscuits and plum pie for dessert, and they were hungrier than bears coming out of hibernation.

It surprised Lydia that Henry had asked earlier if she could cook, saying what they ate wasn't much. This meal was fit for kings. Everyone ate in the ranch house, but afterward the men retired outside where they smoked and sat around watching the sun disappear over the end of the world.

The two cottonwoods out back provided the most shade as the sun went down, and for some time Lydia and Henry sat in two chairs made out of cottonwood limbs. Trying to piece together a decent conversation was awkward work for both of them.

"Living out here on the prairie is going to be a whole lot different than living in Chicago," Henry said.

"I'm sure it will be," she answered.

"I heard Chicago's got buildings four and five stories high."

"It does," she answered, sure that it did.

"You never did write anything about your parents," he said.

"They both died when I was young," she answered, which was the truth.

"Momma Dee's got a bad leg. She's having a hard time getting around lately, so's she ain't always up to cooking for the boys." Henry was silent for some time. "But she sure has taken to you."

"I don't have anything against cooking," she said. "I don't have anything against eating, either," she added, at which they both laughed.

"Well, you look real fine to me," he said, the grin back on his face. "You certainly fit the description you sent me."

Now that Lydia thought back she did have some of the facial features of Miss Summerfield. They both had black hair, dark eyebrows and dark eyes, and both were slim of build. Lydia felt sheepish about having taken on the persona of the dead girl. Worse yet, Henry, after only a half day, was growing on her like moss grows on a tree. What was most painful was that all the comments Henry had made were meant for Miss Summerfield and not her, and none of this was setting well with her. She had lied enough during her lifetime. Now Henry Stouter believed she was Sally Summerfield, and that was the biggest lie of all.

"Mr. Stouter," she began, "I, ah . . ."

"I know," he interrupted. "It's been a long day, and I apologize for keeping you up so long."

Before she could respond Henry escorted her into the ranch house to the bedroom he usually utilized. He had moved most of his belongings to the bunkhouse, she guessed, so that the real Sally Summerfield would have privacy during which she could make up her mind as to whether or not she wanted to stay.

Momma Dee occupied the only other bedroom. Before she retired she made it known, as she had already said several times during the day, that she was happy to have Lydia as a new member of the household.

That night Lydia tossed and turned before she fell asleep. She was not at all certain what the morning might bring, and she was especially wary of what the outcome of this latest adventure might be.

Momma Dee had breakfast in the making when Lydia rose. It was as if she wanted to have everything prim and proper. She was humming and kept a smile on her face all the while she worked. There was no doubt in Lydia's mind that she wanted her to stay.

"I haven't got the stamina I once had," Momma Dee said as she set the table. "Been here over seven years now. Henry takes real good care of me."

"Everyone calls you Momma Dee," Lydia remarked. "Are you Henry's mother?"

"No, child. I only had one boy, but he . . ." She stopped what she was doing, her thoughts obviously miles away from her work. "Well, Jake—that was my boy's name—well, him and Henry was best of friends, and Henry promised he would take care of me if anything ever happened to Jake." She stopped again, and then, "Well, then it happened." She looked at Lydia, her face blank for a moment, and then the smile came back. "Henry's like my own boy now."

She laughed. "All the boys call me Momma Dee, even Curly, and he ain't but a few years younger than me."

Lydia was curious about what had happened to Jake, yet was hesitant to inquire. She heard voices from outside and suddenly the front door banged open and the boys from the bunkhouse rushed in and took their places at the table. They all greeted Lydia, even Andy, whose murmur she accepted as a greeting.

"Miss Sally," Henry said, as he took a chair. "Hope you slept well."

"I did," she responded. When Momma Dee served up pancakes and sausage, the boys gobbled it up as if it was their last meal. After coffee and a few instructions about who was going to do what during the day, they all headed outside to their duties.

A couple of days passed following a similar routine. Lydia busied herself around the ranch house, visited with Curly and Adam, since they were always on hand, and in the evenings after dinner, she got to know the ranch hands better, and Henry as well. He spent a lot of his day riding the range, deeply engrossed in the care of his cattle. It seemed he was always busy, but he showed up periodically during the day and paid significant attention to Lydia when it seemed appropriate. She appreciated the time she was given to adjust to ranch life, knowing well that a week or two was hardly enough time to fully comprehend what ranching really was like.

The only real reservation Lydia had about her role as Sally Summerfield was that she had to constantly cover her real identity. The strain was beginning to take its toll. She had to be careful in her conversations, mindful of her thoughts, and sometimes she simply had to agree with what was said because she did not know otherwise.

Her nights were filled with remorse, and she was not at all convinced that she should continue the charade. The fear stayed with her like some dreaded disease that somehow her real past would eventually surface and wipe away the comfort and solitude that this ranch setting offered.

On the third morning, after another hearty breakfast, the men headed outside, but Henry remained behind.

"Do you ride?" he asked Lydia.

"I have ridden," Lydia answered, "back in . . ." She was about to say Yankton, where she had once ridden Barker, Katrina's horse. "Yes, I've ridden before, but I'm afraid I'm not very good at it."

"Don't have to be with Old Blue. He's nineteen and never threw anybody even when he was young and spunky."

Lydia grabbed her dress front and spread it out. "I don't have any riding clothes."

"Momma Dee will fix you up if you don't mind wearing trousers."

Her thoughts jumped to Katrina and the buckskin clothes she often wore. Lydia had never worn men's pants before, but out here on the prairie the only people who would know about it were the ranch hands, and if Henry didn't care, she didn't, either. Momma Dee obviously had nothing against it since she headed for a trunk in a corner and flipped the lid upward.

"Oh, yes, oh, yes," she said. "Child, I got just the thing for you."

A half hour later Lydia walked out of the house wearing a pair of blue denim pants and a plaid shirt, both loose-fitting.

At the barn Henry had saddled two mounts, one a colorful sorrel, the other a deep black horse, so dark he appeared blue in color. There was no doubt in Lydia's mind that this was Old Blue, the nineteen-year-old horse Henry had talked about.

"Miss Sally," Henry remarked when he saw her in her attire. "You look mighty fine in those clothes. Got to find you a hat one of these days."

Curly and Andy were nearby, watching as Henry helped her put a shoe into a stirrup and then told her to hop up. Lydia sprang a few times, but did not have the rhythm for springing into the saddle.

"You're going to have to help me, I'm afraid," she said to Henry.

Henry asked her to try springing up again, and when she made the next attempt, he put his hand on her rear end and pushed her up into the saddle.

Henry jumped on his horse, and as the two turned and headed toward the creek, Curly was cackling like a proud chicken. "Did ya see how he grabbed her butt, Andy?"

"Yuh, yuh, yuh," Andy blurted out.

"Didn't seem to bother her none, did it?"

"Na, na, na," Andy replied.

Both were still chuckling long after Lydia and Henry were out of sight.

They rode at an easy pace about a mile from the ranch house following the meandering, shallow creek. Once they crossed the creek they rode on for several minutes up an incline to where several good-sized rocks jutted out of the ground, forming a huge circle.

"The Indians call this a medicine wheel," Henry explained as he pointed to the circular configuration. "Got some kind of special spiritual meaning to them. This one ain't been used in years. 'Course, the Indians left a long time back. I suppose that's why."

"Pushed out," Lydia said.

"What's that?" Henry asked.

"The Indians didn't leave on their own. They were forced out."

Henry nodded. "I guess you're right. I got along with them, but a lot of white folks around here didn't."

Lydia gazed across the wide prairie, cherishing the mild breeze that cooled her. They were on a high point from which she could see for miles in every direction. Henry's cattle were scattered all around them. "Where are your cowboys at?" she asked.

"South of here." He pointed off as if she would be able to spot them, but she couldn't. "Got nearly twelve square miles to cover. When the sun ain't shining it's kind of hard to find your way around. Course, the boys know every square inch of this place. If you ever get lost just find the creek and follow it back."

Henry spoke the last sentence as if he expected that she might sometime be riding out here alone.

He pointed off to the west. "Three miles that way is a grove of trees in a ravine. Ain't many trees around here, but whenever you see one, there's usually water." He pointed to the south. "Broadus is about a half day ride that way." He swung around in his saddle. "Elk Crossing is that way, where I picked you up. It's not too far from Powderville. That town ain't as big as Broadus, but it holds a dance once in a while, what can be fun. I believe I wrote to you about that.

"Want to get down and sit a spell?" he asked.

She nodded, and after he dismounted he helped her down. They sat in a patch of tall white flowers that were springing up from the ground.

"These are called violets," Henry said as he picked a flower and twirled the stem. "Kinda strange, a white flower being called a violet."

"Yes, it is," Lydia answered. As she studied Henry she could see a bit of Frank McCann in him, and she had a good idea now how Katrina had so quickly fallen in love with the cowboy. Deep down she felt a pain gnawing at her, a reluctance to go on with this charade she was portraying.

Henry removed his hat and brushed his hair back. "Seem's I'm doing all the talking." He saw the frown on her face. "I hope your silence doesn't indicate your dissatisfaction with the ranch."

She said nothing.

"In my letter I thought I was straightforward about this country." When she didn't respond, he went on. "I know I ain't perfect, either." She was still quiet. "If I misled you, I'm sorry."

She looked into his face and could see the hurt that was building in him. "No, you haven't misled me, but I've been misleading you."

He jerked upright.

"Mister Stouter, I'm not Sally Summerfield. My name is Lydia Pearlman."

He sat as still as a rock, his expression growing in disbelief. "But we wrote to each other. I thought we had an understanding."

"You wrote to Sally Summerfield, not to me. I knew your intended bride for just a few minutes before she . . ."

"Before she what?"

"Before she died."

Henry remained as still as a post.

"About ten days ago Miss Summerfield arrived in Miles City on the stage with a deathly fever. We tried to save her, but she was too far gone. I'm so sorry I didn't tell you earlier."

He hardly moved, his mind mulling over what she had just said. "You're everything I imagined about her. If you hadn't told me, I wouldn't have known."

He was silent, as if he needed to catch his breath, and then asked, "Why did you take her place?"

"It was my way out of Miles City. I thought I could leave behind a life of misery and shame."

"Maybe you can," he said, his face unchanged. "We've all got something in the past we'd like to bury. I'm no different."

He stood and offered his hands, and when he pulled her up he looked into her face and smiled. "Lydia Pearlman. That's a nice name." He smiled. "No, that's a wonderful name.

"Miss Lydia, I've done a lot of things in my lifetime I'm not proud of. I came out to this country to start over. I'm guessing my past is a lot worse than yours, no matter what you say. I'm still looking ahead, and if you want to take the place of Miss Summerfield, I want you to feel free to do so. But if you do, I'm going to call you Lydia from now on."

He looked into her face for the longest time waiting for her response. When she smiled, he knew he had made a wise suggestion.

"Do you mind if I kiss you, Miss Lydia?" he asked.

Her heart fluttered. "Not at all, Henry. Not at all."

Every day that followed filled Lydia's soul with joy. She would never have believed that she could find the open plains to be such a comfort, nor did she ever dream she would accidentally happen upon a rugged cowboy who thought she was the most beautiful woman on earth.

Momma Dee was like a mother, and the men at the ranch were as close to having a family as she could ever imagine. The decision wasn't at all difficult to make, but she allowed another week to slip by just to make sure. She and Henry left for Broadus early one morning and were married late that afternoon. The next day on the way back her heart soared like an eagle. This was the first time in her life that she'd ever felt as if she was going home.

Inside the ranch house her thoughts went back to the closest friends she had made over the years: Katrina, Halona and Tom Hodges, Colleen and Selma from St. Louis, and the Jefferson family as well. She had a lot of letter-writing to catch up on. When she finally set her pen to the task she was confident and ecstatic, and so very happy, since from now on, everything she was about to write would be real.

Henry never did ask about her past, and she never inquired about his.

ABOUT THE AUTHOR

Kent Kamron is a lifetime resident of the Dakotas and finds real comfort on the plains where he can see fifty miles in every direction. *Letters from Lydia* is his fourth novel, followed by *The Baltic Sea Incident, The Prague Double,* and *The Mirror Man.* The earlier three novels and his published plays are under his Christian name, *Delray K. Dvoracek.*

He has also penned three Western short-story collections; *Charlie's Gold and Other Frontier Tales, A Time for Justice and Other Frontier Tales,* and *The Dime Novel Man and Other Frontier Tales.* In the works are another Western short-story collection and a Western novel.

Kent Kamron resides in Fargo, North Dakota, where he writes daily. His Web site is www.dkdbooks.com. His e-mail is dkd@i29.net.